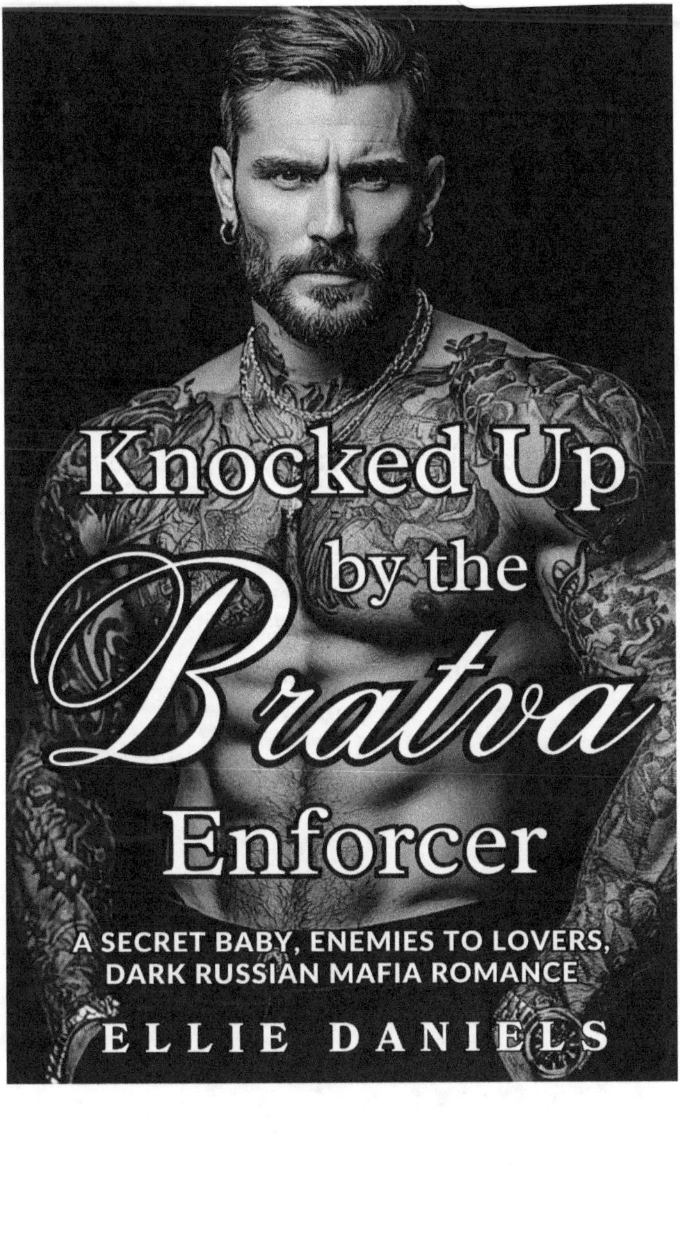

Knocked Up by the *Bratva* Enforcer

A SECRET BABY, ENEMIES TO LOVERS, DARK RUSSIAN MAFIA ROMANCE

ELLIE DANIELS

Scan the QR code to join
the Ellie Daniels Romance
Community for updates
and promotions.

Other Titles by
Ellie Daniels:

Volkov Bratva Series:
Claimed by the Bratva King
Promised to the Bratva
Knocked Up by the Bratva Enforcer
Indebted to the Bratva

Taboo Relationships

My Professor's Secret

Moonlit Desires

Bound by Betrayal

Table of Contents

Chapter 1

Mikhail stepped through the door of Viktor's office, the heavy wood creaking slightly as it swung closed behind him. The air inside was thick with the scent of leather, cigars, and power. Viktor liked to keep his space intimidating—floor-to-ceiling bookshelves lined with old, untouched books, a deep mahogany desk that took up most of the room, and two dim lamps casting long shadows across the floor. There was no comfort here, no warmth, only the weight of expectation and silent authority.

As Mikhail's boots thudded against the plush rug, he surveyed the room with practiced ease. His dark, piercing eyes landed on Viktor, sitting behind the desk, leaning back in his chair as if he had all the time in the world. A small, predatory smile played on Viktor's lips as he regarded Mikhail, his fingers steepled in front of him.

Mikhail, towering over most men at 6'3", was no stranger to this kind of environment. He had been in Viktor's office more times than he could count, each time receiving a task that required his particular set of skills. It never bothered him. The weight of the job, the blood on his hands—it was part of his life. He accepted it without question, without hesitation.

His body was a testament to that life. Muscles rippled under his tight black t-shirt, tattoos snaking across his skin like battle scars. The ink on his arms told stories—some of violence, others of loyalty—but none of sentimentality. Mikhail didn't do sentimentality. His hands, calloused and strong, were always steady, always ready to pull the trigger when ordered. His face, with its sharp jawline and neatly trimmed beard, was unreadable, betraying none of the thoughts that flickered behind his cold, dark eyes.

He stopped in front of Viktor's desk, his posture straight, his expression neutral, waiting for the command. There was no need for pleasantries between them—this was business, nothing more.

"Mikhail," Viktor began, his voice low and smooth, like silk over steel. He leaned forward slightly, his predatory gaze never leaving Mikhail's face. "We've got a situation."

Mikhail didn't respond right away, simply holding Viktor's gaze, waiting. There was no need for him to speak. He was the enforcer, Viktor's right hand when things needed to be done quietly—or not so quietly. He handled the dirty work so Viktor didn't have to.

"Mikhail, you've heard of the Morozov Bratva, I assume?" Viktor asked, his voice cold but casual, as if he were discussing the weather rather than rival factions.

"Of course," Mikhail finally responded, his voice a deep rumble. His words were clipped, to the point, just as Viktor liked it.

"They've been making moves," Viktor continued, his fingers tapping rhythmically on the surface of the desk. "Nothing overt, but we've been watching. They got bold a few days ago. Stole a stash of guns from one of our warehouses."

At this, Viktor leaned back in his chair, studying Mikhail's reaction. But there wasn't much to see. Mikhail's expression remained stone-cold, his jaw set, eyes unwavering. Theft wasn't a new game, especially not between rival Bratvas, but the Morozovs had crossed a line.

"We've tracked them," Viktor said, his smile widening slightly. "To a house in Brooklyn. Small crew, nothing you can't handle."

Mikhail nodded once, barely a movement, signaling he understood the gravity of the task. He had handled much worse. The men inside the house didn't know it yet, but they were already dead. There was no mercy in this business. The minute they touched the Volkov Bratva's weapons, their fate was sealed.

"Kill them all," Viktor said, his voice dropping a little lower, the danger in his tone unmistakable. "No witnesses. I want them wiped out, and I want that house empty when you leave. Bring the guns back."

It was a simple mission, one Mikhail had executed countless times before. Eliminate the threat, retrieve the assets, leave no one alive to tell the tale. It was routine—clean, efficient. He didn't ask questions, didn't hesitate. He followed orders because that's what he did, and that's what made him valuable.

Viktor's eyes gleamed in the low light. "Consider it a message to the Morozovs. They'll think twice next time."

Mikhail's mind was already on the job, calculating his approach, mapping out the possibilities. He would get in, take out the men, gather the guns, and be out within the hour. Easy. He had no reason to linger, no reason to leave any trace behind. The men inside wouldn't even know what hit them.

"I'll handle it," Mikhail said, his voice steady, giving no hint of hesitation. He didn't need to say more. Viktor knew he would follow through.

Viktor smiled, a slow, satisfied grin that never reached his eyes. "I know you will."

Mikhail turned without another word, his boots heavy against the floor as he made his way back out of the office. Behind him, he could feel Viktor's gaze, still sharp and predatory, watching him as he left. Mikhail didn't mind. He didn't need Viktor's approval, only his orders.

The moment the door closed behind him, Mikhail's focus narrowed, his mind already shifting to the task ahead. The house in Brooklyn, the men inside, the guns—they were all that mattered now. He would do what he was sent to do, and then he would disappear into the night, as he always did.

The sound of the engine cut off as Mikhail parked his black SUV halfway down the block, far enough from the house to avoid drawing attention but close enough to strike quickly. The street was quiet, unnervingly so for Brooklyn, where the sounds of the city never truly died down. Tonight, though, there was an eerie stillness in the air. The occasional hum of distant traffic was the only thing disturbing the silence.

Mikhail sat for a moment, his fingers resting on the steering wheel as he surveyed his surroundings. The house stood at the end of the block, dark and unassuming. Its windows were black, casting long shadows across the cracked pavement. It was the kind of house that blended into the neighborhood, the kind people passed without a second glance.

The perfect place for a group of men looking to hide. But they couldn't hide from him.

His eyes narrowed as he checked the mirrors, scanning the area for any signs of movement. There was none. The street was deserted, the other houses on the block dark and silent. Good. It made his job easier when there were no prying eyes. No neighbors to call the cops or ask too many questions. Not that it would matter. By the time anyone noticed anything was wrong, he would be long gone.

Mikhail opened the door and stepped out into the night, the heavy weight of his gun resting comfortably at his side. The cool evening air brushed against his skin, but it didn't faze him. His focus was already on the task ahead. The streetlights cast a dim glow, illuminating the sidewalk in patches of weak yellow light, but Mikhail stayed in the shadows, moving with the practiced ease of a predator stalking its prey.

His steps were soundless, his boots barely making a noise against the cracked pavement. His movements were fluid, calculated. He had done this countless times before, and every step was part of the routine. There was no room for mistakes, no room for hesitation. Each step brought him closer to the house, closer to his target.

The house loomed ahead of him, its worn exterior blending into the darkness. It was an old building, probably built decades ago and left to decay. The paint was peeling, the front porch sagged, and the windows were smudged with grime. But Mikhail wasn't interested in the aesthetics. His eyes were on the front door, slightly ajar, like an invitation waiting for him to accept.

He paused for a moment at the edge of the porch, listening. He could hear faint voices coming from inside—two, maybe three men, speaking in low tones. They were relaxed. They weren't expecting him. That would be their last mistake.

Mikhail's fingers tightened around the grip of his gun as he moved closer. His heartbeat remained steady, his breathing calm. There was no fear, no adrenaline rush. This wasn't about emotion. It was about precision. He approached the door, his body hugging the shadows, blending into the darkness. The voices inside grew louder as he neared, and he could make out snippets of their conversation. It didn't matter. He wasn't here to talk.

With a swift motion, Mikhail pushed the door open and stepped inside, his gun raised, eyes scanning the room. The men inside barely had time to register his presence before the first shot rang out. The sharp crack of the silenced gun echoed through the small space, and the first man fell without a sound. A bullet to the head. Quick, efficient.

The others scrambled, panic flashing across their faces, but Mikhail was faster. His movements were smooth, practiced. Two more shots, and two more bodies hit the floor. Blood pooled beneath them, the room suddenly silent except for the ringing in his ears.

He didn't stop to look at them, didn't hesitate to assess the damage. It was done. Mikhail stepped over the bodies, his boots leaving faint marks in the blood as he moved through the house. His gaze swept the room, taking in the empty liquor bottles, the guns scattered across a table in the corner, the dirty plates stacked in the sink. This wasn't just a hideout. These men had been living here, comfortable in their theft. Comfortable in the belief that they had gotten away with it.

Mikhail felt nothing as he stepped into the back room, where the stash of guns was kept. There was no satisfaction in the kill, no sense of accomplishment. This was his job. These men had stolen from the Volkov Bratva, and they paid the price. Simple as that.

He knelt by the stash, carefully inspecting the weapons. A mix of handguns, assault rifles, ammunition. Everything Viktor had said was there, and more. Mikhail's fingers brushed over the cold metal of the guns, methodically checking each one. This wasn't about greed or revenge. It was about sending a message. No one stole from the Volkov Bratva and lived to tell the tale.

He packed the guns into a large duffel bag, moving with the same calm precision he had used to kill the men. His mind was already on the next step, already thinking about how long it would take to get back to the safehouse, to report the job as done. There was no room for second thoughts, no time for reflection. This was just another job. Another kill.

As he slung the bag over his shoulder, Mikhail glanced down at the bodies one last time. They lay where they had fallen, their faces frozen in expressions of shock and fear. He didn't feel anything for them. They were already forgotten, erased from his mind as easily as he had pulled the trigger.

"Another job. Another kill. They should've known better than to steal from us."

Mikhail's thoughts were as cold and precise as the actions he'd just carried out. The guns were already packed into the duffel, his mind shifting to the next step. His body moved on autopilot, sweeping through the house to ensure nothing was left behind. He walked with the same cold efficiency that had carried him through countless missions—no wasted movements, no unnecessary thoughts.

And yet...

A sound. Faint, barely there. But to someone like Mikhail, whose senses had been honed by years of survival in the Bratva, it was unmistakable.

He froze, muscles tensing, head tilting slightly toward the direction of the noise. It came from deeper inside the house. The back room. His pulse remained steady, his breath even, but his instincts sharpened, every nerve on high alert.

Someone was still here.

His fingers tightened around the grip of his gun, and he moved silently toward the sound. His boots barely made a sound on the creaky floorboards as he approached the door to the back room. His mind was already calculating—whoever was in there was about to die, just like the others. The job was clear: no witnesses.

Mikhail paused at the door, listening. There it was again—a rustling, as though someone was trying to hide, trying to disappear into the shadows. A prey, hoping to escape the predator's notice. His lips tightened into a thin line as he pushed the door open, his gun raised, ready to fire.

The room was dimly lit by the streetlights filtering in through the dirty windows. Dust clung to every surface, and the air was thick with the smell of stale cigarette smoke and sweat. But it wasn't the disarray that caught Mikhail's attention.

It was the figure huddled in the corner.

She was small, barely noticeable, crouched against
the wall with her knees pulled up to her chest. Her
long, chestnut brown hair tumbled over her
shoulders in messy waves, half-covering her face
as she pressed herself into the shadows. Her pale
skin seemed to glow in the dim light, and her
emerald green eyes, wide with terror, locked onto
Mikhail's as soon as the door opened.

For a moment, time seemed to freeze.

Mikhail's gun remained steady, aimed directly at her
head. His finger was on the trigger, ready to pull,
but something stopped him. He stared at her, his
cold, detached mind registering the details like
pieces of a puzzle—young, early 20's at most,
scared, out of place. She didn't belong here. Not
with the bloodied bodies in the other room, not with
the guns and the violence.

Her trembling hands gripped the fabric of her jeans,
her knuckles white with fear. She was trying to
make herself invisible, to disappear into the wall,
but her eyes—those wide, terrified emerald
eyes—gave her away. They pleaded for mercy, for
something Mikhail wasn't used to giving.

Mikhail's expression didn't change, but internally,
something flickered. His mind told him what to
do—what he was supposed to do. He was the
Bratva's enforcer, the one Viktor called when loose

ends needed tying up. And this girl, whoever she was, was a loose end.

No witnesses.

He took a step closer, his shadow falling over her as he towered above her small, fragile frame. She flinched but didn't scream, her breath coming in short, sharp gasps. Her eyes were fixed on him, like a deer caught in the headlights, paralyzed by the fear of what was about to happen.

Mikhail raised the gun, his finger tightening on the trigger.

It should've been easy.

One shot. Clean. Quick. He'd done it a hundred times before. This girl, whoever she was, didn't matter. She was just another witness, another person who had seen too much.

But as his finger hovered over the trigger, something in him hesitated.

For the first time in his life, Mikhail paused.

It wasn't rational. It wasn't part of the plan. He had a job to do, and leaving witnesses alive wasn't an option. But as he stared down at her, something in her wide, tear-filled eyes made him stop. It was like she was silently begging him, pleading for her life without speaking a word.

"I should kill her. It's what I'm supposed to do." His internal voice was cold, insistent. This was his duty, the way things worked in their world. Mercy wasn't part of the job description. Mercy was for the weak.

And yet, he couldn't pull the trigger.

His eyes scanned her again, trying to find something—anything—to justify the hesitation. She was shaking, her body rigid with fear, but there was something else in her face, something he couldn't place. Vulnerability. Innocence.

And those eyes...

His finger hovered over the trigger, but the longer he looked at her, the harder it became to pull. Mikhail clenched his jaw, frustration building inside him. This wasn't how it was supposed to go. She was supposed to be dead by now, just like the others. But here she was, still breathing, still staring at him with those haunting green eyes.

"So why can't I pull the trigger?"

The question echoed in his mind, louder with each passing second. It wasn't logical, wasn't part of the job, but something deep inside him—a part he had long buried—stopped him.

She didn't belong in this world. That much was clear.

And for some reason, Mikhail couldn't bring himself to end her life.

He lowered the gun, frustration bubbling beneath his calm exterior. This was a mistake. He knew it. Viktor's orders had been clear—kill everyone, no witnesses. Yet, here he was, sparing a girl he didn't even know.

Mikhail's expression darkened. He hated this feeling—this loss of control, this hesitation. It made him feel weak, vulnerable. But the decision had been made, and now he would have to deal with the consequences.

Without saying a word, he reached down and grabbed her by the arm, yanking her to her feet. She gasped, too shocked and scared to fight back. Her legs buckled under her, but Mikhail didn't let go. He pulled her close, his grip firm but not painful.

Her breath came in shallow gasps as she stared up at him, wide-eyed and trembling.

"You're coming with me," he growled, his voice low and rough. He didn't explain why—hell, he didn't even know why. But he knew one thing for sure.

This girl was a problem.

And problems like her didn't just disappear.

Mikhail pulled Anya to her feet with little effort, her small frame struggling to stay upright as she stumbled against him. Her wide, terrified eyes stared up at him, but he ignored them, focused on getting her out of the house and away from the bodies that now littered the floor. His grip on her arm was firm, commanding, and left no room for protest.

The smell of blood still lingered in the air as he yanked her toward the front door, his other hand gripping the duffel bag full of guns. Anya's panicked breaths were rapid, her chest rising and falling as she tried to understand what was happening. She opened her mouth to speak, but the words never came. Fear had stolen her voice.

Mikhail didn't stop to explain. There was no time for explanations, no time for rationalizing why he had just spared her life. In his world, there were no loose ends. And yet, here she was—alive, shaking, and following him out the door like a reluctant lamb to slaughter.

The night air hit them as they stepped outside, the darkness swallowing them whole. The quiet Brooklyn street remained just as deserted as when Mikhail had arrived, the houses standing like silent witnesses to the violence that had just unfolded inside. He quickened his pace, dragging Anya with him, her legs barely able to keep up with his long, purposeful strides.

She tripped on the uneven sidewalk, her body lurching forward, but Mikhail didn't stop. His grip tightened, keeping her upright as he reached his SUV. He could feel her trembling under his hold, but he pushed it out of his mind. He couldn't think about her fear, her vulnerability. Not now. Not when he was trying to figure out what the hell he had just done.

Without a word, Mikhail yanked open the passenger door and shoved her inside. She let out a gasp as she hit the seat, her hands scrambling to steady herself. Her breath came in quick, shallow bursts, her wide eyes flicking between Mikhail and the door, as if calculating her chances of escape.

But Mikhail was already moving, throwing the bag of guns into the backseat before slamming the door shut. He circled around the SUV with the same efficiency that had carried him through the mission. Every move was deliberate, controlled. But inside, he was anything but.

He slid into the driver's seat, his jaw clenched as his hands gripped the steering wheel. The engine roared to life, and without hesitation, he pulled away from the curb, the tires screeching against the pavement as the SUV sped down the quiet street.

She was still, her back pressed against the seat, her eyes wide with terror. It took her a moment to gather her thoughts, to process what had just happened. But as the city lights blurred past the window and the distance between them and the house grew, her fear quickly gave way to panic.

"You can't keep me here!" Her voice broke through the silence, frantic and high-pitched. She turned in the seat, her hands reaching for the door handle as if she could somehow throw herself out of the speeding car.

Mikhail's eyes flicked to her, his expression cold. "Shut up."

His voice was curt, leaving no room for argument. It wasn't a request—it was an order. One he expected her to follow. But She wasn't listening. Panic had taken over her body, and she fumbled with the door, her fingers slipping on the handle as she tried to pry it open.

"Let me out!" she screamed, pounding her fists against the door in desperation. "You can't do this! Let me go!"

Mikhail's frustration bubbled under the surface, but he kept his gaze on the road, his knuckles white as they tightened around the steering wheel. He was still trying to process his own decision, still grappling with the fact that she was alive and sitting next to him. He could have ended it, could have pulled the trigger and left her body in that house with the others.

But he didn't.

And now, here she was, yelling at him, fighting against him, reminding him with every frantic word that he had made a mistake. A mistake he couldn't afford.

"I said, shut up," Mikhail growled, his voice low and dangerous. He didn't turn to look at her this time. He didn't need to. The command in his tone was enough.

She froze for a moment, her breath coming in sharp gasps as she stared at him, her green eyes wide with fear. But the panic didn't leave her face. She shook her head, her lips trembling as she fought back tears. "You can't keep me here. I'll—I'll scream. I'll get away."

Mikhail clenched his jaw, the muscles in his neck tightening as her words grated against his already frayed nerves. His mind was a whirlwind of thoughts—why had he spared her? Why had he taken her? None of this made sense. He followed orders. Always. But now, he was going against everything he had been trained to do.

And for what? A girl he didn't know, a girl who was supposed to be dead?

"This was a mistake." The thought echoed in his mind, gnawing at him with each second that passed. He should have killed her. He should have followed through with the plan, just as he had done so many times before.

But he hadn't. And now, he was stuck with her.

The girl let out another cry, her fingers fumbling with the door handle again, but Mikhail was faster. His hand shot out, grabbing her wrist in a firm grip. "Don't," he warned, his voice ice-cold. He didn't need to say more.

For a brief moment, their eyes met—his dark and unreadable, hers wide with fear and desperation. She stilled under his grip, her body trembling as her lips parted, but no words came. The fight seemed to drain out of her, leaving only the quiet, shaking breaths that filled the silence between them.

Mikhail released her wrist and turned his attention back to the road, the city lights casting fleeting shadows across his sharp features. His mind was racing, trying to process what came next, but nothing was clear. His gut had made the decision to spare her, but now his head was paying the price.

"I'm not going back," he thought, the weight of his actions pressing down on him. There was no going back. He couldn't undo the choice he'd made.

The road stretched out before him, dark and winding, just like the path he had chosen. The girl next to him was a problem. One he didn't know how to solve.

Yet.

The SUV crunched to a stop in the driveway of the safehouse, gravel shifting under the tires as Mikhail killed the engine. The dense forest surrounding the property swallowed them in darkness, with no other sign of life for miles. The safehouse loomed ahead, its silhouette barely visible against the blackened sky, worn and hidden from the world. Just like the secrets it kept.

Mikhail glanced at her. She had gone quiet again, but her earlier defiance still lingered in the air between them. The memory of her yelling at him in the SUV—screaming, fighting him with words, unafraid of who or what he was—flashed through his mind. It had been a surprise. Most people, especially after seeing what she had, broke down into tears or silent terror.

But not her.

She had yelled, her voice cracking with anger, not fear. She hadn't begged for her life or cowered under his command. She had fought. Even when she was terrified, she had the audacity to stand up to him, to look him in the eye and dare him to do worse. That fire—that resistance—it was something he hadn't expected. And now, as he stared at her, it stirred something deep inside him.

Mikhail opened the door and stepped out into the cold night air, his thoughts racing as he walked around the car. He couldn't stop thinking about that moment when he'd found her, crouched in the corner of the back room, her wide green eyes pleading with him. There had been innocence there, a kind of vulnerability that had made him hesitate. But now, that same girl was showing a different side—a fierceness he hadn't seen coming.

A flicker of attraction tugged at him, uninvited. He hated that it was there, lingering beneath his frustration. It wasn't just her looks, though they hadn't escaped his notice. Her chestnut hair, the softness of her features—they stood in stark contrast to the defiance in her eyes. No, it was something more. It was her refusal to be broken, her determination not to beg.

He yanked open the passenger door, grabbed her by the arm, and pulled her out. His grip was firm, rough, but not cruel. She stumbled as her feet hit the ground, but she didn't fall. Instead, she squared her shoulders, glared up at him, and for a moment, he could almost see the anger in her eyes igniting again.

"Get moving," he snapped, pulling her toward the house.

Her resistance was immediate, her feet dragging as she jerked her arm back. "You don't know who you're dealing with!" she spat, her voice sharp and filled with fury. "You're going to regret this! You have no idea what kind of trouble you've brought on yourself!"

Mikhail felt the frustration rise inside him like a tide, pushing against the attraction he hadn't wanted to acknowledge. She was fearless in her anger, even when she should have been terrified. It was as if she didn't realize who he was, what he was capable of. Or maybe she just didn't care.

His jaw clenched as he tightened his grip on her arm, pulling her up the crumbling steps of the safehouse porch. The wooden door groaned as it opened, and he dragged her inside, his mind torn between the frustration she provoked and the unwanted desire that stirred every time she looked at him with that fire in her eyes.

"You're going to be sorry you took me!" she shouted again as he hauled her down the narrow hallway. "You think this is going to go your way? You're nothing! My people will come for you, and when they do, you'll wish you had killed me!"

Her words hit him like sparks, igniting something primal. She was relentless, fearless in her fury, and it stirred him in ways he didn't want to admit. Her voice—sharp, biting—was unlike anything he'd expected. No one talked to him like that. No one had the nerve.

He shoved open the door to one of the back rooms, a small, windowless space with nothing but a rickety bed in the corner. She barely had time to react before he pushed her inside, letting go of her arm with a sharp motion.

"Shut up," he growled, his patience fraying at the edges.

She stumbled forward, catching herself against the wall before turning to face him, her eyes blazing with rage. "You don't scare me," she hissed, her breath coming in short, angry bursts. "You think you're in control? You're nothing but a thug, and when my father finds out—"

"Enough!" Mikhail's voice cut through her words like a blade. He stepped forward, his broad frame filling the doorway as he glared down at her, his jaw tight with barely restrained anger. He could feel the heat of his frustration boiling over, mixing with the attraction that had been simmering ever since she'd opened her mouth in the car.

She was right. He should have killed her. This wasn't supposed to happen. She wasn't supposed to live. But something in her—something in the way she refused to back down—had stopped him. And now he was stuck with her, this defiant, fiery woman who couldn't seem to stop testing his limits.

"Stay here," he ordered, his voice rough, thick with the tension that had been building since the moment he found her.

She didn't answer, but the look in her eyes was enough. She wasn't going to stop fighting. And maybe—just maybe—that was part of what intrigued him.

Mikhail turned on his heel, leaving her standing in the room as he slammed the door shut behind him. The sound of the lock sliding into place echoed in the small space, but it did little to calm the storm brewing inside him.

As he leaned against the wall, his hands clenched into fists, Mikhail felt the weight of his impulsive decision settle in. She was more than a complication now. She was a problem—one he didn't know how to fix. But worse than that, she was becoming something he couldn't afford to be distracted by.

This wasn't supposed to happen. She wasn't supposed to live. But I can't take it back now.

The frustration gnawed at him, but so did the unwanted spark of attraction that had ignited when she fought back. He hated it. He hated the way she got under his skin, the way her defiance drew him in.

But there was no turning back now.

Chapter 2

The room was small, suffocating. The walls were bare, cracked in places where time had worn them down, and the single dim bulb overhead cast long shadows that made everything feel even smaller. The air was thick, stale, with the lingering scent of dust and something she couldn't quite place. Anya sat on the edge of the bed, staring at the floor, her arms wrapped around herself, trying to stop the tremors that seemed to ripple through her body. The lack of windows only heightened the sense of being trapped. Nowhere to run. Nowhere to hide.

The bed beneath her was hard, the mattress thin and lumpy, but it was the least of her concerns. Her mind raced, replaying the events of the night over and over again, each memory more jarring than the last. Her breath hitched, heart pounding in her chest as fear clung to her like a second skin.

What had she been thinking?

Anya had only wanted to find Pavel. It had been a routine visit—she had stopped by the house in Brooklyn, expecting to find her cousin lounging with his friends, maybe playing cards or drinking. But Pavel wasn't there. Just a few of his guys, the ones he always hung around with.

Pavel was supposed to be there. He had told her to meet him, but when she arrived, he was nowhere to be found. His absence should have been a sign, a red flag telling her to leave, but she had decided to wait a little bit to see if he would show up.

But then she heard it.

The gunshot.

It echoed through the house, freezing her in place. One shot, then another. Her breath caught in her throat as panic flooded her body, her legs nearly giving out beneath her as the realization hit her: someone was here. Someone dangerous.

She had run without thinking, darting through the back hallway, looking for anywhere to hide. The small room tucked away in the back corner had been her only option. She had slipped inside, her heart hammering in her chest, praying she wouldn't be found. The smell of blood had hung heavy in the air as the minutes ticked by, each one stretching longer than the last. Her mind had raced with a thousand questions, but there was only one that mattered—would she survive?

Anya squeezed her eyes shut, her fingers digging into the fabric of her jeans as the memory clawed at her. The sound of bodies hitting the floor, the low grunts of pain—it all played in her head like a horror film. And then, the footsteps. Slow, deliberate, coming closer.

She swallowed hard, a lump forming in her throat. She could still feel it—the way her body had tensed, every muscle frozen in terror, as the door creaked open. She hadn't dared to breathe, hadn't dared to move, hoping against hope that whoever it was would leave her alone. But she had known, deep down, that they wouldn't.

And then she had seen him.

The man who had found her—his tall, imposing figure filling the doorway. His presence had been suffocating, overwhelming, and the moment their eyes met, her heart had nearly stopped. His gaze had been cold, piercing, like ice cutting through her, but there was something else behind it. Something she couldn't quite place.

Anya shivered at the memory, biting down on her bottom lip as her mind drifted back to that moment. She had felt her fear spike the second their eyes locked, but even in that fear, she couldn't deny the way she had noticed him. His face, sharp and angular, was striking in a way she hadn't expected. His dark hair, short and neat, framed his strong jawline. And his eyes—those cold, intense eyes—had held hers for what felt like an eternity. There was a harshness to him, a violence just beneath the surface. And yet, there was something about the way he looked at her, something that made her pause.

"Why can't I stop thinking about the way he looked at me?"

It didn't make sense. He had been ready to kill her, gun raised, finger on the trigger, and yet… she couldn't stop replaying that moment in her head. Why hadn't he killed her? Why had he hesitated?

The fear that had gripped her so tightly was now joined by something else—something she didn't want to acknowledge. She couldn't help but notice his size, his strength, the way he had handled her, rough but not brutal. There had been control in his actions, a restrained power that made her both terrified and… drawn to him.

"No," she whispered to herself, shaking her head. *"I should fear him."*

She did fear him. Didn't she? He had killed those men—her cousin's friends, people she had known, however briefly. And he had spared her, for reasons she didn't understand. How could she feel anything but fear of him?

And yet, the image of him—standing there, strong and unyielding—refused to leave her mind. The way his muscles had flexed under his shirt, the sharpness of his features, the force of his presence—it all lingered in the back of her thoughts, gnawing at her.

"I should have left when I didn't see Pavel. Why did I stay? I never thought it would end like this."

She was trapped now, caught in a web of confusion and fear, and all she could do was wait. The room felt smaller by the second, the lack of windows making her feel like she was suffocating. She didn't know what he wanted from her. She didn't know if he would come back to kill her, or if he had some other plan in mind. But the uncertainty gnawed at her.

And then there was the attraction.

She hated herself for it. For even thinking about it in a moment like this. But her mind kept drifting back to him. The way he had looked at her—not just with the intent to kill, but with something else behind that cold stare. And on the car ride… she had noticed how close they were. How his body had filled the space beside her, the sheer size of him making her feel small in comparison. She had noticed the way his hands gripped the steering wheel, the way his chest rose and fell with steady breaths.

"How can I want the man who killed those men? Why can't I stop thinking about his touch?"

Anya clenched her fists, shaking the thoughts away. She couldn't think like that. She had to focus on getting out, on finding a way to survive. But even as she tried to push those thoughts aside, they lingered, pulling her back to that moment, to him.

The room felt colder now, the fear settling deep in her bones. She didn't know what was going to happen next, but one thing was clear: she was no longer in control. And the man who held that control… was dangerous.

The stillness of the room weighed heavily on Anya, pressing against her chest with the force of a thousand unspoken thoughts. The faint hum of silence seemed to fill every crevice, every shadow, making the room feel more like a cage than a place to rest. She could still feel the remnants of fear pulsing through her veins, her mind trapped in the aftermath of the night's events. But as she sat there, staring at the cracked walls and worn floors, her thoughts began to drift.

The car ride.

Her breath hitched slightly as her mind replayed it—those agonizing moments when she had been so close to him, so close to the man who had taken her, who had killed the men in that house. She had been terrified, her heart pounding in her chest, her body rigid with fear. And yet, something else had crept in, something she hadn't expected. Something she didn't want to admit.

She closed her eyes, the memory of the car ride filling her senses. He had shoved her into the passenger seat, not gentle, but not brutal either. His movements had been precise, controlled, his strength undeniable. The way his hand had gripped her arm, rough but steady, sent a shock of awareness through her that she hadn't been able to shake. Even now, she could still feel the ghost of his touch on her skin, the lingering impression of his hands as they had held her in place.

She shivered, hugging herself tighter as the memory washed over her.

"He killed those men." Her mind whispered the words, a reminder of the violence she had witnessed, of the danger she was in. *"I should fear him."* She did fear him. Didn't she?

But with each passing moment, that fear felt more and more elusive, slipping through her fingers like sand. Because alongside the fear, the anger, and the confusion, there was something else. An attraction she couldn't explain, an unsettling pull that made her feel both repulsed and… drawn to him.

"Why am I drawn to him?" She clenched her fists, digging her nails into her palms as if the pain might help her focus, might help her banish the feelings that had no place in her heart.

But no matter how hard she tried, she couldn't stop thinking about him—about his size, his strength. He had filled the car, his presence overwhelming, making her feel small and vulnerable in a way she had never felt before. He had been quiet for most of the ride, his jaw clenched, eyes focused on the road, but she had felt the tension radiating from him. Every breath he took had seemed to echo in the small space, making her painfully aware of how close they were.

Her pulse quickened at the memory of his hands gripping the steering wheel, the way his muscles had tensed beneath his shirt. There had been a raw, untamed energy about him, a force that both terrified and captivated her. She had wanted to scream, to yell at him, to demand answers. But fear had kept her silent, fear and something else—something that made her stomach twist in knots.

She hated herself for it.

"I should be planning my escape, thinking about how to get out of here." But all she could think about was him—how his presence had dominated the car, how every inch of him seemed built for control, for power. She had never felt so powerless in her life, and yet, there was a part of her, a dark part, that had been drawn to that. To him.

Anya shook her head, trying to clear her thoughts. She couldn't let herself think like this. She was his prisoner. He had killed those men—men she had known, men who had been part of her cousin's circle. He had killed them without hesitation, without mercy. How could she even entertain the thought of being attracted to him? How could her body betray her like this?

"I hate him." She repeated the words in her mind, trying to make them feel real. *"I hate him for what he's done."* But even as she thought it, she couldn't stop the shiver that ran down her spine at the memory of his voice, the cold command in his tone as he had told her to shut up.

There had been no comfort in his words, no softness. He was a man who lived by violence, who thrived on control. And yet, that control—his dominance—it had stirred something inside her. She hated the feeling, hated the way it lingered even now, in the silence of the room.

She bit her lip, her thoughts drifting back to the way he had handled her in the car. There had been nothing gentle about it, but there had been restraint. He could have hurt her, could have done far worse, but he hadn't. His grip had been firm, his movements precise, as though he was always in control of himself, of everything around him. And that control, that strength, had sparked a response in her that she didn't want to acknowledge.

"How can I want the man who killed those men? How can I think about how his hands felt on me?"

It was madness. But no matter how hard she tried to push the thoughts away, they returned with every breath she took. She had seen the coldness in his eyes, had felt the danger that lurked beneath the surface of his calm exterior. He was not a man to be trifled with. And yet, even knowing that, even feeling the weight of his violence hanging over her, she couldn't stop the rush of heat that came with the memory of his touch.

Her body betrayed her, reacting to him in ways she couldn't control. She hated it, hated the way her skin tingled at the thought of him, hated the way her mind kept drifting back to the car ride, to the moments they had shared in silence, so close and yet worlds apart.

Anya pressed her hands against her face, trying to block out the flood of conflicting emotions that were threatening to drown her. She had never felt so confused, so torn between what she knew was right and what her body seemed to want. How could she be attracted to him? How could she feel anything but fear and anger toward the man who had taken her captive, who had killed without hesitation?

"It's just the fear," she told herself, desperate for an explanation. *"It's just because I'm scared. That's all this is."*

But even as she tried to convince herself, she knew it was more than that. There was something about him, something that had ignited a spark deep inside her, a spark she couldn't extinguish no matter how hard she tried.

And as much as she hated herself for it, she couldn't stop thinking about him—about the way his presence had consumed the space around them, the way his voice had sent a shiver down her spine. The way he had looked at her, cold and calculating, yet somehow… different.

She shook her head, frustrated with herself, but the thoughts wouldn't leave her. She was drawn to him in a way she couldn't explain, and that terrified her more than anything.

Because no matter how much she tried to deny it, she couldn't shake the feeling that this was only the beginning.

The air in the room was thick with tension, every second dragging like an eternity as Anya sat motionless on the bed, her heart pounding in her chest. She couldn't shake the weight of her thoughts, the conflicting emotions that battled for control inside her. Fear still gripped her tightly, but beneath it, anger simmered, threatening to boil over at any moment. She felt trapped, like a caged animal with nowhere to run, and the silence of the room was suffocating.

The sound of the door swinging open was like a gunshot, shattering the stillness. Anya's body tensed, her breath catching in her throat as her eyes darted to the doorway. Mikhail stood there, his large frame filling the entrance, casting a shadow over the room. His presence was overwhelming, the air seemed to shift with his arrival, and despite herself, Anya felt her pulse quicken.

He was different now. His expression was colder, his gaze hard and unyielding as it swept over her. Yet there was something behind the coldness—something controlled, calculated, but not entirely emotionless. He was trying to rein himself in, to maintain the upper hand, and that only made her heart race faster. She wanted to scream at him, to demand answers, but fear kept her frozen in place for a moment longer.

Mikhail's eyes locked onto hers, and for a second, neither of them moved. The tension between them thickened, a silent standoff that stretched impossibly thin. He was the first to break the silence.

"My name is Mikhail," he said, his voice low and measured.

The sound of his voice sent a shiver down Anya's spine, but she pushed the feeling away, trying to focus on the words. Mikhail. So that was his name. The man who had killed those men—her cousin's friends—the man who had spared her life for reasons she couldn't begin to understand. Her mind raced, swirling with questions she wasn't sure she wanted answered.

"Mikhail," she thought, the name ringing in her head. *"The man who spared me."* But why? What was his plan? Why had he hesitated?

Her heart was hammering in her chest, fear and anger colliding like a storm inside her. She was furious, terrified, and yet... there it was again. That strange pull, that inexplicable attraction she couldn't ignore. It made no sense, but it was there, gnawing at her in the midst of the chaos. Her emotions were a tangled mess, and she hated herself for the confusion that clouded her thoughts.

Mikhail stood in the doorway, his expression unreadable, though his eyes held hers with an intensity that made it hard to breathe. He didn't move, didn't make any threatening gestures, but his mere presence was enough to keep her on edge. He was trying to keep the situation under control, trying to be reasonable, but Anya had reached her breaking point.

She was done sitting still. Done being afraid.

Anya's fists clenched at her sides, her anger bubbling up to the surface like a volcano ready to erupt. She rose from the bed, her body shaking with the force of her emotions as she glared at Mikhail, the fury in her eyes burning brighter than the fear.

"You don't know who you're dealing with!" she spat, her voice sharp and filled with defiance. "I'm Anya. Anya Morozov. My father is Konstantin Morozov, head of the Morozov Bratva!"

For a split second, she thought she saw something flicker in Mikhail's eyes—a crack in his cold exterior. His calm facade wavered, just for a moment, and his expression darkened. The weight of her words sank in, and she saw the recognition flash across his face. He knew exactly who she was now, and it made everything infinitely more complicated.

"Fucking hell," Mikhail muttered under his breath, running a hand through his hair as he stared at her with a mixture of frustration and disbelief. "I should have killed you."

The words were like a punch to the gut, knocking the wind out of her, but Anya didn't flinch. She had expected as much. She had known from the moment he found her that her life was hanging by a thread. But hearing him say it, hearing the cold truth in his voice, only fueled her anger.

"Why didn't you?" she demanded, taking a step forward, her fists still clenched. "Why didn't you kill me with the others?"

Her voice shook, but her resolve didn't. She was furious, her fear turning into something sharp and dangerous. She wanted answers, needed to understand why he had spared her. It didn't make sense. Nothing about this made sense.

Mikhail didn't answer immediately. His jaw tightened, and for a moment, he looked like he was struggling with something. His dark eyes flickered, the control he had been trying so hard to maintain slipping for just a second. But then he straightened, his expression hardening once more.

"It would've been easier," he said, his voice rough. "No witnesses. No complications."

"Then why am I still alive?" Anya shot back, her voice rising. "What are you planning to do with me? Keep me locked up until you decide to finish the job?"

Her words hung in the air between them, and for a moment, Mikhail just stared at her, his gaze piercing through the anger and fear that roiled within her. He stepped forward, his presence looming larger as he closed the distance between them.

"You don't understand what's happening here," he said, his voice low and dangerous. "You think you're in control? You think your name will protect you?"

Anya's heart pounded, but she didn't back down. She met his gaze head-on, her defiance burning brighter than her fear. "I'm not some nobody. My father will find out what you've done. You think you can just take me and get away with it? You're the one who doesn't understand."

The air between them was charged, the tension palpable as they stood face to face, neither willing to back down. Anya could feel her pulse racing, could hear the blood pounding in her ears, but she refused to show weakness. She refused to let him intimidate her.

But beneath the fury, beneath the sharp words and the defiance, there was something else. Something neither of them wanted to acknowledge, but it was there, simmering just below the surface. A dangerous attraction that made her skin tingle and her heart race for reasons that had nothing to do with fear.

"Why did you spare me?" she asked again, her voice softer now, almost pleading. "Why didn't you kill me?"

Mikhail's jaw clenched, and for a moment, it looked like he might answer. But instead, he stepped back, his gaze darkening as he turned away.

"I don't know," he muttered, more to himself than to her.

The silence that followed Mikhail's muttered response was thick, charged with tension so palpable it felt like the air between them was sparking. Anya's breath caught in her throat, her mind reeling. His words had been so quiet, so unsure—so unlike the man who had stormed into the room with the weight of death hanging over him. The coldness that had defined him was cracking, and in its place, something darker and more dangerous was emerging.

But Anya wasn't ready to let it end there. She wasn't ready to let him walk away from this without understanding the gravity of what he had done—what he had started by sparing her life. She felt her chest tighten with a new wave of anger, her fear morphing into something sharper, something hotter.

"You don't understand what you've done," she said, her voice trembling with the intensity of her emotions. "You think this ends with me locked in a room? Do you have any idea who my father is? What he'll do when he finds out you've taken me?"

Mikhail didn't respond immediately, but the way his jaw clenched told her he was listening. His dark eyes flickered, and for a moment, she thought she saw a flash of something—uncertainty, perhaps, or hesitation. But it was gone as quickly as it had come, replaced by the same cold, unreadable mask he always wore.

He didn't care. She knew it. He didn't care about her father or the consequences. But what scared her more was that he didn't seem to care about anything. Not even himself.

Anya's fists tightened at her sides, her body trembling with the force of her anger. "You've gotten yourself into something you can't control," she continued, her voice rising. "You think you're untouchable? That nothing can touch you because you're so strong, so powerful?"

She took a step forward, her eyes blazing with fury as she stared up at him. "You're wrong."

Mikhail's eyes narrowed, his gaze hardening as he watched her, his silence only fueling her rage. She could feel the heat between them growing, a tension that was no longer just about anger. It was something else—something she didn't want to admit. But it was there, simmering beneath the surface, threatening to erupt at any moment.

Her breath came faster, her chest rising and falling with the weight of her emotions. She could feel his eyes on her, could feel the intensity of his gaze as it roamed over her, taking in every detail of her defiance, her fury. And despite everything, despite the fear and the hatred she had for him, she couldn't stop the way her body responded.

Her pulse quickened, her skin tingling with a heat that had nothing to do with anger.

"How can I want him right now?" The thought raced through her mind, unwanted and impossible to ignore. *"After everything he's done? After what he is?"*

But she couldn't stop it.

Mikhail took a step closer, his body towering over hers, his presence overwhelming. The room seemed to shrink around them, the walls closing in as the space between them disappeared. Anya's breath caught in her throat, her heart hammering against her ribs as she stared up at him, her hands trembling at her sides.

He was close now, so close she could feel the heat radiating off his skin, could see the way his muscles tensed beneath his shirt, the way his breath came in slow, measured exhales. His eyes were darker than before, no longer cold, but filled with something primal, something dangerous.

She could feel it—the shift between them. The anger was still there, burning hot, but it was no longer the only thing driving them. There was a pull, a magnetic force that neither of them could deny, a desire that had been building since the moment they had locked eyes in that house.

Mikhail's gaze dropped to her lips for a fraction of a second, and Anya felt her stomach twist with anticipation, a heat rising inside her that she couldn't control. Her body was betraying her, reacting to him in ways she didn't want to acknowledge. She wanted to hate him. She did hate him. But her body wasn't listening.

"I shouldn't want this," she thought, her breath coming in shallow, uneven gasps. *"I should hate him."*

But she didn't move. She couldn't.

Mikhail's hand twitched at his side, as though he was trying to resist something. His jaw clenched, his eyes locked onto hers with an intensity that made her knees weak. He was holding back, fighting something within himself, something that was slipping through the cracks of his control.

Anya's breath hitched as he took another step forward, his body so close now that she could feel the heat of him pressing against her. She swallowed hard, her heart racing as she waited, her body tense with a mix of fear, anger, and something else—something she wasn't ready to admit.

"Shut up," he growled, his voice low and rough, the words barely audible over the sound of their ragged breaths.

And then, before she could react, he snapped.

Mikhail's hand shot out, grabbing her by the waist with a force that made her gasp, pulling her against him in one swift motion. His mouth crashed down on hers, rough and demanding, the kiss filled with all the pent-up frustration and desire that had been simmering between them for too long.

Anya gasped as Mikhail's mouth crashed down on hers, the kiss rough and demanding, filled with the pent-up frustration and desire that had been building between them since the moment their eyes first met. For a second, her body tensed, her hands instinctively pushing against his chest, trying to create space between them. But the second her fingers made contact with his hard muscles, the heat between them ignited, and all thoughts of resistance crumbled under the weight of her own need.

The force of his kiss stole her breath, his lips bruising against hers, his hands gripping her waist with a possessiveness that sent a shiver down her spine. She should have pushed him away, should have screamed at him, fought him—but instead, her body betrayed her. A spark of desire flared inside her, overwhelming everything else. She kissed him back with equal fervor, her hands sliding up his chest, fingers curling into the fabric of his shirt as she pulled him closer.

Mikhail growled low in his throat, a sound that sent a rush of heat flooding through her body. His hands were everywhere—gripping her waist, sliding up her sides, fingers digging into her skin as though he couldn't get enough of her. The air between them crackled with electricity, their heated breaths mingling as the kiss deepened, becoming more frantic, more desperate.

Anya's mind was a blur of confusion and desire, her thoughts clouded by the overwhelming sensation of his body pressed against hers. She couldn't think, couldn't reason, could only feel—feel the way his hands moved over her, the way his lips claimed hers with a raw, primal hunger. Her heart pounded in her chest, her pulse racing as the heat between them intensified.

He broke the kiss only long enough to mutter something under his breath, a curse, before his mouth was on her again, devouring her with a ferocity that left her trembling. She could feel his frustration, his desire, his need—all of it pouring into her with every kiss, every touch. It was overwhelming, suffocating, and yet she couldn't stop. She didn't want to stop.

Her hands moved to his shirt, fumbling with the buttons as she tore at the fabric, desperate to feel his skin against hers. Mikhail's lips left hers, trailing down her jaw to her neck, his teeth grazing her skin in a way that made her gasp. Her fingers finally managed to tear open his shirt, pushing it off his broad shoulders, and she ran her hands over his chest, feeling the hard planes of muscle beneath her fingertips.

He was dominant, controlling every moment, but Anya found herself giving in to it, surrendering to the heat of the moment. The power struggle that had defined their every interaction melted away, replaced by something far more primal, far more instinctual.

Mikhail growled again, low and dangerous, as he grabbed her waist, pressing her back against the wall. His body pinned hers in place, his hands roaming over her with a hunger that made her knees weak. His mouth found her neck again, lips and teeth nipping at her skin as his hands slid lower, gripping the hem of her shirt and pulling it over her head in one swift motion. Then came her bra.

Her breath came in ragged gasps as his hands moved to her jeans, the rough fabric of his palms brushing against her bare skin, sending jolts of electricity shooting through her body. She felt the button pop, the zipper sliding down, and before she could even process it, her jeans and panties were gone, discarded on the floor.

Mikhail's hands were on her again, rough and possessive, his fingers digging into the soft flesh of her hips as he pulled her closer with a force that made her gasp. His touch was demanding, as though he was claiming every inch of her body with the strength of his grip, leaving no room for doubt about who was in control. The air between them crackled with heat, and Anya felt her heart race faster as the intensity of his touch sent a shiver down her spine.

His mouth moved lower, trailing hot, open-mouthed kisses down her neck, his breath hot against her skin. When his lips reached her breast, Anya's breath hitched, her body arching involuntarily into him. Mikhail's mouth latched onto her nipple, sucking hard, his tongue flicking over the sensitive bud with a roughness that sent sparks of pleasure shooting through her. Her body jerked in response, a moan escaping her lips before she could stop it.

Teeth grazed the peak of her nipple, the sharp edge of his bite blending pain and pleasure so seamlessly it left her trembling. She gasped, her hands clutching at his shoulders, fingers curling into his skin as her mind spun with the intensity of it all. The sensation of his mouth on her breast, his teeth nipping at her sensitive skin, made her head fall back against the wall, her eyes fluttering shut as she gave in to the overwhelming pleasure coursing through her.

A low, throaty cry escaped her lips, her body reacting to every touch, every flick of his tongue as he continued to lavish attention on her breasts, switching from one to the other, never easing the relentless pressure of his mouth. The roughness of his hands, the possessive way he held her in place, only heightened the desire that pooled deep inside her. She could feel the heat building between her legs, her arousal slick and undeniable, her body responding to him in ways she couldn't control—ways she didn't even understand.

The need was overwhelming. It surged through her, taking over every thought, every sensation, until all she could focus on was the way he made her feel. She wanted him. Desperately. She craved the way his hands claimed her, the way his mouth devoured her, and the way he seemed to stoke a fire inside her that she couldn't extinguish.

Her breath came in short, ragged gasps, her hands trembling as she gripped his shoulders, pulling him closer, needing more of him, more of the pleasure he was giving her. The heat between them was unbearable, and with every rough, possessive touch, Anya found herself sinking deeper into the sensation, giving in to the primal need that coursed through her veins.

"Mikhail…" she whispered, her voice barely audible over the sound of their ragged breaths, but it was enough to make him pause, his dark eyes locking onto hers with an intensity that stole the air from her lungs.

His hand slid between her legs, fingers brushing over the wetness that had gathered there, and he growled, the sound vibrating through her. "I can feel how much you want me," he muttered, his voice thick with desire. "You're so wet for me."

Without breaking the heated contact between them, Mikhail straightened slightly, and Anya felt his hands slip down to his waistband. His fingers quickly unbuckled his belt, the sound of the leather sliding through the loops sharp in the room's silence. The metallic clink of the buckle hitting the floor echoed as he unbuttoned and unzipped his pants in one swift motion. His movements were purposeful, every action infused with the dominance that marked every interaction between them.

Anya's eyes flicked down, taking in the sight of him stripping the rest of the way. His pants dropped to the floor, leaving him standing before her in nothing but his briefs. Her breath caught in her throat as she took in the full view of his body, the hard muscles of his chest, the rigid lines of his abs, and the strain of his erection pressing against the fabric of his briefs. He was overwhelming, larger than life, his presence so powerful it made her knees feel weak.

Her hand reached out almost instinctively, sliding over the bulge in his briefs, and she gasped at the sheer size of him. He was enormous, his cock hard and throbbing beneath her touch, the heat of him radiating through the fabric. Her fingers curled around him, stroking slowly as her desire built to a fever pitch, her body responding to him with an intensity that left her trembling.

Mikhail groaned, the sound low and primal, as he shoved his briefs down, freeing his cock from its confines. The sight of him made Anya's heart race, her body aching with a need so raw it consumed her. He was massive, his cock thick and hard, the veins running along its length pulsing with desire. Her hand moved over him, stroking his length with

slow, deliberate movements, her fingers barely able
to wrap around him fully.

His hands returned to her body, one sliding down
her stomach, his fingers slipping between her legs.
Anya's body trembled as his fingers teased her,
sliding through the wetness that had already
gathered there. His thumb brushed against her clit
with just enough pressure to make her gasp, her
breath catching in her throat as the pleasure shot
through her.

She was panting now, her hands gripping his arms
for support as her mind spun with the intensity of it
all. His fingers were relentless, teasing and stroking
her in a way that left her desperate for more. Her
hips bucked against his hand, her body moving of
its own accord, seeking the pressure and friction
that would send her over the edge.

Mikhail's fingers slid deeper, thrusting inside her
with an expertise that made her head fall back, her
lips parting in a soft moan. His thumb pressed
harder against her clit, rubbing slow, firm circles
that made her body arch toward him, every nerve
on fire.

Anya's free hand moved down between them,
finding the solid length of him again, and she
gripped him tightly, stroking him with more urgency
now. She could feel the heat radiating from him, the
raw power of his arousal pulsing under her hand as

she stroked him harder, her hand moving in time with the rhythm of his fingers inside her.

Mikhail groaned again, his fingers thrusting deeper, matching the movements of her hand on him. His body was rigid, every muscle tense with the effort to maintain control, but Anya could feel him beginning to lose it. His breathing was ragged, his chest heaving as their movements became more frantic, more desperate.

She was close, the tension in her body building to an unbearable peak as his fingers worked her clit with ruthless precision. Her hips moved in time with his hand, her body writhing against him as she chased the release that hovered just out of reach. She was moaning now, her voice low and breathless, her mind too consumed by the sensations coursing through her to think about anything else.

Mikhail's cock throbbed in her hand, his hips bucking slightly as she stroked him harder, her fingers gliding over his rigid length. She could feel the slick wetness gathering at the tip, her thumb brushing over it as she squeezed him, her desire growing with every passing second.

His fingers thrust deeper, curling inside her, and Anya cried out, her body tightening around him as the pleasure became too much. She was on the edge, her body trembling as his thumb pressed harder against her clit, the pressure sending her spiraling toward release. Her hips rocked against his hand, her free hand clutching at his shoulder for support as her entire body tensed.

Mikhail's eyes darkened, his jaw tight as he watched her unravel beneath him. "You want this," he growled, his voice low and rough, the words barely audible over the sound of their labored breathing. "I can feel how much you want me."

Anya could only nod, her body too overwhelmed by the pleasure to form words. She wanted him more than she had ever wanted anything, the need for him so deep it was almost painful. Her mind was a blur of sensation, every thought drowned out by the intensity of his touch, by the way his fingers drove her closer and closer to the edge.

With a growl, Mikhail pulled his fingers from her, grabbing her by the waist and throwing her onto the bed. The world spun for a moment as she landed on the mattress, her body still trembling with need, but the moment she looked up at him, she knew what was coming next. And she wanted it.

She barely had time to catch her breath before he was on top of her, his body pressing hers into the mattress, his hands gripping her thighs as he positioned himself between her legs.

Her heart was racing, her skin on fire as she felt the head of his cock pressing against her entrance, teasing her, making her squirm with need. He was so large, so thick, and she could already feel the stretch of him, the overwhelming sensation of being filled.

And then he thrust into her, deep and hard, filling her completely.

Anya screamed, her nails digging into his back as the intensity of it all washed over her. He was so big, so deep inside her that it took her breath away. But the pain quickly gave way to pleasure, a raw, primal pleasure that made her body arch beneath him, her hips moving to meet his thrusts.

Mikhail's hands gripped her hips with a bruising force, his fingers digging into her soft skin as if he were staking his claim on every inch of her body. His thrusts were deep and relentless, each one harder and faster than the last, the raw power behind his movements driving her closer to the edge with every stroke. Anya gasped, her head falling back against the pillows as the intensity of it all threatened to overwhelm her.

He was everywhere—filling her completely, his body heavy and solid above hers, every movement a deliberate act of control. His cock thrust deep inside her, the friction igniting a heat so intense she could barely stand it. Each time he filled her, it was as though the breath was knocked from her lungs, the sensation of his size and power sending shockwaves of pleasure coursing through her body.

Her moans echoed through the room, mixing with his deep, guttural groans, their ragged breaths the only sound between them. The room was thick with the heat of their bodies, the tension between them building to a fever pitch with every thrust. She could feel the muscles in his back tensing and flexing beneath her hands as he drove into her, his body moving with a force that bordered on brutal but never crossed the line. He was in complete control, every motion precise, calculated, as though he was determined to push her to the very limit of what she could handle.

Anya's hands roamed over the hard planes of his back, her fingers desperate to hold on to something as the pleasure built inside her. Her nails dug into his skin, leaving red, angry marks in their wake as she clung to him, her body arching beneath him as each thrust brought her closer to her breaking point. Her breath came in sharp gasps, her moans growing louder, more desperate, as the intensity between them reached an almost unbearable crescendo.

His cock stretched her in ways that left her trembling, the thickness of him filling her completely, hitting her in all the right places with every thrust. His hands were rough and commanding, his grip on her hips so tight she knew she'd be left with bruises, but the thought of it only fueled the fire inside her. His mouth found her neck, his lips brushing against her damp skin as he groaned into her ear, the sound sending a fresh wave of arousal pooling between her legs.

Mikhail's rhythm grew faster, more erratic, his body surging into hers with a primal urgency that made her entire body quake. He was relentless, each thrust pushing her closer to the edge, and she could feel him losing control, his own need driving him forward as his hands held her firmly in place. Her body met his with equal fervor, her hips moving in time with his, desperate to take him deeper, harder, until there was nothing left but the raw, unfiltered pleasure that consumed them both.

Her nails dragged down his back, leaving red welts in their wake as the pleasure mounted, her body tightening around him as her orgasm loomed closer. She was lost in the sensation of him—the way he filled her so completely, the way his hands gripped her as though he owned her, the way his mouth claimed her skin with every kiss and bite. The connection between them was electric, every thrust sending shockwaves of pleasure through her body, her mind spiraling with the intensity of it all.

The tension in her body coiled tighter and tighter, her muscles tensing as the pleasure built to a point of no return. Mikhail's pace quickened, his thrusts becoming deeper, harder, as his own control slipped further away. She could feel the weight of him pressing down on her, his breath hot against her neck as he groaned, the sound sending a fresh wave of heat coursing through her veins.

"Fuck," he growled, his voice thick with need, the word barely audible over the sound of their labored breaths.

Anya's response was a moan, her voice broken and breathless as her body tightened around him, her nails sinking deeper into his flesh as the pressure inside her reached its breaking point. She could feel it building, the wave of pleasure threatening to consume her entirely, and with every thrust, every moan, she edged closer to that final, blinding release.

And then, with one last hard thrust, it hit her.

Her body exploded with pleasure, her back arching off the bed as her orgasm ripped through her with a force so intense it left her gasping for air. Her nails raked down Mikhail's back as she cried out, her voice raw and hoarse as wave after wave of pleasure crashed over her, leaving her trembling and breathless beneath him. She could feel every inch of him, the way his body pulsed inside her as he pushed her to the very brink of ecstasy, her entire body consumed by the heat of their connection.

Mikhail groaned, his movements growing frantic as her orgasm pushed him over the edge. His hands gripped her hips even tighter, his thrusts becoming erratic as he followed her into that same, dizzying release. He drove into her one last time, deep and hard, and then she felt him shudder above her, his own release ripping through him with a force that made his entire body tense against hers.

They were both lost in the overwhelming intensity of it, their bodies trembling with the aftershocks of their shared release, the room still filled with the sound of their ragged breaths. Mikhail's grip on her hips finally loosened, his body collapsing on top of hers as they both struggled to catch their breath, their hearts pounding in unison as they came down from the overwhelming high of their connection.

The room was still thick with the scent of their shared release, the air heavy with the lingering heat of their bodies. Anya lay beneath Mikhail, her chest rising and falling as she tried to catch her breath, her mind reeling from the intensity of what had just happened. Her skin was slick with sweat, her heart still pounding in her chest, but the rush of pleasure that had consumed her moments ago was already beginning to fade, replaced by a torrent of conflicted emotions.

What had she done?

Her body still trembled with the aftershocks of their encounter, but her mind was spinning with confusion, guilt swirling in her chest like a storm. She had given herself to him—completely. To the man who had killed without hesitation, who had taken her prisoner. And worse, she had wanted it. She had wanted him. Every desperate, heated touch, every rough thrust had only driven her need for him higher, and now that it was over, she couldn't understand how it had come to this.

"How could I have let this happen? How could I want him after everything he's done?"

Anya's breath hitched as the questions tore through her, her chest tightening with a mix of regret and desire she couldn't shake. She had no answer, no explanation for why her body had betrayed her, why she had given in to the heat between them so willingly. She should hate him. She should feel disgusted. And yet, as she lay there, her body still humming with the remnants of pleasure, all she could think about was the way he had made her feel. The way he had filled her so completely, so perfectly, that it left her wanting more.

"What have I done? Why do I want more?"

Mikhail shifted above her, his breath still labored, but his expression was unreadable. He didn't speak as he pulled away from her, his movements slow and deliberate, as though he were gathering himself, pulling the walls back up around him. The connection they had just shared—the raw, primal intensity of it—seemed to fade as he stood and reached for his clothes, his demeanor shifting back to the cold, controlled man she had first met. But there was something different in his eyes now, a flicker of something she couldn't place.

Anya watched him silently, her emotions a tangled mess. She wanted to say something, to break the heavy silence that had settled between them, but the words wouldn't come. She didn't know what to say. What could she say?

Mikhail pulled on his pants, his shirt still hanging open as he glanced at her once more, his dark eyes lingering on her for just a moment longer than they should have. He said nothing, but the tension between them hadn't disappeared. It had simply shifted, becoming something far more complicated than it had been before.

They had crossed a line, and there was no going back. The desire they had shared was undeniable, but it only made the situation more dangerous, more unpredictable.

Anya's heart pounded as she lay there, still too breathless to move. She knew this wasn't over. Not by a long shot.

Chapter 3

Mikhail was ripped from sleep by the unmistakable sound of an engine roaring to life outside. His eyes snapped open, the fog of sleep clinging to him as his mind struggled to catch up. For a brief, blissful moment, he wasn't sure where he was. The bed beneath him felt foreign, his senses dulled by the comfort of sleep. And then, like a punch to the gut, the events of the night before crashed into him.

Anya. Her body beneath his. The heat between them. The way she had cried out his name as he thrust into her, her body trembling with need and desire. He could still feel the ghost of her hands clawing at his back, her moans filling the room as they lost themselves in the intensity of the moment. His mind replayed it all in vivid detail, and for a split second, he let himself drown in the memory.

But the roar of the engine dragged him fully into the present.

His heart slammed against his ribcage as he shot up from the bed, his muscles stiff from the previous night's exertion. He glanced toward the small window, the light filtering through the cracks in the wall casting pale beams across the room. That was when the realization hit him. The engine outside wasn't just any car. It was *his* SUV.

"Fuck!" Mikhail cursed under his breath, his heart rate spiking as he leapt out of bed, his bare feet slamming against the cold wooden floor.

He lunged toward the window, yanking the flimsy curtain aside. The sight that met him sent a surge of fury rushing through his veins. His SUV was tearing down the dirt road, the back wheels kicking up dust and gravel as it sped away. The sight of it—a blur of dark metal against the early morning light—made his stomach turn with a sickening mix of anger and disbelief.

How had he let this happen?

His mind raced as he tried to piece together what had gone wrong. He hadn't tied her up. That much was obvious now. After everything that had happened the night before—after the raw, primal encounter that had left them both breathless—he'd let his guard down. He'd been too distracted by her, too consumed by his own lust and the way she'd made him feel, and in doing so, he'd made the most dangerous mistake of all: he'd trusted her not to try and escape.

"How could I have been so careless?" The thought rang in his head, an accusation that only fueled the fury building inside him.

She'd stolen his fucking car. *His* car. Not only had she escaped, but she'd taken his only means of transportation with her. Mikhail's jaw tightened, his teeth grinding together as he ran a hand through his disheveled hair, the frustration bubbling up inside him like molten lava.

For a moment, he stood frozen in place, the cold morning air biting at his skin as he tried to process what had just happened. Anya—the woman he should have killed the moment he found her—was now speeding away, slipping further and further out of his grasp with every passing second. She wasn't just a loose end. She was the daughter of Konstantin Morozov, head of the rival Bratva. A witness to the brutal murders he had committed. And now, she was gone.

His fingers itched to reach for his gun, to chase after her and fix the colossal mistake he had made. But it was too late. She was already too far gone, and his SUV was quickly disappearing into the distance. There was nothing he could do but watch helplessly as the vehicle vanished from sight, leaving him standing there, alone and exposed.

"Fuck! I didn't tie her up. I didn't fucking tie her up!" The thought kept repeating itself in his mind, each repetition a hammer blow to his pride.

He could feel the fury building inside him, threatening to boil over. Mikhail had prided himself on being in control—of every situation, every job.

He was the enforcer for the Volkov Bratva, the one who took care of loose ends without hesitation. He never slipped, never made mistakes. But Anya had slipped through his fingers, and now she was a danger not just to him, but to the entire Bratva.

His hands curled into tight fists, his knuckles turning white as the anger consumed him. He should have killed her. It had been the plan from the start—kill everyone, leave no witnesses. And yet, when he'd found her cowering in that back room, something had stopped him. Something in those defiant, emerald green eyes of hers had stayed his hand. And now, because of that moment of weakness, she was out there, a liability.

Mikhail growled under his breath, turning away from the window as he began to pace. He couldn't call Viktor. Not yet. The second Viktor or Nikolai found out what had happened, there would be hell to pay. He needed to get her back, clean up this mess before word spread that he had let her escape. Before the Bratva found out he had let a witness, a Morozov, slip away.

But even as the fury and frustration churned inside him, there was something else—a feeling he couldn't shake. Despite everything, despite the danger she posed, he couldn't get her out of his head. The way her body had felt beneath his, the way she had moved against him, the raw fire in her eyes. The night they had shared was burned into his memory, and no matter how much he tried to focus on the problem at hand, her image kept flashing through his mind.

"I should have killed her," he thought bitterly. *"But fuck, I can't stop thinking about her."*

The conflict inside him was unbearable. He had a job to do—a responsibility to the Bratva. She was a threat. But in that moment, as he stood there, torn between anger and something else.

As he made his way to the front porch, the anger that had been simmering under the surface now boiled over, his fists tightening at his sides as he struggled to regain control of his thoughts. He should have known better. She was smarter than he'd given her credit for—more dangerous, too. He had underestimated her, and now he was paying the price.

His mind raced, cycling through the events of the night before. She had been so defiant, so strong-willed, even when faced with death. He had expected her to beg, to break, but she hadn't. Even in the heat of their argument, she had held her own, and the tension between them had ignited into something far more primal. And in that moment, Mikhail had let his guard down. He'd allowed himself to be swept away by her, by the intensity of their connection. It was a mistake, and now she was gone.

This is on me.

The thought hit him like a punch to the gut. He had let her live when he should have killed her. She was a loose end—an unpredictable one—and he had let her slip through his fingers. And now she was out there, free, with every reason to run straight back to her father and reveal everything.

Mikhail's hands twitched at his sides, the urge to punch something—anything—growing stronger with every passing second. But he forced himself to remain still, his breath coming in short, sharp bursts as he stared down the empty road.

There was nothing he could do right now. The SUV was already long gone, and he had no way of catching her on foot. He needed a plan. He needed to figure out his next move. Viktor and Nikolai would be furious if they found out—*when* they found out. This wasn't just a screw-up; it was a disaster waiting to happen.

What the fuck am I going to tell them?

The question gnawed at him, the weight of his failure settling heavily on his shoulders. He could already picture Viktor's reaction, the cold fury in his eyes when he learned that Mikhail had let the daughter of the Morozov Bratva get away. Nikolai, too, would be livid. Mikhail knew he had fucked up in ways that went beyond letting her escape.

And yet, despite the chaos swirling in his mind, there was something else—something he couldn't shake. The memory of her—Anya—was still fresh. Her emerald green eyes. The defiance, the strength. The way her body had moved against his, the heat between them, the way she had moaned as he took her.

Fuck.

The conflict inside him was unbearable. He had a job to do—a responsibility to the Bratva. She was a threat. But in that moment, as he stood there, torn between anger and something else he couldn't quite name, all he could think about was her. The way she had challenged him. The way her body had felt against his, the fire in her eyes that had matched the fire in his blood.

It was maddening.

He should hate her. He should be plotting her death—planning how to clean up this mess before it spiraled any further out of control. But instead, he was thinking about her skin, her lips, her body moving beneath him with that raw, animalistic desire. He couldn't help it.

Why didn't I just kill her?

That was the real question. He had every opportunity. But the moment he had seen her—really *seen* her—something had shifted. And now she was gone, speeding away in his SUV, and all he could think about was the way she had felt, the way she had looked at him, the way she had made him feel.

Mikhail shook his head, pushing those thoughts away as best he could. There was no time for this. He needed to fix this. Now.

Without another moment of hesitation, he turned back toward the house, determination hardening in his gut.

 The safehouse felt emptier now—colder. It was as though her absence had sucked the heat out of the room, leaving behind only the ghost of what had happened between them the night before. Mikhail could still smell her on his skin, still feel the faint sting of her nails dragging down his back, still hear the way she had moaned his name. He shook his head, trying to clear the thoughts.

Focus. You have bigger problems now.

He found his phone on the bedside table, still lying where he'd tossed it the night before. Next to it was his wallet, untouched. He grabbed both, shoving them into his pockets as he tried to push the memory of Anya out of his mind. He needed to think—needed to focus on the task at hand. She had gotten away. And that meant he needed to retrieve his car, track her down, and clean up the mess before Viktor and Nikolai found out. Because if they did…

They'll kill me, he thought grimly, his jaw tightening as the weight of his failure sank in.

The consequences were clear. He had let her live when he should have killed her, and now she was a liability. A witness to multiple murders, the daughter of Konstantin Morozov, and the one woman who had slipped through his fingers. He should be angry. Furious. But instead, all he could think about was her—about the night they'd shared, about the way her body had responded to his, the way she had fought him, defied him, and ultimately surrendered to him.

Mikhail cursed under his breath as he grabbed his keys from the counter and slammed the door shut behind him. What the hell was wrong with him? He should be focusing on the fact that she was a threat, that she had stolen his car, that she could be running straight to her father at this very moment. But his thoughts kept drifting back to her—back to that fiery defiance in her emerald eyes, to the heat of her body pressed against his.

I should have killed her…

The thought echoed in his mind, a cold reminder of what he should have done. He had known it from the moment he found her in that house—no witnesses. No loose ends. That was the job. That

was his responsibility to the Bratva. But the second
he had looked into her eyes, something had
changed. Something inside him had shifted, and for
reasons he couldn't explain, he had spared her.
And now, she was running. And all he could think
about was the way she had felt beneath him, the
way her lips had parted as she moaned his name,
the way her hands had clawed at his back,
desperate for more.

Why can't I stop thinking about her?

Mikhail clenched his fists, his knuckles turning
white as he stalked down the dirt road. His feet
moved on autopilot, heading toward the main road
where he could catch a cab. His mind, however,
was elsewhere. He couldn't shake the memory of
her—of the way she had challenged him, the way
she had made him feel something he hadn't felt in a
long time. Desire. Not just lust, but something
deeper, something more dangerous.

Fuck.

He cursed again, this time louder, the frustration
bubbling up inside him like a volcano ready to
erupt. He should be thinking about the
consequences, about what Viktor and Nikolai would
do if they found out. They would tear him apart for
this. He had one job—one fucking job—and he had
blown it. But even the thought of Viktor's fury
couldn't drown out the memory of Anya—the way

she had looked at him, the fire in her eyes, the strength in her defiance.

No woman had ever fought him like that. No woman had ever made him feel this way. And it was driving him insane.

His thoughts raced as he continued walking, the early morning air cool against his skin. He couldn't help but replay the events of the night before, over and over in his mind. He had been so close to killing her. He had had his gun to her head, ready to pull the trigger, but then those green eyes had locked onto his, and he had hesitated. That hesitation had been his downfall. It had cost him his car, his control, and now, she was out there, running.

Why didn't I just pull the fucking trigger?

The question gnawed at him, but deep down, he knew the answer. It wasn't just about the job anymore. It was about her. There was something about her that had gotten under his skin, something he couldn't ignore. Her strength, her fire, the way she had fought back even when she knew she was in danger. Most women would have begged for their lives, would have crumbled under the weight of his dominance. But not Anya. She had faced him with defiance, with that stubborn will that had both infuriated and captivated him.

And that was the problem. She wasn't just some girl he could toss aside, some witness he could silence. She was different. She was more dangerous than he had ever anticipated, not just because of who she was, but because of what she made him feel.

Mikhail's jaw tightened as he approached the main road. He had no choice but to deal with this. He couldn't let her get away—not just because of the mess she would create, but because he couldn't let her slip through his fingers again. He needed to get her back.

And yet, even as that thought crossed his mind, another one lingered in the back of his head.

What then?

What would he do when he found her? Kill her? Or would he give in to the desire that still burned inside him, the desire that had been simmering beneath the surface since the moment he laid eyes on her?

He didn't know. And that was what scared him the most.

Chapter 4

The steering wheel felt cold and unfamiliar beneath Anya's hands as she gripped it tightly, her knuckles white against the leather. Her heart was still pounding, her chest tight with adrenaline as she drove through the quiet streets. The early morning light bathed the city in a pale, eerie glow, casting long shadows that seemed to stretch endlessly across the road ahead of her. The engine of Mikhail's SUV hummed beneath her, a steady reminder of her escape, of how close she had come to being trapped again.

She kept her foot steady on the gas, resisting the urge to speed, knowing that drawing attention to herself was the last thing she needed right now. Her mind was a whirlwind of thoughts, fragmented memories from the past night flashing through her head—Mikhail's hands on her, the heat of his body, the way his gaze had pierced through her when he found her. The contrast between the man who nearly killed her and the one she had willingly given herself to left her reeling.

What just happened?

Anya's chest tightened, her breath catching in her throat as she realized the weight of it all. She had managed to escape. She had taken his car and run. But as she drove through the empty streets, the feeling of freedom wasn't as overwhelming as she had hoped. Instead, it was shadowed by guilt—guilt she couldn't quite explain.

She glanced down at the dashboard, seeing the clock ticking steadily forward. The city was beginning to wake up around her. In a few more minutes, the streets would start to fill with people, the hum of everyday life taking over the early morning stillness. Anya didn't have much time.

I can't keep this car. I have to get rid of it before someone finds me.

Her mind made up, she took a quick left down a narrow side street, far enough away from the main roads to avoid being seen. She needed somewhere discreet, somewhere no one would notice her ditching a black SUV in broad daylight. Her pulse quickened as she scanned her surroundings, her eyes darting to the quiet corners of the neighborhood.

Finally, she spotted a small, deserted parking lot behind an old building, the perfect place to abandon the car without attracting attention. She pulled the SUV into the lot, her hands shaking as she shifted the gear into park. The moment the engine cut off, the silence hit her like a wave, the sudden absence of noise amplifying the pounding of her heart in her ears.

Anya sat there for a moment, her breathing unsteady as the reality of what she had done sank in. She had escaped Mikhail. She was free. But instead of feeling relief, all she felt was a heavy pit in her stomach. Her mind was still racing, still trapped in the confusion of the night before.

I have to get out of here.

Her hand trembled as she reached for the door handle, her fingers cold and stiff from gripping the steering wheel too tightly. She hesitated for just a moment, her eyes scanning the rearview mirror to make sure no one had followed her, before pushing the door open and stepping out into the crisp morning air. The sudden chill sent a shiver through her, but it wasn't just the cold that made her shake—it was the weight of everything that had happened.

She glanced around the empty lot, her eyes darting to every corner, looking for any sign of movement. Nothing. No one was watching. Still, her heart raced with paranoia, a creeping sense of dread settling in her bones as she hurried away from the SUV.

I can't keep his car. Someone will recognize it. Someone will find it.

She quickened her pace, trying to put as much distance between herself and the vehicle as possible. Her breath came in short, uneven bursts, her pulse throbbing in her neck as she walked away, leaving the car behind like a ghost of the night before. But with every step she took, the nagging feeling in her chest grew stronger.

What am I doing? Why do I feel like this?

Anya's mind swirled with conflicting emotions. She had escaped—she had done what she needed to do to survive. But her thoughts kept circling back to Mikhail. He could have killed her. He should have killed her. But he didn't. And even though she had run from him, from the danger he represented, she couldn't shake the memory of his touch, the way his hands had gripped her, the way her body had responded to him.

I wanted him. Even after everything, I wanted him.

The thought made her stomach twist, guilt gnawing at the edges of her mind as she turned the corner and spotted a small convenience store ahead. A lone cab sat parked near the entrance, its driver sipping coffee from a paper cup, oblivious to the world around him.

Anya's feet slowed as she approached, her hand still trembling slightly as she raised it to hail the cab. She knew she needed to get home, to leave this part of the city behind and return to her father's estate where everything would feel safe, where she could pretend that none of this had happened. But the closer she got to the cab, the more uncertain she felt.

Her hand hovered over the door handle, her thoughts racing.

Do I go back? Do I tell my father what happened?

A part of her wanted to spill everything—to tell him about Mikhail, about the kidnapping, about the way she had barely escaped with her life. But then what? Her father would be furious. He would hunt Mikhail down. He wouldn't rest until the man was dead. And the thought of that—of Mikhail dead because of her—made her chest tighten with something she didn't want to acknowledge.

I don't want him dead.

Her fingers curled around the door handle, the weight of her decision pressing down on her as she hesitated. She was torn. Torn between the safety of home and the chaos of what had just happened, between the need to tell the truth and the desire to keep the memory of Mikhail's touch to herself.

Anya took a deep breath and opened the door, sliding into the backseat. She gave the driver her father's address, her voice steady, but inside, she felt anything but calm.

Anya sat back in the cab, the soft hum of the engine vibrating through the seat beneath her as the city passed by in a blur. She leaned her head against the cool glass of the window, watching the streets roll by, barely registering the familiar landmarks of home. Her mind was too crowded, too full of everything that had happened, to focus on anything but the storm of emotions swirling inside her.

The silence in the cab was heavy, punctuated only by the occasional sound of the driver clearing his throat or the rustle of his jacket as he shifted in his seat. For Anya, the silence only amplified the noise in her head—her thoughts racing, conflicting emotions battling for dominance as she tried to make sense of what had happened.

Do I tell him what happened? Can I?

The question hung heavy in her mind, weighing her down as she considered what she would say to her father when she finally arrived home. How could she possibly explain it? How could she make sense of it when she barely understood it herself? She had been kidnapped by Mikhail, taken against her will—he had almost killed her, for God's sake. But that wasn't the whole truth, was it?

Anya's brow furrowed as she leaned her forehead against the glass, the coolness of it doing little to calm her. She closed her eyes, trying to block out the world around her, trying to replay the events in her mind to make sense of them.

Mikhail had taken her, yes. She had been terrified, trapped in a situation she couldn't control. And yet, when the time had come, when the tension between them had snapped, it hadn't felt forced. She hadn't felt like a victim. She had wanted it—wanted *him*.

Her breath hitched in her throat as the memories rushed back, unbidden and unwanted. She could still feel the roughness of his hands on her skin, the heat of his body pressing against hers, the way he had kissed her—hard, desperate, like he couldn't get enough of her. And she had responded in kind. She hadn't fought it. In fact, she had reveled in it, craved it even. Every touch, every kiss, every thrust had been as much her choice as his.

What does that make me?

Anya opened her eyes, her gaze unfocused as the city continued to pass by outside the window. She felt a wave of heat rise to her cheeks, her body betraying her as she remembered the intensity of their connection. She had never felt anything like it before—so raw, so consuming. The way her body had responded to him had been almost primal, as though something deep inside her had awoken for the first time.

But how could she explain that? How could she tell her father about the desire she had felt for the man who had kidnapped her? How could she confess to the way Mikhail had made her feel—like she had lost control of herself, of her own body? How could she admit that part of her didn't regret it, that part of her still wanted him?

If I tell my father the truth… he'll kill Mikhail. He'll hunt him down and destroy him.

Her heart clenched at the thought, her stomach twisting into knots as she considered the inevitable consequences of telling her father everything. He wouldn't understand. He wouldn't care about the nuances of what had happened—he would see only one thing: his daughter had been taken, threatened, and hurt. And Mikhail would pay the price for that.

Her father was a powerful man, and when he was angry, he was unstoppable. She had seen it before—had seen the lengths he would go to in order to protect what was his. And she knew that if he ever found out about Mikhail, about what had happened between them, there would be no mercy. Mikhail wouldn't stand a chance.

Can I live with that?

Anya's chest tightened at the thought of Mikhail dead—of him lying lifeless on the ground, the fire that had burned so intensely between them snuffed out forever. The image sent a pang of guilt through her, guilt she didn't quite understand. Why did she care? Why should she care? He had kidnapped her. He had threatened her life. He was the enemy.

But then again, he hadn't killed her. He hadn't forced her. And in those moments when they had been together, it hadn't felt like they were enemies. It had felt like something else entirely—something dangerous, yes, but also intoxicating, something she couldn't quite explain or push away.

I don't want him dead.

The realization hit her like a punch to the gut. As much as she should have wanted him dead, as much as she should have wanted revenge for what he had done, the thought of Mikhail being hunted down, being destroyed, left her feeling hollow. She didn't want that blood on her hands, didn't want to be responsible for his death.

But what was she supposed to do? How could she go home, look her father in the eye, and pretend that nothing had happened? How could she keep this secret when the memory of Mikhail's touch haunted her, when the guilt gnawed at her insides every time she thought about him?

The cab turned down another street, the familiar neighborhoods of her childhood coming into view. Her father's estate wasn't far now. Soon, she would have to make a decision—soon, she would have to face her father and decide what to tell him. But the closer she got to home, the more conflicted she felt.

What am I going to say?

Anya leaned back against the seat, her fingers fiddling with the strap of her bag as her mind continued to race. She had always trusted her father, always believed in his ability to protect her, to make things right. But this time, things weren't so simple. She wasn't sure she wanted her father's protection—not if it meant Mikhail's death.

Her thoughts drifted back to Mikhail, to the way he had looked at her with those piercing eyes, the way he had touched her as though he couldn't get enough. She had felt something in those moments, something she couldn't ignore, something that had left her reeling. And despite everything, despite the danger, she couldn't deny that part of her wanted to feel that again.

How could I want him?

The question burned in her mind, fueling the guilt that gnawed at her. She shouldn't want him—she should be angry, furious even. But instead, all she could think about was the way he had made her feel, the way her body had responded to him, the intensity of it all. It was like nothing she had ever experienced before, and it scared her as much as it excited her.

The cab pulled up to the gates of her father's estate, the grand iron bars standing tall against the backdrop of the mansion beyond. Anya's heart thudded in her chest as the driver rolled down the window, speaking briefly into the intercom before the gates swung open, allowing them access.

As the cab drove up the long driveway, Anya felt the weight of her decision pressing down on her shoulders. She knew she couldn't keep this secret forever, but she also knew that telling the truth would set events in motion that she wasn't ready for.

What am I supposed to do?

The cab came to a stop outside the front entrance, and Anya paid the driver, her hands trembling slightly as she pulled her bag onto her lap. She hesitated for a moment before stepping out of the car, her mind still spinning with questions, with guilt, with desire.

She didn't have any answers—not yet. But she knew one thing for sure.

Mikhail was still a part of her story. And no matter how hard she tried, she couldn't shake the feeling that this wasn't over. Not by a long shot.

The cab's tires crunched softly over the gravel driveway as it slowed to a stop in front of the imposing gates of her father's estate. Anya's heart thudded in her chest as she stared up at the massive iron gates, her breath catching in her throat. The sight of her family home, usually a source of comfort and safety, now felt foreign—overwhelming. The familiar looming presence of the mansion, with its pristine lawns and towering facade, stood stark against the pale morning sky, but today, something was different.

It wasn't the house that had changed. It was her.

She paid the driver quickly, her hands trembling slightly as she fumbled for cash in her bag. The driver gave her a brief nod, oblivious to the storm of emotions raging inside her, before pulling away, leaving her standing alone on the driveway. The grand gates swung open with a quiet hum, triggered by the security system, but as Anya stepped forward, the weight of her secret seemed to press down harder on her shoulders with every step.

The mansion loomed closer, a cold reminder of the life she was returning to—a life where secrets had no place. But she couldn't help it. The secret of what had happened with Mikhail clung to her, refusing to let go, no matter how desperately she tried to shake it off.

I'm home. I'm safe. But why doesn't it feel like it?

The thought gnawed at her as she made her way through the grand gates, her footsteps quickening as if she could outrun the memories chasing her. The sprawling estate, with its neatly manicured lawns and glistening marble facade, was bathed in the soft light of early morning, but instead of offering her the comfort it usually did, it felt distant—like a place she no longer belonged.

Anya slipped through the front door as quietly as possible, her heart still pounding, her breath coming in short, shaky bursts. The house was silent, the early hour keeping the usual bustle of the staff at bay. It wasn't uncommon for her to stay out all night at nightclubs with friends, so she didn't worry about questions, she just didn't want to face anyone yet. The familiar scents of expensive wood polish and fresh flowers filled the air, but none of it seemed to calm her. Instead, she felt suffocated by the stillness, as though the walls themselves were closing in on her.

She moved quickly through the hallways, her feet light against the polished floors as she headed for her room. The mansion's grandeur was as it always had been—richly decorated with artwork and tapestries, the height of luxury—but today, it felt colder. Each step seemed to echo louder in the empty halls, and every shadow seemed to stretch longer, as though the house itself knew she was hiding something.

By the time Anya reached her room, her nerves were frayed, her body on edge from the weight of the secret she carried. She slipped inside, closing the door softly behind her, before leaning against it and letting out a long, shaky breath. For a moment, she allowed herself to feel relieved. She was home.

She was safe. But the sense of relief was fleeting—overpowered by the knowledge that she couldn't keep hiding what had happened forever.

I need to forget about Mikhail. I need to pretend none of this ever happened.

Anya closed her eyes, pressing her palms against the door as though she could push the memories away. But the more she tried to force them out of her mind, the more they clung to her—like shadows she couldn't escape. His face, his voice, his touch—it was all still so vivid, so real, as though he were standing in the room with her.

She could still feel the weight of his hands on her skin, the roughness of his fingers gripping her waist, the way his breath had brushed against her neck when he whispered her name. Her body still remembered the heat of him, the way he had made her feel things she had never felt before—desire, confusion, fear.

I shouldn't feel this way. He's the enemy.

But even as she thought it, Anya knew it wasn't that simple. Mikhail was the enemy—her father's enemy, her family's enemy—but in those moments they had shared, it hadn't felt like that. It had felt like something else—something more dangerous. She had wanted him, had craved his touch, and even now, standing alone in her room, she could still feel the echo of his hands on her body.

The guilt gnawed at her, twisting in her stomach like a knot she couldn't untangle. How could she feel like this? How could she be standing in her father's house, in the place where she had always felt protected, and still be thinking about the man who had kidnapped her, who had nearly killed her?

I need to stop. I need to forget.

But the more she told herself to forget, the more her thoughts drifted back to Mikhail. She couldn't push him away, couldn't erase the way he had made her feel, the way her body had responded to him. It was as though a part of her had awakened that night—something she hadn't known existed—and now that it had, it refused to be silenced.

Anya opened her eyes, staring at the familiar surroundings of her room. The soft, plush bed, the elegant furniture, the large window that overlooked the estate's sprawling gardens—it was all the same, but none of it felt like hers anymore. The safety she had once felt within these walls was gone, replaced by the cold weight of guilt and confusion.

What am I supposed to do?

The question echoed in her mind, but there were no answers. She had come home, but it didn't feel like home. Not with the weight of her secret pressing down on her, not with the memories of Mikhail haunting her every thought. She couldn't tell her father—not yet. He would never understand. But how could she keep this to herself? How could she walk around this house, pretending everything was fine, when nothing felt fine anymore?

Anya pushed herself off the door, walking slowly toward the window. The morning sun was higher in the sky now, casting a warm glow over the estate, but even the beauty of the gardens couldn't calm the storm inside her. She stared out at the neatly trimmed hedges, the fountains, the winding pathways that led to nowhere, feeling more lost than ever.

I need to forget.

But she knew she wouldn't. Mikhail wasn't someone she could forget. He had gotten under her skin, into her thoughts, and no matter how hard she tried, she couldn't shake the feeling that this wasn't over. That he wasn't done with her yet.

By the time Anya made her way downstairs a few hours later, the house had come to life. The kitchen staff moved about with practiced efficiency, the smell of fresh coffee and breakfast wafting through the air. Normally, this would bring her a sense of comfort—home always had that effect. But today, as she entered the breakfast room where her father sat at the long, polished table, the sense of unease that had settled in her chest refused to leave.

Konstantin Morozov was seated at the head of the table, reading over a newspaper with a casual intensity. He looked up as she entered, his sharp, blue eyes locking onto hers, and for a brief moment, Anya hesitated. She felt a familiar pang of guilt, sharp and unrelenting, twisting in her gut as she sat down across from him.

Her father's estate had always been a symbol of power and wealth—a place where Anya had felt safe, protected from the harsh realities of the world outside. And her father, the man who had built his empire from the ground up, had always been her shield, the one person she trusted above all others. She had been his "little girl" for as long as she could remember, the one person who could do no wrong in his eyes. He had always looked after her, always protected her. If there was one person she knew would go to any length to keep her safe, it was her father.

But now, as she sat across from him, trying to act like everything was normal, the weight of her secret pressed down harder than ever.

The room felt too bright, the sunlight streaming in through the large windows casting harsh shadows on the table. Anya could hear the faint clinking of silverware as one of the maids set down a plate of food in front of her, but she barely registered it. Her father's gaze was still on her, as if he could see through the surface, through the layers she was trying to hide behind.

"Good morning," Konstantin said, his voice calm, but there was a hint of curiosity there, as though he could sense that something was off. "You were out late last night."

Anya swallowed, trying to keep her expression neutral as she picked up her cup of coffee, her hands trembling slightly as she brought it to her lips. She could feel her father's eyes on her, studying her in that way he always did, his gaze sharp and perceptive.

He knows something's wrong.

"I went to a club with some friends," she said, her voice steady, though inside she felt anything but. "I lost track of time."

It wasn't a complete lie, but it wasn't the truth either. She had lost track of time, but not with friends. And now, sitting here with her father, the man she trusted more than anyone, she couldn't bring herself to say more. She couldn't tell him what had happened last night—couldn't tell him that she had been kidnapped, that she had been nearly killed. And she certainly couldn't tell him about Mikhail.

Konstantin set his newspaper aside, his full attention now focused on her. His face was calm, but his eyes were watchful, a flicker of concern passing over his features. "You seem tired, Anya," he said slowly, his voice measured. "Is everything alright?"

Anya's heart skipped a beat, her pulse quickening as she forced a smile. "I'm fine, Papa," she said, her voice soft but steady. "Just a late night, that's all."

Her father's gaze didn't waver. He had always been able to read her—sometimes better than she could read herself. And now, as he studied her, Anya could feel the tension in the room thickening, the weight of her unspoken words hanging in the air between them.

I should tell him everything. He was going to hear about the shootings soon from someone. But then I'd have to admit what happened… and I don't even understand it myself.

Her stomach twisted as the guilt gnawed at her. She knew she should trust him, should tell him the truth. After all, her father had always protected her. He had always been there for her, no matter what. But how could she explain this? How could she tell him about Mikhail without admitting her own guilt, her own desire? How could she tell him that, even after he killed people and kidnapped her, she had wanted what had happened, that she had wanted Mikhail, even after everything?

Her father reached for his coffee, taking a slow sip as he continued to watch her. "You know you can tell me anything, right?" he said after a long pause, his voice quiet but firm.

Anya nodded, feeling a lump form in her throat as she tried to swallow the rising tide of emotion. She knew she could tell him anything. That had always been true. But this? This was different. This wasn't something she could just confess and have him fix. This was a secret that carried consequences—consequences she wasn't sure she was ready to face.

"I know," she said softly, her fingers gripping the edge of the table as she forced herself to meet his gaze. "I know I can tell you anything."

Her father studied her for a moment longer, his eyes narrowing slightly as though he could sense the battle waging inside her. The tension between them was palpable, but Anya held her ground, refusing to let the truth slip out. Not yet. She wasn't ready to talk about it. She wasn't ready to admit what had happened—not to herself, and certainly not to him.

Konstantin finally leaned back in his chair, his gaze softening just a fraction as he gave her a small nod. "Alright," he said, his voice gentle but with an edge of finality. "But if something is wrong, Anya, you tell me. Understand?"

Anya nodded again, though the knot of guilt in her chest tightened even further. She could feel the weight of his words pressing down on her, the unspoken expectation that she would eventually come to him, that she would tell him the truth. But how could she?

As she picked at her breakfast, her mind wandered back to Mikhail—back to the way his hands had felt on her skin, the way his body had pressed against hers, the way she had wanted him. The memory made her stomach flip, a mixture of guilt and desire swirling inside her like a storm she couldn't control.

How could I tell my father that I wanted the man who kidnapped me? That I wanted him in ways I've never wanted anyone?

She pushed the thoughts away, focusing instead on the calm, steady rhythm of her father's voice as he talked about business—about meetings and plans for the day. But even as she listened, even as she nodded in all the right places, the thoughts of Mikhail lingered, refusing to be pushed aside.

Her father didn't press her any further, but the tension between them didn't fade. Anya could feel it in the air, could sense that he knew something was off, even if he didn't know what it was yet. She knew that if she didn't tell him soon, if she didn't confess what had happened, the weight of her secret would only grow heavier. But for now, she wasn't ready.

As the conversation moved on, Anya forced herself to relax, to pretend that everything was normal. She smiled, laughed at her father's jokes, and listened as he talked about the plans for the week. But inside, her mind was spinning, her thoughts tangled in a web of guilt and secrecy that she wasn't sure she could escape from.

I'm still Daddy's little girl, she thought, her chest tightening with the lie. *But how long can I keep pretending?*

Chapter 5

Mikhail's boots echoed on the hardwood floor as he paced the length of his small, sparse apartment, his hands balled into fists at his sides. The air in the room felt thick, suffocating, every breath he took weighing heavier in his chest. His mind raced, his thoughts a tangled mess of guilt and frustration, and no matter how hard he tried to focus, his mind kept circling back to the same thing: Anya.

I should have killed her.

The thought pulsed through him, sharp and bitter. It would have been clean. Quick. One shot, and all of this would have been over. There wouldn't be a stolen car, no loose ends, no woman from the rival Bratva haunting his every waking thought. If he had just done what he was supposed to do—what he had been trained to do—none of this would be happening. And now? Now, he had to deal with the fallout of his own failure.

Mikhail's jaw clenched, the muscles in his neck tensing as the full weight of the situation pressed down on him. He had let her go. Worse than that—he had fucked her, and now she was out there, a witness to his crimes, the daughter of Konstantin Morozov, no less. His hand twitched toward the scar that ran along his jawline, an old habit when he was stressed. But nothing could ease the tension simmering inside him.

His eyes flicked to the duffel bag of guns lying on the floor by the door. At least he had those. At least he had that one part of the mission accomplished. But as he stood there, staring at the bag, the sense of accomplishment was drowned by the far greater failure that loomed over him. The fact that Anya had slipped through his fingers, that he hadn't killed her when he had the chance.

What the fuck was I thinking?

He hadn't been thinking. That was the problem. The moment he saw her, cowering in that dark corner of the room, something inside him had shifted, something he didn't recognize. He should have pulled the trigger, should have ended it right there. But those wide, green eyes had looked up at him, and his resolve had cracked. Now, he was left with the consequences of that crack. She was gone, and he was left standing here like a fool, with nothing but a bag of guns and the memory of her body still fresh in his mind.

That was what infuriated him the most—how much she was still on his mind. He could feel her, still, the heat of her body, the softness of her skin, the way she had moaned his name. He had told himself it was just another fuck, just another way to release the pent-up tension, but deep down, he knew it wasn't that simple. He had wanted her. Still wanted her, and that weakness made him sick to his core.

I let her go. I let her fucking go, and now she's out there, running back to her father. I should've put a bullet in her skull.

Mikhail's fists tightened, his anger bubbling just beneath the surface, ready to explode. He had made a mistake. A huge fucking mistake. And now, he had to face the consequences. Viktor wouldn't let this slide. There was no way he could spin this. No way to make it look like anything other than what it was—an unforgivable fuck-up.

His feet stilled, and he turned his gaze toward the small window at the far end of the room. The early morning light was filtering through the blinds, casting long shadows across the floor. His pulse thudded in his ears, his mind still reeling as the reality of what he had to do settled over him like a heavy cloak.

I have to tell Viktor.

There was no way around it. He couldn't keep this from him, couldn't lie his way out of this one. The moment Viktor found out who she was—and Viktor always found out—it would be over. No, Mikhail needed to face this head-on. He needed to own up to what he had done, and hope to God that Viktor didn't tear him apart for it.

This is going to be fucking brutal.

Mikhail bent down and grabbed the duffel bag, slinging it over his shoulder with a grunt. The weight of the guns inside was nothing compared to the weight of what he was about to do. He moved toward the door, his steps heavy, each one filled with the knowledge that he was walking straight into a firestorm.

I have to get her out of my head. He couldn't afford to be distracted by her anymore. She was gone, and he needed to focus. But no matter how hard he tried to shake the memory of her, she lingered in the back of his mind—those defiant eyes, the way her body had felt beneath his.

I need to focus on what's coming. Viktor is going to tear me apart for this. And I deserve it.

Mikhail's hand hovered over the doorknob for a moment, his chest tight with the weight of what he had to do. His mind raced, the guilt gnawing at him like a rabid dog, but there was no going back now. He had made his choice, and now, he would have to face the consequences.

He tightened his grip on the duffel bag as he walked down the empty corridor toward Viktor's office. Each step was heavy with the knowledge of what was coming, but no matter how much he prepared himself, he knew nothing could soften the blow.

The heavy door to Viktor's office creaked open as Mikhail stepped inside, the weight of the duffel bag pulling at his shoulder. The room was dimly lit, the cold light filtering through the half-closed blinds casting sharp lines across the floor. Viktor's office always felt too still, too silent—like the calm before a storm. The smell of leather and expensive cigars clung to the air, but today, even the familiar scents did nothing to ease the knot of tension in Mikhail's gut.

Viktor sat behind the massive oak desk, his expression unreadable as he watched Mikhail enter. His sharp eyes flicked briefly to the bag of guns before returning to Mikhail's face. There was no warmth in Viktor's gaze—only expectation. The silence stretched on for a moment too long, the air between them growing thick with the weight of what wasn't being said.

Mikhail didn't speak as he crossed the room, his footsteps echoing in the stillness. He dropped the duffel bag onto the desk with a thud, the sound shattering the quiet like a gunshot. His jaw clenched as he straightened, forcing himself to meet Viktor's gaze. He could feel the tension radiating off Viktor, a coiled snake ready to strike, but for now, the older man remained eerily calm.

The silence hung heavy in the air, thickening with every passing second. Mikhail could feel the pulse of his heart, the thrum of adrenaline still racing through his veins. His body was taut, every muscle coiled, knowing that the conversation ahead wouldn't go well.

Viktor finally broke the silence, his voice low and steady, but there was an edge to it—something cold and dangerous lurking beneath the surface. "Did you kill all the men in the house?"

Mikhail's mouth went dry. He knew this was coming—the question that would rip open the gaping wound of his mistake. His gut churned as the words lingered in the air, waiting for his response. For a split second, he considered lying. He considered telling Viktor exactly what he wanted to hear, burying the truth beneath layers of false confidence. But he knew that wouldn't work. Viktor always found out the truth. And when he did, the consequences would be even worse.

Mikhail swallowed, his voice flat as he replied. "Yes. I killed all the men."

The words tasted like ash in his mouth, his stomach tightening with the weight of the lie. It wasn't a full lie—he had killed the men. But the truth—the whole truth—was far more complicated. He could feel

Viktor's gaze boring into him, waiting for more, waiting for the full story.

For a moment, Viktor didn't respond. He leaned back in his chair, his fingers steepled under his chin as he studied Mikhail in silence. The tension in the room spiked, the quiet unbearable as Mikhail stood there, his pulse racing. He could feel his hands beginning to tremble, but he clenched them into fists, forcing himself to stay still.

Viktor's eyes narrowed slightly, a flicker of something unreadable passing over his face. "And what about any women?"

Mikhail froze, the question hitting him like a punch to the gut. His heart stuttered in his chest, his body going rigid as Viktor's words sank in. Of course, Viktor knew. He always knew. The man was too perceptive, too sharp to miss something as important as that.

For a second, Mikhail said nothing, his mind scrambling for the right words, for a way to explain the mess he had created. But the truth was, there was no way to explain it. No way to make it right. He had fucked up, and there was no getting around it.

His throat tightened as the truth clawed its way out. "There was a woman," he said, his voice rough with the admission. "She wasn't supposed to be there. Wrong place, wrong time."

The temperature in the room seemed to drop as Viktor's expression darkened. His gaze sharpened, the anger flickering behind his eyes like the first spark of a fire. Mikhail could feel the weight of Viktor's disappointment bearing down on him, suffocating him.

"And what did you do with this woman?" Viktor asked, his voice calm, but there was a dangerous edge to it. Mikhail could hear the barely contained fury beneath the surface, ready to explode.

Mikhail's jaw clenched, his pulse pounding in his ears. He hated this—hated the way Viktor was dragging the truth out of him, piece by piece, as if he were a child being scolded for some petty mistake. But this wasn't petty. This was a fuck-up of epic proportions, and he knew there was no escaping it.

"I couldn't kill her," Mikhail admitted, his voice tight. "She wasn't a threat. Just... wrong place, wrong time."

Viktor's eyes flashed, his hands gripping the arms of his chair as he leaned forward slightly, the tension between them thick enough to cut with a knife. "You couldn't kill her?" he repeated, his voice low and dangerous. "Since when do we let people walk away because they're in the wrong place at the wrong time?"

Mikhail could feel the anger rolling off Viktor in waves, the older man's composure slipping as his fury began to build. He hated himself for what he had done, hated himself even more for the weakness that had led him here.

"I should have killed her," Mikhail said, his voice harsh. "I know that."

Viktor's eyes narrowed, his voice a growl. "But you didn't. Did you?"

"No," Mikhail muttered, his hands curling into fists at his sides. "I didn't."

The silence that followed Mikhail's admission was deafening. Viktor sat there, his eyes locked on Mikhail's face, a slow-burning fury building behind the cold mask of his expression. Mikhail's hands were at his sides, clenched into fists, but his face remained impassive. Inside, though, the weight of his mistake was crushing him, pressing down harder with every second that passed in silence.

Finally, Viktor leaned forward in his chair, his voice low and razor-sharp. "You didn't kill her?" he repeated, his tone laced with disbelief and growing rage. "Why not?"

Mikhail swallowed, his gaze hard as he met Viktor's eyes. He had to keep this clinical, detached. If there was one thing Viktor despised more than incompetence, it was weakness. And Mikhail wasn't about to show weakness—not here, not now.

"I couldn't kill her," Mikhail said, his voice as flat and emotionless as he could make it. "I fucked her."

Viktor's reaction was immediate. His eyes blazed with fury, his fist slamming down on the desk with a force that rattled the papers scattered across its surface. The sound reverberated through the room like a gunshot, but Mikhail didn't flinch. He stood his ground, his jaw set, his eyes steady, even as Viktor's anger exploded.

"You defied orders for some pussy?" Viktor shouted, his voice harsh, the words slicing through the tension in the room like a blade. "You thought with your dick instead of your head, and now you've left a fucking witness?"

Mikhail didn't speak. He knew there was no point in defending himself—not when Viktor was like this. The older man's fury was palpable, filling the room with a violent, almost tangible energy. Mikhail could feel the weight of it pressing down on him, but he remained silent, standing rigid and unmoving as Viktor's words continued to cut into him.

"You had one job, Mikhail," Viktor spat, his hands gripping the edges of the desk so tightly his knuckles turned white. "Kill everyone. No witnesses. No loose ends. That's what we do. That's what we've always done. And now? Now you've left us vulnerable. You've jeopardized everything we've built for some girl?"

Mikhail's stomach twisted at the word *girl*, but he forced his expression to remain neutral. Viktor didn't need to know the details. He didn't need to know about the fire in Anya's eyes, the way she had looked at him, the way she had fought back. All Viktor needed to know was that Mikhail had fucked her. That was all that mattered.

"I didn't plan it," Mikhail said, his voice still flat, devoid of emotion. "It just happened."

Viktor's eyes narrowed, his lips curling into a snarl. "Just happened? What the fuck are you talking about, Mikhail? You don't fuck up like this because something just happens. You don't let a witness walk away because you had a moment of weakness."

Mikhail's jaw clenched, the tension coiling in his muscles as he stood there, feeling the full weight of Viktor's disappointment, his fury. He knew this was coming. He knew Viktor would tear into him, would make him feel every inch of his mistake. And he deserved it. He deserved every harsh word, every ounce of anger Viktor threw at him.

But even now, standing in the midst of Viktor's rage, Mikhail couldn't stop thinking about Anya. The way she had felt beneath him, the way her lips had tasted, the fire in her eyes as she had fought him.

No matter how hard he tried to push the memories away, they lingered, taunting him, reminding him of his weakness.

Viktor's voice cut through his thoughts like a blade. "Where is she now?"

Mikhail hesitated for the briefest of moments, the words catching in his throat before he forced them out. "She stole my car. She's gone."

The silence that followed was suffocating. Viktor stared at him, his eyes wide with disbelief, his lips curling into a sneer of disgust. "She *stole* your car?" he repeated, his voice dripping with venom. "You let her steal your fucking car, Mikhail?"

Mikhail nodded, his face still blank, though inside, he could feel the shame burning in his chest. He had let her go. He had let her slip through his fingers, and now, he was paying the price.

Viktor pushed himself up from the desk, his movements slow and deliberate, the fury simmering just below the surface. "Let me get this straight," he said, his voice low and dangerous. "Not only did you defy my orders, not only did you let a witness walk away, but you let her steal your fucking car and disappear? What the fuck were you thinking, Mikhail?"

Mikhail stood silent, his eyes fixed on a point just past Viktor's shoulder. He didn't have an answer for that. He didn't have an excuse. All he had was the knowledge that he had fucked up, that he had let his emotions—his desire—get the better of him, and now, they were both paying the price.

Viktor paced behind his desk, his hands clenching and unclenching as he tried to rein in his temper. The room was thick with tension, the weight of Mikhail's mistake hanging heavy in the air between them. Viktor's face was a mask of fury, his eyes sharp with accusation.

"I trusted you," Viktor said finally, his voice barely above a whisper, but the anger in it was unmistakable. "I trusted you to handle this, and you fucked it up. You put the entire Bratva at risk because you couldn't keep your dick in your pants."

Mikhail's stomach churned, the guilt twisting inside him like a knife. He knew Viktor was right. He had let Anya get under his skin, had let his desire for her cloud his judgment, and now, they were all at risk because of it. He had defied orders, and there was no coming back from that.

But even now, with Viktor's anger scorching him, with the consequences of his actions looming over him like a death sentence, Mikhail couldn't get Anya out of his head. The way she had looked at him, the way she had fought him, the way she had made him feel alive in a way he hadn't felt in years. It was a distraction—one that could get him killed.

But it was there, and no matter how much he hated himself for it, he couldn't shake it.

"I know I fucked up," Mikhail said, his voice low, but steady. "I'll fix it."

Viktor stopped pacing, his eyes narrowing as he stared at Mikhail, the rage still burning behind his gaze. "You'd better, Mikhail. Because if you don't, Nikolai will have your fucking head. You left a witness, and not just any witness—a witness who can take down the entire Bratva if she wants to. You clean this up, or you're dead. Understand?"

Mikhail nodded, his jaw tight. "I'll handle it."

But as he stood there, facing Viktor's wrath, the only thing he could think of was Anya—her face, her eyes, her body. And despite everything, despite the consequences he knew were coming, a part of him didn't want to handle it. A part of him didn't want her dead.

The air in Viktor's office was thick with tension, vibrating with the fury simmering just beneath the surface. Mikhail stood still, his muscles coiled tight as Viktor's voice rose to a shout, filling the room with a harsh, biting anger. The older man was pacing now, his hands gesturing wildly as he raged, every word dripping with disbelief and fury.

"You let her go? You let a fucking witness escape, and now you've put the entire Bratva at risk. For what? For some girl you found in a goddamn house raid?" Viktor's voice cracked with the force of his frustration, his movements sharp and erratic. He slammed his fist against the desk again, the sharp sound reverberating through the room. "What the fuck were you thinking, Mikhail?"

Mikhail said nothing, his face blank, his gaze steady. Inside, his emotions were a tangled mess of guilt, shame, and anger, but he wouldn't let them show. Not now. Not when Viktor was tearing into him, the full weight of his mistake crashing down on him like an avalanche. He deserved this. He knew he did.

"You know what you've done?" Viktor continued, his voice a mix of disbelief and rage. "You've just handed Konstantin fucking Morozov leverage over us on a silver platter! You've given him a reason to come after us, to dismantle everything we've built, and for what? For some pussy?"

Mikhail felt the sting of the words, but he remained silent. Viktor's fury was justified. He had fucked up. Big time. And now, the consequences of that failure were spiraling out of control.

"You should have killed her!" Viktor shouted, his voice shaking with anger. "You should have put a bullet in her fucking head, like you were supposed to, but no! You let her go! You let her take your car, for fuck's sake! You let a witness slip through your fingers, and now we're all at risk. Do you even understand the gravity of what you've done?"

Mikhail stayed still, his fists clenched at his sides. His heart pounded in his chest, the weight of Viktor's words crashing down on him like hammer blows. But he knew better than to interrupt. Viktor needed to get it out, needed to rage, and Mikhail needed to take it.

"She could be anywhere by now, telling anyone what she saw," Viktor went on, pacing behind the desk, his hands running through his hair in frustration.

Mikhail's stomach twisted with guilt, the reality of what he had done settling over him like a suffocating fog. Viktor was right. He had let Anya go, and now, everything was spiraling out of control. He had made a mistake—a catastrophic mistake—and now, they were all paying the price.

Viktor stopped pacing, turning to face Mikhail with a look of pure, seething rage. "Do you have any idea what Nikolai is going to do when he finds out about this?" he spat. "He's going to have your head, Mikhail. He's going to rip you apart for this fuck-up, and I won't be able to stop him. No one will. You've put all of us in danger, and for what?"

Mikhail let Viktor's words wash over him, the weight of the truth settling deep in his gut. He had made a mistake, and there was no taking it back. But there was something Viktor didn't know. Something that made this mess even worse than it already was.

Mikhail took a deep breath, his hands curling into fists at his sides as he prepared himself for the final blow. His voice was calm, measured, as he spoke. "It gets worse."

Viktor stopped dead in his tracks, his eyes narrowing as he stared at Mikhail. The room fell deathly silent, the tension thick and oppressive. For a moment, neither of them moved, the words hanging in the air like a bomb waiting to go off.

"What do you mean, it gets worse?" Viktor asked, his voice low and dangerous, his fury barely contained.

Mikhail swallowed, the truth heavy on his tongue. He had fucked up, but this was the part that would make Viktor realize just how badly. There was no way around it. No way to soften the blow. He had to tell him.

"She's Konstantin Morozov's daughter."

The silence that followed was absolute. It was as if the entire world had come to a screeching halt. Viktor's face went pale, his mouth slightly open in disbelief. His eyes widened, the fury in them replaced by something much colder—something like shock.

For a moment, Viktor didn't speak. He just stared at Mikhail, his mouth opening and closing as if trying to process what he had just heard. The reality of the situation was sinking in, but the full weight of it hadn't hit yet. When it did, Mikhail knew it was going to be explosive.

Viktor finally managed to find his voice, though it was low and shaky. "She's what?"

Mikhail's jaw clenched as he forced himself to repeat it. "She's Konstantin Morozov's daughter."

The words hit Viktor like a freight train. His face twisted into a mask of shock and fury, his hands shaking as he slammed them down onto the desk. "You fucking idiot!" he roared, the sound echoing through the room like a thunderclap. "You fucked Konstantin Morozov's daughter?"

Mikhail didn't answer. There was nothing left to say.

The silence that followed was suffocating, the air thick with the realization of what had just been revealed. Viktor stood there, his chest heaving, his face flushed with rage and disbelief. He looked like a man on the edge, ready to explode at any second.

"This… this is worse than I thought," Viktor muttered, his voice shaky. "Do you have any idea what you've done?"

Mikhail nodded, his jaw tight. "I know."

Viktor stared at him for a long moment, his eyes wide with shock and fury. Then, slowly, he sank back into his chair, his hands covering his face as the weight of the situation settled over him like a heavy fog.

"We're all fucked," Viktor whispered, his voice barely audible. "We're all so fucked."

The room felt like it had been plunged into ice, the explosive fury of moments ago replaced by a chilling silence. Viktor sat at his desk, his fingers steepled in front of him, his breathing heavy as he wrestled with the enormity of what Mikhail had just revealed. The rage that had burned so brightly in his eyes had dulled to something colder—something much more dangerous.

Mikhail stood in front of the desk, his body tense, waiting for Viktor's next words. He knew what was coming. There was only one way this could go, and no matter how much he wanted to fight it, no matter how much his stomach twisted at the thought, he knew there was no escaping it.

Viktor lifted his head slowly, his gaze locking onto Mikhail's. When he spoke, his voice was low, but it carried a deadly weight. "You need to take care of this, Mikhail," he said, his words like ice. "You need to kill the bitch and finish what you started."

The words hit Mikhail like a hammer to the chest. He had expected them, but hearing them aloud, hearing them said with such cold finality, made the weight of his duty feel all the heavier. His hands clenched into fists at his sides, his pulse quickening as the reality of what Viktor was asking him to do set in.

"I don't care how you feel about her," Viktor continued, his voice steady, unyielding. "I don't care if she's Konstantin Morozov's daughter or the fucking Queen of England. You need to kill her, Mikhail. Because if you don't, we're all dead. Nikolai will have your head for this mess if it's not cleaned up, and if Konstantin finds out, he'll come after us with everything he has."

The silence that followed was suffocating. Mikhail felt the weight of Viktor's words pressing down on him, the enormity of the task he had been given tightening like a noose around his neck. He had to do it. There was no other choice. This was the Bratva way—loose ends were tied up, witnesses were silenced. It was as simple as that. And Anya... Anya was a threat.

But the thought of killing her made something inside him twist painfully. He could still see her in his mind, the fire in her emerald green eyes, the defiance in her voice as she had fought against him. He remembered the way her body had felt against his, the heat of her skin, the sound of her moans. And now, Viktor was asking him to take her life—to end something that had barely begun.

"You know what has to be done," Viktor said, his voice hardening. "If you don't do this, you're dead. We're all dead. There's no room for weakness, Mikhail. Not in this life. Not in the Bratva."

Mikhail swallowed, his throat dry. He knew Viktor was right. There was no room for weakness. He had been raised in this world, trained to do what had to be done, no matter how difficult. He had killed before—many times. He had pulled the trigger without hesitation, taken lives without remorse. But this… this felt different. Anya wasn't just some random woman caught in the wrong place at the wrong time anymore. She had become more than that. And that was the problem.

He forced himself to nod, the motion stiff, mechanical. "I'll handle it," he said, his voice tight, strained. The words felt foreign on his tongue, but they were the only ones that would satisfy Viktor.

Viktor's gaze didn't waver. He studied Mikhail for a moment longer, as if searching for any sign of hesitation, any sign that Mikhail wasn't fully committed to the task at hand. But Mikhail had learned long ago how to mask his emotions, how to hide the conflict raging inside him.

Finally, Viktor nodded, leaning back in his chair. "Good," he said, his voice calm now, cold. "Make sure it's done quickly. Clean. No loose ends this time."

Mikhail gave a curt nod, then turned on his heel and left the office, his steps heavy, his mind spinning. As he made his way down the long hallway and out of the building, the weight of Viktor's words echoed in his ears. *Kill her. Finish what you started.*

But no matter how many times he repeated the words to himself, they didn't feel real. The thought of Anya, dead by his hand, felt like a nightmare he couldn't wake from. He should have killed her back at the house, should have ended it before any of this became an issue. But he hadn't. And now… now he was in deeper than he had ever intended to be.

As he stepped out into the cold air, his breath visible in the early morning light, Mikhail's mind raced with conflicting emotions. His loyalty to the Bratva, to Viktor, to Nikolai—it all demanded that he follow through with this. It was his responsibility. His duty. If he didn't do it, someone else would. And then, he would be next.

But the image of Anya wouldn't leave his mind. The way she had looked at him, the fire in her eyes, the raw, primal attraction between them. He could still feel her body pressed against his, the memory of her soft skin, her scent lingering in his thoughts like a drug he couldn't quit.

He cursed under his breath, running a hand through his hair as he tried to clear his head. He couldn't afford to be distracted by her. She was the enemy. She was a threat. And he had to take care of her before she became an even bigger one.

But despite his best efforts, no matter how much he tried to tell himself it had to be done, he couldn't get her out of his head. And that… that scared him more than anything.

The cold air hit Mikhail's face the moment he stepped out of Viktor's office, but it did nothing to cool the storm raging inside him. His footsteps were heavy, echoing through the quiet compound as he walked away from the building, his mind spinning with the weight of Viktor's ultimatum. Every step he took felt like he was sinking deeper into a pit he couldn't crawl out of, the edges of it closing in around him.

He clenched his fists as he walked, the tension coiling tighter and tighter in his chest. He knew what he had to do. He had been given a direct order—an order that couldn't be ignored, not without consequences. He had to kill Anya. It was the only way to clean up the mess he had created, the only way to make sure the Bratva stayed intact, and that his own head stayed firmly on his shoulders.

I should kill her. I should have killed her already.

The thought gnawed at him, relentless and sharp. It would have been simple. Quick. A clean shot, and everything would have been over. No loose ends, no complications. He would have walked away from that house without a second thought, just another mission completed, another problem erased.

But he hadn't done it. He had hesitated. He had let her live, and now he was paying the price for that moment of weakness.

And now I can't stop thinking about her.

That was the part that infuriated him the most. No matter how hard he tried to focus, no matter how many times he told himself that she was a threat, that she needed to die, her image still lingered in his mind. Her face, those emerald green eyes burning with defiance, the way her body had responded to his touch… it was driving him mad. Every time he closed his eyes, he saw her. Every time he tried to push her out of his mind, she crept back in, taunting him, reminding him of the weakness he had allowed to take root.

Mikhail gritted his teeth, his jaw clenching as he walked through the compound. His body was rigid, his movements stiff as he tried to shake the thoughts away, tried to clear his head, but it was useless. She was there, always there, haunting him with every step he took.

I need to focus. I need to end this.

But even as the thought crossed his mind, his stomach churned with the idea of it. The thought of putting a bullet in her head made him sick in a way that no other kill had before. He had killed countless men—women too. It was the job. It was what he did. And he had never hesitated, never questioned his orders before. But Anya was different. She wasn't just another loose end to tie up. She had gotten under his skin, and no matter how much he tried to deny it, the truth was there, staring him in the face.

She's making me weak.

The realization hit him like a punch to the gut, his fists tightening at his sides. She was a threat—not just to the Bratva, but to him. She was making him vulnerable, distracting him, pulling him away from the life he had built, from the duty he had sworn to uphold. And that was dangerous. That was something he couldn't afford.

But even knowing that, even feeling the weight of his responsibility pressing down on him, he couldn't bring himself to do it. He couldn't bring himself to kill her. Not yet.

Why? The question echoed in his mind, and for the first time in a long time, Mikhail didn't have an answer. He didn't understand why he couldn't pull the trigger. Why he couldn't just finish it. All he knew was that something inside him wouldn't let him.

He stopped walking, his breath visible in the cold air as he stared out at the compound, his mind a whirlwind of conflicting emotions. His loyalty to the Bratva was absolute, his commitment to his duty unwavering. But when it came to Anya, everything was different. She had changed something in him, something he didn't want to admit was even there.

I need to figure this out. I need to end this before it gets any worse.

But as he stood there, fists clenched and heart pounding, Mikhail knew that killing Anya wasn't something he could do. Not yet. And that terrified him more than anything.

Chapter 6

The thumping bass of the nightclub reverberated through Mikhail's body as he stepped through the darkened entrance. The flashing lights, strobing in shades of red and blue, cut through the darkness in quick bursts, casting fleeting shadows over the writhing crowd. Bodies pressed together in dance, the air thick with sweat, alcohol, and the kind of reckless abandon that thrived in places like this.

But Mikhail wasn't here to lose himself. He was here to kill.

It had been a week since his tense meeting with Viktor, a week filled with internal battles that left him restless and frustrated. Despite telling himself that his night with Anya had meant nothing, she haunted him. Every day, she was there—in his mind, in his blood. It twisted something deep inside him, something dark, something he couldn't control. And he hated it.

I need to kill her.

The thought echoed through his head as he moved through the crowd, his steps calculated, his expression cold. She was a threat. He knew it. Viktor had made it clear that leaving her alive was a

liability, a loose end that needed to be dealt with.
Yet Mikhail had hesitated before, and that hesitation
had cost him. He couldn't afford it again. Not
tonight.

This is my chance. No more hesitation.

His hand hovered near his jacket, where the cold
steel of his gun was tucked away, hidden but
ever-present. It had always been his weapon of
choice—clean, quick, final. The thought of using it
on Anya sent a strange pulse through him, a
mixture of duty and dread, but he pushed it aside.
This was what he had been trained for. There was
no room for emotion in this line of work.

She's a threat. I need to kill her.

His jaw tightened as he found a dark corner near
the back of the club, away from the pulsating lights
and the frenzied dancers. The shadows clung to
him like an old friend, obscuring his face from the
crowd as he surveyed the room. The music
pounded through the walls, shaking the floor
beneath his feet, but his focus remained
razor-sharp. He was waiting for her.

He had been tracking her all week. Following her
movements through the city, learning her routines,
her habits. She wasn't easy to find alone. Anya was
always guarded—whether it was by her father's
men or by the walls she had built around herself.
But tonight, she was here, vulnerable, surrounded

by her friends but not by the security detail that usually trailed her.

This was his moment.

Mikhail scanned the sea of faces, each one blurring together under the flashing lights. His senses were heightened, his mind sharp, as he hunted her from the shadows. The club was packed, filled with people who were oblivious to the predator in their midst, people who had no idea that someone was about to die tonight.

The thought of it should have steeled him, should have reminded him of his mission. But the conflict within him was growing stronger with each passing second. Every time he thought of her—those defiant green eyes, the way her body had felt against his—it stirred something inside him, something dangerous. He couldn't afford distractions like that. Not now. Not when he was so close.

It was just one night. It meant nothing.

He had told himself that over and over again, but the memory of her still clung to him, refusing to let go. He had made a mistake that night, letting her live. And now, here he was, trying to clean up the mess he had made. But no matter how much he tried to harden his heart, to remind himself that this was just another job, the thought of pulling the trigger on Anya felt… wrong.

This is my chance, he told himself again, his hand tightening around the grip of his gun. *I won't fail this time.*

The pounding music surged again, making the walls vibrate as the crowd erupted in cheers. Mikhail's pulse quickened, his eyes narrowing as he scanned the entrance. Any moment now, she would walk through those doors, completely unaware of what was waiting for her. And when she did, he would make his move.

He shifted slightly, his body blending into the shadows. He needed to stay calm, to stay focused. This wasn't the first time he had been in this situation. He had killed before. Countless times. But somehow, this felt different. This wasn't just about loyalty to the Bratva. This was personal. Anya had gotten under his skin, and that was something he couldn't afford.

She's a threat, he reminded himself, his mind fighting to drown out the thoughts of her that kept creeping in. *A threat that needs to be eliminated.*

And yet, beneath the cold resolve, something darker simmered. His obsession with her—the way she had challenged him, the way she had ignited something in him—was clouding his judgment. He had never hesitated like this before. Never. But with Anya, it wasn't just about duty anymore. It was about something much more dangerous.

The minutes dragged on, each one pulling Mikhail deeper into his internal conflict. The urge to kill her was there, but so was the desire to see her again. To touch her. To lose himself in the fire that burned between them, even if it meant betraying everything he stood for.

No more hesitation, he told himself, his eyes sharp as he watched the crowd, his pulse racing. *She's a threat. And threats need to be eliminated.*

But even as the thought repeated in his mind, Mikhail knew the truth—he wasn't sure if he could do it.

Mikhail's eyes locked onto the entrance the moment she walked in. Even through the swirling bodies and flashing lights, he saw her—Anya. His heart skipped a beat, and his pulse quickened as she stepped into the nightclub, her figure immediately commanding his attention. She wore a tight, low-cut dress that clung to her body like a second skin, hugging every curve. The fabric shimmered under the neon lights, and the cut was just revealing enough to make every man in the room look twice.

Including him.

His jaw tightened as he watched her move with effortless grace, her lips curving into a smile as she laughed with her friends, completely unaware of the danger lurking in the shadows. Mikhail's hand twitched near his jacket, where the cool metal of his gun was concealed, but despite the tension coiling in his chest, his fingers didn't move. He couldn't take his eyes off her.

She was supposed to be his enemy. He had come here with one goal in mind—kill her. But the sight of her now, bathed in the flashing lights, surrounded by the pulsing energy of the club, stirred something else inside him. Something darker. More dangerous. Desire.

She's the enemy. I need to kill her. Why the fuck can't I stop looking at her?

His internal dialogue battled against the urge that was building inside him. Every step she took, every time her hips swayed, every time she laughed, it clawed at him, dragging him deeper into the conflict that had been tearing him apart for the past week. His mind screamed that she was a threat, that she needed to be eliminated, but his body… his body remembered what it felt like to touch her. To taste her.

She moved through the crowd, her friends surrounding her, unaware of the deadly intent that followed her from the shadows. They were laughing, drinks in hand, their carefree energy a stark contrast to the storm brewing inside Mikhail. He watched them closely, his eyes tracking Anya's every movement. She was so alive, so full of fire.

And yet, in his world, that fire made her dangerous. Deadly.

This is my chance, he reminded himself, his heart pounding in his chest. *She's not guarded tonight. This is the moment I've been waiting for.*

But even as the thought formed in his mind, it felt hollow. There was a time when he wouldn't have hesitated. When pulling the trigger would have been second nature. But now? Now, every time he looked at her, every time he thought of ending her life, something inside him pulled back.

Mikhail's hand clenched into a fist, his knuckles white as he struggled to maintain control. The memory of her body pressed against his, her breathless moans in his ear, the way she had moved under him—it all crashed into him like a tidal wave, overwhelming his senses. It was infuriating. He should have killed her back at the safehouse. He should have walked away without looking back. But he hadn't. And now, she was here, tempting him, teasing him, driving him mad with the knowledge that he still couldn't pull the trigger.

Why is she making this so hard?

He hated himself for feeling this way. For wanting her. For craving the same thing that had put them both in this mess. But even as the anger bubbled inside him, it wasn't enough to shake the attraction that lingered just beneath the surface. His body remembered her. His mind fought against it, but the pull was undeniable.

For nearly an hour, he watched her from the shadows, his eyes following her every move. She danced with her friends, her body swaying to the rhythm of the music, the lights casting her in an almost ethereal glow. She was beautiful. Too beautiful. The way her dress clung to her hips, the way her laughter floated above the pounding bass, the way she seemed so completely unaware of the storm she had set off inside him—it was maddening.

His eyes narrowed as he observed her, the cold rational side of him calculating her every move. She was mingling, chatting with different groups, her smile never fading. But there was something about the way she held herself, something deeper that told Mikhail she wasn't completely oblivious. Maybe she was hiding it, masking it behind that carefree facade, but he could see it—the way her eyes flicked toward the shadows now and then, as if she could feel the danger creeping closer.

She knows, Mikhail thought, his grip tightening around the edge of his jacket. *She knows someone's watching her.*

But did she know it was him? Did she know that the man who had saved her life—and almost taken it—was standing just a few feet away, torn between his loyalty to the Bratva and the undeniable pull she had over him?

Mikhail's jaw clenched as he watched her break away from the group. His pulse quickened, his body tensing as she moved through the crowd, her hips swaying as she made her way toward the back of the club. Toward the bathrooms.

This is it, he told himself, his heart pounding in his chest. *I'll end it here.*

The time for hesitation was over. He had already waited too long. Every second she remained alive was a risk to the Bratva, a risk to his own survival. Viktor had been clear—kill her or face the consequences. And Mikhail had always followed orders. He didn't have a choice. Not now. Not anymore.

His hand moved to the gun hidden under his jacket, his fingers brushing against the cold metal. He felt the familiar weight of it, the power it gave him, the finality it promised. All he had to do was wait for her to pass. He would follow her to the back, where the shadows were darker, where the noise of the club wouldn't mask the sound of the gunshot. It would be clean. Quick.

But as he moved through the crowd, following her path, that familiar tension twisted in his gut again. His eyes were locked on her, watching the way her dress clung to her body, the way her hair fell down her back in waves, the way her confidence radiated from her like heat. And despite everything, despite the gun in his hand and the mission in his mind, Mikhail couldn't deny the truth.

I don't want to kill her.

It was the first time he had admitted it to himself, the first time he had allowed himself to feel it. He had come here with every intention of ending her life. But as he closed the distance between them, all he could think about was the night they had shared. The fire that had burned between them. The way she had looked at him, not with fear, but with something else. Something he had never seen in the eyes of anyone else.

And now, as she disappeared down the hallway toward the bathrooms, Mikhail knew one thing for certain—this wasn't just another mission. This was something else. Something he couldn't control.

Mikhail moved through the crowd with purpose, his body slipping between dancing couples, groups of friends, and drunk strangers without a second glance. His focus was razor-sharp now, every step he took bringing him closer to the moment he had been waiting for. The back hallway was just ahead, dimly lit and far enough from the deafening music to feel like a different world. Quieter. More intimate. More deadly.

His heart pounded in his chest, the rhythm matching the bass of the club's music, but his hands were steady. His mind was clear. This was what he had come for. This was why he had followed her here, why he had spent the last week tracking her every move. He had to end it. Anya was a threat—a threat to his life, to the Bratva, to everything he had built. And threats had to be eliminated.

No more hesitation, he reminded himself as he reached the hallway, his back pressing against the cool wall, hidden in the shadows. He was good at this. He was born for it.

His hand went to the gun under his jacket, the familiar weight of it grounding him, giving him the cold assurance he needed. He knew what had to be done, even if some part of him still resisted the idea. He had been here before—on the edge of making a kill—but this time felt different. This time, the stakes were higher. Not just because she was Konstantin Morozov's daughter, but because of what she had stirred in him.

It's just a job. She's just a loose end.

The hallway was quiet, the distant sound of the club's music muffled by the walls. It was the perfect place. The perfect moment. Mikhail's grip tightened around the gun as he waited, his breath steady, his pulse thrumming beneath his skin. His mind was set—he was going to do it. He was going to end this, like he should have done a week ago.

The sound of footsteps echoed softly down the hallway, drawing closer, and Mikhail's muscles tensed. He knew it was her. He could feel it. The scent of her perfume, the quiet click of her heels against the floor, the soft rustle of her dress. She was coming, unaware of the danger that waited for her just a few feet away.

This is it, he thought, his finger brushing the trigger of the gun. *One shot. No more loose ends.*

But as Anya walked past, something inside him snapped.

Instead of drawing the gun, instead of pulling the trigger like he had been trained to do, Mikhail's body moved on its own. His hand shot out, grabbing her arm in one swift motion. The gun remained under his jacket, untouched.

Anya gasped, her body stiffening as his grip tightened around her arm. Her wide eyes met his, shock flashing across her face as she struggled against him, trying to pull away.

"Let me go!" she demanded, her voice sharp and full of defiance.

Mikhail's grip only tightened, pulling her closer to him, dragging her into the shadows where they wouldn't be seen. His heart was pounding in his chest, his mind a chaotic mess of emotions, but he kept his face cold, unreadable.

"Who have you told?" he growled, his voice low and dangerous. "What does your father know?"

Anya stopped struggling, her eyes narrowing as she looked up at him. She was breathing hard, her chest rising and falling rapidly, but she wasn't afraid. Not like the others had been. Not like he expected her to be. There was no fear in her eyes—only fire.

"I haven't told anyone," she replied, her voice steady, defiant.

For a moment, Mikhail didn't believe her. His mind raced, every instinct telling him that she was lying, that she had already gone to her father, that the Bratva was in danger because of her. But then, something shifted. He stared into her eyes, and for the first time in a week, he felt it again—the pull.

It was the same pull that had kept him from killing her before. The same pull that had made him hesitate when he had found her hiding in that back room. The same pull that had led to that night, to the heat between them, to the way she had made him feel things he had never allowed himself to feel.

Their eyes locked, and for a moment, it was like the rest of the world disappeared. The club, the Bratva, the gun beneath his jacket—it all faded into the background, leaving only the two of them standing there, staring at each other. And in that moment, Mikhail realized something. He wasn't the only one who felt it.

Anya's expression softened, just for a second, as if she could see the conflict raging inside him. Her eyes, still bright with defiance, held a quiet understanding. They shared something now, something that went beyond words. A secret. A connection.

Mikhail's breath hitched in his throat, his grip on her arm loosening just slightly. He could still feel the warmth of her skin beneath his fingers, the softness of her body so close to his. And for the first time, he wasn't sure what he wanted more—to kiss her or to kill her.

I should kill her, he thought, his mind screaming at him to do it. *I have to.*

But his body refused to listen. Instead of reaching for the gun, instead of ending it right there in the dark hallway, Mikhail did something else. Something reckless. Something he would regret.

He kissed her.

It happened before he could stop himself, his lips crashing down on hers with a force that surprised them both. Anya stiffened at first, caught off guard by the suddenness of it, but then she melted into him, her hands reaching up to grip his shoulders as she kissed him back.

Mikhail's hands roamed over her body, his fingers digging into her waist, pulling her closer as the kiss deepened. The heat between them was instant, electric, just like it had been that night. Every part of him screamed that this was wrong, that he was betraying the Bratva, betraying everything he stood for, but he couldn't stop. He didn't want to stop.

Anya responded just as fiercely. Her hands flew to his chest, fingers pressing against the firm muscle beneath his shirt as if grounding herself in the chaos of the moment. A soft moan escaped her lips, muffled by the intensity of the kiss, and it sent a jolt of desire straight through him.

Her body pressed against his, her curves fitting perfectly against him, as though they had been made for each other. She wasn't resisting—if anything, she was pulling him in, her grip on his chest tightening, her breath quickening in sync with his. They were lost in each other, the world around them forgotten, drowned out by the pounding music and the frantic beat of their hearts.

Mikhail's hands slid up her sides, his fingers brushing against the fabric of her dress, and he could feel the rapid beat of her heart beneath his palms. Every touch, every movement was electric, sparking between them with a force that neither of them could control. Her body trembled slightly against his, not from fear, but from the intensity of the moment, from the raw, unrestrained desire that surged between them.

Anya's lips parted, her breath hot against his mouth as she kissed him back with just as much hunger, just as much need. It was mutual, the same pull that had ignited between them that night now consuming them both. Her fingers curled into his shirt, pulling him closer, as if she couldn't bear the distance between them. And in that moment, it didn't matter who they were, what side they were on—there was only the heat, the undeniable attraction that bound them together.

They were lost, wrapped up in the intensity of the kiss, the connection between them overpowering everything else. For that moment, nothing else mattered—not the Bratva, not their loyalties, not even the danger that lurked in the shadows. All that existed was them, the fire that burned between them, too strong to be ignored.

But then, reality came crashing back in.

Mikhail pulled away, his breathing ragged, his mind spinning with the weight of what he had just done. His hands were still on her, holding her close, but the cold realization of his mistake was already creeping in.

I'm supposed to kill her. I have to kill her.

But as he looked into her eyes, the fire still burning there, he knew he couldn't do it. Not tonight.

Mikhail's breathing was still ragged as he pulled back from her, the heat of their kiss lingering in the air between them. For a moment, all he could do was stare at her, his chest rising and falling rapidly as his mind raced to catch up with what had just happened. He was supposed to kill her. That was why he had come here. It was supposed to be simple—pull the trigger, clean up the loose end, and walk away.

But it wasn't simple anymore. It hadn't been from the moment he found her in that room. And now, standing here in the dark hallway, the memory of her lips on his still fresh, he knew with certainty that it never would be.

His hand trembled as it moved to his jacket, not for the gun this time, but for something else. Something he had no business giving her. Something that would betray everything he stood for. Yet, even as his mind screamed at him to stop, his body moved on its own, pulling out the small, unmarked card that he always kept hidden in a secure pocket of his jacket.

The card was simple—just a number. A lifeline. A safe way to make contact. It was something he only gave to people he trusted, people he knew would need it one day. And now, he was about to hand it to the woman he should be killing.

His hand shook as he extended the card toward her, his eyes locking onto hers. "You need to protect yourself," he said, his voice low, urgent. "Get out of town. Disappear. Don't let anyone find you."

Anya's brow furrowed in confusion, her eyes flicking down to the card and then back up to him. She didn't take it right away, her hesitation clear as she tried to make sense of what he was doing. Her lips parted slightly, but no words came out at first. He could see the questions swirling in her eyes, the fear, the uncertainty. But there was also something else—something deeper. She trusted him, despite everything. And that trust made him feel even worse.

"Why are you doing this?" she asked, her voice barely above a whisper.

Mikhail swallowed hard, his throat tightening as he tried to find an answer. But he couldn't. There were no words that could explain the war raging inside him. How could he tell her that he didn't understand it himself? That he was supposed to kill her, that it would have been the smart thing, the right thing to

do, but every time he thought about it, his chest
twisted in a way that made it impossible?

"I..." he began, but the words died in his throat. He
shook his head, knowing that any explanation he
gave would only complicate things further. He didn't
know why he was doing it. He didn't know why he
couldn't pull the trigger. All he knew was that the
thought of her dead, of her lifeless body on the
ground because of him, was something he couldn't
stomach.

So, instead of answering, he pressed the card into
her hand, closing her fingers around it. His touch
lingered for a moment, a silent acknowledgment of
the choice he was making. A choice that would
have consequences. A choice that would change
everything.

"Call the number if you need something," he said,
his voice rough. "It's safe."

Anya looked down at the card in her hand, her
fingers trembling as she held it. She didn't say
anything at first, her gaze lifting to meet his once
more, her confusion etched into every line of her
face. "You're not going to kill me," she whispered,
as if only now realizing the weight of what he had
done.

Mikhail's jaw clenched, the reality of her words
sinking in. No, he wasn't going to kill her. Not
tonight. Not ever. He had made his choice. And that

choice meant betraying everything he had stood for up until now.

"I should," he muttered under his breath, his frustration bleeding into his tone. "But I can't."

It was the truth, as much as he hated to admit it. She had gotten under his skin, into his head in ways no one else ever had. And now, instead of eliminating the threat like he had been trained to do, he was giving her a way to survive. A way to escape. A way to protect herself.

He was letting her go again.

His stomach twisted at the thought, the weight of his decision settling heavily on his shoulders. Viktor would kill him if he found out. Nikolai would do worse. He had disobeyed a direct order, and the consequences for that were unforgiving in their world. But even as the fear of what was to come gnawed at him, Mikhail couldn't bring himself to regret it.

Anya's eyes searched his face, trying to read the emotions he was desperately trying to hide. For a moment, he thought she might say something—ask him again why he was doing this, why he was betraying his loyalty to the Bratva for her. But instead, she simply nodded, her expression softening as she clutched the card tighter in her hand.

"Thank you," she whispered, the words barely audible, but they struck him harder than anything else she could have said.

Mikhail nodded, his throat too tight to respond. He didn't deserve her gratitude. He wasn't the hero in this story. He was the man who had come here to kill her, and the only reason she was still breathing was because of his own selfish weakness.

He turned away from her, his body rigid as he forced himself to leave. Every step felt heavier than the last, the weight of his choice pressing down on him like a physical force. His mind was screaming at him to turn back, to finish what he had started, to follow the orders he had been given. But his heart, traitorous as it was, wouldn't let him.

As Mikhail exited the club, the cold night air hit his face like a slap, jolting him back into the harsh reality of what he had done. He had let her go. Again. And this time, there would be no turning back. The consequences of his actions would come crashing down on him soon enough, and he wasn't sure if he'd be able to survive them.

But as he walked away, the only thing he could think about was Anya—the way she had looked at him, the way her lips had felt against his, the way her body had responded to his touch. And the fact that, despite everything, he had made his choice.

And now, they were both going to have to live with
it.

Chapter 7

Anya sat on the edge of her bed, her fingers trembling as she stared at a simple, plain card with nothing but a phone number printed on it. Mikhail had given it to her a week ago. He had spared her life again and warned her to run. He had been so conflicted, his dark eyes filled with something raw, something dangerous, but also something protective. Why couldn't she get him out of her head? Why had he spared her when it would have been so easy for him to kill her?

Her gaze drifted down to the other object in her hand— a small innocuous-looking stick in her hand. The pregnancy test. The lines on it were unmistakable, as if mocking her with their certainty. Positive. The truth stared back at her, cutting through the fog that had clouded her thoughts for days.

How could this have happened?

She felt the weight of her situation press down on her chest like a heavy stone. They had their one night of unbelievable passion a few weeks ago. Then she had gone to the club last week trying to forget everything about Mikhail—the man who had upended her life in more ways than she could ever have imagined. But instead of finding release,

instead of pushing him out of her mind, she had
found herself back in his arms. Now, here she was,
the undeniable proof of their connection held
between her trembling fingers.

She tossed the pregnancy test onto the bed and
ran her fingers through her hair, trying to calm the
chaotic thoughts swirling in her mind. The memory
of his touch haunted her, the way he had kissed her
in the shadows of that nightclub hallway, the way
his hands had claimed her body like she was his. It
had felt so right in the moment, but now, with the
consequences staring her in the face, she didn't
know how to feel.

Anya squeezed her eyes shut, trying to push away
the memories. She had been so reckless, so
foolish. But no matter how hard she tried to deny it,
her body had responded to him in ways she had
never felt before. Her heart raced just thinking
about the way he had looked at her, the way his lips
had moved against hers with such possessiveness.
How could she be so drawn to the man who was
supposed to kill her?

He's dangerous, she reminded herself, *but I still
want him.*

The thought made her sick to her stomach, but it
didn't make it any less true. Mikhail was dangerous.
He had killed men in front of her, and yet here she
was, pregnant with his child, unable to stop thinking
about him. It didn't make sense, and the more she

tried to unravel her emotions, the more confused she became.

Anya stood up abruptly and paced the length of her room, her bare feet making soft sounds against the plush carpet. Her mind raced with possibilities, with questions she didn't know how to answer.

What do I do now?

The question gnawed at her, over and over, without reprieve. She had always been able to rely on her father—her protector, her guiding force in life. He had always shielded her from the dangers of their world, always kept her safe from the chaos that came with being the daughter of a Bratva leader. But could she trust him with this? Could she tell him that she was pregnant with the child of one of their enemies?

She stopped pacing and glanced at the pregnancy test on her bed, the sight of it sending a fresh wave of anxiety crashing over her. *No. I have to tell him. He'll understand. He has to. He's always protected me.*

Her father had always been there for her. No matter what happened, no matter how complicated things got, he had never let her down. He was a powerful man, commanding and dangerous to others, but to her, he had always been her rock. Her protector. She was his little girl, even now, and she knew that he would want to help her.

But telling him about the baby? About Mikhail?

Anya swallowed hard, her throat dry with fear. This wasn't like anything she had ever dealt with before. Her father was bound by the same rules of loyalty and vengeance as the rest of the Bratva. What if he saw this baby as a threat? What if he reacted badly? The Volkov Bratva was their enemy. How would her father react to the news that she was carrying the child of one of their enforcers?

Her eyes fell back to the card on the bed, the lifeline Mikhail had given her. She hadn't called the number. She hadn't been able to bring herself to do it, not even to ask what it all meant. What would she say if she called him? Would he even care? Would he try to use her for leverage? Or would he protect her and the baby? The confusion swirled in her head until it became too much.

With a sharp breath, Anya sat down on the edge of the bed again, clutching her stomach protectively. It was strange to think that a new life was growing inside her, a life created with Mikhail. Her hand rested on her abdomen, a sudden sense of responsibility washing over her. She wasn't just thinking about herself anymore. She had a child to protect. *His child.*

The thought was terrifying, and yet, deep down, she felt a strange attachment to the baby already. It wasn't something she had planned, and it certainly wasn't something she had ever imagined happening under these circumstances, but she wanted this baby. She wanted to protect it, no matter what.

But how could she do that on her own? She needed help. She needed guidance. And the only person she had ever been able to rely on was her father.

Anya stood up once more, determination hardening in her chest. She had to tell her father. She couldn't keep this secret, not from him. He had always been there for her, and he would be there for her now. She was sure of it. He would understand. He had to.

She walked to the mirror on her wall and stared at her reflection, trying to gather the courage she needed to face her father. Her reflection looked back at her with wide, fearful eyes, but behind the fear, there was something else. Strength. She had been through so much already—survived so much. She could do this.

With one final look at the card and the pregnancy test, Anya made her decision. She would tell her father about the baby. He would protect her, just like he always had.

Anya stood outside her father's office, her heart racing. She had faced tough situations before—dangerous, life-threatening moments that tested her resolve—but none of them compared to the fear gnawing at her now. This was different. This was personal. This was her father, and the stakes were higher than ever.

The heavy oak door stood closed in front of her, the familiar scent of her father's study—leather, wood, and the faint smell of expensive cigars—wafting through the air. This room had always been her father's domain, a place of power where he made decisions that shaped their world. She had never felt like an outsider here, but now, standing at the threshold with a secret that would shake the very foundation of their family, she felt vulnerable.

Taking a deep breath, she knocked softly and pushed the door open. Her father was seated behind his imposing desk, papers spread in front of him, his attention focused on some business matter. He looked up when he heard her enter, his brow lifting slightly as he acknowledged her presence.

"Anya," he greeted her, his voice deep and steady. "What brings you here?"

She swallowed hard, her fingers curling nervously by her sides as she crossed the room to sit down across from him. She could feel her pulse pounding in her ears, the weight of the pregnancy test in her pocket a constant reminder of the life-altering news she was about to deliver.

"Daddy," she began, her voice faltering for a moment. She cleared her throat, trying to gather her strength, but the fear still clung to her like a second skin. "I need to tell you something important."

Her father leaned back in his chair, his eyes narrowing slightly as he observed her. He was always calm, always in control. But she could see the shift in his expression, the way his posture straightened as he sensed the seriousness of what she was about to say.

"What is it?" he asked, his tone still measured, but with a hint of curiosity.

Anya's hands shook as she reached into her pocket and pulled out the pregnancy test, placing it gently on his desk. She couldn't bring herself to look him in the eyes as she set it down, the two small lines staring up at her like an accusation.

The room grew heavy with silence. She felt her father's gaze on her, his shock radiating across the desk. For a moment, neither of them said anything. The tension hung in the air like a weight pressing down on them both.

Finally, her father spoke, his voice quieter now, more measured. "Is this... what I think it is?"

Anya nodded, unable to find her voice. Her heart was racing, her stomach twisted in knots. Even at 23, she was still his little girl, the one he protected from the cruel realities of their world. But now… now she wasn't sure how he would react.

She glanced up at him, and for the first time in her life, she saw a flicker of something she hadn't expected: hesitation. His brow furrowed, and his hands gripped the arms of his chair tightly, as if grounding himself to the moment. His shock was clear, but so was his internal struggle. She could see it in his eyes—the clash between his protective instincts as her father and the cold, calculating nature of a man who had built an empire in the shadows.

"Anya…" he began slowly, his voice cautious. "This is… a lot to take in."

She could feel her pulse quicken at his words, and she braced herself for the worst. Would he be angry? Would he see this baby as a threat to the family's legacy, to everything he had worked so hard to build? Would he demand that she get rid of it?

"I know it's a lot," she said quietly, her voice shaking. "But I'm keeping the baby. I want to keep it."

Her father's eyes darkened slightly, and for a moment, she thought she saw a flash of something hard and cold behind his gaze. But then, just as quickly as it had appeared, it was gone, replaced by the same calm, reassuring presence she had known all her life.

"Anya," he said again, his tone softening. "This wasn't planned, was it?"

She shook her head, biting her lip to keep from crying. "No… it wasn't."

He nodded slowly, his fingers tapping rhythmically on the armrest as he processed her words. "And the father? Is he involved?"

Anya hesitated, her heart clenching painfully in her chest. She had been dreading this question, knowing that once she said Mikhail's name, everything would change. But she couldn't lie to her father. Not about this.

"No," she said softly. "He isn't involved. It was… a one-time thing. I'm doing this on my own."

Her father's expression softened again, and for the first time since she had entered the room, he reached across the desk and took her hand in his. His grip was firm but comforting, the way it always was when she needed him most.

"Anya," he said, his voice filled with something she hadn't expected—compassion. "This is a lot to take in, but… you're my daughter. I'll always protect you and help you anyway I can."

Tears welled in Anya's eyes as she heard his words. She had been so afraid that he would be angry, that he would see this baby as a mistake. But here he was, holding her hand, reassuring her that everything would be okay.

"If this is what you want… if this is what will make you happy, then we'll figure it out," he continued. "I'll do whatever it takes to protect you and the baby."

The relief washed over her in a wave, and she felt herself exhale a breath she hadn't realized she had been holding. "Thank you, Daddy," she whispered, her voice trembling with emotion. "Thank you."

Her father gave her a small smile, though there was something about it that felt slightly off. It wasn't the smile she was used to—warm and genuine. This one felt… strained. But she didn't dwell on it. She was too overwhelmed by the relief that he was on her side, that he was going to protect her and the baby.

After a moment of silence, her father asked the inevitable question. "Who is the father?"

Anya's heart skipped a beat, but she forced herself to answer. "His name is Mikhail."

Her father's smile faltered slightly. "Mikhail who? Do I know him"

She shook her head, bracing herself for the next part. "No, you don't know him. He works for the Volkov family."

The change in her father's expression was subtle, but she saw it. His grip on her hand tightened slightly, and his eyes darkened for just a moment before he quickly masked his reaction. But Anya knew him well enough to know that the mention of the Volkov family had rattled him.

"Mikhail from the Volkov family," he repeated, his voice calm but colder than before. "I see."

Anya looked down, her heart pounding in her chest. "It was a one-time thing. He's not in the picture."

Her father was silent for a long moment, his fingers still gripping hers tightly. Then, slowly, he nodded. "Don't worry, Anya," he said softly, though there was something unsettling in his tone now. "Everything will be alright. I'll take care of you. We'll handle this together."

He released her hand and stood up, walking around the desk to pull her into a hug. Anya felt a wave of relief wash over her as he embraced her, his arms strong and reassuring. He had always been her protector, and now, despite everything, she knew he would be there for her.

"Thank you," she whispered again, burying her face in his chest.

Her father stroked her hair, his touch gentle, but beneath the surface, Anya sensed something had shifted. She just couldn't tell what.

As Anya left her father's office, she felt a lightness she hadn't expected. The burden of keeping her pregnancy a secret had been lifted, and now, she was reassured.

Her father, the man she had trusted all her life, was going to protect her—just like he always had. As she walked down the hallway toward the grand staircase, her shoulders relaxed, and a faint smile tugged at her lips. *He understands,* she thought, repeating the comforting words in her mind.

He'll take care of me. Everything will be okay.

Each step she took away from his office felt like a step toward safety. Anya's mind raced with thoughts of the future—of her baby, of how her father's support would make everything easier. She pictured the moment she would tell her father the baby's name, or when he would cradle his grandchild in his arms.

He'll be there for me. He'll protect us both.

But as she neared the bottom of the staircase, a sudden thought struck her. *Maybe we should talk more about this. Maybe we can have dinner tonight?* She spun on her heels and retraced her steps, heading back toward his office, her heart lighter than it had been in days.

As she reached the door to his office, she stopped in her tracks. Her father's voice, so kind and protective just moments earlier, was now sharp and unyielding. Her hand froze on the door handle as she heard the cold edge in his words.

Anya's heart skipped a beat. She pressed her back against the wall, just outside the door, and listened.

"This baby cannot be born," her father's voice said, flat and chilling. "It's a Volkov bastard created from my daughter's betrayal. I won't allow it."

Her breath caught in her throat, her stomach twisting violently. She pressed closer to the door, desperate to hear more but dreading every word that followed.

"I will not have some bastard as the heir to my empire," he continued, his tone dripping with disdain. "I don't care what Anya wants."

Her entire body went numb as she clutched her hand to her chest, her pulse pounding in her ears. *He doesn't care what I want?* The words repeated in her mind, the betrayal sinking in deeper with each breath.

"I don't care what it takes—she won't give birth to that child," her father's voice continued, colder and more detached than she had ever heard him before. "Arrange a doctor. This problem will be taken care of."

The words hit her like a sledgehammer, knocking the air from her lungs. *This problem…* Was that what she and her baby had become to him? A problem to be taken care of? She pressed a hand over her mouth to stifle a sob, her knees threatening to give way beneath her.

Her father—the man who had always protected her, the man she had trusted with her life—was plotting to take everything from her. He didn't care about her happiness. He didn't care about her child. All that mattered was his empire. His legacy. And he would do anything to protect it. Even if it meant killing her baby.

Anya's heart broke as the realization sunk in. He didn't care about her. Not really. The love she had believed was unconditional, the trust she had placed in him, it was all shattered in an instant. She had thought he would protect her no matter what. But now, she knew the truth. He would destroy her if it meant preserving his legacy.

Her knees buckled, and she stumbled back from the door, her body shaking as tears streamed down her face. She had been so naive to trust him, so foolish to believe that he would put her above his empire.

He lied to me. He doesn't care about me. He only cares about the family's legacy. He'd sacrifice me for it.

The thought was like a dagger to her heart. Anya had no one now. No one to protect her. Not even her own father.

Her world crumbled around her as she stood in the hallway, trembling with fear and heartbreak. Her father was willing to do whatever it took to ensure that the baby was never born, and if that meant forcing her to lose it—or worse—he wouldn't hesitate.

Anya wiped at her tears, her mind spinning as she tried to come to terms with the betrayal. She wasn't safe here. Not anymore.

I can't stay. He'll kill my baby… maybe even me.

With her heart pounding, she turned and fled down the hallway, her mind racing with fear and desperation. She had to get out of here. She had to protect her baby. But where could she go? And who could she turn to now that the one person she had trusted most had turned against her?

Anya barely registered the sound of her footsteps as she fled down the hallway, her mind consumed by a single, overwhelming thought: *I have to leave. Now.* Tears blurred her vision as she stumbled into her bedroom, slamming the door behind her. Her breath came in sharp, ragged gasps as she leaned against the wall, trying to process everything she had overheard.

He's going to kill my baby. The words echoed in her mind, slicing through her like a blade. The man she had trusted her entire life, the man who had always promised to protect her, was willing to destroy the one thing she had left—her child. Her body trembled with a mix of fear and heartbreak, her pulse pounding in her ears. The betrayal was suffocating, wrapping around her like a vise, threatening to choke her.

She had to get out. She had to run.

Anya wiped at her tears with shaking hands, but the panic clawed at her chest, making it hard to breathe. She moved to her closet, yanking open the door and pulling out a duffel bag. Her movements were frantic, fueled by sheer desperation. Clothes, money, anything she could find—she stuffed it all into the bag without a second thought. There was no time to plan, no time to think. She had to leave before her father made good on his threat. Before he took everything from her.

Where will I go? The question hit her like a wave, and for a moment, she froze, staring blankly at the mess of clothes spilling from her bag. She had no plan, no destination. All she knew was that she couldn't stay here. *I have no one.*

The realization sank in, heavy and cold. The man who was supposed to protect her had betrayed her in the worst way. He didn't care about her, not really. He cared about the legacy, the empire, the name. And she was nothing but a problem—a problem her father would stop at nothing to eliminate. Anya bit her lip, tasting blood, as she tried to suppress the sobs that threatened to escape. She had no one to turn to, no one to help her. She was completely, utterly alone.

I have to protect my baby. I have to survive.

With renewed determination, she zipped up the bag and swung it over her shoulder. Her gaze drifted around the room, the room she had called home for as long as she could remember. The soft curtains, the plush bedding, the family photos that lined her dresser—it all felt foreign now. Alien. This wasn't home anymore. It was a prison, and her father was the warden, willing to do anything to keep his perfect world intact.

She lingered for only a moment longer before turning her back on the life she had known. With her heart pounding in her throat, she crept to the door, every muscle tensed with fear. Her father's words played over and over in her mind as she tiptoed down the hallway, making her way toward the back exit. She couldn't risk being seen by any of the staff. They were loyal to her father. If anyone saw her leaving, she'd be dragged back, and she couldn't let that happen.

Her breaths came faster as she approached the door that led to the garden. The house was eerily silent, the only sound the soft rustle of her clothes as she moved. She placed her hand on the doorknob, hesitating for the briefest moment. Once she walked out that door, there was no going back. She would be on her own, with no idea of what lay ahead. But staying meant losing her child, and she couldn't live with that.

I'm not safe here. I'll never be safe here.

Steeling herself, she turned the knob and slipped out into the evening. The cold air hit her like a slap, chilling her to the bone, but it also brought a sense of clarity. She was free—for now. The garden was dimly lit, shadows casting eerie shapes across the lawn. Anya kept to the edges, moving as quickly and quietly as she could, her bag clutched tightly to her side. Her heart raced as she reached the back gate, her mind screaming at her to run faster, to get farther away.

Once she was outside the estate, standing alone on the dark street, she paused for a breath, her hands shaking. She was free. But the fear gnawed at her, deep and unrelenting. Where would she go? What was her next step? She had no money, no plan, and no safe place to hide. The city suddenly felt enormous and dangerous, a vast, cold landscape where she was utterly exposed.

Who can I trust? The thought came unbidden, and before she could stop herself, one name flashed in her mind—Mikhail.

Anya's breath hitched at the memory of him, the feel of his hands on her, the way his eyes had pierced through her the night they had shared. He had been tasked with killing her, yet he hadn't. He had let her go. And then at the club, he had given her a chance, even warning her to disappear before it was too late. He could have killed her then, but instead, he had given her that card. The small, plain card with only a phone number, stashed in her wallet. She had dismissed it at the time, telling herself she would never need it. But now, standing alone in the dark, she realized he was her only hope.

I don't have a choice. He's the only one who can help me.

Anya clutched the bag tighter and began walking, her feet carrying her forward on instinct. She didn't know what Mikhail would do when she called him. She didn't even know if he would answer. But there was no other option. Her father wanted her baby dead, and Mikhail… he had shown her more mercy than anyone else in her life. He had spared her once. Maybe, just maybe, he would help her again.

With fear clawing at her throat and the weight of
betrayal pressing down on her, Anya disappeared
into the night, the darkness swallowing her whole.
She had no idea where she was going, but one
thing was certain—she couldn't go back. Not now.
Not ever.

Chapter 8

Mikhail gripped the steering wheel so hard that his knuckles blanched. The dark streets of New York City blurred past him, but his mind was somewhere else entirely. The growl of the engine echoed in the quiet of the car, matching the simmering tension that had been building inside him for days. He hadn't felt this conflicted in years—maybe ever.

It had taken some time, but he'd finally tracked down his SUV after Anya had ditched it in a parking lot. He'd found it sitting untouched, the cold metal a stark reminder of the moment she'd slipped away from him. Now, behind the wheel of his reclaimed vehicle, the weight of everything seemed heavier.

It had been a week since he'd given Anya the card, telling her to disappear. A week of dodging Viktor's questions, avoiding eye contact, and lying through his teeth about why the job wasn't done yet. Every day that passed without him finishing what he was supposed to do, the weight of his choice pressed harder on his chest.

I should have killed her.

The thought kept coming back, gnawing at the edges of his mind. It would have been clean, simple. She had been a threat—still was, technically. Viktor had been clear: no witnesses. No complications. Just a clean job, like all the others. But instead of pulling the trigger, he'd let her go. Worse than that—he'd warned her to run.

Mikhail's grip tightened, the leather of the steering wheel creaking under the pressure. *What the fuck was I thinking?* He replayed the moment over and over in his head. The way she'd looked at him, those green eyes wide with fear and something else—something that had stopped him cold. He hadn't hesitated like that in years. But with Anya… everything was different.

I gave her a chance. She should be gone by now. So why can't I stop thinking about her?

That was the real problem, wasn't it? Even now, after all this time, she was still in his head. He couldn't shake the memory of her. The feel of her body against his. The way she had kissed him back, as if they were caught up in the same madness. He'd warned her to disappear, told her it was her only chance, but deep down, part of him had wanted her to stay.

This isn't me, Mikhail thought, jaw clenched. He wasn't the type to hesitate. He wasn't the type to get distracted, least of all by a woman. And yet here he was, driving through the city at night, his mind consumed by thoughts of the one person he should have already forgotten.

He knew Viktor was getting impatient. He could feel the noose tightening around his neck. Viktor was starting to ask more questions, starting to press him harder for answers, and Mikhail's excuses were wearing thin. *I'm running out of time.*

The glow of the streetlights reflected off the windshield as he drove through the empty streets, but it did nothing to illuminate the path forward. The more he tried to push thoughts of Anya away, the more they consumed him.

She's a Morozov. She's the enemy. I should have killed her. I should have finished this a week ago.

But he hadn't. And now, everything was unraveling.

Mikhail was still lost in the tangled mess of his thoughts when the sharp ring of his phone cut through the quiet hum of the car. His pulse quickened as he glanced at the screen. An unknown number. He should ignore it—he always did—but something gnawed at him this time, telling him to answer.

Reluctantly, he picked up the phone, pressing it to his ear. "Yeah?" His voice was rough, filled with tension. He wasn't in the mood for whatever this was.

There was a brief pause on the other end, and then a voice—soft, hesitant—filled the silence. "Mikhail... it's me."

For a moment, he froze, the familiar sound of her voice sending a jolt through him. *Anya.* His mind raced, heart pounding harder as conflicting emotions surged inside him. This was the last thing he needed. He had told her to disappear.

Why did I give her that damn card? He cursed himself for the impulsive decision that now felt like a mistake. He should hang up. Pretend he hadn't answered. But something kept him on the line, his grip tightening on the phone as he waited for her to continue.

"There's something… something's happened," Anya's voice was shaky but controlled, clearly trying to maintain some semblance of calm. "I didn't know who else to call."

Her words hung between them, heavy with meaning. She didn't explain further, didn't offer any details, but he could hear the fear in her voice. Mikhail clenched his jaw, his mind whirling. *What the hell does she expect me to do?*

Everything inside him screamed to walk away from this. It was a complication he couldn't afford—a risk that could get him killed. If Viktor or Nikolai found out he was even speaking to her, let alone considering helping her, it would be over. His life, his loyalty to the Bratva—all of it shattered. And yet… he couldn't bring himself to hang up.

"This is the last thing I need," he muttered under his breath, running a hand through his hair in frustration. He fought the urge to end the call, to stop himself from getting sucked further into this mess. But despite his better judgment, despite everything, he stayed on the line.

"Where are you?" he asked, his voice sharper than intended. The words came out before he had time to think them through.

There was a moment of silence on the other end, and then she gave him the address, her voice barely above a whisper. Mikhail cursed under his breath, knowing full well what he was getting into. The knot in his stomach tightened as he realized just how deep he was going.

He made a quick U-turn, the engine roaring as he sped in the direction of her location. His mind was a storm of thoughts, each one worse than the last. This was a bad idea—a fucking terrible idea. He knew it. Anya was trouble, and getting involved with her again could cost him everything.

I should have killed her. I should have ended this when I had the chance.

But he hadn't. And now here he was, driving to pick her up like some kind of savior, when he knew he shouldn't be getting involved at all.

This is my fault. He gritted his teeth, the weight of the situation pressing down on him. He knew this wasn't going to end well, but deep down, something in him couldn't ignore her call. Not after everything that had happened between them. He couldn't just let her fend for herself—not now.

And that scared him more than anything.

Mikhail's foot pressed harder on the gas, the car surging forward as the city lights blurred past. His thoughts were a chaotic mess, spiraling deeper with every mile he drove. He had no business getting involved in this. *She's a Morozov,* he reminded himself, the name laced with danger and betrayal. Every instinct screamed that he should turn around, let her deal with her own problems, but something kept pulling him toward her.

He cursed under his breath, his grip tightening on the steering wheel as memories of Anya flooded his mind. The look in her eyes that first night—terrified, yes, but with a defiance that had sparked something inside him. She wasn't like the others. There was a fire in her, something raw and real that he couldn't ignore. And then there was the way her body had responded to him, the way she'd moaned his name, arching beneath him.

What the fuck am I doing? Mikhail's jaw clenched. His mind was split in two—one part telling him to turn back, to forget about her and let her fend for herself. But the other part... the other part kept driving forward, the image of her burning in his thoughts.

She was a Morozov, and that made her the enemy. Viktor had given him clear orders. He should have killed her a week ago. He'd had plenty of chances. But instead, he'd kissed her, let her go, and now he was speeding toward her, risking everything.

Viktor will gut me for this. The thought flashed through his mind like a warning, but it wasn't enough to stop him. He knew Viktor wouldn't understand. Hell, he didn't even understand it himself. But the closer he got to her location, the less his anger mattered. It was being replaced by something else—something more dangerous.

I should be angry. I should hate her for putting me in this position. But all he could think about was how scared she had sounded on the phone, how vulnerable her voice had been. She needed him. And despite everything, he couldn't shake the feeling that he needed to protect her.

His knuckles were white against the wheel, the tension coiling tighter and tighter inside him. This was wrong. He knew that. But it didn't change the fact that he was driving toward her. It didn't change the fact that when he thought about her, the heat between them, the way she had looked at him in the club, his heart sped up.

This is your fault. He scowled at his own weakness. If he had killed her when he had the chance, none of this would be happening. But he hadn't. And now, here he was, on his way to rescue a woman he shouldn't care about, a woman he couldn't stop thinking about.

The city streets blurred past as he approached the address she had given him, his mind racing faster than the car. His heart pounded in his chest, a knot of anxiety and desire twisting together. She was trouble—he knew that. But he couldn't let her face this alone. Not after everything they'd been through.

With every passing second, the protective instinct inside him grew stronger, pushing aside the doubts, the anger, and the fear. Whatever happened next, he was already too deep in this to turn back. He was in trouble. She was in trouble. And now, like it or not, they were in this together.

The car slowed to a stop on a quiet, dimly lit street corner. Mikhail scanned the area, his heart pounding as he searched for her. His eyes locked onto a figure standing in the shadows, small and vulnerable. It was Anya. She had her arms wrapped tightly around herself, her body language screaming fear and desperation.

For a moment, he didn't move. He just sat there in the car, watching her. She looked so fragile, so out of place in this cold, dangerous world. The streetlights cast long shadows, and she seemed to shrink into them, her form barely visible except for the occasional glint of light catching her hair. It was the first time he'd seen her like this—completely defenseless. And something about it twisted in his chest.

She's scared. She's alone. And it's my fault.

The realization hit him hard, and for a brief second, he was overwhelmed with guilt. He had done this. If he had killed her when he should have, she wouldn't be here now—standing on a street corner in the middle of the night, terrified and alone. He had given her that card, told her to run, but instead of protecting herself, she had come to him.

What the fuck am I doing? Mikhail clenched the steering wheel, the weight of the situation crashing down on him. He wasn't supposed to feel anything for her. She was a Morozov. He was supposed to kill her, not protect her. And yet, the moment he saw her standing there, something inside him shifted.

It wasn't just guilt anymore—it was something darker, something more dangerous. *I should turn around. Leave her here.* But the thought was fleeting, drowned out by the growing urge to protect her. To keep her safe. And it scared the hell out of him.

With a frustrated sigh, Mikhail shoved open the car door and stepped out into the night. The cool air hit him, but it did nothing to cool the fire burning inside him. His footsteps echoed softly on the pavement as he walked toward her, every step increasing the tension building between them.

Anya looked up as he approached, her wide, green eyes meeting his. For a moment, they just stood there, staring at each other, the world around them fading into the background. Mikhail's heart hammered in his chest as he fought to keep his expression neutral, but there was no denying the pull between them. He had felt it since that first night, and it hadn't gone away.

She was still beautiful, even in her fear. Maybe more so because of it. Vulnerable, yet strong. Mikhail cursed under his breath as his emotions tangled into a knot he couldn't untie.

"Get in," he growled, his voice gruffer than he intended. He motioned to the car, not giving her a chance to argue. The last thing he needed was more complications, and yet here they were, standing together in the shadows once again.

Anya hesitated for a moment, her arms tightening around herself as if she could shield herself from whatever was coming. But when she looked into his eyes, she seemed to understand that there was no running anymore. She was in this, and so was he.

Without a word, she walked toward the car, her steps tentative but certain. Mikhail watched her, feeling that same pull tugging at his gut. He wasn't just in trouble anymore—he was fucking drowning in it.

The car door shut with a quiet thud, and for a moment, the world outside faded into nothing. Inside the car, the silence between Mikhail and Anya was thick, pressing down on them like a heavy blanket. Mikhail stared ahead, gripping the steering wheel, his mind spinning in a thousand directions. He didn't know what to say, didn't even know where to start.

He glanced at her from the corner of his eye. She sat there, quiet, her hands fidgeting in her lap. There was something more, something she wasn't telling him. He could feel it, the weight of her unspoken words hanging in the air between them. He wanted to ask, wanted to demand an explanation for why she'd called him, but something held him back.

Instead, they drove in silence, the tension growing with each passing second. His chest tightened, his thoughts warring between frustration and something else—something he didn't want to acknowledge. She was supposed to be the enemy, supposed to be dead by now. And yet, here she was, sitting beside him again.

What the fuck am I doing? He clenched the wheel harder, trying to shake off the confusion swirling inside him. He had been reckless before, but this was something else entirely.

Finally, after what felt like an eternity, Anya broke the silence. Her voice was soft, hesitant, but her words cut through the quiet like a blade. "I'm pregnant."

The world seemed to stop. Mikhail's grip on the steering wheel loosened, his heart pounding so loud in his ears that for a moment he thought he hadn't heard her right. He blinked, staring straight ahead, as the words settled into his brain.

Pregnant? His mind raced, trying to process the bombshell she had just dropped. He turned to look at her, his chest tightening with a mixture of shock, confusion, and something dangerously close to panic. "What did you say?"

"I'm pregnant," she repeated, her voice steadier this time but no less heavy with emotion.

Mikhail's pulse quickened, and for a moment, he couldn't respond. A baby. His baby. The thought slammed into him like a sledgehammer, knocking the wind out of him. This couldn't be happening. It didn't make sense. He had never even considered the possibility. He wasn't... *fuck,* he wasn't prepared for something like this.

A kid? I can't be a father. What the fuck am I supposed to do with a pregnant woman?

His thoughts spiraled, and suddenly he felt like he couldn't breathe. His own childhood flashed in his mind—the violent outbursts from his father, the nights spent wondering if his old man would even come home. Mikhail had sworn he'd never be like that. He had told himself from a young age that he wasn't cut out for fatherhood. It wasn't in him. He was broken—too scarred, too fucked up to ever raise a kid.

And now, Anya was sitting here, telling him she was pregnant. With his child. His heart pounded in his chest as he fought to make sense of it all. What the hell was he supposed to do with a pregnant woman?

He stared at her, at the way her shoulders slumped slightly, like she was carrying the weight of the world on her own. And in that moment, as the realization hit him, something shifted inside him. This wasn't just about her anymore. It wasn't just about the mess they had created. There was a life at stake. A child.

My child.

The thought sent a wave of something unexpected through him—something close to protectiveness, something primal. But almost immediately, the fear and confusion returned, crashing over him like a tidal wave. This was a disaster. A fucking disaster. If Viktor or Nikolai found out about this, they would kill him. Hell, they'd kill both of them.

He clenched his fists, trying to keep control of the rising panic. *I should walk away. I should have killed her before any of this happened.* But it was too late for that now. There was no going back.

"What the fuck am I supposed to do with this?" Mikhail finally muttered, his voice harsher than he intended. He didn't know what to say, didn't know how to react. He wasn't prepared for this.

Anya looked at him, her eyes filled with a mix of fear and determination. "I don't know," she admitted, her voice barely above a whisper. "But I need your help, Mikhail. I can't do this alone."

Her words hung in the air, and Mikhail felt the weight of them settle on his shoulders like a crushing burden. *Help her? I can't even help myself right now.* But the look in her eyes, the vulnerability, the plea for protection… it gnawed at him.

His heart pounded in his chest, his mind still reeling. But one thing was clear—this wasn't going away. He was responsible, whether he liked it or not. He couldn't just walk away from this.

I should kill her. I should end this. But I can't.

He let out a long breath, trying to process what the fuck he was supposed to do now. He couldn't deny the responsibility he felt, the sense that this was his mess to clean up. But with every second that passed, that responsibility grew heavier, threatening to crush him.

He glanced at Anya again, his jaw tight. "I'll help you," he finally said, the words feeling foreign in his mouth. "But this… this is a fucking mess."

Anya nodded, relief flashing across her face for a brief moment. But they both knew it wasn't over—not even close.

The car hummed along the dark streets, the silence between them thick and heavy. Mikhail gripped the steering wheel, his knuckles white with tension. His mind raced, struggling to make sense of the situation. Anya sat beside him, small and vulnerable, with his child growing inside her. It was a reality he hadn't expected, hadn't prepared for. And it terrified him.

He hadn't been raised to handle this. The old Mikhail, the one who had thrived in the cold, violent world of the Bratva, would have killed her without hesitation. He wouldn't have thought twice. Viktor had made it clear—there could be no loose ends. And yet, he hadn't pulled the trigger. Instead, he'd given her a chance, a card, and now, he was deeper into this mess than he could've imagined.

I should've killed her. I should have done it a week ago. The thought repeated in his mind like a broken record, each time followed by a sharp pang of regret. But he hadn't. And now, he couldn't. Not when she was carrying his baby.

His eyes flicked to her for a brief second. She was staring out the window, her arms wrapped around her body, as if trying to protect herself from the world. She looked fragile, but he knew better. Anya was stronger than she appeared. He had seen that in her defiance, in the way she'd fought against him at every turn. And yet, the fear was still there, etched into her features.

Mikhail's anger simmered beneath the surface, but it wasn't directed at her anymore. It was directed at himself. *This is my fault. I should have handled this. I should have taken care of her. But now…*

He clenched his jaw, the weight of responsibility pressing down on him. This wasn't how things were supposed to go. He wasn't supposed to feel anything for her, wasn't supposed to care. But every time he looked at her, something inside him twisted. The thought of her being pregnant—of a child, *his* child, growing inside her—stirred something deep and primal within him. It scared the hell out of him.

Mikhail's voice broke the silence, rough and tense. "Why did you come to me? Why aren't you at home?"

Anya turned to face him, her eyes filled with a mix of fear and something else—something vulnerable. Her voice was soft as she spoke, explaining everything. She told him about her father, about how he had turned against her, how he wanted to force her to get rid of the baby. Each word sent a surge of anger through Mikhail, his grip tightening on the wheel.

Konstantin Morozov. The name alone sent a wave of fury through him. He knew men like Konstantin all too well—men who saw their children as nothing more than pawns in a larger game. It wasn't so different from his own father, a violent bastard who had left scars on Mikhail that had never fully healed. Hearing Anya's story, hearing how her father had betrayed her, struck a deep chord in him.

Just like my father. The thought was bitter, and it only fueled the anger bubbling up inside him. He glanced at Anya again, watching as she recounted the events with a quiet pain in her voice. She had trusted her father, believed that he would protect her. And he had turned on her, just like Mikhail's father had turned on him.

Mikhail's jaw clenched, his anger shifting into something more focused, more determined. He wasn't sure what to do about any of this—he wasn't prepared to be a father, and he sure as hell wasn't prepared to go against Viktor or Nikolai. But one thing was clear: he wasn't going to let anyone hurt her. Not her father. Not Viktor. No one.

He exhaled slowly, trying to steady his thoughts, his voice coming out gruff. "We'll figure this out."

Anya looked at him, her eyes wide and uncertain. He could see the fear there, the worry that she was putting her trust in the wrong person. And maybe she was. Mikhail wasn't a good man. He wasn't someone who should be trusted, least of all by a woman like her. But right now, none of that mattered. She needed him. And whether he liked it or not, he was involved now.

Mikhail tightened his grip on the wheel, the weight of the situation pressing down on him. He had been in impossible situations before—dangerous situations, life-or-death situations—but this… this was different. This wasn't just about him anymore. It wasn't just about survival.

This was about a child. His child.

The thought sent another wave of confusion crashing over him. Mikhail had never even considered the idea of fatherhood. His own father had been a monster, a man who had cared more about his own power than his family. Mikhail had spent his entire life trying not to become like him, distancing himself from any possibility of having a family of his own. And now here he was, on the verge of fatherhood with a woman he was supposed to have killed.

I can't be a father. I don't even know how. But as much as the thought terrified him, there was no denying the growing sense of protectiveness that had been building inside him since the moment he had first seen Anya again. She wasn't just another woman to him now. She wasn't just a job he had to clean up. She was carrying his child, and that meant something.

Mikhail glanced at her again, the tension in his chest easing just slightly. He had no idea what the fuck he was doing, but one thing was clear—he couldn't walk away from this. He couldn't turn his back on her.

His voice softened, though the resolve in it remained. "I'll help you."

Anya nodded, her relief palpable, but Mikhail knew this was only the beginning. They had a long way to go, and the road ahead was filled with danger. But for now, for this moment, he had made his decision.

He wasn't going to let anyone hurt her. Not ever.

Chapter 9

Mikhail pulled up to the curb outside a nondescript building, the car rumbling to a stop as the silence between them deepened. Anya glanced out of the window, feeling a knot form in her stomach. The building was unremarkable, its facade cold and uninviting, a stark contrast to the opulence and grandeur she had grown up with. Her pulse quickened as Mikhail stepped out of the car, moving around to her side without a word. The tension between them was suffocating, thick with unspoken words, unresolved anger, and something else—something darker, something she couldn't quite name.

When she finally stepped out of the car, she felt the weight of Mikhail's gaze on her, intense and unreadable. She avoided meeting his eyes as she followed him into the building, her breath coming in short, nervous bursts. The cold metal door swung open, and they stepped into a small, dimly lit lobby. It was bare, almost claustrophobic, with walls that seemed to close in around her. This was his world, his space. So different from the one she had grown up in, and now, for reasons she could barely comprehend, she was standing right in the middle of it.

What am I even doing here?

Anya couldn't shake the question from her mind. The practical part of her knew she shouldn't have come. This was a mistake, another in a long string of choices she hadn't been able to control. But what was the alternative? Go back home to her father, the man who had betrayed her in the worst possible way? She didn't have a choice. Not really.

Mikhail walked ahead of her, his steps heavy as he led her up a narrow flight of stairs. She followed, the tension in her shoulders building with every step. She didn't know what was going to happen next, didn't know if she was walking into danger or something else entirely. But one thing was certain—she was in too deep to turn back now.

When they finally reached his apartment, Mikhail pushed the door open, revealing a space that was as cold and minimalistic as the rest of the building. The dim lighting cast long shadows across the walls, and the air was thick with the scent of leather and something distinctly masculine. Anya stepped inside, her eyes scanning the room. It was smaller than she had imagined, intimate in a way that felt unsettling. She could sense the weight of his presence here, the way the apartment seemed to reflect who he was—cold, distant, and yet undeniably powerful.

Her gaze lingered on the sparse furnishings: a worn leather couch, a small kitchen in the corner, and a few shelves filled with an assortment of books and weapons. It was bare, functional, and utterly devoid of warmth. Yet, it was strangely fitting for Mikhail. This was the life he had built for himself—solitary and dangerous.

Anya moved further into the room, trying to find something to focus on, anything to ground her in the midst of the confusion swirling inside her. She wasn't used to spaces like this, places that felt so devoid of life. It made her hyperaware of how far she was from the world she had always known.

Mikhail stood by the door, watching her. The silence between them grew heavier, each of them seemingly waiting for the other to break it. Anya shifted uncomfortably, searching for something to say, anything that would fill the oppressive quiet.

"This place is… different from what I expected," she said finally, her voice more uncertain than she had intended.

Mikhail's lips twitched slightly, but the expression never quite reached his eyes. "It's not the palace you're used to."

His words stung, but she didn't respond. It wasn't worth the argument, not now. Instead, she looked away, her eyes landing on the darkened windows across the room. The view outside was just as bleak as the inside. She crossed her arms over her chest, suddenly feeling cold.

Mikhail moved toward her, his steps slow, deliberate. "Why didn't you listen?" he asked, his voice low but sharp. "Why didn't you leave when I gave you the chance?"

Anya tensed, her heart racing at the question. She knew this was coming, knew that eventually the thin thread of civility between them would snap. But she still didn't have an answer—at least not one that made sense to her. How could she explain the pull she felt toward him, the way she was torn between wanting to hate him and needing him to protect her?

"I don't know," she said, her voice barely above a whisper. The words felt pathetic, even to her. But they were the only truth she had right now.

Mikhail's eyes narrowed, and the space between them felt suffocating. "You don't know?" He stepped closer, his presence overwhelming. "That's not good enough."

Anya met his gaze, frustration building inside her. She wanted to yell at him, to scream that this was all his fault—that he was the reason her life was in shambles. But she couldn't find the words. She was too tired, too confused, and too scared of the truth she had been running from.

What am I even doing here?

Mikhail finally broke the silence, his voice low and filled with restrained frustration. "Why didn't you leave when I told you to? What do you expect from me?"

The words slammed into Anya, reigniting the simmering anger that had been bubbling beneath the surface ever since she'd called him for help. How could he stand there, acting like she was the one at fault for everything?

Her temper flared, and she turned to face him, fists clenched, unable to hold back. "What do I expect? Are you serious, Mikhail? You're the reason I'm in this mess in the first place! You're a killer. You've ruined my life!"

Her voice rose, filled with fury and desperation. "I didn't ask for this! I didn't ask for you to barge into my world and turn everything upside down!"

She could feel her chest tightening as the words came tumbling out, her breath quickening with the intensity of her emotions. She was angry at him, at her father, at everything, but underneath it all was the sheer weight of her fear—the fear of being alone, of facing a future that now included a baby, all because of Mikhail.

Mikhail's expression remained hard, but there was a flicker of something in his eyes as she yelled at him—something raw, barely contained. He took a step closer, his voice harsh, but quieter than before.

"You think I wanted any of this? You think I wanted to be here? You should've been long gone by now, Anya. I told you to disappear. You should have listened."

The words stung, but Anya wasn't about to back down. Not now. Not when everything felt so completely out of control.

Her eyes flashed with fury. "Disappear? Where the hell was I supposed to go? My father wants me dead! I have no one left. And you—" Her voice cracked, betraying the emotion behind her anger. "You're the reason I'm in this position. You're the reason I'm carrying your child."

She didn't want to admit it, but she felt utterly lost. She wanted to believe Mikhail had a plan, that he could fix this somehow, but the truth was, she didn't know what to expect from him. He was dangerous—she knew that—but there was something about him, something beneath the surface that kept drawing her in.

Mikhail's jaw tightened, his frustration barely contained. "You could have gone anywhere. Anywhere but here."

Anya's hands trembled as she stared at him, her emotions swirling in a mess of anger, fear, and something else she refused to name. "And what? You'd have just killed me then, right? You think I don't know what you're supposed to do?"

The accusation hung in the air between them, and for a brief moment, Mikhail's mask slipped. His expression hardened, but his silence was telling. She'd hit a nerve.

"You should've gone, Anya," he muttered, his voice quieter now. "But you didn't. And now... I can't fix this."

The way he said it, as if the weight of their entire situation was pressing down on him, made something inside her chest twist. She wanted to hate him. She should hate him. But there was something else—something she couldn't shake.

And then, the tension between them shifted, almost imperceptibly. The anger that had been boiling over a moment ago seemed to change into something deeper, something more dangerous.

The air between them felt charged, thick with emotions that neither of them could name but both of them felt. Anya's pulse raced as Mikhail stepped even closer, his body looming over hers. She could feel the heat of his presence, and despite everything, her body reacted to it.

Her breathing hitched, the adrenaline from their argument mixing with the undeniable pull that had been building between them since the night they first met. She didn't want to admit it, but there was an attraction—one that scared her as much as it consumed her.

Mikhail's voice dropped lower, his eyes locking onto hers. "You shouldn't have stayed. But now... we're in this."

Anya's heart pounded in her chest, her skin prickling with the awareness of how close he was, how intensely his gaze was fixed on her. She hated him for what he'd done. She hated him for the way he made her feel. But she couldn't ignore the way her body responded to his nearness, the heat building between them despite the chaos of the situation.

"Why are you even helping me?" she whispered, her voice softer now, filled with frustration and confusion. "You're supposed to be a killer. You're supposed to hate me."

Mikhail's expression shifted, his eyes darkening with something she couldn't place. "I don't know why I'm helping you," he admitted, his voice rough. "But I can't stop."

The space between them seemed to vanish entirely, the tension shifting into something charged with desire. Anya's breath caught in her throat as the intensity of his gaze pinned her in place. She felt her body lean toward him before her mind could stop it, the need for him—despite everything—taking over.

Their heated words hung in the air, unresolved, but something else was growing between them now—something primal, undeniable.

Anya could feel the air between them growing heavier, the tension that had simmered all this time finally boiling over. It was as if everything they had been through, all the fear, anger, and confusion, was pulling them toward this moment, a collision they couldn't avoid.

Without warning, Mikhail's hands were on her, gripping her waist with a force that made her gasp. His pull was rough, desperate, and his lips crashed into hers with an intensity that sent a shiver down her spine. The kiss was fierce, more a battle than an embrace, his teeth grazing her bottom lip as he devoured her mouth.

Anya instinctively pushed against him for a brief moment, but that only made him pull her tighter against his hard chest. The resistance melted away as her hands found their way to his shirt, fisting in the fabric as she clung to him. The heat between them was undeniable, and despite her inner voice telling her to stop, she couldn't.

Mikhail growled low in his throat as he broke the kiss, only to trail his mouth down the side of her neck, biting at her skin in a way that sent jolts of electricity through her body. His hands were everywhere—on her waist, then sliding up her back, gripping her so hard she knew she'd have bruises, but she didn't care.

She moaned when his mouth found the sensitive spot below her ear, and her own hands began pulling at his shirt, desperate to feel his skin beneath her fingers. "Take it off," she murmured breathlessly.

Mikhail stepped back for a moment, eyes locked on hers, his pupils dilated with lust. In one swift motion, he yanked the shirt over his head, revealing his muscular torso. Anya's breath hitched at the sight of him—his chest and arms covered in dark tattoos, the lines and swirls of ink telling a story of violence and loyalty. His body was like a map of the life he led, and every inch of him exuded power and danger.

Her eyes roamed over his chest, the hard ridges of his muscles, the inked symbols marking him as a Bratva enforcer. She couldn't help but feel a surge of attraction, her body responding even though her mind screamed at her to stop. But it was too late for that.

He reached for her shirt, his fingers brushing against her skin as he grabbed the hem and pulled it over her head. The cool air hit her bare skin, but she didn't feel cold—not with the way Mikhail was looking at her, his gaze dark and hungry.

His hands were on her again, sliding down to her waist and pulling her closer. He kissed her again, this time slower, more deliberate, as his fingers worked the clasp of her bra. It fell away easily, and Anya felt a rush of heat as Mikhail's gaze lowered, his eyes locked on her breasts.

"Goddamn," he muttered under his breath, his voice rough with desire.

His hands cupped her breasts, thumbs grazing over her nipples, which hardened instantly under his touch. Anya arched into him, her breath coming in short gasps as his mouth followed, taking one nipple into his mouth, sucking and biting gently. The sensation sent a wave of pleasure coursing through her, and she moaned, her fingers tangling in his hair, pulling him closer.

Mikhail groaned against her skin, his hands gripping her hips as he pulled her even tighter against his body. She could feel the hard length of him pressing into her stomach, and the knowledge of how much he wanted her only fueled her desire.

His mouth moved to her other breast, his tongue flicking over the sensitive bud as his hands began working at the button of her jeans. Anya gasped as he yanked them down her legs, his movements rough and urgent, but the thrill that shot through her was undeniable. She kicked off her jeans, standing there in nothing but her panties, her skin flushed with heat.

Mikhail didn't wait long. His hands found the waistband of her panties and in one swift motion, he pulled them down, leaving her completely bare before him. His eyes roamed over her body, taking in every curve, every inch of skin, as if memorizing her.

Her fingers fumbled with the button of his jeans, but she was desperate now, her body aching for him. Mikhail's hands were on her again, gripping her hips as she finally freed him from his pants. She gasped at the sight of him, his cock hard and thick, twitching in her hand as she stroked him.

Mikhail groaned at her touch, and in one quick movement, he lifted her off the ground, her legs instinctively wrapping around his waist. She clung to him, their mouths colliding once more in a fierce kiss as he carried her toward the bedroom.

The world around them blurred as they stumbled through the door. Mikhail laid her down on the bed, her legs falling open as he positioned himself between them. His gaze flickered up to hers, holding it for a moment before he lowered his head between her thighs.

Anya gasped as his tongue slid between her folds, swirling around her clit in a way that made her whole body tremble. Each flick of his tongue sent a surge of heat through her veins, making her legs shake. The roughness of his beard brushing against her sensitive skin was a delicious contrast to the softness of his tongue, heightening every sensation as he worked her over. She could barely keep still, her hips arching off the bed as her body sought more contact, more friction, more of the unbearable pleasure he was giving her.

A loud moan escaped her lips, uncontrollable, as Mikhail's tongue circled her swollen clit with expert precision. The pleasure was too much, too intense, making her body writhe beneath him as she gasped for breath. Her hands flew to his head, tangling in his hair, desperate to pull him closer, to keep him exactly where she needed him most. Her thighs trembled around his head as he continued his relentless assault on her senses, his tongue flicking and swirling with an intensity that left her breathless.

His fingers joined the fray, slipping inside her with ease, and Anya's back arched off the bed as he began to thrust, slow at first, then faster, deeper. Her body clenched around his fingers, the rhythm perfect, matching the sensual strokes of his tongue as he sucked gently on her clit. Each movement pushed her closer to the edge, her breath hitching in her throat as the pleasure built higher and higher, like a tidal wave crashing through her.

"Mikhail," she moaned his name, her voice breathless, desperate, as he drove her toward the brink of release. His fingers curled inside her, hitting the perfect spot with each thrust, sending shockwaves of pleasure radiating through her. Her hips moved in sync with him, her body completely lost to the sensations he was drawing out of her.

Her breath came in short, ragged gasps, each one more frantic than the last. She was teetering on the edge, her entire body trembling, her thighs tightening around his head as the tension coiled tighter and tighter inside her. Every nerve in her body was on fire, each flick of his tongue and thrust of his fingers bringing her closer to the point of no return.

She could feel the climax building, her muscles tensing, her toes curling, as her body prepared to let go. But just when she thought she was about to fall over the edge, Mikhail pulled back, his tongue leaving her clit, his fingers stilling inside her.

Anya cried out in frustration, her body aching for the release he had so cruelly denied her. She was panting, her breath coming in desperate, ragged gasps, her entire body trembling with unspent desire. The fire inside her still burned, but Mikhail had left her on the brink, teetering precariously, aching for more.

Her hands remained tangled in his hair, tugging him back toward her as her body screamed for the pleasure to continue.

"Not yet," he growled, his voice thick with lust.

Her mind was foggy with lust, and the anticipation of what would come next made her heart race. She heard Mikhail's low, rough voice break the silence, thick with command. "Roll over."

Anya didn't hesitate. Her body was his to command, her every sense heightened by the primal desire coursing through her. She rolled over, her body trembling with both fear and excitement. She felt Mikhail's hands grip her hips roughly, pulling her up onto all fours. His fingers dug into her skin, leaving marks she would feel for days, but she welcomed the pain—it only heightened her pleasure.

The weight of him behind her was intoxicating, his presence overwhelming. She could feel the heat of his body, his breath heavy as he positioned himself. The tip of his cock slid against her slick folds, teasing her, making her gasp as the pleasure built again. His hand held her firmly in place, her back arched, her ass pressed against him, leaving her completely at his mercy.

Mikhail's voice was a growl, deep and dangerous, sending shivers down her spine. "Tell me you want it," he demanded, his cock still teasing her, sliding against her wetness without entering.

Anya's breath caught in her throat. Part of her wanted to resist, to maintain some sense of control, but the need inside her was too strong. She bit her lip, trying to hold on to the last shred of her pride, but when he pressed harder against her, the pressure just shy of what she craved, she couldn't hold back any longer.

"I want it," she whispered, her voice barely audible, thick with lust.

Mikhail's grip tightened on her hips. "Louder," he demanded, his voice a dangerous growl.

"I want it," she moaned, louder this time, her voice filled with desperation and need. She was panting now, her body trembling, every inch of her on fire, begging for him to take her.

With a growl, Mikhail thrust into her, hard and deep, filling her completely in one swift motion. Anya screamed out in both surprise and pleasure, her body clenching around him as he started to move. He began slowly, his thrusts deep and controlled, each one sending a shockwave of pleasure through her. She could feel every inch of him inside her, stretching her, filling her so completely that it was almost too much to bear.

The room was filled with the sound of their moans and the rhythmic slap of skin on skin as Mikhail picked up speed, driving into her with increasing intensity. His grip on her hips was bruising, his fingers digging into her flesh as he pulled her back against him, meeting each of his thrusts. Anya's moans grew louder, her body completely out of her control, her mind consumed by the overwhelming pleasure of being taken by him.

Mikhail leaned over her, his body pressing down against her back as he pounded into her, his breath hot against her neck. She could feel the tension in him, the raw desire as he moved faster, harder, his cock hitting deeper with every thrust. Her hands clutched at the sheets, her knuckles white as she tried to anchor herself, her entire body shaking with the force of his movements.

She was lost in the sensation of him, her mind blank, her body completely overtaken by the need for release. Her moans mixed with his grunts, the sound of their ragged breaths filling the room. Each thrust pushed her closer, each stroke of his cock inside her driving her to the edge of oblivion.

Anya could feel the heat building, the tension winding tighter inside her. Her body was on fire, every nerve alive with pleasure, her senses overwhelmed by the intensity of the moment. She could feel herself spiraling, feel the climax rising, unstoppable, as Mikhail continued to thrust into her, his movements growing more erratic, more desperate.

"Fuck," Mikhail growled, his voice hoarse with lust as he pounded into her, his hands gripping her hips with bruising force. "You're so tight. So fucking perfect."

Anya's body tightened around him, her muscles clenching as the pleasure reached a fever pitch. She was so close, so close to the edge, and with one final thrust, she shattered. Her climax hit her with the force of a tidal wave, her body convulsing as the pleasure ripped through her. She screamed out, her body shaking, her fingers clawing at the sheets as the release consumed her.

Mikhail groaned loudly behind her, his own release hitting him at the same time. His cock pulsed inside her, filling her with his heat as he thrust into her one last time. His body tensed, his fingers digging into her hips as he held her in place, the two of them lost in the overwhelming intensity of their shared climax.

For a moment, time stood still. The world fell away, and there was only the sound of their labored breathing, the feeling of their bodies pressed together, and the aftershocks of their release still coursing through them.

The room was thick with the lingering scent of sex, their bodies still entwined in the quiet aftermath of their frenzied passion. Mikhail's arm rested heavily over Anya's waist, his fingers lightly grazing her skin, almost absentmindedly, as though even in his sleep, he couldn't help but keep her close. Anya's body felt limp, exhausted, her legs tangled with his under the sheets. The intensity of what had just happened left her breathless, but her mind refused to settle.

Her heart pounded against her ribs, not from the physical exhaustion but from the storm of emotions swirling inside her. She lay there, unable to comprehend how everything had changed so drastically. She should be repulsed, terrified even. And she was—part of her was still screaming inside, begging her to get out, to run far away from this man who had torn her life apart. But another part of her felt something she didn't expect. Something she didn't want to admit.

Safety.

How did it come to this? How did she end up here, lying next to the man who should be her enemy, the man who had kidnapped her, killed men for a living, and now was somehow wrapped around her like a protective shield? Her thoughts wouldn't stop racing, no matter how much she wanted to sink into the oblivion of sleep.

Mikhail shifted slightly beside her, his breathing steady, his body warm and firm against hers. His presence was overwhelming in every sense of the word. His strength, his danger, his power—it should terrify her. And yet, the weight of his arm over her waist felt like an anchor, keeping her grounded in this strange, twisted reality she now inhabited.

Anya tried to make sense of the pull she felt toward him, the undeniable connection that had bloomed from the most impossible of circumstances. He had killed those men. She had watched him do it, heard the sound of the gunshots ringing through the air. He had kidnapped her, torn her from her world, leaving her alone and vulnerable in his. Yet, here she was, wrapped up in his arms like she belonged there.

It made no sense.

Her fingers lightly traced the tattoos on his chest, the inked lines a reminder of the life he lived—a life that she had no part of before. But now, everything was different. He wasn't just some enforcer for the Bratva. He wasn't just the man who had been sent to kill her. He was the father of her child. The thought sent a jolt through her, a reminder of the impossible situation they now faced.

She didn't know if she could trust him. Mikhail was dangerous—deadly, even. Yet, when he had learned about the baby, he hadn't pushed her away. He hadn't turned his back. In fact, he had made it clear that he would help her. He had promised to protect her, and for reasons she couldn't understand, she believed him.

Anya's mind reeled with the contradiction of it all. How could she feel so safe in the arms of a man like Mikhail? How could she, after everything, trust him with her life? With her baby's life? The questions twisted inside her, but no answers came.

Her fingers curled slightly against his chest, and she closed her eyes, trying to focus on the steady rise and fall of his breathing. Every time she thought she had found her footing in this mess, something pulled her under again. How could she be drawn to him like this? It wasn't just physical. That much was obvious. There was something deeper, something raw and magnetic between them that had been there since the first time their eyes met.

She hated it. She hated the way her body responded to him, the way her heart beat faster when he was near, the way she found comfort in his presence. And yet, it was undeniable.

Her thoughts drifted to her father, and a wave of bitterness washed over her. The man who had protected her her whole life, who had always been her rock, her shield, had turned on her. The betrayal still stung, leaving a hollow ache in her chest that no amount of Mikhail's warmth could fill. She had nowhere to go now, no one she could truly rely on—except the man lying next to her.

It made no sense, but in that moment, wrapped up in Mikhail's arms, she felt more protected than she ever had with her father. There was a vulnerability in the way he held her, a possessiveness that was terrifying and comforting all at once. She didn't understand it, didn't know what it meant, but she couldn't deny the safety she felt when he was close.

Anya's heart fluttered with an unspoken fear. What would happen next? Could she really trust him? Or was she simply clinging to the only option she had left?

She knew, deep down, that she couldn't stay in this limbo forever. Sooner or later, the reality of their situation would crash down on them both. Her father, his Bratva—they wouldn't just let this go. But for now, in this moment, with Mikhail's body wrapped around hers, she let herself forget all of that.

For now, all she could do was lie there, listening to the steady beat of his heart and wondering how much longer this fragile peace between them could last.

Chapter 10

Mikhail woke up to the soft, rhythmic sound of Anya's breathing beside him. The early morning light crept through the blinds, casting long shadows across the room. He lay still, staring up at the ceiling, trying to get his thoughts in order, but they remained as jumbled as ever. Beside him, Anya shifted slightly in her sleep, her hand resting protectively over her belly. That sight, more than anything, sent a shock through him—a visceral reminder of what had changed.

My baby, he thought, his chest tightening in a way that was both unsettling and unfamiliar.

This wasn't supposed to happen. His life had been simple before—kill when ordered, follow Bratva code, survive. Now everything was different. He'd allowed Anya to live, even after knowing what that would mean for him. And now she carried his child, a reality that gnawed at the corners of his mind, forcing him to confront truths he wasn't prepared to face.

Mikhail shifted slightly, careful not to wake her as his eyes traced the outline of her body beneath the sheets. Her hair fanned out across the pillow, the peacefulness of her sleep in stark contrast to the chaos that surrounded them. She had been so

vulnerable when she came to him, so broken, yet
so strong. He hated how much he noticed these
things now. How much she was starting to matter to
him.

*I should have walked away. This isn't my life. It's
not supposed to be,* he thought bitterly.

But deep down, he knew he couldn't walk away.
Not now. Not anymore. Anya wasn't just a woman
caught up in Bratva business; she was something
else entirely. She was carrying his child, and that
fact changed everything. The possessiveness that
had been simmering inside him since their night
together was now an unshakable force.

He sat up carefully, running a hand through his dark
hair, still damp with sweat from a restless night. His
fingers brushed against the tattoos on his arm, a
constant reminder of the life he had built for
himself—the life he was bound to. A life filled with
blood and violence. A life that had no room for
someone like Anya.

But here she was, lying in his bed, and he couldn't
shake the overwhelming urge to protect her. To
protect *them.*

Mikhail clenched his fists, feeling the familiar heat
of anger flare in his chest, not at her, but at himself.
How had he let it get to this? How had he lost
control? He should have killed her when he had the
chance. It would have been cleaner, easier. But

now, she and their unborn child had become his responsibility.

He turned to look at her again, and for a brief moment, the anger dissipated, replaced by something far more unsettling: fear. Not fear for himself—he had never feared death or the dangers that came with his line of work. But the thought of failing to protect Anya, of losing her or the baby... That terrified him in a way he hadn't anticipated.

They're mine, he thought, a wave of possessiveness rising in his chest. *No one is taking them from me.*

The weight of it all pressed down on him—the betrayal to the Bratva, the inevitable confrontation with Viktor and Nikolai, the impossible situation he'd created. He couldn't hide her forever, and he knew it. Sooner or later, he would have to face them, and when he did, he would have to make a choice. The Bratva demanded loyalty above all else, and betraying that loyalty would cost him everything.

But there was no question in his mind anymore. He'd already made his choice, even if he hadn't realized it until now. Anya wasn't just some loose end to be tied up. She was his. And he would protect her at all costs, even if that meant going against the Bratva—against the only family he had ever known.

The thought made his stomach churn with unease. Viktor would demand answers soon. He wasn't a man to be left in the dark for long, and Mikhail had already pushed the boundaries of his patience. But what could he say? What excuse could he give for sparing her life, for keeping her hidden away like this? Viktor wouldn't understand. Nikolai certainly wouldn't. And Mikhail couldn't afford to show weakness. Not in front of them.

He pressed a hand to his forehead, the weight of it all crashing down on him. Protecting Anya meant going against everything he had been trained to believe. It meant severing ties with the Bratva, something that wasn't just dangerous—it was suicidal. But there was no other choice now. His loyalty had shifted, and it wasn't just about survival anymore.

His eyes returned to Anya's sleeping form, her chest rising and falling steadily. She didn't know the war that raged inside him, didn't understand the depth of what was coming. But Mikhail knew. He had already crossed a line, and there was no going back.

She's mine, he thought again, the possessiveness taking root deeper than before. *No one will touch her. Not Viktor. Not Nikolai. Not her father. No one.*

He stood up from the bed, the decision solidifying in his mind. He would face Viktor and Nikolai soon. He'd have to. But he would do it on his terms. He would protect Anya, protect their baby, and he would do whatever it took to keep them safe. Even if it meant going to war with the very men he had sworn to follow.

As he left the room, Mikhail took one last look at Anya, his jaw tightening with resolve. She was no longer just a complication. She was his responsibility. And he wouldn't let anyone take her from him.

Mikhail moved through the small kitchen, his mind already working through the steps he would need to take. The dull sound of coffee brewing filled the room as he leaned against the counter, staring out the window but seeing nothing. His thoughts were miles away, already anticipating the storm that was heading his way.

He knew Viktor and Nikolai wouldn't wait much longer for answers. Mikhail had been dodging Viktor's calls for the past week, using excuses about scouting and planning, but Viktor wasn't stupid. The man was calculating, ruthless, and above all, he valued loyalty. And Mikhail was dangerously close to betraying that loyalty.

The Bratva wasn't forgiving. There were no second chances when it came to defying orders. He knew what was coming. If Viktor found out about Anya—about the baby—there wouldn't be any understanding, no negotiation. The Bratva's law was simple: anyone who posed a threat had to be eliminated. No exceptions.

I should've told them by now, Mikhail thought as he took a long sip of coffee, the bitter liquid doing little to ease the tension gnawing at him. *I should've ended this.*

But as he stood there, staring at the black surface of the coffee in his mug, he knew the truth. He wasn't going to tell Viktor. He wasn't going to turn Anya over, and he sure as hell wasn't going to let anyone touch her.

It had been easier before, when he'd only thought of her as a loose end—a witness who needed to disappear. But now? Now everything was tangled up in a mess of emotions he hadn't expected, hadn't prepared for. She was carrying his child. The possessiveness he felt toward her, toward the baby, was like nothing he'd experienced before. It consumed him, driving out the cold, calculated side of him that had kept him alive for so long.

She's mine, he thought again, gripping the edge of the counter. *They're mine.*

The sound of soft footsteps broke into his thoughts, and he turned to see Anya standing in the doorway, her hair tousled from sleep, her eyes still heavy with it. She gave him a small, sleepy smile, one that should have felt out of place in the world he lived in but somehow didn't.

"Morning," she murmured, her voice thick with sleep as she made her way over to him.

Mikhail nodded, watching as she moved toward the coffee pot, instinctively grabbing a mug and pouring herself a cup. It was such a simple, normal action, but in that moment, it struck him how much had changed. He wasn't alone anymore. He wasn't just some enforcer, living from one kill to the next, waiting for orders. He had someone to protect now—someone who depended on him. And that meant everything had changed.

Anya leaned against the counter next to him, taking a slow sip of her coffee, her gaze wandering out the window. For a moment, there was a comfortable silence between them, the quiet of the morning settling in around them. But Mikhail's mind never stopped racing.

She's still in danger. Every second she's here, she's a target.

He glanced at her from the corner of his eye, his jaw tightening with frustration. As much as he wanted to keep her hidden here forever, he knew that wasn't realistic. The Bratva would come for him eventually, and when they did, he wouldn't be able to protect her if they were unprepared.

Anya must have sensed the tension in him because she turned to look at him, her brow furrowing slightly. "Are you okay?" she asked, her voice soft but laced with concern.

Mikhail didn't respond immediately, his thoughts too tangled to offer her any real reassurance. He set his coffee mug down on the counter with a bit too much force, the sound breaking the morning stillness.

"I have to figure out how to deal with this," he muttered, more to himself than to her.

Anya tilted her head, watching him closely. "Deal with what?"

He met her gaze, his blue eyes sharp with an intensity that made her swallow nervously. "Viktor's not going to wait forever," he said, his voice low. "I've been putting him off, but he's going to demand answers soon. And when he does…"

Her face paled slightly, and Mikhail could see the fear flash in her eyes. He hated that fear. He hated that he was the reason for it, but it was also what kept him anchored. That fear reminded him that she wasn't just some woman caught in the crossfire—she was tied to him now, and that made her a target.

"Mikhail…" she began, but he shook his head.

"I'm not letting anything happen to you or the baby," he growled, his voice rough with emotion. "But I can't hide you forever. Viktor will come looking. He'll ask questions, and I'm running out of lies."

Anya's hand trembled slightly as she set down her coffee, her gaze dropping to her stomach. "What… what are we going to do?"

He moved closer to her, his hand reaching out to cup her face, his thumb brushing gently over her cheek. "I'll figure it out," he said, his voice softer now, but filled with determination. "You and the baby… you're my responsibility now. I'll handle Viktor and Nikolai. You just stay here."

She looked up at him, her eyes wide and uncertain, but she nodded. "I trust you."

Those words hit him harder than they should have, digging deep into his chest. It had been a long time since anyone had said that to him. Trust wasn't something he was used to, and it felt foreign, unsettling. But in her eyes, he saw the truth—she did trust him. And that only made his need to protect her burn stronger.

He leaned down, pressing a brief kiss to her forehead, trying to ignore the way his heart tightened at the feel of her soft skin against his lips. As he pulled back, he gave her one last, hard look.

"I'm going to fix this," he said, his voice a low growl. "I swear to you, I'm going to keep you safe."

Anya nodded, her hand resting over her stomach. "I know."

Mikhail turned away, already thinking about what needed to be done. He couldn't keep putting off Viktor. He needed to face this head-on. And he would. For her. For their child. He would do whatever it took to protect them.

Mikhail paced the length of his small apartment, his mind a whirlwind of conflicting thoughts. Every instinct in him screamed that this wasn't sustainable, that hiding Anya from the Bratva was only delaying the inevitable. Sooner or later, Viktor would come knocking, demanding answers—and lies wouldn't save him then.

He glanced back at Anya, still sitting at the kitchen table. She looked calm on the surface, but he could see the way her hands fidgeted in her lap, how her eyes darted toward him every few seconds. She was afraid, and Mikhail hated that she had every right to be. It made him feel weak—something he despised.

But what could he do? His entire life had been built around a single, unwavering loyalty to the Bratva. His job was to protect the organization, to follow orders without hesitation. That was his role as an enforcer, and he had always done it well. He had killed for the Bratva, lied for them, bled for them.

But now... now it wasn't so simple.

Viktor's orders had been clear. Kill the witness. Eliminate the threat. That was how things were done. And yet, here he was, defying the very rules he had lived by for so long. Worse than defiance, this was betrayal. He was protecting Anya, hiding her from the men who expected him to be loyal to them, not to her.

What the hell have I done? Mikhail thought, dragging a hand down his face. He wasn't supposed to be this man—this man who put one person above his duty, above his loyalty to the family that had given him everything.

But he couldn't shake it. Couldn't push away the possessive need to keep Anya safe. Not just because she was pregnant, but because she was his now. His responsibility. His woman.

He couldn't let anything happen to her.

But I can't hide her forever.

The realization hit him hard. He couldn't keep playing this game. Viktor would find out eventually, and when he did, the consequences would be severe. He would lose everything—his position, his power, maybe even his life. But the worst part was that they would come for Anya. And Mikhail knew, deep down, that the Bratva wouldn't just stop at her. They would make sure she never had the baby.

That thought alone filled him with a rage he couldn't contain. His fists clenched, his muscles tight with barely contained fury. He wasn't going to let that happen. He couldn't. Anya's father may have betrayed her, but Mikhail wasn't going to let anyone take her or their child from him.

But how do I do this without bringing Viktor's wrath down on us?

The silence in the apartment grew heavier, the air thick with unspoken tension. Mikhail knew he needed to act, and soon. He couldn't wait for Viktor to come to him—he had to go to Viktor first, make a stand, no matter how dangerous it was.

"You're leaving, aren't you?" Anya's voice broke the silence, soft but steady.

Mikhail turned toward her, seeing the understanding in her eyes. She wasn't stupid—she knew the stakes just as well as he did. It made him respect her more, even as he hated that she was in this situation at all.

"I have to," he said, his voice rough. "I can't keep dodging Viktor forever. Sooner or later, he's going to demand answers. And when he does…"

He trailed off, the weight of what he was about to say settling over him like a heavy fog.

Anya stood, crossing the room toward him, her expression a mixture of fear and something else—something that looked like trust. Mikhail's heart clenched at the sight of it.

"What are you going to tell him?" she asked quietly, her eyes searching his.

"I don't know yet," he admitted, the frustration clear in his tone. "But I can't keep lying. Sooner or later, they'll find out I'm hiding you. And if they do, Viktor and Nikolai… they'll come for us. For you. For the baby."

Anya's hand moved to her stomach, a gesture that was so instinctual and protective that it tugged at something deep inside Mikhail. It made him more resolute, more determined to keep her safe.

"Will they…" she hesitated, her voice catching. "Will they try to kill me?"

The question hung in the air, heavy and cold. Mikhail wanted to lie, to tell her that everything would be fine, but he couldn't. Not with something like this.

"Yes," he said, his voice barely above a whisper. "They'll kill you. They'll kill the baby. And if I don't handle this… they'll kill me too."

Anya's face paled, but she didn't crumble. She stood tall, her hand still resting protectively over her stomach. "Then you have to handle it. Whatever it takes."

Her strength, in that moment, took him by surprise. He had expected fear, maybe even panic, but Anya wasn't like other women. She had been through too much, seen too much, to fall apart now.

And maybe that's what drew him to her in the first place—the fire inside her, the strength that defied the world she had been thrust into. She wasn't weak. She wasn't someone who needed constant protection. She was his equal, even if she didn't realize it yet.

"I will," Mikhail promised, stepping closer to her. His hand reached out, cupping her cheek as he looked into her eyes. "I'll handle it. I'll make sure they don't come for us."

The "us" hung in the air between them, a quiet acknowledgment of the bond they now shared. They weren't just two people tangled in a dangerous web. They were more than that now—connected in ways that went beyond simple survival.

Anya leaned into his touch, her eyes closing for a moment as she let out a soft breath. "I trust you," she whispered, the words slipping out before she could stop them.

Mikhail's heart clenched at the admission. Trust. He had never expected it from her, but now that she had given it, he felt the full weight of responsibility that came with it. He couldn't let her down. He couldn't fail her.

Without another word, Mikhail dropped his hand and turned toward the door. He had a plan forming in his mind, one that would give them a fighting chance, but it wouldn't be easy.

He paused at the door, his hand resting on the knob. "Lock the door behind me," he said quietly. "Don't answer it for anyone but me. Understand?"

Anya nodded, her eyes wide but determined.

Mikhail took a deep breath, steeling himself for what was to come. Viktor was waiting, and Mikhail knew he was walking into the lion's den. But he would face it. For her. For the baby.

For them.

Chapter 11

Anya sat at the small table by the window, the morning sunlight casting a soft glow over the city skyline. The warmth of the coffee cup seeped into her palms as she stared out at the world beyond the glass, but her mind was miles away. Mikhail had left the apartment not long ago, his departure quiet but lingering. The weight of their earlier conversation hung in the air, replaying in her head over and over.

He had promised her safety—had reassured her in his usual gruff, almost dismissive way. But something was different this time. His eyes, cold and hardened by the life he lived, had softened when he spoke about protecting her and the baby. That shift in him, subtle yet unmistakable, sent a flutter of uncertainty through her. *Can I really trust him?*

It felt strange without him there. The apartment was still, the only sound the faint hum of the city below. Anya wasn't used to this kind of silence, this sense of calm. For so long, her life had been consumed by fear, by the constant dread of what her father would do, by the looming threat of the Bratva. But now, there was something new—an unexpected stillness that should have brought her comfort but instead left her grappling with emotions she wasn't ready to confront.

She traced her finger along the rim of the coffee cup, letting her thoughts swirl in the quiet space. *How did it come to this?* Just weeks ago, her world had been so different. She had been Konstantin Morozov's daughter, untouchable in her own right, surrounded by luxury and security. And now? Now, she was pregnant, on the run, and entangled with a man who had turned her life upside down.

But Mikhail was more than just a danger in her life. He had saved her, more than once. She wasn't sure when it had happened, but she had started to see him as something more than the violent enforcer who had kidnapped her. There was a depth to him, something he kept hidden behind that steely exterior.

I shouldn't feel this way, she thought, her chest tightening. *I should hate him for what he's done—for what he's capable of. But I don't.*

Anya stood, the movement jarring her out of her thoughts. She placed the empty coffee cup in the sink, wiping her hands absently on a towel as she wandered through the apartment. It was minimalist, functional—nothing like the grand, opulent spaces she had grown up in. Yet there was something comforting about the simplicity. It was Mikhail's world, and somehow, she felt herself fitting into it.

But can I really trust him? The question lingered in her mind, stubborn and persistent. Mikhail was nothing like her father, yet the shadows of doubt still clung to her. Her father had been the center of her universe for as long as she could remember, and now, he was the one who had betrayed her in the worst possible way. Mikhail had promised her protection, but promises were fragile things, easily broken. What if he turned on her, too? What if this was just temporary, and she was fooling herself into thinking he cared?

The thought of Mikhail turning on her made her stomach twist. She was carrying his child, a life that bound them together in ways she couldn't fully understand yet. And that scared her more than anything. She pressed a hand to her abdomen, the subtle swell beneath her fingers a reminder of everything that had changed.

What if I'm just a responsibility to him? Anya's heart pounded at the thought. Mikhail had always been clear about one thing—he was an enforcer, a man who followed orders and dealt with problems efficiently. Was that all she was to him? A problem to solve? A loose end he couldn't bring himself to cut?

Her mind raced through every interaction they had shared. She remembered the way he had looked at her, the way his touch had ignited something deep inside her. There was more than just responsibility there—she had felt it. But could she trust it? Could she trust herself?

Anya sighed, leaning against the counter. Her feelings were a tangled mess, and no matter how hard she tried to make sense of them, she kept circling back to one undeniable truth—Mikhail had become more than just her protector. She wasn't sure when it had started, but she felt something for him, something that scared her as much as it excited her.

But feelings were dangerous. She knew that better than anyone. Her father had used her emotions against her, had manipulated her love and loyalty to suit his own needs. And now, that same father wanted her gone, wanted her baby gone. The betrayal still stung, raw and painful. Could Mikhail do the same? Was she walking into another trap, this time one of her own making?

She pushed herself off the counter, pacing the length of the kitchen. *No, this is different,* she told herself, her mind flashing to the look in Mikhail's eyes earlier. He wasn't like her father. He was ruthless, yes, but there was a darkness in him that came from survival, not manipulation. He had killed, yes, but not out of cruelty—out of necessity.

But is that enough? Could she trust that the man who had kidnapped her and killed without hesitation would truly protect her and their child? The uncertainty gnawed at her, refusing to let go.

Anya paused by the window again, staring out at the city streets far below. Whatever her feelings were for Mikhail, whatever this strange connection between them was, one thing was clear—she couldn't afford to make a mistake. Her life, and the life growing inside her, depended on her making the right choice.

And right now, that choice was Mikhail.

Anya swallowed hard, her fingers tightening around the windowsill. It wasn't love—not yet, anyway. But it was trust. Fragile, uncertain trust. And for now, that would have to be enough.

Anya had been pacing for what felt like hours, her restless energy filling the apartment. The quiet had settled around her like a weight, pressing down on her thoughts, stirring up emotions she didn't want to face. She paused near the window, her fingers grazing the cool glass as she tried to calm her racing mind.

I need to stop thinking so much.

The tension in her body was impossible to ignore, a reminder of the emotional chaos she had been plunged into since her life collided with Mikhail's. As much as she tried to push it away, the growing feelings she had for him only made everything more confusing. Could she really trust him? Could she trust anyone?

Suddenly, the sharp ring of her phone cut through the silence, and Anya jumped, startled. Her heart leapt into her throat when she saw the name flash across the screen—*Father.*

For a moment, she stood frozen, staring at the phone as her stomach twisted into knots. She considered ignoring it, letting it ring until the call went to voicemail. But something in her hand moved on instinct, and before she could stop herself, she had answered the call.

"Anya," her father's voice boomed through the speaker, cold and commanding, the way it always had been. There was no warmth, no gentleness—just an edge of impatience and control. "Where are you?"

His tone was enough to send a shiver down her spine. The familiar tightness crept into her chest, the instinct to obey, to fall in line, pressing at her from all sides. But this time, something was different. This time, she didn't feel the fear that usually came with his demands. She felt anger. Deep, seething anger.

"I'm not coming home," she said, her voice surprising even herself with how steady it was. The tension coiled around her, but she didn't falter. She couldn't. Not anymore.

There was a heavy pause on the other end of the line before Konstantin's voice returned, sharper, more menacing. "Anya, this is not a discussion. You will come home, and we will fix this mess."

Fix this mess? The words hit her like a blow to the chest, knocking the air from her lungs. Her grip tightened on the phone, and for a moment, she struggled to find her voice. But then the anger flared again, hotter and brighter than before.

"Fix it?" she spat, her voice laced with venom. "You mean get rid of the baby, don't you? You think I don't know what you planned for me?"

There was a silence on the other end, the kind that felt like a gathering storm, dark and heavy with unspoken threats. Then came a sharp intake of breath. "Anya, listen to me—"

"No!" she cut him off, her voice breaking, raw with emotion. "You betrayed me! You tried to control me, to take away my choice—just like always!"

Her body shook, every word tearing at her insides. She had spent her entire life trying to earn her father's approval, trying to be the daughter he expected her to be. But now, standing on the other side of that divide, she saw it for what it really was—control. Domination. He didn't care about her. He cared about the power she represented, the legacy she could continue for him.

Konstantin's voice grew darker, more dangerous. "You don't understand what you're doing, Anya.

You are making a mistake—a mistake that will destroy everything."

"No, you're the one who doesn't understand," she shot back, her heart pounding in her chest. "This is my life! It's my choice! You can't decide for me anymore. I won't let you."

The silence that followed was deafening, filled with the weight of everything unspoken between them. Anya's breathing was ragged, her heart racing as she waited for his response. She could practically feel the fury radiating from the other end of the line.

"You are my daughter," Konstantin said finally, his voice low, but seething with barely restrained anger. "You do as I say, *always.* You will come home, and we will deal with this—one way or another."

Anya's stomach churned, bile rising in her throat as the threat in his words sank in. Her father wasn't asking—he was ordering her to come home, to give up everything for his plans. He didn't care about her, didn't care about the baby she was carrying. She had no doubt that he would force her to get rid of the baby if it meant protecting his empire, even if it meant hurting her.

Her hands trembled as she clutched the phone, tears burning the back of her eyes. *How did it come to this?* Her father—the man who had raised her, who had taught her everything about strength and loyalty—had become a monster in her eyes. A monster who would destroy her without a second thought.

"I'm not coming back," she whispered, her voice barely above a breath. But there was resolve in her words.

Konstantin's voice turned cold, as sharp as a knife. "Then you've chosen sides, Anya. And you've chosen wrong."

Her heart cracked wide open at the finality of his words. Her father was no longer her protector. He was her enemy. And the realization was like a knife in her chest, cutting deeper than she thought possible.

Anya couldn't take it anymore. The pain, the betrayal—it was too much. Without another word, she hung up, her hand shaking as she ended the call.

Anya collapsed onto the couch, the phone still clutched tightly in her hand as if it might anchor her to reality. Her chest heaved, and the sobs that wracked her body came harder and faster. Her world had just been shattered. The man she had relied on for her entire life, her protector, her father, had disowned her.

It was more than a rejection—it felt like a violent severing, as if the very fabric of her identity had been ripped away. Her father, Konstantin, had been the center of her world for so long that she had never even imagined what life would be like without him.

But now, here she was, truly and utterly alone.

How did it come to this? she thought as the tears continued to spill down her cheeks. *How did I lose everything so quickly?*

Her sobs echoed in the quiet of Mikhail's apartment, the walls closing in on her. The weight of her father's words pressed down on her chest, suffocating her. She had always believed her father would protect her, that no matter how far she strayed, he would welcome her back with open arms. But now, she realized just how wrong she had been. He wasn't the man she thought he was. He wasn't her protector, her guide. He was a tyrant, willing to sacrifice her and her child to maintain his power and legacy.

The thought made her stomach churn, and she pulled her knees to her chest, hugging herself tightly as if she could somehow shield herself from the crushing reality. *I meant nothing to him,* she thought, bitterness creeping into her sorrow. *I was just another piece in his game—a pawn he was willing to sacrifice.*

Her body trembled as she wept, each sob tearing at the fragile threads holding her together. The emotions flooded her in waves—first sadness, then disbelief, and finally, anger. The sadness remained, but it slowly morphed into something darker and more potent: rage.

Her father hadn't just abandoned her; he had *betrayed* her. He had thrown her away like she was nothing, like her life—and the life of her unborn child—were insignificant. The man she had loved and trusted, the one who had taught her strength and loyalty, had been lying to her all along. She had been nothing more than a tool for him to use, a means to an end.

As the realization hit her, a fiery anger began to bubble up inside her, burning away the grief. Anya sat up straighter on the couch, wiping the tears from her face. She was done crying over a man who didn't deserve her loyalty or love. Her father had made his choice, and now, she was making hers.

He had freed her from the chains that had bound her to him for so long. No more living under his control, no more being his obedient daughter. She was her own person now, capable of making her own choices.

I don't need him. I'm stronger than this, she thought, a surge of determination pushing back the lingering grief.

Anya stood, her legs shaky but firm, and walked over to the window. The city sprawled out before her, endless and full of possibilities. It was intimidating, but at the same time, it felt liberating. There was no one left to hold her back. For the first time in her life, she was truly free.

As she stared out at the skyline, her thoughts drifted to Mikhail. He was dangerous, violent, and a part of a world that terrified her. But even so, there was something about him that drew her in, something that made her feel safe in a way she had never felt before.

How can that be? she wondered, her mind swirling with confusion. *How can I feel safe with a man like him, when he's the very thing I should fear?*

And yet, Mikhail wasn't like her father. Yes, he was dangerous. Yes, he had killed men, and yes, he had kidnapped her. But he had also protected her, fought for her, and made her feel seen in a way her father never had.

When she had confronted her father earlier, she had expected him to be angry, to try to control her like he always did. But she hadn't expected the cruelty, the sheer lack of love and compassion in his voice. It was as if she had never mattered to him at all—as if her entire existence was merely a tool for his ambitions.

Mikhail, on the other hand, had shown her a side she hadn't expected. He had been rough with her, yes, but he had also shown her moments of tenderness, of protectiveness. He had risked his life for her.

Is that what this is? she asked herself. *Do I feel safe with him because, in his own way, he cares about me?*

It was an unsettling thought, but she couldn't deny it. The way he had looked at her last night, the way he had held her, made her feel like she wasn't just a responsibility to him. She was *his*—not in the possessive way her father had always tried to claim her, but in a way that felt protective, secure.

Her mind raced with questions, with possibilities. Could she trust him? Could she trust her feelings for him? Or was she just fooling herself, falling into the same trap she had with her father?

Anya placed a hand on her stomach, thinking of the life growing inside her. This wasn't just about her anymore. She had a baby to protect, a life to nurture. And if she had learned anything today, it was that she couldn't trust her father to keep her safe.

But Mikhail… Mikhail was different. As dangerous as he was, she believed—*needed* to believe—that he would protect her and the baby. He had shown her more loyalty than her own father had.

Wiping away the last of her tears, Anya took a deep breath, trying to steady herself. The apartment felt empty without Mikhail, but she no longer felt lost. She was starting to see things more clearly, starting to understand that she had the power to make her own choices now.

And she was choosing Mikhail. She had to. There was no one else she could trust.

The thought brought a strange sense of peace. She wasn't out of danger yet—far from it. But for the first time in what felt like forever, she felt like she was finally on the right path.

I won't let my father control me anymore. I won't let him take this from me.

Anya walked back to the couch and sat down, her mind still spinning but with a newfound clarity. The tears had dried, and with them, the last remnants of her obedience to her father. She was no longer Konstantin Morozov's daughter.

She was her own person now, and she was going to fight for herself—and for her baby.

Whatever it took.

Anya sat in Mikhail's apartment as the sun began its slow descent beyond the horizon. The day had been filled with intense emotions—fear, betrayal, heartbreak—but now, in the soft glow of the fading afternoon light, she felt something new. A quiet strength she hadn't felt before. Her world had shattered, but she hadn't. She had survived.

The weight of her father's rejection still lingered, but it didn't crush her. Instead, it steeled her resolve. For so long, she had lived under her father's influence, doing what was expected, being the obedient daughter, fulfilling his expectations. Now, all of that was gone. It hurt, but there was freedom in that loss, too—a realization that she no longer had to live her life according to anyone else's rules.

By the time the soft glow of the afternoon sun began to fade into early evening, Anya had made peace with one thing: she was no longer Konstantin Morozov's daughter, at least not in the way that mattered. That part of her life was over, and she wasn't looking back. For the first time, her future was hers to shape.

Her thoughts drifted to Mikhail. Despite everything—despite his dangerous life, his violent nature, the chaos that surrounded him—he had become something unexpected in her life: a protector. She had seen sides of him that conflicted with the brutal enforcer he appeared to be. He had saved her, not just physically but emotionally. He had given her space, safety, and, in his own way, a sense of belonging.

It wasn't something she had anticipated. She had wanted to hate him, but she couldn't. Instead, a strange connection had formed between them—something that went beyond physical attraction. It was as if, in their shared danger, they had become tethered to one another. Mikhail had given her something that her father never could: a sense of trust.

Can I trust him completely? she wondered, her mind wandering over the complexities of their relationship. She didn't have the answer to that yet, but she knew that Mikhail had shown her more loyalty and protection in these few weeks than her father had in a lifetime.

And she needed to show him that she wasn't just a burden to him. He had done so much for her, and she wanted to find a way to repay that kindness, even in the smallest of ways.

The idea hit her suddenly—something simple, yet meaningful. *I'll cook him dinner.*

It wasn't grand, but it was something she could do to show her appreciation. Mikhail was constantly on guard, always protecting her, always making sure she was safe. He deserved to come home to something comforting, something that made him feel as though he had a place to rest, if only for a brief moment.

She stood, her resolve building, and quickly searched the apartment for a pen and paper. She found them tucked in a kitchen drawer, and she scribbled a quick note:

Went to grab some groceries. Will be back soon. – Anya.

Satisfied, she placed the note on the counter where Mikhail would easily spot it. The thought of surprising him with something as simple as dinner filled her with a renewed sense of purpose. Maybe it wasn't much, but it was her way of saying thank you.

As she grabbed her purse and headed for the door, Anya felt a growing sense of calm. She wasn't powerless. Despite the chaos swirling around them, she could do something to make life feel normal, if only for a moment.

Opening the door, she stepped out into the hallway, and the fresh air greeted her as she made her way to the street. There was a slight chill in the air, a reminder that autumn was on its way, and with it, a new season—both in the world and in her life.

For the first time in what felt like forever, hope began to stir in her chest. Things weren't perfect, and the road ahead was uncertain, but for now, there was a glimmer of something better.

Maybe—just maybe—things would be okay.

The weight of her father's words, the betrayal she had endured, the fear for her unborn child—they were all still there, but they didn't control her anymore. She had made her decision, and it was a decision to move forward, to build something new, something that wasn't dictated by anyone but herself.

As she walked down the street toward the grocery store, her thoughts settled on Mikhail once again. He had shown her that he was more than just an enforcer. He had shown her that he cared—maybe in ways he didn't fully understand yet. She knew she wasn't ready to fully embrace her feelings for him. It was all too complicated, too intense. But at least she could start with this.

Dinner.

It wasn't much, but it was a start. A way of telling him that she saw him, that she appreciated him, and that she wanted to take care of him in the smallest of ways, just as he had taken care of her.

And as she walked, a smile tugged at the corners of her lips—a small, tentative smile, but one filled with the promise of something more.

For now, it was enough.

Chapter 12

Mikhail sat in front of Viktor, watching the older man as he thumbed through some papers on his desk. The ticking of the clock on the wall was the only sound in the room, a constant reminder that time was running out for him. He had avoided this moment for as long as he could, but it was time. There was no more delaying.

Viktor finally glanced up, his sharp, calculating eyes locking onto Mikhail. He raised an eyebrow, clearly expecting him to speak.

Mikhail kept his tone steady, knowing that any hesitation would be seen as a weakness. "I need a meeting with Nikolai."

Viktor's expression didn't change, but there was something behind his eyes—something close to curiosity. "A meeting with Nikolai," he repeated, his voice even. He set down the papers, leaning back in his chair as he studied Mikhail with an unreadable gaze.

Viktor didn't ask for explanations right away, but Mikhail knew what he was thinking. You don't just request a meeting with Nikolai. Not unless you have a damn good reason.

After a moment, Viktor leaned forward slightly, folding his hands on the desk. "Is this about the girl?"

Mikhail's jaw tightened for a fraction of a second, but he nodded. There was no point in hiding it from Viktor. He had been in the game long enough to know when something didn't add up.

Viktor watched him for another long moment before sighing and shaking his head. "I'll set it up. You know this won't be easy, Mikhail. You'll need more than excuses when you sit in front of Nikolai."

"I'm ready," Mikhail said simply, though inside, his thoughts were swirling.

Viktor didn't press him further. He had his own way of understanding the stakes without needing the details. "Fine. I'll let you know when the meeting is set." Viktor's tone carried a finality, and Mikhail stood, giving a curt nod before turning to leave.

He was halfway to the door when Viktor spoke again, his voice low but carrying a weight that demanded attention. "Mikhail... be careful. You know what Nikolai expects from us."

Mikhail paused but didn't turn back. He simply nodded again before stepping out of the office and into the cool hallway. The weight of Viktor's final words hung over him like a shadow, pressing down on his chest. There was no escaping the truth of

what he was about to face—the moment he had
been dreading was now looming on the horizon.

As he stepped outside into the crisp city air, he took
a breath, feeling the tension coil tighter inside him.
His mind was already racing ahead, the cold reality
of his situation beginning to settle in.

Sliding into the driver's seat of his car, Mikhail
gripped the steering wheel, his knuckles white as
he sped through the narrow city streets, the weight
of the upcoming confrontation with Nikolai sitting
heavy on his chest. He had known from the
moment he decided to protect Anya that this day
would come. But it didn't make it any easier to face.

He couldn't help but think back to the first night he
had found her, the way she had looked at him with
a mix of defiance and fear. He had expected her to
be like the rest—just another pawn in the endless
cycle of Bratva power plays. But she wasn't. From
the moment he had laid eyes on her, something
had shifted inside him.

What the hell am I doing? He thought, his mind
racing as the city blurred by in his peripheral vision.
This wasn't how things were supposed to go. He
wasn't supposed to care about her—wasn't
supposed to let her into his life. But now, everything
was different.

He couldn't kill her. That much was clear. Viktor
might have let it slide for now, but Nikolai would

demand answers. Hard answers. And if Mikhail didn't have the right ones, they both knew what would happen.

His jaw clenched at the thought. Nikolai wasn't a man who tolerated failure, and Mikhail had been skating the edge of that for weeks now. Each day he kept Anya hidden, each time he let her stay alive, he was crossing a line. And yet, he couldn't bring himself to stop.

The memory of her, curled up in his bed last night, flashed through his mind. The way she had looked so vulnerable, so trusting, even after everything. She should hate him—should be terrified of him. But instead, there was something in her eyes, something that told him she didn't see him as the monster he had always believed himself to be.

That's the problem, isn't it? She makes me feel like I'm more than this. But I'm not. I'm not built for this life—for protecting people, for family.

The streetlights cast long shadows across his face as he drove, his thoughts consumed by the upcoming meeting. Nikolai was the head of the Volkov Bratva for a reason. He didn't give second chances, didn't make exceptions. The fact that Mikhail hadn't completed his mission would be seen as a weakness, a betrayal of everything the Bratva stood for.

But then, there was the baby.

Mikhail's grip tightened on the wheel. That had changed everything. Anya wasn't just a girl caught up in a mess anymore. She was carrying his child—his responsibility. It was a fact that gnawed at him constantly, making it impossible for him to think clearly. He had always avoided the idea of family. His own father had been a nightmare, a violent man who had torn his life apart, leaving scars that Mikhail still carried to this day.

I swore I'd never be like him. And now here I am, with a kid on the way.

The thought sent a chill down his spine, but at the same time, it stirred something deep inside him. A primal, possessive urge that he had never felt before. Anya and the baby—they were his. And no one was going to take them from him. Not Nikolai, not Viktor, not Konstantin.

Mikhail's heart pounded as he neared his apartment, the looming confrontation with Nikolai only heightening the tension in his chest. He had never gone against the Bratva before. But for Anya, for the baby, he would.

There's no turning back now. I have to protect them, no matter what it costs me.

As he pulled into the driveway of his building, a strange sense of calm washed over him. He didn't have all the answers yet, didn't know how the meeting with Nikolai would play out. But one thing was certain: he wasn't going to lose them. He would fight for them, even if it meant going to war with the very people he had once sworn his loyalty to.

Stepping out of the car, Mikhail's focus shifted to his apartment. As he entered, the quiet of the space hit him, the silence a stark contrast to the storm of thoughts raging in his mind. He expected to find Anya inside, maybe resting or reading. But instead, the apartment was empty—eerily empty.

That's when he saw it: the note sitting on the kitchen counter.

Mikhail's heart sank as he quickly picked it up, reading the hastily scribbled words.

Went to grab some groceries. Will be back soon. – Anya.

Mikhail's heart rate spiked, his blood turning cold. She wasn't here. She wasn't in the apartment, where he could keep her safe. She was out there, alone.

His first instinct was to grab his phone and call her, demand that she come back, but he stopped himself. No, he hadn't explicitly told her she couldn't leave—but she should have known. After everything, how could she not realize the danger lurking just beyond the safety of his walls?

His pulse quickened as his mind raced through a hundred worst-case scenarios. She's vulnerable. Her father is after her. Konstantin's men are out there somewhere, and if they get their hands on her…

He moved to the window, eyes darting across the street below. His gaze locked on the grocery store a few blocks down, and there she was, carrying a bag, walking as if the world wasn't ready to snap at her heels. For a split second, relief coursed through him. She's okay. She's almost home.

But then, his heart lurched painfully in his chest.

A black car pulled up to the curb, its windows dark and menacing. Two men stepped out, their movements too purposeful, too fast. They weren't there by accident.

Mikhail's blood ran cold. He knew exactly what this was.

No hesitation. His body moved before his mind could catch up. He grabbed the gun tucked in the waistband of his jeans and bolted from the apartment. His heart pounded in his chest, his breath ragged as he tore down the stairs, muscles tensed, already bracing for the fight ahead. He could hear his pulse hammering in his ears, the adrenaline flooding his veins as he sprinted down the street toward Anya.

She was still oblivious, her head turned away as the men closed in on her. Mikhail's breath came in harsh gasps, his feet pounding against the pavement, but his only focus was reaching her before they did.

He was too far. Too far. His lungs screamed for air, his muscles burning as he pushed harder. But the men were fast, already at her side. He saw one of them reach out, grabbing her by the arm, yanking her toward the car.

A flash of fear crossed Anya's face as she twisted around, panic flooding her features as she struggled against the man's grip. The grocery bag fell from her hand, its contents spilling across the sidewalk in a surreal scatter of mundane things—fruit, bread, a carton of milk—while the world around her shattered into violence.

"No!" Mikhail's shout ripped from his throat, his voice raw with fury. The men's heads snapped up, their eyes narrowing as they spotted him barreling toward them.

He was too late. He saw the second man move, his hand reaching into his jacket—going for a gun. Mikhail's body surged with rage, his vision narrowing as the distance between him and the attackers closed in what felt like slow motion.

The man holding Anya was already dragging her toward the car, her screams piercing the air as she fought back. The other man drew his gun, pointing it straight at Mikhail.

Everything inside him went cold.

But then instinct took over.

Mikhail dropped low as he ran, his hand yanking his own gun free in one fluid motion. In the next heartbeat, he fired. The deafening crack of the shot echoed through the street, and the man's gun clattered to the ground as he dropped, blood pooling from a wound in his shoulder.

Mikhail didn't stop to think. He was on the second man before the first body had even hit the ground. His fist collided with the man's face, a sickening crack as bone met bone. The man staggered back, still clutching Anya's arm, trying to hold her against him.

"Let. Her. Go." Mikhail's voice was a growl, each word dripping with barely controlled rage. His eyes blazed with fury as he grabbed the man by the collar and slammed him against the side of the car. The man's grip on Anya faltered, and she stumbled back, gasping as she tried to regain her footing.

Mikhail didn't let up. His fists flew, one after another, until the man slumped to the ground, unconscious. Blood dripped from Mikhail's knuckles, but he didn't feel the pain. All he could think about was Anya—keeping her safe.

He turned to her, his breath heavy, adrenaline coursing through his veins. Anya stood frozen, her eyes wide and terrified as she took in the scene before her—the unconscious men, the blood, Mikhail standing like a force of nature between her and danger.

"You're safe now," Mikhail said, his voice still rough with the remnants of the fight. He stepped forward, reaching for her. "Let's get you home."

Anya didn't say a word, just nodded, still trembling from the ordeal. Mikhail slid his gun back into his waistband and wrapped an arm around her shoulders, guiding her away from the carnage and toward the safety of the apartment.

As they walked in silence, Mikhail's mind was already spinning. This wasn't just a warning. This was Konstantin making his move. And now, the war between the Morozov and Volkov Bratva was more than inevitable—it had already begun.

But one thing was certain: he wouldn't let anyone touch Anya again. Not while he was still breathing.

Mikhail closed the door behind them, locking it with a sharp click. The silence inside the apartment was suffocating, a stark contrast to the chaos that had just unfolded outside. He could still hear the rapid thud of his heart in his chest, his adrenaline pumping through him like wildfire. His hands, stained with blood and bruised from the fight, twitched at his sides.

Anya stood frozen by the entrance, her eyes wide, her body trembling from the aftermath. Her hands clutched at the strap of her purse, as if holding on for dear life. She hadn't said a word since they left the scene, but Mikhail could feel her fear, her shock, and something else—a new awareness, maybe, of the reality of the danger that now surrounded her.

Mikhail turned to her, trying to force himself to breathe. His chest still heaved from the sprint, the fight, and the blind panic he had felt the moment he saw her being dragged toward that car. He wasn't a man easily shaken, but the sight of Anya in danger had triggered something primal in him, something he hadn't felt in years.

He had been too late. She could have been taken. And the thought of that—it made his blood boil.

"You should never have left," Mikhail growled, his voice low but heavy with the anger he had tried to suppress since seeing her outside. His fists clenched, and he paced a few steps, unable to stay still, the tension still coiled inside him.

Anya flinched at his words, the tremor in her body more pronounced. She hadn't expected his anger, and yet, she couldn't blame him.

"I just wanted to get groceries," she whispered, her voice hoarse. "I didn't think…"

Mikhail snapped his head toward her, his eyes blazing. "That's the problem. You didn't think."

His words cut through the room, sharp and harsh. He knew he shouldn't be yelling at her, not after what she'd been through, but the fear still twisted inside him, turning to frustration. He had told her before that it wasn't safe. She should have known better.

Anya's eyes flashed with sudden defiance, breaking through her fear. "I just wanted to do something for you! I didn't think I needed permission to leave the apartment."

Her words hit him, making him stop in his tracks. The tension between them thickened. He could see the hurt in her eyes, the anger rising in her chest. But there was something else too—something that made Mikhail's own chest tighten.

This wasn't just about her leaving. It wasn't even about the groceries. It was about the fact that she didn't feel safe, not really. She hadn't understood the depth of the danger she was in until now.

"I'm sorry," Anya said, quieter now. "I just… I just wanted to cook for you, to show you that I appreciate what you've done for me."

Mikhail's anger faltered. The look in her eyes—it wasn't just fear. There was something deeper there. Vulnerability. Guilt. And, beneath all of that, a hint of gratitude.

He couldn't let his rage, his fear, consume this moment. She was already scared enough.

He sighed heavily, running a hand through his hair. "I don't need you to do that," he muttered, his voice softer but still laced with frustration. "I need you to be safe."

Anya's eyes shimmered with unshed tears. She turned away, her hands twisting together nervously as she moved further into the apartment. The tension still hung between them, thick and heavy, neither of them knowing how to bridge it.

"I didn't realize…" she began, her voice trembling. "I didn't understand how dangerous it really was. But I do now."

Mikhail watched her as she spoke, his jaw tightening. She was still so naive in some ways, still trying to navigate a world that had been thrust upon her without warning. And now, after what had just happened, he could see the realization dawning on her—the gravity of her situation, of who her father was and what that meant for her future.

"They're coming for you, Anya," Mikhail said, his voice calm but firm. "Your father isn't going to stop.

You're in the middle of a war, and the only thing keeping you alive right now is me."

Anya's shoulders tensed at his words, and she swallowed hard. She knew he was right. She had seen it with her own eyes—the men sent by her father, ready to drag her back whether she wanted to go or not.

"I know," she whispered. "I know that now."

Mikhail took a step closer to her, the urge to comfort her warring with the need to keep his walls intact. But as he stood there, watching her struggle with her emotions, something inside him shifted.

He had failed to protect her today. He had let her slip away, and it had nearly cost them everything. But he wouldn't let it happen again. The fierce protectiveness he felt for her—the same feeling that had driven him to nearly kill those men—had taken root inside him, growing stronger with every moment.

This wasn't just about keeping her safe for the sake of the Bratva. This was personal now. Anya was his, and no one would touch her. No one would take her from him.

"Come here," he said, his voice softening. He reached out, his hand hovering for a moment before resting gently on her arm. She looked up at him, her eyes searching his face.

"I won't let anyone hurt you," Mikhail said quietly. "Not again. You're mine to protect."

Anya's breath hitched at his words. There was something in the way he said it—possessive, yes, but also… caring. For the first time since this all began, she felt truly safe.

Mikhail's thumb brushed against her skin, and Anya leaned into his touch, her fear slowly ebbing away. She wasn't alone. Not anymore.

They stood there for a moment, the tension between them shifting into something else—something deeper, more intimate. Mikhail's presence, once terrifying and cold, now felt like a shield, protecting her from the world outside.

"You have to stay close to me, Anya," he said, his voice a low growl. "No more going out alone. No more risks."

Anya nodded, the weight of his words sinking in. She wasn't just surviving anymore. She was part of something bigger—something dangerous and all-consuming. But she wasn't afraid, not with Mikhail by her side.

"I won't," she whispered, her voice barely audible. "I won't make that mistake again."

Mikhail's hand slid down her arm, his fingers entwining with hers for a brief moment before he let go. "Good," he said, his voice firm. "Because I won't let anything happen to you."

Chapter 13

Anya's body trembled as she sat on the edge of the couch, her hands still shaking from the events of the last hour. The adrenaline was slowly draining from her system, leaving behind a cold, hollow fear that gnawed at her insides. She was back in the safety of Mikhail's apartment, the door locked behind them, but that sense of security felt fragile, as if it could be shattered by the weight of her own guilt.

Across the room, Mikhail stood with his back to her, his broad shoulders rigid with tension. His hands were clenched into fists at his sides, and even though he wasn't looking at her, she could feel the waves of anger radiating off him, hot and suffocating. But beneath that anger, there was something else, something she couldn't quite name—a deep, raw fear. The kind of fear that came from nearly losing something precious.

"You don't get it," Mikhail finally snapped, his voice sharp, each word cutting through the heavy air between them. He spun to face her, his eyes blazing with frustration. "You can't just walk out of here like everything is fine. Do you know what could've happened? They almost took you, Anya."

His words hit her like a slap. She felt her chest tighten as tears welled in her eyes, her throat constricting as she fought them back. Mikhail's anger was justified—she knew that. She had been reckless, stupid even, for thinking she could just slip out for groceries like nothing was wrong. But the way he spoke to her, the intensity of his voice, made her feel like a child being reprimanded for making a mistake she didn't understand the gravity of.

"I just…" she tried, her voice faltering. She glanced down at the floor, unable to meet his piercing gaze. "I thought it would be okay. I didn't think they'd find me."

Mikhail's scoff was bitter, filled with frustration and disbelief. "You didn't think," he repeated, his tone biting. He resumed his pacing, his hands flexing open and closed as if he were trying to calm himself down. But it was clear that he couldn't.

He stopped again, turning back to her, his eyes softening only slightly as he looked at her, the anger simmering just beneath the surface. "I told you this wasn't a game, Anya. Your father isn't going to stop. He's not going to give up on getting you back, and if he can't… he'll kill you."

Anya's breath caught in her throat, her heart pounding at the stark truth in his words. She knew her father was ruthless, but hearing Mikhail say it out loud like that, the cold reality of it, was suffocating. She hadn't truly understood just how dangerous her situation was until now. Her father was a man of control, a man who saw her as a pawn in a much larger game, and if he couldn't have her, he wouldn't hesitate to destroy her life—or worse.

Tears pricked at her eyes again, and this time, she couldn't stop them from spilling over. "I know," she whispered, the words barely audible through the lump in her throat. "I know that now."

Her admission hung in the air between them, thick with regret and guilt. She knew she had messed up. She had risked everything—not just her own life, but Mikhail's as well. She had been naive to think she could slip away unnoticed, that her father wouldn't come after her.

Mikhail's gaze softened further as he looked at her, the hard lines of his face easing just enough to show the depth of his worry. The anger that had filled the room moments ago began to dissipate, leaving behind something else—something raw, vulnerable. His fury wasn't just born out of frustration; it was rooted in fear. Fear of what could have happened, fear of losing her.

He let out a long breath, running a hand through his hair, his movements less sharp now. "Anya, you don't understand," he said, his voice lower, more controlled. "I almost lost you today."

Her heart clenched at the vulnerability in his voice,
the admission that seemed to surprise even him.
Mikhail wasn't a man who showed weakness—he
was strong, unbreakable, always in control. But in
this moment, she saw the cracks. She saw how
close he had come to losing control entirely, how
the thought of her being taken, of her being hurt,
had shaken him to his core.

"I'm sorry," Anya whispered, her voice trembling. "I
didn't mean to—"

"It's not just about you," Mikhail interrupted, his
voice still tense but softer now. "It's about both of
us. If something happens to you, your father will
come after me next. He'll destroy everything."

She looked down, shame washing over her in
waves. She hadn't thought of that. She hadn't
thought about the consequences of her actions
beyond herself. Mikhail was risking everything to
protect her, and she had nearly thrown it all away
for something as trivial as groceries.

"I didn't realize," she murmured, her voice thick with
regret. "I didn't think about what this would mean
for you."

Mikhail's hand shot out, gently cupping her chin
and lifting her face so their eyes met. His
expression was hard, but there was something soft
in his eyes, something she hadn't seen
before—something almost tender.

"I'm not angry because you left, Anya," he said, his voice low, his thumb brushing gently over her jaw. "I'm angry because I was scared. I've never… I've never felt like this before."

The confession sent a jolt through her, her heart skipping a beat as she stared up at him. The anger in his voice had melted away completely now, replaced by something deeper, something that made her chest tighten with an unfamiliar ache. Mikhail wasn't just angry at her. He was scared—scared because he cared.

"You don't have to be scared for me," she whispered, her voice barely audible. "I'm not worth that."

Mikhail's grip on her chin tightened slightly, his eyes blazing with intensity as he leaned closer. "Don't ever say that again," he growled, his voice rough with emotion. "You're worth everything."

Her breath hitched at his words, the weight of them crashing down on her like a tidal wave. She had never thought of herself as someone worth fighting for, someone who could inspire this kind of protectiveness in a man like Mikhail. But here he was, telling her—no, demanding that she see herself the way he saw her. As someone worth protecting. As someone worth saving.

The silence stretched between them, thick with emotion, and Anya's heart raced as she stared into

Mikhail's eyes, feeling the intensity of his gaze like a physical touch. She had never been this close to anyone before, never felt this kind of raw connection. And in that moment, she realized just how deep Mikhail's feelings for her went.

But with that realization came fear. Fear of what it meant for both of them. Fear of how much she was coming to care for him in return.

"I won't let anyone hurt you," Mikhail said, his voice low, rough with promise. "Not your father, not anyone. You're mine now."

His words sent a shiver down her spine, but it wasn't a shiver of fear. It was something else, something primal that stirred deep inside her. Mikhail's protectiveness, his fierce determination to keep her safe, made her feel something she hadn't expected—something she hadn't allowed herself to feel in a long time.

Safe.

Despite everything, despite the danger, despite the violence that seemed to follow Mikhail wherever he went, she felt safe with him.

Mikhail stepped closer to her, his expression softening as the anger drained from his features. His towering frame, which had just moments ago felt so intimidating, now felt like a shield—an impenetrable force between her and the outside world. Anya's breath hitched as he reached out, his large hand gently cupping her cheek. The rough callouses on his fingers contrasted with the tenderness of the gesture, and when his thumb brushed a stray tear from her face, something inside her nearly broke. The tenderness, the care, it was almost too much to bear.

"I won't let anyone hurt you," Mikhail said quietly, his voice thick with conviction. The roughness of his tone sent shivers down her spine, not from fear but from something deeper—something she wasn't quite ready to name. "Not ever. Do you understand?"

Anya nodded, her throat tight, a knot of emotion forming that made it hard to speak. There was something about the way he said it—so fierce, so certain—that made her believe him without question. He wasn't just saying words to comfort her; he was making a promise, one that felt etched into the very air between them. For the first time in days, maybe even weeks, Anya felt a sense of safety, a sense of protection.

She had never felt this with anyone, not even her father, who had been her protector for so long. There was something different about Mikhail—his presence, the raw intensity of his emotions. It was as if he was ready to tear the world apart just to keep her safe, and in that moment, it made her feel something that terrified and comforted her all at once.

"You're mine to protect now," Mikhail continued, his hand never leaving her cheek. His voice was softer now, but the intensity remained. "And I don't take that lightly."

The words struck her deeply. The possessiveness in his voice would have sent her running before, but now… now it sent a thrill through her. Not because it was about control, but because it was about something more—something deeper. He wasn't trying to claim her like a possession; he was telling her that she was precious to him, that she mattered.

Her breath caught in her throat, her heart racing as the weight of his words settled into her. She didn't feel trapped by his claim; she felt protected, shielded in a way she hadn't been in a long time. Mikhail wasn't just talking about physical safety; he was talking about all of her—her heart, her mind, her future.

His thumb brushed against her cheek again, the roughness of his touch sending heat through her body, and she shivered, the tension between them shifting. The intensity of the moment wrapped around them like a blanket, cocooning them from the rest of the world. Everything they had been through—the danger, the fear, the uncertainty—melted away, leaving only the two of them, bound together by a force neither of them could ignore.

Anya's heart raced as she tried to make sense of it all. She shouldn't trust him—he was a killer, a man whose life was filled with violence and bloodshed. He had turned her world upside down, and yet… here she was, falling for him.

Her mind screamed at her to be careful, to keep her guard up, but her heart had already begun to betray her. She felt it every time she looked at him, every time she caught a glimpse of the man beneath the hardened exterior. This was the same man who had kidnapped her, who had killed without hesitation, and yet… he was the man who had saved her, who had promised to protect her and the child they now shared.

Mikhail's eyes were still on her, dark and intense, and she felt the pull between them like a current, drawing her closer. The heat between them was undeniable, and the longer they stood there, the more the tension built, like a fuse waiting to be lit.

She couldn't stop the way her body responded to him. Her skin tingled where his hand touched her, and the closeness of him, the heat radiating from his body, made her pulse quicken. Anya knew this moment was about more than just physical attraction—there was something deeper between them, something that had been building since the first time their eyes met.

But could she trust it? Could she trust him? Could she trust herself?

Anya's mind whirled with the questions, her internal conflict gnawing at her, but even as her thoughts spiraled, her body moved on its own. Her hand came up to rest on his chest, the fabric of his shirt rough beneath her palm, and she felt the steady beat of his heart beneath her fingertips. It was faster than she expected, as if his pulse mirrored her own.

"Mikhail…" she whispered, her voice trembling with the weight of everything she was feeling.

He didn't respond with words. Instead, his hand moved from her cheek to the back of her neck, pulling her closer until their bodies were nearly flush against each other. The space between them, already small, disappeared entirely as his forehead rested against hers.

The moment felt fragile, like it could break at any second, but neither of them pulled away. They were connected now, in a way that went beyond the physical. It was emotional, visceral, and it terrified Anya just as much as it thrilled her.

The heat between them, the intensity of their connection, continued to build, wrapping around them until it was impossible to tell where one of them ended and the other began. Anya's breath came in shallow gasps as she struggled to hold onto her thoughts, but they slipped away like sand through her fingers.

She was falling. Falling for a man who was dangerous, unpredictable, and deadly.

And she didn't know how to stop.

Mikhail's voice broke the silence, his breath warm against her lips. "You're safe with me, Anya. I swear it." His voice was a promise, a declaration that made her chest ache with emotions she wasn't ready to name.

She nodded, unable to speak, her throat too tight with unshed tears. She believed him. God help her, she believed him.

In that moment, the world outside didn't matter. The danger, the threats, the violence—it all faded away, leaving only the two of them, bound together by something neither of them could control.

And for the first time, Anya felt like maybe, just maybe, she had found the place where she belonged.

The tension between them shifted, the charged air between their bodies becoming something far more primal. The heat in Mikhail's eyes was unmistakable—dark, burning, and raw. It matched the fire growing in Anya's chest, spreading like wildfire through her veins. The fear, the guilt, everything that had weighed her down only moments ago, vanished in the wake of this overwhelming desire. Every breath between them was thick with an unspoken promise, the intensity of their emotions boiling over.

Mikhail moved toward her without hesitation, his rough hands cupping her face with a surprising tenderness, a softness that was at odds with the fierce need simmering just beneath the surface. His touch, despite its gentleness, ignited something deep inside her. Their lips crashed together in a kiss that was anything but soft—a battle for control, for dominance. Anya met him with equal fervor, losing herself in the urgency of the moment.

His mouth claimed hers, hot and demanding, his lips firm as they molded against her own. Her heart raced, the adrenaline of their argument still coursing through her veins, mixing with the unmistakable rush of lust. Their kiss deepened with every second, their mouths moving in sync, breaths mingling in desperate gasps. She felt Mikhail's hands move down her body, his fingers leaving a trail of heat in their wake as they explored her waist, her hips, her back, pulling her closer until there was no space left between them.

Anya's hands, trembling slightly from the rush of emotions, found their way to his chest. Her fingers skimmed over the hard planes of muscle beneath his shirt, feeling the power contained within his body. The fabric was too much, a barrier she couldn't stand for a second longer. With a low, frustrated growl, she tugged at his clothing, needing to feel the warmth of his skin against hers. Mikhail didn't resist—he responded with the same urgency, pulling his shirt off over his head in one swift movement, revealing the body she had only glimpsed before.

For a moment, Anya paused, her breath catching in her throat as her eyes drank him in. His chest was broad, the muscles perfectly defined, a testament to the strength that lay beneath the surface. But it wasn't just his body that captivated her—it was the intricate tattoos that adorned his skin, wrapping around his arms and chest, telling stories of battles fought and survived. The ink seemed to pulse with life, each pattern a reminder of the danger he carried with him. But none of that scared her. Not now.

The hunger that had been simmering within her intensified as her gaze lowered to his abdomen, her pulse quickening at the sight of the hard ridges of his stomach, the way his body seemed to radiate power.

Mikhail's eyes never left hers, watching her every move, his gaze darkening with lust. The tension between them was palpable, electric, and it spurred her forward, her body aching for more of him. She didn't care about anything else right now. All she cared about was the way he made her feel, the way her body seemed to come alive under his touch.

Anya reached for him, her hands moving instinctively to his chest again, feeling the heat of his skin beneath her palms. He was so warm, so solid, and the contact sent a shiver of anticipation down her spine. She dragged her fingers over the tattoos etched into his flesh, feeling the slight ridges where the ink had settled into his skin, a part of him forever.

Her touch stirred something deep inside Mikhail, and his hands found their way to her waist, tugging her closer with a possessiveness that sent a thrill through her. His touch was rougher now, less restrained, as if he couldn't hold back any longer. His hands roamed upward, tracing the curve of her body until they reached her breasts. Anya gasped when his thumbs brushed over her nipples through the thin fabric of her shirt, sending jolts of pleasure straight through her core. She arched against him, her body instinctively seeking more of that delicious friction.

It wasn't enough. She needed more. Craving the feel of his skin against hers, she yanked her own shirt over her head, discarding it without hesitation. The cool air hit her exposed skin, making her shiver, but it was nothing compared to the heat that blazed between them.

Mikhail's eyes darkened even further as they fell to her breasts, his gaze hungry and appreciative. He wasted no time in reaching for her again, his large hands cupping her breasts, his thumbs brushing over her hardened nipples with deliberate pressure. The sensation sent waves of pleasure through her, and she moaned softly, her body arching toward him as if begging for more.

Their hands moved with a kind of frenzied desperation now, neither of them able to get enough of the other. Mikhail's fingers fumbled with the waistband of her jeans, tugging them down over her hips with a roughness that only served to heighten her desire. Anya kicked them off, and in one fluid motion, Mikhail rid himself of his own pants.

For a brief moment, they both paused, standing completely exposed to one another. Anya's breath hitched in her throat as she took in the sight of him—every inch of him. The tattoos that wrapped around his muscular arms and chest, the dark trail of hair leading down from his navel to his impressive cock, already thick and fully hard.

Her pulse raced, her heart pounding in her chest as she drank him in. Mikhail was breathtaking, and the hunger she felt for him was overwhelming, an insatiable need that consumed her. Without hesitation, she stepped forward and pushed him back onto the bed.

Mikhail allowed her to guide him, his body falling back onto the mattress with a soft thud, his gaze never leaving hers as he lay there, sprawled out and ready for her.

Anya knelt beside him, her heart pounding in her ears as she reached for him, her fingers wrapping around his thick length. The feel of him in her hand—so hard, so heavy—sent a fresh wave of desire coursing through her.

Mikhail's breath hitched, a low groan escaping his lips as her fingers stroked him slowly, teasingly. The sight of him lying there, his body taut with anticipation, his cock throbbing in her hand, filled her with a sense of power she'd never felt before.

She wasn't just his to claim. Right now, he was hers.

Anya's hand moved with deliberate slowness, sliding along the thick length of Mikhail's cock. Her fingers squeezed gently, reveling in the heat and hardness of him. Every touch, every flick of her wrist was a tease, a promise of more to come. Mikhail groaned, the deep sound sending a shiver of excitement through her, making her all the more eager to push him further toward the edge. She lowered her head, her lips brushing the tip of his cock, teasing him with soft, barely-there licks.

Her tongue flicked out, tasting the salty bead at the tip. She closed her eyes, savoring the flavor of him before she took him deeper into her mouth. He was so big, she could barely take him all, but that only spurred her on. Her lips stretched as she wrapped them around him, sucking gently, feeling the weight of him pressing against her tongue.

Mikhail's hand slid into her hair, his fingers tangling in the strands, guiding her gently but firmly as she began to bob her head. His control was slipping, she could tell from the way his hips bucked slightly, from the soft curses that escaped his lips. His groans grew deeper, more guttural, as she moved her mouth up and down, working him with practiced precision.

Anya hollowed her cheeks, increasing the suction as her tongue swirled around his tip. His taste filled her senses, intoxicating her, driving her to push him closer to that breaking point. She wanted to watch him fall apart, to feel the power of reducing him to a trembling mess beneath her. The thought thrilled her, made her heart race with the sheer thrill of it.

Her free hand moved to his balls, massaging them gently, and Mikhail's breath hitched in response. She could feel the tension building in his body, his muscles tightening beneath her touch. His hips bucked again, this time harder, the movement involuntary as he gave in to the pleasure she was giving him.

But it wasn't just Mikhail who was losing control. Anya could feel the wetness between her own legs growing, the heat pooling low in her belly. Her body ached for release, the same release she was driving him toward. Every moan that escaped him sent a surge of heat through her, and she found herself clenching her thighs together in a desperate attempt to relieve the pressure building inside her.

Mikhail's grip on her hair tightened slightly, not enough to hurt, but enough to remind her that he was still holding on, still guiding her, even as he teetered on the brink of losing himself. His breath came in ragged gasps, his chest rising and falling rapidly as she worked him over with her mouth, taking him deeper with each bob of her head.

As she sucked him, her hand slid down his shaft, stroking him in time with the movement of her mouth. She let out a soft moan around his cock, the vibrations sending a shockwave of pleasure through him. His hips jerked in response, a rough groan tearing from his throat.

But Mikhail wasn't content to let her have all the control. His other hand moved from her hair to her breast, his fingers rolling her nipple between them, teasing her until she let out a soft gasp. The pleasure shot through her, making her knees weak, but she didn't stop. She couldn't. She was as lost in the moment as he was.

His hand trailed down her body, sliding over her stomach, and then lower. Anya's breath caught as his fingers found her slick folds, parting them with ease before slipping inside her. She gasped around his cock, her head spinning as the dual sensations overwhelmed her.

Mikhail's fingers thrust inside her, curling just right, hitting that sweet spot that made her hips buck against his hand. She moaned again, this time louder, the sound muffled by the thickness of him in her mouth. Her body trembled as he worked her, his fingers moving in perfect rhythm, matching the pace of her mouth on his cock.

She sucked him harder, her lips tightening around him as her free hand continued to massage his balls, rolling them gently in her palm. Mikhail groaned, the sound low and primal, as his hips bucked again, his cock twitching in her mouth. She could feel how close he was, how badly he wanted to let go, but he was holding back, just like she was.

His fingers slid out of her, only to find her clit, rubbing it in slow, deliberate circles. Anya's entire body jerked in response, her hips grinding against his hand as he brought her closer and closer to the edge. She was panting now, her breath coming in short, desperate gasps as her head spun with the pleasure he was giving her. But she didn't stop. She kept sucking him, kept stroking him, determined to push him over the edge with her.

The feeling of his fingers inside her, combined with the taste of him in her mouth, was almost too much to handle. She could feel herself unraveling, her body trembling as she teetered on the brink of release. Her legs shook, her muscles tightening as the pleasure mounted, growing stronger with each passing second.

Mikhail's fingers moved faster, rubbing her clit in quick, deliberate strokes, while his other hand tangled in her hair, guiding her mouth up and down his cock. She moaned around him, the vibrations of her voice sending him dangerously close to the edge. He was holding on by a thread, but she could feel him slipping, feel the way his body tensed beneath her.

Anya was right there with him, her body on fire, the pleasure building to a breaking point as she sucked him harder, faster. Her tongue swirled around his tip, teasing him just as she had before, but now with more urgency, more desperation.

And then, just as she felt herself about to tip over the edge, Mikhail's hand stilled on her clit, and he gently pulled her head away from him. His cock slipped from her mouth, still fully hard and pulsing, but he hadn't come. Not yet.

Anya looked up at him, her chest heaving, her body trembling with unfulfilled desire. She could see it in his eyes—the hunger, the need. He was still holding on, still waiting, but not for long. The look he gave her was filled with raw, primal need, and she knew that this was far from over.

Mikhail's fingers slid from inside her, leaving Anya trembling and breathless. The absence of his touch was immediate and maddening, a void that only made her body throb with need for more. Her breath came in short, uneven gasps as she moved over him, positioning herself above his hips, straddling him with her legs spread wide. The room seemed to still for a moment, their heated breaths the only sound, as she gazed down at him, her heart pounding in her chest.

His cock stood hard and ready between them, the thick length of him brushing against her slick folds, sending sparks of pleasure shooting through her. Her hand trembled slightly as she reached for him, guiding him to her entrance. The thick head of his cock pressed against her, and she bit her lip, her heart racing with anticipation as she began to lower herself slowly.

The sensation of him filling her was overwhelming. Inch by inch, he stretched her, his girth pushing deep inside, making her gasp. Anya could feel every inch of him, the way he filled her so completely, and her body shuddered with the intensity of it. She stopped for a moment, fully seated on him, her body adjusting to the size of him inside her.

Mikhail's hands gripped her hips tightly, his fingers pressing into her skin as he held her steady, his eyes dark with lust as he watched her. His chest rose and fell rapidly, his breath coming in harsh gasps as she began to move. Slowly at first, her hips rolled in gentle circles, the friction between their bodies driving her wild.

"Fuck," Mikhail groaned, his voice raw, filled with need.

Anya's own need built with every movement, the desire mounting inside her as she found a rhythm, her hips moving faster, riding him harder. The way he stretched and filled her was incredible, each thrust pushing her closer to the edge. The sensation of his cock sliding in and out of her, rubbing against her sensitive walls, sent waves of pleasure coursing through her, building with each roll of her hips.

Her breath hitched as Mikhail sat up suddenly, his hands moving from her hips to her breasts, cupping them roughly before his mouth latched onto her nipple. He sucked hard, his teeth grazing her tender skin, sending a sharp jolt of pleasure straight to her core. Anya moaned loudly, her head falling back, her body arching into him as he teased her nipple with his tongue and teeth.

The heat between them was unbearable, consuming, and Anya gave herself over completely to the moment. She ground down against him, her body moving instinctively, chasing the release that felt so close she could almost taste it. Mikhail's mouth moved to her other breast, his lips closing around her nipple, and the sensation was enough to drive her wild.

"More," she gasped, her hands fisting in his hair as her hips bucked wildly against him.

Mikhail growled low in his throat, the sound sending a shiver down her spine as his hands gripped her waist again, pulling her down hard onto his cock, thrusting up into her at the same time. The new angle sent shockwaves of pleasure rippling through her, making her cry out as she rode him harder, faster.

The tension between them built with every thrust, their bodies moving together in a perfect, frantic rhythm. The sound of their moans filled the room, mingling with the wet slap of their bodies colliding over and over again. Mikhail's hands roamed over her, gripping her waist, her breasts, pulling her closer, as if he couldn't get enough of her.

Anya's whole body was trembling now, the tension coiling tighter and tighter inside her, ready to snap at any moment. She could feel Mikhail's cock twitching inside her, his hips bucking up harder, faster, as he neared his own release. They were both so close, teetering on the edge, and all it would take was one final push to send them both tumbling over.

"Anya," Mikhail groaned, his voice thick with need, his hands digging into her hips as he thrust up into her one last time, pushing her over the brink.

Her climax hit her like a tidal wave, crashing through her body with such force that she could only scream his name as her muscles clenched tightly around him, her inner walls pulsing as wave after wave of pleasure washed over her. Mikhail followed her, his release coming seconds later as his hips bucked uncontrollably beneath her. His hands tightened on her hips as he came inside her, filling her with hot, thick pulses of his seed.

They moved together through the aftershocks of their release, their bodies trembling, their breaths coming in ragged, uneven gasps. Anya's head fell forward, her forehead resting against Mikhail's chest as she tried to catch her breath, her heart still racing from the intensity of it all.

For a long moment, neither of them moved. They stayed tangled together, Mikhail's cock still buried deep inside her, their bodies slick with sweat, their breaths mingling in the quiet aftermath of their shared pleasure. The world outside seemed distant, far removed from this moment, where only the two of them existed.

Anya could still feel the aftershocks of their climax pulsing through her, but more than that, she felt the weight of the connection between them. It wasn't just physical anymore. It was something deeper, something she hadn't expected, something that scared her as much as it thrilled her.

She had fallen for him. Hard.

But with that realization came fear. Fear of what it meant, fear of the dangerous world they were tangled in, fear of what loving Mikhail could cost her. He wasn't just a man—he was an enforcer, someone capable of violence, someone whose loyalty lay with a criminal empire. Yet, here he was, holding her as if she were the most precious thing in the world.

Mikhail's arms wrapped around her, pulling her closer, and for a brief moment, all of her fears melted away. In his arms, she felt safe, protected, cherished. And that was all that mattered, at least for now.

Chapter 14

The room was dimly lit, the soft glow from the lamp on the bedside table casting warm shadows over the space. Mikhail and Anya lay tangled together, their bodies still intertwined after the intensity of their lovemaking. The weight of what had just passed between them lingered in the air, thick and palpable. Yet, the silence wasn't heavy. It wasn't awkward or uncomfortable, but intimate—charged with the kind of unspoken emotion that neither of them could yet articulate.

Mikhail felt the steady rise and fall of Anya's chest against him, her breath warm and soft as she rested her head on his chest. He gazed down at her, the weight of his own emotions pressing harder than he'd ever felt before. His hand reached up instinctively, brushing a loose strand of her hair from her face. The gesture was gentle, almost tender, and as he did it, a strange tightness wrapped itself around his chest.

Her vulnerability hit him hard. She was so delicate in this moment, so open and trusting. It felt foreign to him, this quiet intimacy. He had been with women before, had shared beds and fleeting moments of passion, but this… this was different. The way she fit against him, the way her presence filled the space beside him, was different. And what she represented now—his child growing inside her—made everything feel all the more real, and all the more terrifying.

He stared up at the ceiling for a moment, his thoughts a chaotic mess. He was a man built for violence, raised in a world that had no room for softness or love. He had spent years crafting a version of himself that was impenetrable, untouchable—emotionally distant from anyone and anything that could make him vulnerable. But now, lying beside Anya, that armor was crumbling, and he wasn't sure how to handle it.

His arm tightened around her reflexively, pulling her closer as if she might slip away if he didn't. The weight of his emotions—the need to protect her, to care for her—was overwhelming. He had never felt like this before, never felt this… protective. He had been trained to be cold, to distance himself from emotional attachments. It was safer that way. But now, with Anya, that training meant nothing.

Anya stirred slightly against him, her hand resting softly on his chest, her fingers tracing idle patterns over his skin. The gentle contact only deepened the pull he felt toward her, a pull that both frightened and compelled him. He looked down at her again, his heart pounding with an intensity he hadn't expected. Could he really do this? Could he open himself up to her, knowing what that meant—knowing how much it would change him?

A battle waged inside him. Part of him, the part that had been shaped by years of living in a world of violence and betrayal, told him that this was dangerous. That he couldn't afford to let her in like this, that he couldn't afford to care—not when the stakes were so high. Caring made him vulnerable. It made her vulnerable. And in their world, vulnerability could get them both killed.

But the other part of him, the part that had been slowly waking up since the moment Anya had entered his life, pushed back. He *wanted* to care. He wanted to protect her, not just out of obligation or instinct, but because she had become important to him in a way no one else had. And the baby… their baby… He couldn't deny the fierce possessiveness that welled up inside him whenever he thought of the child growing in her womb.

He wasn't sure how to be a father. He wasn't even sure how to be a partner, how to care for someone beyond the physical, beyond the fleeting moments of passion and release. But he *did* know one thing: he couldn't let anything happen to her. She was his now. His to protect, his to care for, whether he was ready for it or not.

Mikhail's fingers found their way to her chin, gently tilting her face up so he could look into her eyes. Her gaze was soft, filled with a quiet vulnerability that sent a pang through his chest. He saw the trust there, the trust she had placed in him—despite everything he had done, despite the life he led. She trusted him to keep her safe. And for the first time in his life, he found that trust terrifying. Because what if he failed?

The idea of losing her, of losing the child, clawed at his insides. He had failed to protect before—his mother, the only person who had ever tried to protect him. And he had sworn never to be that weak again, never to let someone he cared about suffer. But this… this was different. Anya wasn't just someone he cared about. She was becoming a part of him, a part of his world, and that scared him more than anything.

Anya shifted again, her eyes meeting his, and she smiled softly, her hand moving to rest over his heart. The simplicity of the gesture, the warmth of her touch, melted something inside him. He leaned down, pressing a kiss to her forehead, lingering there for a moment as he tried to gather his thoughts, tried to make sense of the chaos swirling inside him.

"I'll keep you safe," he whispered against her skin, his voice rough with emotion he couldn't suppress. "You and the baby. No one's going to hurt you."

He meant every word. He would lay down his life for her if it came to that. He would fight—kill—anyone who tried to take her from him. That much was clear to him now. But as he lay there, holding her close, he couldn't help but wonder if he was capable of being more than just her protector. Could he be what she needed? Could he be a father?

The weight of that question hung in the air between them, unspoken but deeply felt. Mikhail wasn't sure if he had the answer yet. But one thing was certain: his life had changed the moment Anya had walked into it. And there was no going back.

He tightened his hold on her, his lips brushing against her temple as he closed his eyes. For now, he would take things one step at a time, one moment at a time. But deep down, he knew—he wasn't the same man he had been before. Anya and the baby had changed him, and for the first time in his life, he didn't want to fight that change.

Mikhail lay back against the pillows, the weight of the moment heavy on his chest. His thoughts swirled in a storm, tugging him toward a part of his past he had kept hidden for years, even from himself. His mind was telling him to shut it down, to stay silent. But when he looked at Anya, resting beside him, her body still soft and warm from their lovemaking, something cracked open inside of him.

He'd never let anyone in—not fully. Not even the brothers from his bratva that he trusted with his life. But this was different. She was different. He couldn't explain it, but the need to share his story, the darkest parts of himself, rose up and refused to be ignored.

He closed his eyes for a moment, trying to suppress the urge to speak, but it gnawed at him, growing stronger by the second. The last thing he wanted was to burden Anya with his past. She had already endured so much—her father's betrayal, the danger that constantly hovered over her—and now, with their child on the way, it felt wrong to drag her into the darkness he had lived through. But something in him had shifted since meeting her, something that made him feel… different. Vulnerable, but in a way that felt almost necessary. Like she needed to understand where he came from if they were going to share a life together.

"I haven't told anyone this," he said, his voice low and rough, breaking the silence between them. His eyes stared at the ceiling as if the words would be easier to say if he didn't have to look at her. "But you should know."

Anya turned her head slightly, her eyes curious and cautious as she sensed the weight of what he was about to share.

"If you're going to be part of this life with me," Mikhail continued, swallowing the knot forming in his throat, "you need to know what kind of man I come from."

The words felt like they were being ripped from somewhere deep inside, but once they started, there was no stopping them. Mikhail could feel Anya's eyes on him, but he couldn't bring himself to meet her gaze just yet. His chest felt tight, constricted with the memories he'd kept buried for so long.

"My father…" Mikhail started, his jaw tightening as the old anger flared. "He wasn't a man. Not really. He was… a monster. A violent, hateful bastard who didn't care who he hurt as long as he had control."

Anya stayed silent, her fingers resting lightly on his arm, a soft touch that seemed to anchor him.

"He used to beat the hell out of me and my mother," Mikhail continued, his voice thick with emotion. "For no reason. Because the dinner wasn't hot enough. Because I looked at him wrong. Or because he was drunk and needed something to hit." He paused, his breathing deep and steady, as if trying to maintain control of the memories that threatened to pull him under.

"I was just a kid," he said, bitterness seeping into his tone. "Too small, too weak to do anything about it. But my mom… she was the one who took the brunt of it. Every damn time." His voice wavered for a moment, the raw pain of those memories cutting deep.

Anya's fingers tightened slightly on his arm, her silent support giving him the strength to keep going.

"She would throw herself in front of me, just to keep him from turning his fists on me. She… she took every punch, every kick, because she thought she could protect me from him." Mikhail's voice cracked, and he clenched his jaw, trying to rein in the flood of emotion that threatened to overwhelm him. "And I let her."

He turned his head slightly, looking at Anya for the first time, searching her face for any hint of judgment. But there was none. Only empathy. Only understanding.

"That's not your fault, Mikhail," Anya whispered, her voice soft but firm. "You were a child. You couldn't have stopped him."

Mikhail shook his head slightly, the old guilt rising up like bile. "Maybe. But I should have done something. I should have stopped it sooner."

He took a deep breath, the air in the room feeling heavy, stifling. "The night everything changed, I was sixteen. It was one of those nights—he came home drunk, more drunk than usual, and I could hear them fighting in the other room. My mom's voice, begging him to stop, and his... roaring like a fucking animal."

Anya watched him carefully, her eyes wide, not with fear but with a deep sadness. She could feel the weight of his pain, the years of carrying this burden alone.

"I don't know what snapped in me that night," Mikhail said, his voice low and dark. "Maybe I'd just had enough. Maybe it was because I'd gotten bigger, stronger, and I wasn't the small, weak kid I used to be. I don't know. But I grabbed a bat... and when I saw him hit her again, something inside me just... broke."

He clenched his fists, the memory of that moment flashing in his mind like it was happening all over again. "I swung that bat at him so hard, I thought I'd kill him. I wanted to kill him."

Mikhail's chest heaved slightly, the intensity of the memory overwhelming him for a moment. He didn't look at Anya, didn't want to see the look on her face as he confessed the darkest part of himself.

"I didn't stop," he said quietly, his voice barely audible. "I just kept swinging. Over and over again, until he wasn't moving anymore."

There was a long pause, the silence heavy and suffocating. Mikhail's heart pounded in his chest, the rage and fear from that night surging up inside him once more. But this time, there was no outlet. Only the memory.

"I thought I'd killed him," he whispered, his voice breaking slightly. "I wanted to."

Anya's breath hitched, and she reached out, her hand gently touching his face, her thumb brushing softly against his jaw. "But you didn't."

Mikhail closed his eyes, leaning into her touch for a moment. "No. He survived. And he disappeared after that. I never saw him again."

Another long silence stretched between them as Mikhail let the weight of his confession settle. He felt raw, exposed in a way he hadn't expected. But more than that, he felt… lighter. Like speaking the truth had taken some of the burden off his shoulders, even if only for a moment.

"I don't know why I'm telling you this," Mikhail admitted, his voice rough and unsteady. "Maybe because I don't want you to think I'm something I'm not. Or maybe because…" He paused, struggling to find the right words. "If we're going to raise this child together, you should know what kind of man I am. Where I come from."

Anya shifted closer to him, her hand moving to rest on his chest, feeling the steady thump of his heartbeat beneath her palm. "You're not your father, Mikhail," she whispered, her voice filled with quiet certainty. "You protected your mother. You protected me. You're nothing like him."

Mikhail's throat tightened at her words. He wanted to believe her, wanted to let her words wash away

the guilt and the anger that had lived inside him for
so long. But it wasn't that simple. It never had been.

Still, as he held Anya close, her body pressed
against his, the warmth of her touch soothing the
jagged edges of his past, Mikhail allowed himself to
hope. Maybe, just maybe, he could be the kind of
man she believed he was. The kind of man who
could protect her, who could be a father to their
child.

And for the first time in a long time, he felt the faint
stirrings of something he hadn't felt in years—hope.

Mikhail exhaled deeply, the heavy silence between
them settling like a thick fog. His chest tightened,
but not from the pain of his past—rather, it was the
weight of his own truth, the realization that he had
laid himself bare in front of Anya. His fingers traced
idle patterns on her skin, needing that connection,
that grounding reminder that she was still there,
listening.

Anya shifted, her palm still pressed against his
chest, her eyes locked on his with a softness that
nearly unraveled him completely. The intensity of
her gaze, filled with empathy and understanding,
was something he wasn't prepared for. He'd braced
for judgment, for disgust even. But what he saw in
her eyes was something else entirely—acceptance.

"I had to become strong," he finally said, his voice
gravelly and low. "After that night, I knew what the

world was. Brutal. Unforgiving. If you don't fight,
you don't survive."

His words hung in the air, and as he spoke them,
they felt like a mantra he'd been reciting all his life.
He'd lived by that creed—brutality, violence, and
survival, over and over again. That was his life.
That's what had led him to the Bratva.

"When I was a kid," he continued, his hand
tightening slightly on her waist as he spoke, "I
thought maybe there was something more for me.
Something… different. But after that night with my
father, after I nearly killed him, I knew. Violence was
the only thing I'd ever be good at. Giving and taking
a beating."

He could still remember the raw satisfaction he'd
felt as he laid his father out on the floor, the blood
dripping from the bat, his knuckles aching from the
force of each swing. For years, he'd questioned
whether that night had been his breaking point or
his salvation. It didn't matter anymore.

He hadn't left the violence behind. He'd walked
straight into it.

"The Bratva…" Mikhail's voice trailed off as he
searched for the right words, unsure of how to
explain it. "They didn't make me like this. I was
already this way when they found me. They just
gave me a place to use it."

Anya's fingers brushed lightly against his cheek, bringing him back from the dark memories. She didn't pull away or recoil from the raw truth of his words. Instead, she held him closer, her touch like an anchor pulling him back to the present.

"You don't have to carry that weight alone," she whispered, her voice steady and soothing, as though her words could unravel the years of violence and pain he had endured.

Mikhail closed his eyes, the conflict inside him raging like a storm. He wanted to believe her—wanted to let go of the idea that his only value was in the brutality he could unleash. But it wasn't that easy. He'd lived in this world too long, fought too many battles, and become too hardened. His life was built on blood and violence. It was all he knew.

"You're not that boy anymore, Mikhail," Anya continued, her voice firm but gentle. "You don't have to keep fighting like this. You've already proven yourself—more than anyone should have to."

Mikhail's eyes opened slowly, meeting hers once again. There was a tenderness in her gaze that shook him to his core, and for a moment, he let himself imagine what it would be like to be free of the burden he carried. To let someone in. To let her in.

"I don't know how to be anything else," he admitted, his voice cracking with the weight of his admission. "This is who I am. It's what I'm good at."

Anya's lips curved into a soft, understanding smile. "Maybe it's who you've had to be. But that doesn't mean it's all you are."

Her words hit him hard, and Mikhail felt the cracks in his armor widen, exposing the raw vulnerability underneath. He'd spent so long keeping people at arm's length, building walls around himself, convinced that the only way to survive was to stay detached, to never let anyone close enough to see the broken parts of him. But Anya had already seen them. She wasn't running.

"I've spent years fighting for the Bratva, killing for them, bleeding for them," he continued, his voice quieter now. "But when I look at you... and the baby…" His throat tightened, the words getting stuck as he struggled to put his emotions into words. "I don't know how to protect you from this life. I don't know how to be anything more than the man they've turned me into."

Anya's hand slid down to rest on his chest, right over his heart. "You're already more, Mikhail. You're protecting me. And you're protecting our baby."

The words hit him like a punch to the gut, the reality of what she was saying sinking in. She believed in him. She trusted him to protect her and their unborn child. Despite everything—despite the blood on his hands, the violence in his past—she saw something in him that he couldn't see in himself.

Mikhail's hands trembled slightly as he pulled Anya closer, his forehead pressing against hers. He breathed her in, the warmth of her skin, the softness of her body against his. For the first time in years, he felt something other than anger, other than rage and violence. He felt… peace. And it terrified him.

"I don't want to fail you," he whispered, his voice rough with emotion. "I don't know if I can be what you need me to be."

Anya's fingers threaded through his hair, her touch gentle but firm. "You won't fail me. We'll figure this out together."

Her words were a lifeline, pulling him from the depths of his self-doubt. He wasn't used to needing anyone, let alone depending on them for emotional support. But with Anya, it was different. She was different. She didn't just see him as the enforcer, the brutal killer that everyone else saw. She saw the man beneath, the one who was scared and uncertain, the one who had spent his life fighting to survive.

"You make me want to be better," Mikhail said quietly, his voice raw. "For you. For the baby."

Anya's lips brushed softly against his, her kiss light but filled with meaning. "Then be better, Mikhail. Not for me. For yourself."

The words settled deep inside him, planting a seed of hope that had been buried for far too long. He wasn't just the sum of his violence. He wasn't just the enforcer for the Bratva. He was a man who had something worth fighting for—something more than blood and survival.

He had her. He had their baby. And for the first time, that was enough.

Chapter 15

Mikhail stood near the window, the dim light from the city casting long shadows across the room. Days had passed since that night—since he'd opened up to Anya, sharing pieces of his past he hadn't spoken of in years. In the time since, they'd settled into a routine of sorts, but the tension had grown with each passing day. His eyes scanned the streets below, as if searching for invisible threats lurking in the dark corners. The apartment felt stifling tonight, the air heavy with the weight of the choices he was about to make. Behind him, Anya moved quietly, her presence a calm within the storm of his thoughts.

Since she had come into his life, everything had changed. He wasn't the man he'd once been—calculating, cold, with nothing to lose. Now, with her and the baby, his world was different. Fragile, yet precious. And that terrified him.

Anya deserved more than the cage he'd created for her. He could see it in her eyes every time she looked out the window or down the hall. She was trapped, and despite her efforts to keep herself occupied, there was a part of her that longed for normalcy, for the outside world she used to know. He couldn't blame her. Hell, he didn't want her to feel like a prisoner in his world, but keeping her safe meant control—control over where she went, who she saw, what risks she was exposed to.

But tonight, that control felt more like a weight around his neck.

Mikhail clenched his jaw, staring harder out the window, as if the answer would reveal itself in the dark skyline. He hated the idea of taking her outside, where danger lurked behind every corner. He knew the men who followed Konstantin, knew what they were capable of. He had spent years with men like that—ruthless, without conscience. And the Volkov Bratva? He could trust Nikolai and Viktor to a point, but there were always eyes in his world, always someone ready to exploit a weakness. And Anya, now more than ever, was his biggest weakness.

His mind warred with itself. Taking her out was a risk, one he wasn't sure he was ready to take. But there was a part of him—a part that was growing louder with each passing day—that wanted to see her smile, to give her even a moment of reprieve from the constant fear. She had been through enough. And so had he.

Behind him, he heard the soft shuffle of Anya's feet. She had been quiet, giving him space, sensing the turmoil inside him. That was the thing about her—she always knew when to speak and when to simply be present. Her patience was one of the things that drew him to her, one of the reasons why his feelings for her had grown beyond anything he had anticipated. She understood him in a way no one else did, even without words.

Mikhail turned around, his gaze locking with hers. She stood by the counter, her hands idly tracing the edge of the table. Her eyes held questions, though she hadn't voiced them. He knew she was trying to understand him, to gauge his mood, and he couldn't blame her. He had been distant ever since their emotional conversation, and the protective walls he'd built around himself were slipping, leaving him exposed in ways he wasn't used to.

"How would you feel about going out tonight?" The question slipped out before he had time to second-guess it.

Anya blinked, clearly taken aback by the sudden shift in conversation. "Out?" she echoed, as if she hadn't heard him right.

Mikhail nodded, moving away from the window and closer to her. "I've been thinking about it. It's been a long time since you've stepped outside. I thought you might want a change of scenery. Somewhere quiet."

Her eyes softened, and for a moment, the exhaustion and fear that had been weighing her down lifted, replaced by a flicker of something he hadn't seen in a while—hope. "You mean it?" she asked quietly, as if afraid to believe it.

He nodded again, though the knot in his stomach tightened. "We'll be careful. I'll take you somewhere no one will recognize us. A small place, out of the way. Just for a few hours."

Anya's expression shifted, a mixture of excitement and trepidation. "But... what about the danger? What if someone sees us?"

Mikhail felt the gravity of her question. He couldn't deny the risks. He had spent his life calculating threats, analyzing every move with precision. But this was different. This was personal. And that made it all the more dangerous.

"I'll make sure no one does," he said, his voice low and steady. "I won't take you anywhere unsafe. But I want you to have this. Even if it's just for a little while."

Anya's lips curved into a small smile, and something inside him loosened. It was small, but it was enough. In that moment, he knew he was making the right decision. He couldn't shelter her forever. She needed to feel like herself again, even if just for one night.

"Thank you," she whispered, her gratitude evident in her eyes. "I'd like that."

Mikhail nodded, already mapping out the route in his mind. He would take her to a quiet restaurant he knew, far from the prying eyes of the Bratva. It was secluded, intimate, the kind of place where no one asked questions and the patrons minded their own business. A few hours of normalcy. That's all it would be.

But even as he made the plan, the tension in his chest didn't fully dissipate. He could feel it, the tightening of his instincts, the sense that something was waiting around the corner. It was the feeling that had kept him alive all these years, the sixth sense that whispered warnings before danger struck.

Still, he pushed it aside for now. Tonight wasn't about him. It was about her. And he'd give her this moment of freedom, even if it went against every instinct he had.

"We'll leave soon," he said, his tone final. "Just stay close to me."

Anya nodded, her trust in him absolute. And that trust was what scared him the most.

Mikhail led Anya into the small, dimly lit restaurant, his hand gently resting on her lower back. The place was tucked away in a quiet corner of the city, a place he had carefully chosen for its seclusion and the privacy it offered. The faint glow of candles flickered on the tables, casting a warm but muted light over the intimate space. Mikhail had called ahead, securing a private table at the back, far from the few other diners. It was the first time in days they'd stepped out of the apartment, and though he'd been adamant about staying hidden, something in him wanted to give Anya this—just a brief moment of normalcy.

As they settled at the table, Anya glanced around the room, her expression soft but curious. The setting felt worlds apart from the danger they lived in, a strange contrast to the tension that had filled their days. She smiled faintly at Mikhail, the flicker of candlelight reflecting in her eyes. For a moment, it felt like a date—a quiet, intimate dinner that a couple might share, free of the burdens that weighed so heavily on their lives. But the undercurrent of tension still hummed in the air, a constant reminder that danger was never far away.

Mikhail, however, couldn't fully relax. His sharp eyes flicked around the room, assessing every detail, every movement, every shadow. He was alert, his instincts never quieting, even here in this secluded place. But beneath the layers of vigilance, there was a part of him that longed to let his guard down, just for a moment. To be here with Anya, without the constant threat looming over them.

Anya seemed to sense his unease, her gaze meeting his as she gently touched his hand across the table. "It's nice here," she said softly, her voice soothing. "Quiet."

Mikhail nodded, forcing himself to focus on her. "Yeah, it is," he replied, though his tone was still cautious. "I thought you could use a break from being locked inside. Even if it's just for a little while."

She smiled, appreciating the gesture. For a few moments, they sat in comfortable silence, the soft clinking of silverware and quiet murmurs of other patrons filling the space around them. It was surreal, almost peaceful, but the heaviness between them lingered.

After the server brought their drinks, Mikhail leaned back slightly, letting the tension in his shoulders ease, even if just a fraction. He glanced at Anya, watching her as she took a sip of her soda and lime, and for the first time in a long time, he felt the pull to talk about something that wasn't centered on survival or the Bratva.

"You know, before all of this," Mikhail began, his voice low, "I used to like nights like this. Quiet places, good food... things I never really had time to enjoy." He paused, looking down at the glass in his hand, his thumb tracing the edge. "This life... it doesn't allow for much of that."

Anya tilted her head slightly, her eyes soft with interest. "What do you mean?" she asked, her voice gentle, encouraging him to continue.

He took a breath, his fingers tightening slightly around the glass. "When I was younger, before I got into the Bratva... I used to dream about a life that wasn't always about violence. I used to think about what it would be like to have normal things—quiet nights, good food, maybe even a family. But once I got pulled into this world... those dreams faded." His words were honest, and it surprised him how easily they came out. He wasn't used to talking about his past or his desires, but with Anya, it felt different.

Anya listened intently, her heart aching for him. She hadn't expected this side of Mikhail—the man who craved something more than the cold, violent life he'd been living. It made her see him in a new light, not just as the protector she'd come to rely on, but as someone who had once yearned for the same things she did.

"You could still have that," Anya said softly, her gaze never leaving his. "Maybe not the way you imagined, but... you could have it with me. With our baby."

Mikhail's heart clenched at her words, and for a moment, the weight of everything he was fighting for hit him all at once. He had never allowed himself to think about the future like that—not in any real sense. But now, sitting across from Anya, the woman carrying his child, the possibility felt closer than it ever had before.

"I don't know how to be that kind of man," he admitted, his voice rough. "This life... it's all I've ever known. I'm not the kind of person who's built for peace."

Anya reached for his hand again, her fingers intertwining with his. "You don't have to be perfect," she whispered. "Just be with me. We'll figure it out together."

Her words stirred something deep within him, something he hadn't let himself feel in years. Mikhail looked into her eyes, and for the first time, he allowed himself to believe that maybe, just maybe, there was a way out of the darkness for him. But as much as he wanted to hold onto that hope, the reality of their situation pressed down on him like a vise.

"I want that," he said, his voice barely audible, "but I can't stop looking over my shoulder. The danger... it's always there."

Anya nodded, understanding the burden he carried. She knew their path wouldn't be easy, and the threats surrounding them wouldn't disappear overnight. But she also knew that they were stronger together, and if anyone could protect her and their child, it was Mikhail.

For a brief moment, they allowed themselves to imagine what life could be like if things were different. The world outside faded away, leaving just the two of them at that small table, sharing a quiet meal, dreaming of a future where they weren't constantly looking over their shoulders.

But Mikhail's gaze still flicked around the room, his instincts never fully shutting off. He knew that even in moments of calm, the threat was never far away. Yet sitting there with Anya, he felt a sense of purpose that he hadn't felt in a long time. He wasn't just fighting for survival anymore—he was fighting for her, for their baby, and for the chance at something better.

Mikhail and Anya continued their meal, falling into a natural rhythm of conversation that felt surprisingly easy. Mikhail had ordered something simple—a steak and potatoes, a dish he'd always enjoyed but rarely had the chance to savor—and Anya chose a light pasta dish, which she picked at while they talked. Their conversation flowed effortlessly, moving between small details of daily life, like the quirks of living in a cramped apartment, to more intimate topics, such as their shared love for quiet nights. It was the first time in days they had allowed themselves to simply exist without the weight of their situation pressing down on them.

Anya smiled as she listened to Mikhail recount a time when he had to cook for himself, burning nearly everything in the pan. "I thought if you just turned up the heat, it would cook faster," he chuckled, shaking his head at the memory. His hand rested on the table, fingers absentmindedly brushing the rim of his glass, and for a moment, Anya found herself captivated by the simple ease in his movements.

She laughed, the sound soft and genuine as she leaned in a little closer. Her arm brushed lightly against his, sending a faint warmth through her. It was moments like this that made her realize how much more there was to Mikhail than the hardened enforcer she'd first known. The way his face softened when he talked, the flicker of vulnerability in his eyes—it was a side of him she hadn't seen often, but one she found herself drawn to more and more.

"I can't picture you in a kitchen," she teased, letting her fingers brush against his as she reached for her glass. The brief touch made her heart skip a beat, a reminder of the growing connection between them. "But I bet you've learned a thing or two by now."

Mikhail's lips curved into a smirk, and his gaze locked with hers for a heartbeat longer than necessary. "Not much," he admitted, his deep voice tinged with amusement. "But I've gotten better. I'd still rather leave the cooking to someone else."

Their shared laughter filled the space between them, a quiet bubble of intimacy that wrapped around them like a warm blanket. Anya's hand lingered just slightly closer to his, their fingers occasionally brushing, each subtle touch sending a spark of awareness through her. The tension of their situation seemed to melt away, if only for a short while.

As Mikhail looked at her across the table, her emerald green eyes bright with laughter, a strange softness settled over him. For a brief moment, he let himself imagine what their life could be like if this was the norm. Quiet dinners in the dim glow of a restaurant, small talk that meant nothing and everything at the same time, the gentle warmth of her presence beside him. He could picture it so clearly—a life where the Bratva's threats and constant danger didn't hang over their heads like a storm cloud, where peace wasn't just a fleeting illusion but something they could truly hold on to.

Mikhail's hand brushed against Anya's once more, this time deliberately, his thumb tracing the delicate curve of her fingers. It was a small gesture, almost unnoticeable, but to Anya, it felt intimate, grounding. She let her hand rest against his, and when their eyes met again, there was an understanding between them—one that didn't need words.

"You're different tonight," Anya said softly, her smile fading into something more thoughtful as her thumb lightly stroked his knuckles. "Like...you're letting yourself breathe."

Mikhail hesitated, the vulnerability flickering behind his eyes as he dropped his gaze for a moment, staring down at their joined hands. Her touch was soft but steady, and it anchored him in a way he hadn't expected. She was right. There was something about being with her here, outside of the apartment's suffocating safety, that made him feel… lighter, more human.

But even now, with her across the table, her presence calming, the weight of everything lingered just below the surface—always threatening to pull him back into the reality of their lives. His gaze lifted, meeting hers once more, and for a moment, he allowed the truth to slip past the walls he had built.

"I guess I am," he replied, his voice quieter now, raw in its honesty. His fingers squeezed hers gently, a silent acknowledgment of the fragile peace they'd found. "It's nice to forget, even for just a little while."

Anya's lips curled into a soft smile, her eyes never leaving his. She felt it too—that fragile peace, the fleeting escape from the danger that lurked outside these walls. Her other hand reached across the table, resting on his forearm, and she felt the strength beneath his skin, the steady beat of his pulse thrumming against her fingertips. He was still so guarded, still so closed off in so many ways, but moments like this, when the walls between them crumbled, made her believe they could find something real together.

They lingered over their meal, the conversation growing lighter, the silences comfortable. At one point, Mikhail said something that made Anya laugh—a genuine, carefree laugh that made his heart twist in his chest. Her laughter was contagious, and for a brief moment, he allowed himself to enjoy it, to feel the warmth it brought.

As they finished their dinner, the moment felt almost surreal. For the first time in what felt like forever, they had simply enjoyed each other's company—no threats, no fear, just the quiet intimacy of two people discovering each other. And as they stood to leave the restaurant, Mikhail's hand settled at the small of her back, guiding her through the door and into the cool night air. His touch was possessive yet gentle, and Anya felt a strange sense of comfort knowing he was there, always watching, always protecting.

The street outside was quiet, the evening casting long shadows over the buildings as they walked side by side. Anya took a deep breath, feeling a strange sense of calm after their night together. "Thank you," she said softly, glancing up at Mikhail as they strolled. "I needed this. It's been a long time since I felt...normal."

Mikhail's lips pressed into a thin line, his gaze flicking from the street ahead to the shadows around them. "Don't get too comfortable," he warned gently, his voice tinged with that familiar edge of protectiveness. "It's not safe yet."

Anya nodded, understanding. She knew better than to think their lives could change overnight, but for now, she was grateful for the reprieve. They walked in silence for a moment, their footsteps echoing in the stillness of the night.

But something caught Mikhail's attention. His sharp eyes darted toward the road, his body tensing as he noticed a car creeping slowly along the curb behind them. It was subtle, the way it moved, almost too casual. But to Mikhail, it screamed danger.

His heart began to race, and his mind immediately shifted into survival mode. He gripped Anya's arm a little tighter, his steps quickening. "Stay close," he murmured, his voice low and urgent.

Anya sensed the shift in his mood immediately, her pulse quickening as she followed his lead. She glanced over her shoulder, her breath catching when she saw the car that had drawn Mikhail's attention. It was too slow, too deliberate, and her stomach twisted with unease. "What is it?" she whispered, her voice trembling.

"Just keep walking," Mikhail said, his voice a calm command. But inside, his instincts were screaming. They were being followed. He had to get Anya out of sight, fast.

The car crept closer, and Mikhail's grip on Anya tightened. Without hesitation, he guided her toward a narrow alley just a few paces ahead. His eyes scanned the street, calculating the distance, the time they had. They couldn't afford to be seen.

As soon as they reached the alley, Mikhail pulled Anya into the shadows, pressing her back against the brick wall. His body shielded hers as he kept one eye on the street, waiting to see if the car would follow.

Anya's heart pounded in her chest, her breath coming in short, shallow gasps. She had no idea what was happening, but the tension radiating from Mikhail told her everything she needed to know—*they were in danger.*

"Stay quiet," Mikhail whispered, his voice barely audible, a low growl in her ear as he pressed her tighter against the wall. His body was firm, unyielding, and Anya could feel the raw tension in every inch of him. His hand gripped her waist with a quiet strength, holding her close, shielding her from the outside world as if he could absorb any danger before it reached her. The heat of his chest seeped through her thin clothing, and despite the fear coursing through her veins, there was an odd comfort in the solidity of him—an immovable force protecting her.

Mikhail's gaze never left the street. His sharp eyes tracked the car with a predatory focus, like a wolf on the hunt, every muscle in his body coiled and ready to strike. His stillness was unnerving, like the calm before a storm, as if he could explode into action at any moment. She could hear the tension in his breathing, slow and controlled, but ready to quicken at the slightest sign of threat.

Anya's heart pounded against her ribs, each beat echoing in the quiet alley. The air between them was thick with anticipation, her breath coming in shallow gasps as she fought to stay silent. She felt the rough texture of the brick wall against her back, but all her senses were tuned to Mikhail—his warmth, his strength, the feel of his arm wrapped around her, grounding her in the storm of fear swirling around them.

She could feel the subtle movements of his muscles beneath his shirt, the tension in his arms as he stayed poised, waiting. His body was a fortress against the chaos that lurked just beyond the shadows, and despite everything—the danger, the fear—she trusted him. She trusted the way he stood so still, the way he watched the car with laser-sharp focus, never wavering. There was no hesitation in him, no doubt.

Her eyes flicked to his face, and what she saw stole her breath. His expression was carved from stone, every line sharp and defined, his jaw clenched as he stared at the car with an intensity that sent a shiver down her spine. His eyes were cold, calculating, as if he were already planning what he would do if the car stopped. There was something primal about him in that moment, something that reminded her of a predator, dangerous and controlled but ready to unleash hell if necessary.

He radiated power and danger, but at the same time, there was something deeply protective in the way he stood, his body forming a shield around her. His presence was a paradox—both terrifying and comforting in its certainty. He would kill for her if it came to that. She had no doubt about that now.

The seconds stretched on, the tension between them heightening as the car inched past the alley. Anya's body trembled, but it wasn't just from fear. It was the feel of him against her, the quiet strength he emanated, the way his hand gripped her waist as if anchoring her in place. She was hyper-aware of every inch of him—the press of his hard chest against her back, the warmth of his breath brushing her skin as he whispered, the steady beat of his heart against her shoulder.

She held her breath, waiting for something to happen, her heart thundering in her chest. Mikhail's stillness was unnerving, his focus absolute. His grip on her waist tightened for a moment, a silent reassurance as the car crept along the street. Anya could feel the tension rolling off him in waves, his body practically humming with readiness. He was prepared for the worst, and the way he watched that car, like a predator tracking prey, made her believe he was ready to unleash whatever violence was necessary.

But then, slowly, the car began to pass. Mikhail's breath remained controlled, his body still braced for action, but as the vehicle continued down the street without stopping, the tension in him lessened—just slightly. He didn't relax fully. He wouldn't—not until he knew they were safe. But Anya felt the moment the car disappeared from sight, the subtle shift in his posture as the immediate threat seemed to pass.

Still, Mikhail's grip on her didn't loosen, and he didn't move from his protective stance. His sharp eyes swept the street once more, ensuring the danger was truly gone before he spoke again, his voice low, gruff. "Stay still. Just for a moment longer."

His command held an edge of caution, but there was something else in it too—something protective, possessive. Anya nodded, her breath shaky but slowly evening out as she stayed pressed against the wall, her body still sheltered by his.

The danger might have passed, but the way Mikhail held her told her that his protectiveness would never waver.

He kept his body close to hers for another moment, his heart still pounding in his chest as the tension slowly began to ebb away. He released a slow breath, but the weight of the near miss clung to him. With one last glance down the street, he pulled away, taking her hand in his and leading her out of the alley.

"Let's get out of here," he muttered, his voice still low and tight.

They walked quickly, and though Anya could feel the fear still pulsing beneath her skin, there was something about the way Mikhail held her hand that steadied her. They made their way back to the car in silence, both shaken but unwilling to show it. Mikhail opened the door for her, watching her closely as she slid into the passenger seat. Once inside, he moved swiftly to the driver's side, casting one last look around before they drove off.

Mikhail's hands gripped the steering wheel tightly as they drove back to the apartment in tense silence, the hum of the car the only sound between them. The calm they'd briefly shared over dinner had been shattered by the near encounter on the street, and the weight of that close call hung heavily in the air. His jaw was clenched, his knuckles white from the force of his grip, and Anya could feel the tension radiating off him in waves.

She sat quietly in the passenger seat, still processing what had happened. Her heart hadn't stopped racing since Mikhail had pressed her into the shadows, shielding her from the unknown threat. The way his body had covered hers, the intense focus in his eyes—it had been terrifying and reassuring all at once. But now, as they drove through the darkened streets, the gravity of the situation settled over her like a heavy blanket.

Mikhail hadn't said a word since they'd slipped into the car. His silence was deafening, thick with the guilt and frustration she could see brewing inside him. Anya shifted in her seat, her hands resting lightly in her lap as she tried to figure out what to say. She wasn't angry at him—not even close—but she could tell that he was furious at himself.

Finally, she broke the silence, her voice soft but steady. "Mikhail… it wasn't your fault."

He didn't respond right away, his eyes fixed on the road ahead, his muscles tense as if holding himself together by sheer will. When he finally spoke, his voice was low, thick with restrained emotion. "I should have known better."

"Mikhail—"

"I almost lost you again," he interrupted, his tone harsher than he intended. His grip on the steering wheel tightened further, as though he could hold the world at bay through sheer force of will. "I never should've taken you out. I put you in danger, and that's on me."

Anya turned to him, her brow furrowing as she watched the conflict play out in his expression. She reached out, her hand resting gently on his arm. "You were trying to give us a moment of normalcy. You couldn't have known someone would follow us."

He shook his head, the guilt gnawing at him. "I should have known. I shouldn't have taken the risk." His voice was rough, his frustration boiling over. He slowed the car as they neared the apartment, parking on the street and cutting the engine. The sudden silence felt suffocating.

Anya shifted toward him in her seat, her hand still on his arm. "You can't protect me from everything, Mikhail."

His eyes darkened, his expression hardening as he turned to face her. "I can't afford not to." His voice was sharp, but beneath the anger was something deeper—a raw, desperate need to keep her safe. "You don't get it, Anya. Every time I close my eyes, every time I let my guard down, I see you getting taken from me. I can't... I won't let that happen."

The vulnerability in his voice cut through her. She could see how deeply this weighed on him, how much responsibility he carried, and it made her heart ache. This wasn't just about the physical danger—they were both fighting an emotional battle, too. She reached out, cupping his face with both hands, her thumbs brushing gently over his tense jawline. "I'm here, Mikhail. I'm safe. You saved me."

His eyes searched hers, and for a moment, he allowed himself to lean into her touch, to absorb the warmth and comfort she offered. But it didn't erase the fear clawing at him—the fear of losing her, of failing her. His mind replayed the events over and over again, the image of those men stepping out of the car and heading toward her, the panic that had gripped him in those heart-stopping moments. He'd been so close to losing her.

"I can't let this happen again," he said, his voice a low growl, as if speaking the words aloud solidified his resolve. "From now on, no more risks. I'm not letting you out of my sight, not until I know it's safe."

Anya's heart swelled with both gratitude and concern. She understood why he was saying this—his need to protect her had become more than just a responsibility; it had become something visceral, something deeply personal. She could see the conflict in his eyes, the war between his desire to give her a semblance of normalcy and his fear of losing her to the dangers that surrounded them.

She moved closer, her face just inches from his as she looked into his eyes. "You don't have to do this alone," she whispered. "We're in this together."

His breath hitched at her words, the sincerity of her gaze hitting him harder than he expected. He wasn't used to this—to someone standing beside him, sharing the burden. But Anya wasn't like anyone else. She wasn't just someone he needed to protect; she was someone who had come to mean more to him than he could have ever anticipated. The thought of losing her was unbearable.

"I know," he said, his voice quieter now, the fury softening as he let her words sink in. His hand covered hers where it rested on his cheek, and he held it there, drawing strength from her presence. "But I can't lose you, Anya. Not you. Not the baby."

Anya felt her throat tighten with emotion. Hearing him speak those words, acknowledging the life they were creating together, sent a rush of warmth through her. She leaned in, pressing her forehead against his, her breath mingling with his in the stillness of the car. "You won't," she promised, her voice steady and full of conviction. "We'll get through this. Together."

For a long moment, they sat like that, their foreheads resting against each other, their breaths syncing in the quiet of the night. It was a simple moment, but it was filled with all the unspoken emotions they hadn't yet dared to name—fear, love, hope, and the weight of the unknown future that loomed ahead.

Mikhail closed his eyes, letting himself just be with her, letting himself believe that maybe—just maybe—they could find a way through this. But the fear lingered, a shadow that would never quite leave. Because in his world, love came with a price. And he wasn't sure how much more he was willing to risk.

Chapter 16

Mikhail sat at the small kitchen table, his eyes focused on the half-empty plate in front of him. The morning light filtered through the curtains, casting a warm glow over the room, but despite the peaceful scene, Mikhail's mind was anything but calm. Breakfast had been quiet, filled only with the sounds of clinking silverware and the steady hum of the refrigerator. Anya sat across from him, unaware of the storm brewing inside him, the weight of what he was about to say settling like a heavy stone in his chest.

He set his fork down carefully, his movements slow and deliberate, as if trying to delay the inevitable. His eyes lifted to Anya's, watching her as she took another sip of coffee. Her face was soft in the morning light, a calmness about her that Mikhail wished he could feel. But this calm, this brief moment of peace, was about to be shattered.

"I have a meeting with Nikolai today," Mikhail said finally, his voice quiet but firm. There was no point in hiding it. The decision had been made, and there was no turning back now.

Anya's reaction was immediate. She froze, her coffee cup halting midair, her eyes snapping up to meet his. The flicker of worry that crossed her face was subtle, but Mikhail saw it. He felt it, like a sharp stab to the gut.

"Today?" she asked, her voice barely above a whisper, her hand tightening around the cup as if bracing herself for what was coming.

Mikhail nodded, his throat tight as he forced the words out. "Viktor texted me this morning. It's happening in a couple of hours."

The silence that followed was suffocating. Anya didn't speak, didn't move for a long moment. Mikhail watched her process the information, her lips parting slightly as if to ask more questions but closing again when the weight of it all seemed too much. He could see the fear lurking behind her eyes, a fear she was trying to keep hidden, but Mikhail could read her better than anyone. He knew what this meant to her—what it could mean for both of them.

"What do you think he'll say?" Anya asked finally, her voice fragile, betraying the strength she was trying so hard to maintain. She set her coffee cup down, her fingers trembling just slightly.

Mikhail reached across the table, his large hand enveloping hers. The contact was grounding, and for a moment, it eased the tension in his chest. "I don't know," he admitted, his thumb gently brushing the back of her hand. "But I have to do this. I can't hide you forever, Anya. The longer we keep this a secret, the more dangerous it becomes—for both of us. I need Nikolai on our side."

He could feel Anya's fear like it was his own. Her hand was cold in his, her grip tightening as she tried to steady herself. The reality of the situation was sinking in for both of them. This wasn't just a meeting. This was a moment that could decide their future—or end it.

Mikhail's stomach twisted as he thought of all the possible outcomes. Nikolai could refuse. He could see Anya and the baby as liabilities, a threat to the Volkov Bratva. And if that happened... Mikhail didn't want to think about it. He couldn't allow himself to consider the possibility of losing her. Not now.

Mikhail struggled with the fear gnawing at the back of his mind. He was used to being in control, used to managing dangerous situations with cold precision. But this was different. This was Anya—his future, his family. The stakes were higher than they had ever been, and the weight of that responsibility pressed down on him like a vice. What if Nikolai said no? What if he decided that Anya and the baby were too much of a risk? The thought alone made Mikhail's blood run cold.

But there was no way around it. He had to face this, had to confront the Bratva head-on if he wanted any hope of keeping Anya safe. Hiding wasn't an option anymore.

Anya's fingers squeezed his, pulling him from his thoughts. Her eyes met his, and in them, he saw not just fear but trust. Trust in him. Trust that he would find a way to protect her, no matter what.

"Just... be careful," she whispered, her voice barely audible.

Mikhail's chest tightened at the softness in her voice, the vulnerability she rarely let show. He didn't deserve her trust—at least, not fully. He had dragged her into this world, into a life she hadn't chosen, and now he was asking her to believe in him, to believe that he could navigate the deadly politics of the Bratva and keep her and their child safe. The truth was, he wasn't sure if he could. But he would die trying.

"I will," he promised, his voice low, but filled with a conviction he wasn't entirely sure he felt. His thumb traced slow circles on the back of her hand, trying to offer her some semblance of comfort.The fear between them was palpable, but it wasn't the kind of fear that drove people apart. It was the kind of fear that pulled them closer, binding them together in a shared understanding of the danger they faced. They didn't need to say it out loud—they both knew what was at stake. But there was also something else in that silence. Trust. Anya trusted him to handle this, to face Nikolai and come back with a future for them both. And despite the uncertainty gnawing at him, Mikhail felt a flicker of something more. Hope. Hope that this wasn't the end, but the beginning.

"I'll come back," Mikhail said, his voice firmer now, the promise settling between them like a quiet vow. "I'll make sure we're safe."

Anya nodded, her eyes softening as she held onto his hand a little tighter. "I know you will."

And for the first time that morning, Mikhail felt a sense of calm. It was fleeting, but it was there, buried beneath the layers of fear and responsibility. He didn't know what the outcome would be, but he knew one thing with certainty: he wasn't alone in this. Anya's eyes, full of concern and trust, lingered in his mind as he stood by the door, taking one last look at the apartment before stepping outside.

The cool air hit him as he descended the stairs, the familiar scent of the city waking around him. His steps were steady, deliberate, despite the rising tension within him. Mikhail reached his SUV, its black, imposing frame a stark contrast to the pale morning light. As he opened the door and slid into the driver's seat, the leather interior felt cold beneath his touch, grounding him in the moment.

The hum of the engine vibrated through him as he started the car, pulling out onto the quiet street. Mikhail's SUV moved quietly through the still morning streets, the hum of the engine the only sound breaking the silence. The city had yet to fully wake, its usual chaos subdued under the early light. His fingers curled tightly around the steering wheel, the leather creaking under the pressure of his grip. He felt the weight of everything he was about to face—he always did before a confrontation—but today, the stakes felt higher. It wasn't just about him anymore.

He tried to focus on the road ahead, but his mind kept circling back to the apartment he had just left. Anya, her worried eyes following him to the door, her whispered "be careful" still lingering in his ears. That quiet moment they had shared over breakfast felt miles away now. The memory of it felt fragile, something that could be shattered depending on how this meeting with Nikolai played out.

The reality was simple but devastating: the moment he stepped into that club, his world could tilt in a direction he couldn't control. If Nikolai deemed Anya and their child a threat, it could all be over. He couldn't let that happen, but the thought gnawed at him, a darkness creeping in from the edges.

Mikhail's jaw clenched. He had always been able to rely on his strength, his loyalty, his ability to get the job done. But this was different. He wasn't asking for leniency for a mistake or mercy for a misstep—he was asking for his future, for the lives of the people who mattered more to him than anything ever had. The thought of Anya and the baby being labeled a "liability" made his stomach churn. But he couldn't show fear. Not to Nikolai, not to anyone.

He shook his head, trying to dispel the negativity. He had spent years proving his loyalty to the Volkov Bratva, standing by Nikolai's side, taking on the dirtiest jobs, making sure that the family business stayed protected. And now he was hoping that loyalty would mean something more—that it would buy him time, buy him safety for Anya.

His knuckles whitened as he thought about Anya's father, Konstantin. That man had started all of this. If it weren't for him, Mikhail wouldn't be caught in this dilemma. His anger simmered just beneath the surface, but he forced himself to focus on the task at hand. Nikolai wasn't the enemy today, but that didn't mean he could let his guard down. Nikolai was calculating, and he didn't make decisions lightly. The only thing that might convince him to allow this was the certainty that Mikhail would do whatever it took to protect not just his family but the Bratva as well. There couldn't be any doubt in Nikolai's mind.

Mikhail replayed what he would say in his head, over and over, sharpening the points he would make. The car rumbled beneath him, a steady rhythm that did nothing to calm the storm building in his chest. He caught his reflection in the rearview mirror, his eyes darker than usual, more intense.

"Family." The word reverberated in his mind. Anya and the baby—*his* family. It had been a long time since he'd thought about what that word truly meant. He had fought for the Bratva, spilled blood for them. But it had never felt like family in the way Anya and their unborn child did. This was different. This was his responsibility.

A red light brought his car to a stop, and Mikhail exhaled slowly, trying to let go of the tension coiling inside him. He could feel the muscles in his shoulders stiff, his body already bracing for the worst. *No.* He couldn't allow himself to think like that. Anya needed him to be strong. The baby needed him to come back alive and with answers.

The light changed, and he pressed down on the accelerator, the SUV surging forward again. His thoughts continued to churn, cycling between strategies for the meeting and flashes of what his life would look like if things didn't go as planned. He wondered briefly if this was what it felt like for his father, always making decisions that impacted more than just himself. His father had been a selfish man, but Mikhail wasn't his father. He would *not* fail them.

As he neared the club, the familiar building came into view. It was quiet now, nothing like the bustling nightlife it hosted after hours. The stillness outside only heightened his awareness of the tension pulling tighter in his chest. The parking lot was nearly empty, making it easy for Mikhail to find a spot. He killed the engine and sat for a moment, staring at the brick façade of the club.

He couldn't shake the feeling that this was a pivotal moment. Everything could shift in the next hour, and that pressure, heavy and suffocating, settled over him like a shroud. The faces of men he had known—men who had failed the Bratva—flashed in his mind. Those were the ones who hadn't come back from meetings like this. He had to remind himself: he wasn't going in as a man who failed, but as one who had built his life on loyalty, respect, and calculated strength. That had to count for something.

Mikhail took a deep breath and reached for the door handle. The morning sun had started to rise higher in the sky, but it brought him no comfort. He stepped out, the sound of his boots crunching lightly on the asphalt, and slammed the door behind him. He stood for a moment, staring up at the building, the club where he had spent so many nights enforcing orders, maintaining control.

Now, he had to surrender some of that control. He hated the feeling of being vulnerable, hated the idea that his fate—and Anya's—could be decided by someone else. But he was a soldier in this life, and sometimes that meant trusting the hierarchy.

He could almost feel Anya's gaze, her worry as she had gripped his hand before he left. He could still hear her voice, the soft tremor of fear in it. But there had been trust too. She trusted him to make this right.

Mikhail took one last deep breath before making his way inside. There was no room for doubt now. He had to protect what was his.

Mikhail moved through the dimly lit hallway, the familiar scent of leather and cigars clinging to the air, though the usual noise and chaos were absent. Instead, the only sound was the echo of his footsteps on the polished floor, each step carrying him closer to the inevitable confrontation.

The silence pressed in on him, wrapping around his thoughts like a vice. This wasn't just a typical meeting—this was a reckoning, a moment where everything he'd been hiding would be laid bare. There was no turning back. Every step he took was heavy, burdened with the knowledge that what happened in the next hour would determine his future. It wasn't just about him anymore. Anya, the baby—his family's safety was now tied to the outcome of this conversation. The pressure mounted, intensifying with every echo of his footsteps.

As Mikhail walked through the empty hall, he passed a few familiar faces. Guards stood at their posts, watching him with knowing glances, but there was something different in their eyes this time. Their gazes weren't just curious; they were calculating. Some of them gave him a small nod of acknowledgment, while others merely stared, silent and unmoving. These were men who had worked beside him, men who had witnessed his loyalty firsthand. But even they understood the delicate balance Mikhail was walking into. Today, loyalty would be questioned. Trust would be tested.

The stakes were high, and it wasn't lost on anyone.

Mikhail kept his expression neutral, though his stomach tightened as he neared the office. His heart beat with a steady, controlled rhythm, but beneath that exterior, tension coiled like a snake ready to strike. This wasn't just about explaining himself—this was about facing the consequences of stepping outside the lines, about daring to keep something so personal hidden from the Bratva. A secret that could unravel the fragile peace they held with the Morozov family.

The large, heavy wooden door stood before him like a barrier between the past and the future, one that he was about to cross. The deep, grainy wood was imposing, carved with intricate details that reminded him of the power that lay on the other side. Behind this door was Nikolai Volkov, the man who held Mikhail's fate in his hands. A man who could, with a single word, condemn everything Mikhail had built.

He hesitated for the briefest moment, feeling the weight of the situation pressing on his chest like a thousand-pound stone. In that second of pause, a flood of thoughts rushed through him—memories of the first time he had walked into this building as a low-level enforcer, hungry to prove his worth. Back then, the idea of sitting across from Nikolai was a distant dream, something he believed he would never achieve. But now, here he was, standing on the precipice, his entire life teetering on the edge.

Would Nikolai see this as betrayal? Would he see the risk that Mikhail had taken as unforgivable?

With a steadying breath, he lifted his hand and knocked.

The sound was solid, a firm reminder that there was no turning back now. The door opened almost immediately, as if they had been waiting for him. Stepping inside, Mikhail was greeted by the sight of Nikolai sitting behind his large oak desk, a formidable presence even in the stillness of the room. The space was minimalist but luxurious—dark wood, rich leather, and the faint scent of tobacco hanging in the air. Despite the calm setting, the air itself felt heavy, charged with tension.

Nikolai's sharp eyes, cold and calculating, met Mikhail's as he entered. His gaze was like a blade, cutting through the silence and landing squarely on Mikhail, weighing him. Off to the side stood Viktor, arms crossed over his broad chest, his expression unreadable but his posture tense. Viktor had

always been difficult to read in these moments, but
there was something in the way he stood that let
Mikhail know he wasn't here just as a witness—he
was here as part of the judgment.

Mikhail's gut twisted. The atmosphere in the room
was thick, almost suffocating. The air felt heavy,
charged with an unspoken tension that weighed
down on Mikhail's shoulders. Every inch of the
space was laced with power dynamics—Nikolai's
control over the room, Viktor's quiet strength, and
Mikhail's precarious position between them.

Nikolai leaned back in his chair, his fingers tapping
lightly on the desk in a slow, methodical rhythm.
The sound filled the quiet room, amplifying the
tension with each soft tap. It was a reminder of who
held the power here, of who controlled the outcome
of this meeting.

"You've been keeping secrets," Nikolai said finally,
his voice low and even, though the undercurrent of
authority was unmistakable. It wasn't a question. It
was a statement of fact, and one that carried an
edge of accusation. Nikolai's gaze never wavered
from Mikhail's, and in that moment, Mikhail knew
this was the beginning of his reckoning.

The silence that followed Nikolai's words was
deafening, and for a split second, Mikhail wondered
if this was how it would all end—with a few simple
words and a quiet order to have him taken out. His

mind raced, considering all the possible outcomes, but his face remained as still as stone.

He nodded slowly, acknowledging the truth in Nikolai's words without offering any excuses. This was not a time for explanations. It was a time for truth—raw, unfiltered, and dangerous.

Mikhail stood his ground, his heart pounding in his chest as the weight of the moment settled on his shoulders. The room felt smaller now, as if the air itself was closing in on him, thick with tension. Across from him, Nikolai remained seated, his eyes sharp, unreadable, while Viktor leaned against the wall, his arms still crossed, though the flicker of interest in his gaze had grown. This was it—the moment Mikhail had been preparing for, the moment where everything he'd kept hidden would be brought into the light.

Taking a steadying breath, Mikhail began. "It's about Anya."

Nikolai's gaze didn't shift, but something in the room tightened. The name alone carried weight, and both Nikolai and Viktor knew it. Anya Morozov. Konstantin's daughter. The very fact that Mikhail had kept her hidden for so long was already a transgression, but Mikhail wasn't here to apologize. He was here to protect her.

"She's not just any woman," Mikhail continued, his voice low but firm. "She's Konstantin Morozov's daughter. And... she's carrying my child."

The words hung in the air like a guillotine ready to fall. Mikhail watched for any reaction from Nikolai, but the Bratva leader's face remained impassive, a mask of cold indifference. Viktor, however, shifted ever so slightly, his brow furrowing in thought. The silence was suffocating, but Mikhail held his ground, knowing this was only the beginning of the storm.

"Konstantin knows," Mikhail said, pushing forward. "He's made it clear. He wants the baby gone—he's willing to sacrifice his own daughter to ensure it."

Still, Nikolai said nothing. He simply sat there, the rhythmic tapping of his fingers on the desk the only sound in the room. Each tap felt like a countdown to Mikhail's fate, and the longer the silence stretched, the more the tension built within him.

"I've kept her safe," Mikhail added, his voice growing rough with the emotion he had been trying to keep in check. "I've protected her, and I will continue to protect her—no matter what it takes. This isn't just about Anya anymore. It's about my family. It's about the life she's carrying. My child. Our future."

For the first time, Nikolai's gaze shifted, just slightly, enough to let Mikhail know that he had finally captured his full attention. But still, the silence lingered. Mikhail could feel the weight of Nikolai's scrutiny, the way the Bratva leader was assessing, calculating. What was going on behind those sharp eyes? Was he weighing the risks? Was he considering how much Mikhail's decision might cost the Bratva?

Viktor remained silent, his eyes darting between the two men. The air was thick with unspoken words, with the tension of loyalty being tested.

Finally, after what felt like an eternity, Nikolai leaned back in his chair. His fingers stopped tapping, and he folded his hands in his lap, his gaze locked on Mikhail. When he spoke, his voice was low, measured, but it carried the weight of years of power and control.

"You know what this means, don't you?" Nikolai said, his eyes narrowing slightly. "You're not just risking yourself. You're putting the entire Bratva at risk. Konstantin Morozov won't let this go easily."

Mikhail's jaw clenched. He had expected this. He had known from the start that this wasn't just about his personal life—this was about the delicate balance of power between the Volkov and Morozov Bratvas. But there was no turning back now. He had made his choice, and he was ready to face the consequences.

"I know," Mikhail said, stepping forward slightly, his posture strong, his voice unwavering. "And I'm prepared to face him. Whatever comes, I'll deal with it. But I need to know that I have your backing. I need to know that the Volkov Bratva is with me."

The room fell silent once more. Mikhail could feel his pulse in his throat, the tension like a vice around his chest. If Nikolai refused him now, if the Volkov Bratva decided that Anya and the baby were too much of a liability, it would mean the end—for all of them. He could fight Konstantin on his own, but without the backing of his family, without the Bratva behind him, he knew the odds were slim. They needed this protection.

Nikolai stood from his chair slowly, the movement deliberate, and walked over to the window, staring out at the city skyline. His back was to Mikhail, but Mikhail didn't move, waiting with bated breath. The seconds stretched into what felt like hours, the tension growing heavier with each passing moment.

"You're asking me to put the full weight of the Volkov Bratva behind this," Nikolai said, his voice quiet, yet firm. "Do you understand what that means? If Konstantin retaliates—and he will—you're asking me to wage war."

Mikhail's hands clenched into fists at his sides. He didn't flinch. "Yes," he said simply. "I understand."

Nikolai was silent for a moment longer before turning back to face Mikhail. His eyes were cold, calculating, as if measuring Mikhail's worth in this moment. He walked back to his desk, his steps slow, deliberate, before finally meeting Mikhail's gaze.

"You have it," Nikolai said at last, his voice decisive. "But understand this—if you fail, if you let this blow back on us, I will be the one to end it. And I will make sure there's nothing left of you or anyone you care about."

Mikhail nodded, the weight of the moment hitting him full force. He had expected this. He knew the risks going into this, knew that he had placed not just himself, but Anya and their unborn child in the hands of the Bratva. But he had no choice. This was the only way to protect them, the only way to make sure they had a future.

"Thank you," Mikhail said, his voice steady despite the tension still coiling inside him.

Nikolai waved him off. "Don't thank me yet. The real fight is only beginning. Konstantin won't back down. He'll come for you—and for her."

"I know," Mikhail said quietly. "I'm ready."

Nikolai gave him a long, hard look before nodding once. "Good. Then you'd better make sure you don't fail."

Mikhail nodded again, a sense of relief flooding through him despite the gravity of the situation. He had Nikolai's backing. The Volkov Bratva was with him. For the first time since this nightmare had begun, Mikhail felt a glimmer of hope. He wasn't alone in this anymore. He had his family behind him—both the Bratva and the one he was building with Anya.

But as Nikolai had warned, the real fight was only just beginning.

Mikhail rose from his seat, feeling the tension of the confrontation still humming through his veins. He gave a firm nod to Nikolai, acknowledging the gravity of the decision, and turned toward the door. As he stepped out of the office, Viktor offered a brief look—one of silent approval, but with the underlying warning that the battle was far from over. Mikhail returned the look, then left, his footsteps echoing through the now eerily quiet hallway.

The weight of the encounter clung to him as he moved toward the club's exit. The silence in the corridors was almost oppressive, amplifying the thoughts racing in his mind. But with each step toward the door, Mikhail could feel the tension begin to unravel. By the time he stepped into the cool morning air outside, a sense of determination had replaced the anxiety that had gripped him since the meeting was first arranged.

Mikhail made his way to his SUV, his mind still sharp, always scanning his surroundings out of habit. He slid into the driver's seat, the familiar creak of the leather beneath him grounding him as he took a steadying breath.

As the engine roared to life, the sound seemed to clear the last remnants of tension from his body. He shifted the car into gear, pulled out of the parking lot, and into the quiet streets. A weight slowly began to lift from his chest. The hum of the engine was the only sound, a steady rhythm that mirrored the calm slowly settling inside him. His knuckles were no longer white against the steering wheel, and for the first time in days, he allowed himself to take a deep breath.

He had done it.

Nikolai had given his blessing, and with that, Mikhail knew he had the full force of the Volkov Bratva behind him. The fear that had clawed at him, the fear of being turned against by his own family, was gone. He no longer had to worry about facing the Volkovs alone. They were with him. Nikolai, for all his stern warnings, had made his position clear—Mikhail's loyalty was valued, and his fight was now the Bratva's fight.

But as the tension eased from his body, the lingering shadows of danger still remained. Konstantin Morozov wasn't just going to disappear. The man was relentless, ruthless. Mikhail had seen

that first-hand. He knew that the moment
Konstantin learned of Nikolai's decision, the battle
lines would be drawn. Konstantin would stop at
nothing to destroy what Mikhail had
claimed—Anya, the baby, their future together.

Mikhail clenched his jaw at the thought. Their
future. He could see it now, clearer than he ever
had before. Anya and the child—they were his
family. The realization hit him like a wave, washing
over him with a strength that nearly took his breath
away. He had never thought of himself as a man
who could have something like this, something so
fragile yet so powerful. But now, there was no
turning back. He was tied to them both, bound by
more than blood or duty.

He had fought for them, and he would keep
fighting.

As the sun began to rise higher, casting a warm,
golden light across the city, Mikhail's thoughts
shifted. For the first time in days, his mind wasn't
clouded with doubt or fear. He had secured the
backing of the Bratva—his family. Now, his focus
was solely on protecting Anya and the baby from
the threats that still loomed.

The streets began to grow busier as the city awoke
around him. Mikhail navigated through the morning
traffic with ease, his focus sharp but his heart a little
lighter. The lingering adrenaline from the meeting
still coursed through his veins, but with it came a

newfound sense of resolve. He had done what needed to be done, and now, with Nikolai and Viktor's support, he was ready to face the next battle—one that would come soon, he was sure.

Konstantin wouldn't give up easily. But neither would Mikhail.

As he turned onto the street that led to his apartment, Mikhail let out a long breath. There was still so much ahead, but he felt stronger now. More determined. He had a purpose beyond the Volkov Bratva, a reason that ran deeper than any loyalty to the organization. Anya and the baby. They were his to protect, his to care for. And with Nikolai's approval, he knew he could stand his ground.

He pulled into the parking lot of the apartment building, the familiar sight of the concrete structure bringing him a sense of stability. It was strange how this place—this small, cramped apartment—had become a haven in the middle of all the chaos. But it wasn't the apartment itself, Mikhail realized. It was what was inside. Who was inside.

As he cut the engine, the stillness of the morning surrounded him, and for the first time in what felt like forever, the weight on his chest loosened just a little. Anya was waiting for him, and with Nikolai's approval, he had given her and their unborn child a fighting chance.

This was his family now. His future. And no matter what came next, Mikhail was ready.

Chapter 17

Anya paced the small apartment, her bare feet silent against the cool floor as her heart raced, mirroring the relentless cycle of worry that consumed her thoughts. Mikhail had left hours ago, the weight of his mission palpable even before he walked out the door. She knew what was at stake—the meeting with Nikolai, the decision that could either secure their safety or unravel the fragile existence they were clinging to. Every second that passed without him felt like a dagger to her chest, the fear gnawing at her like a persistent shadow. She glanced at the clock on the wall, the hands moving far too slowly, taunting her with their steady, indifferent march.

The apartment, which had once seemed like a refuge, now felt suffocating. Each piece of furniture, each familiar sight, only reminded her of the uncertainty that lay beyond the walls. She had tried to distract herself, to sit down with a book or busy her hands with a task, but nothing could quiet the storm inside her. She found herself constantly listening for the sound of the door opening, waiting for Mikhail to return, praying that he would walk back in unharmed.

What if he doesn't? The thought intruded, unwelcome and insidious, curling around her like a snake. Her stomach twisted, bile rising in her throat as the possibility that he might not come back hit her. Mikhail was strong, he was capable, but she knew better than anyone that in the world they were living in, strength wasn't always enough. It wasn't just about physical power—there were forces, decisions, and dynamics that could shift at any moment, leaving even the strongest man vulnerable.

Anya paused, leaning against the edge of the kitchen counter, her fingers gripping the cool surface for support. Her mind raced back to the beginning, to the moment everything had changed. She had stolen his car, desperate to escape the life that was spiraling out of her control, and Mikhail had been nothing more than an enforcer to her back then—dangerous, ruthless, someone she couldn't afford to trust. But now... now everything was different.

She closed her eyes, letting the memories flood in. Mikhail had proven himself time and again—not just as her protector, but as someone she could lean on, someone who cared for her in ways that she hadn't expected. Her fingers absently grazed her stomach, the tiny swell barely noticeable beneath her shirt, but the life inside her was real. It tied them together in ways deeper than just survival. She wasn't just fighting for herself anymore, and neither was he.

But what if Mikhail doesn't come back? What if Nikolai sees her and the baby as a liability, a threat to the Bratva? The fear dug deeper, twisting her insides until she felt like she couldn't breathe. The idea of being left alone, without Mikhail to guide her through this dangerous world, was terrifying. She had never wanted to rely on anyone, and yet now, her very survival—her future—depended on him.

She rubbed her hands over her face, trying to shake the helplessness that clung to her. She hated feeling like this—powerless, as if her life was suspended on the edge of someone else's decisions. It wasn't who she was. She had always fought for control, always found a way to make her own choices, but now… everything was different. Mikhail had taken her in, promised to protect her, but the cost of that protection weighed heavily on her.

A memory surfaced, one she hadn't thought about in a long time. Her father's voice, sharp and commanding, telling her what her role was, what she was meant to do for the family. She had always been the obedient daughter, always followed the rules—until she hadn't. Until she had realized the truth—that her father would sacrifice her in an instant if it meant securing his power. She had run from that life, from the manipulation and control, and now… now she was running toward something just as dangerous.

But this time, it was different. Mikhail wasn't her father. He wasn't using her, wasn't manipulating her for his own gain. At least, that's what she told herself. Mikhail had risked everything for her—his place in the Bratva, his loyalty to Nikolai, his life. He had put himself between her and the storm that her father had unleashed, and she knew, deep down, that he wasn't just doing it out of obligation.

But how could she be sure? Anya wrapped her arms around herself, feeling the cold seep into her skin. The love she was beginning to feel for Mikhail scared her almost as much as the dangers outside these walls. It was one thing to trust him to protect her—it was another to trust him with her heart. And yet… wasn't that what had already happened? Slowly, piece by piece, she had given herself over to him, to the life they were building together, even if it was wrapped in danger and bloodshed.

What kind of future could they even have? Anya's mind drifted to the baby growing inside her. Would they ever know peace? Could she raise a child in a world like this? Mikhail had said he would protect them, but what would that protection cost? She couldn't help but think of the countless enemies lurking in the shadows, the threats that could come from both inside and outside the Bratva. The reality of it was overwhelming.

She glanced out the window, the city spread out below her like a jungle of concrete and steel. Somewhere out there, Mikhail was facing a decision that could change everything. And all she could do was wait. Wait and hope that he would come back to her, that they would be given a chance to build something real, something lasting.

Anya exhaled slowly, trying to steady her racing heart. She needed to believe in him, to trust that Mikhail would do whatever it took to make sure they were safe. But even as she tried to calm herself, the fear lingered, gnawing at the edges of her mind, whispering that nothing in this world was certain.

She paced the apartment once more, each step heavier than the last.

Anya's heart nearly stopped when she heard the familiar sound of Mikhail's key turning in the lock. For a moment, she stood frozen, her breath caught in her throat, unsure if she could trust her ears. Then the door creaked open, and he stepped inside. Relief washed over her like a wave, the tension that had been tightening her chest for hours finally loosening.

He was home.

Mikhail's face was hard, his expression unreadable as he closed the door behind him, but there was something in his eyes—something that told her it hadn't been a disaster. He was alive, and by the looks of him, the meeting hadn't gone badly. Still, Anya's pulse raced, her mind not yet ready to let go of the fear that had gnawed at her all morning.

"Mikhail…" she whispered, her voice shaky, almost unsure if she should speak or if the moment required silence.

He didn't say anything at first. Instead, he crossed the room in a few long strides and pulled her into his arms. His embrace was tight, fierce, as if he was holding on to her for dear life. Anya felt herself melt into him, her body sagging against his in relief. The familiar scent of him, the steady rise and fall of his chest, the warmth of his skin—everything about him grounded her, pulling her back from the edge of panic that had consumed her in his absence.

His hand slid up to cradle the back of her head, his fingers threading through her hair. For a moment, they just stood there in the quiet apartment, holding on to each other as if nothing else existed. Anya could feel his heart beating against hers, the solid, steady rhythm soothing the anxiety that still clung to her.

"You're safe," he murmured into her hair, his voice rough but filled with something tender. "We're safe."

Anya pulled back just enough to look up at him, her eyes searching his. "What happened? Did it…?"

"It's done," Mikhail cut her off, his voice low but firm. "Nikolai's given us his backing."

A rush of air escaped Anya's lungs, the weight of her fears lifting just a little more. Nikolai had agreed. That meant they weren't alone. They had the Volkov Bratva behind them now, a layer of protection she hadn't dared to hope for. But as the relief began to settle in, she couldn't shake the underlying tension, the knowledge that while one hurdle had been cleared, many more still lay ahead.

Her hand instinctively moved to her stomach, her fingers splaying protectively over it. Mikhail's eyes followed the movement, and something shifted in his expression—something softer, more vulnerable. His hand came down to cover hers, their fingers intertwining over the life they were both fighting for.

"Anya…" His voice trailed off, as if he couldn't find the words, or maybe he didn't need to say them. His eyes, deep and intense, told her everything she needed to know.

She nodded, tears welling up in her eyes. "I was so scared," she admitted, her voice barely more than a whisper. "I didn't know if… I didn't know if you'd come back."

Mikhail's grip on her tightened, his jaw clenching as if the very thought of her fear caused him pain. "I'll always come back for you," he said, his voice rough but resolute. "I'll never let anything happen to you or the baby. You're mine, Anya. Both of you."

The possessiveness in his voice wasn't threatening. It didn't feel like control or dominance—it felt like protection, like a vow, and it sent a shiver down her spine. She felt safe with Mikhail in a way she hadn't expected. He wasn't just her protector, though. He was so much more.

The realization hit her then, a sudden clarity that had been creeping up on her for days. She wasn't just grateful to him for keeping her safe. She wasn't just leaning on him because of their circumstances. She was falling for him—had already fallen, in fact. And that scared her more than anything else.

Her heart pounded in her chest, her mind racing as she stared up at him, trying to figure out how to say what she was feeling. But the words wouldn't come. Instead, she raised her hand, cupping his cheek, feeling the rough stubble beneath her palm. His eyes softened at the touch, his thumb brushing over her hand where it still rested on her stomach.

For a long moment, neither of them spoke. They didn't need to. The connection between them had deepened in ways that words couldn't describe. It was more than just physical attraction now, more than just the bond formed by shared danger and survival. It was something real, something strong.

Mikhail leaned down, his forehead resting against hers. His breath was warm on her lips, and Anya closed her eyes, savoring the closeness. For the first time since this nightmare had begun, she allowed herself to feel hope. Hope that maybe, just maybe, they could get through this. Together.

The tension in the room began to shift, the fear and uncertainty giving way to something else—something deeper, more intimate. Anya's heart raced as Mikhail's hand slid up her back, pulling her even closer. She could feel the heat of his body against hers, the steady thrum of his pulse beneath his skin. Her fingers curled into his shirt, holding on to him like he was the only thing keeping her grounded.

"I need you," Mikhail whispered, his voice barely audible, but the weight of his words hung heavy in the air.

Anya's breath hitched at the raw vulnerability in his tone. She had always seen Mikhail as strong, as someone who never faltered, never wavered. But in this moment, she realized that he needed her just as much as she needed him. He wasn't invincible, wasn't immune to the fear and uncertainty that came with their situation. And that made her love him even more.

"I'm not going anywhere," she whispered back, her voice trembling with the weight of the promise. "I'm yours."

The words felt right, felt true. Because they weren't just surviving together anymore—they were living. And no matter what dangers still lay ahead, they would face them side by side.

Mikhail's eyes, dark and intense, never wavered from hers as he gently tilted her chin up with his hand. The room seemed to shrink around them, the weight of the world outside their walls falling away as if nothing else mattered. Anya could feel his breath on her lips, and her heart pounded in her chest, a heady mix of desire and emotion flooding her senses.

"You're mine," Mikhail whispered, his voice low and rough, sending a shiver down her spine. There was no hesitation in his words, no question. It was a declaration, an undeniable truth that left no room for doubt.

It wasn't the first time he had spoken those words, but tonight, they carried a different meaning. Tonight, they were laced with something more, something deeper. The possessiveness in his tone wasn't harsh or controlling—it was protective, born out of a need to claim her as his in the purest sense. To let her know that she wasn't just under his protection, she was his. His to care for, his to cherish, his to love.

Anya's heart raced, a dizzying rush of emotions flooding her all at once. She felt overwhelmed, not by fear, but by the intensity of it all. The way his gaze held hers, so unyielding, so certain. It was as if he could see straight into her soul, stripping away the layers of doubt and insecurity that had plagued her for so long. There was no mistaking what he meant. He wasn't just saying the words—he was living them, embodying the promise in every look, every touch.

For a moment, Anya was speechless, her mind swirling with everything that had happened, everything she had felt since she first crossed paths with Mikhail. She had been afraid, angry, lost—but now, standing here in his arms, none of that mattered anymore. All the fear, all the uncertainty melted away, replaced by a deep, undeniable sense of belonging.

She was his. And somehow, that made her feel more secure, more wanted, than she had ever felt in her life.

Mikhail's hand slid down from her chin to the small of her back, pulling her even closer until their bodies were pressed together, the heat of his skin seeping into hers. His other hand found its way to her cheek, cradling her face as if she were the most precious thing in the world. His touch was gentle but firm, and Anya couldn't help but lean into it, her eyes fluttering shut as she absorbed the moment.

"I'll protect you, Anya," he murmured, his lips brushing against her temple. "Always."

The sincerity in his voice was enough to bring tears to her eyes. She believed him—she believed every word. There was no room for doubt anymore. She had seen the lengths he was willing to go to for her, the risks he had already taken. This wasn't just about survival anymore. It was about them. About the life they were building together, even if it had been born out of chaos and danger.

Her breath hitched, and she opened her eyes to find him watching her, his hungry gaze burning with a raw intensity that sent a thrill through her. There was a vulnerability in his expression, too—a crack in the hardened facade he usually wore. He was letting her in, letting her see the man behind the enforcer. And that was something he didn't do for anyone else.

Anya swallowed, her voice trembling as she whispered, "I'm yours, Mikhail."

The words came out before she could stop them, but once they were spoken, they felt right. They hung in the air between them, binding them together in a way that words alone could never fully capture. It wasn't just an acknowledgment of what he had said—it was her acceptance of it. She was his. And the realization filled her with a warmth she hadn't expected.

Mikhail's lips quirked into a small smile, his hand slipping into her hair as he pulled her in for a kiss. It was slow, tender, but filled with an underlying heat that made her head spin. His mouth moved against hers with a hunger that echoed the depth of his feelings, and she responded in kind, her hands tangling in his shirt, pulling him closer.

The kiss deepened, the tension between them shifting from emotional to physical as the fire that had always been there flared to life. Anya could feel the hard planes of his body against hers, the strength in his arms as he held her, the steady beat of his heart beneath her palm. It was intoxicating, the way they fit together, like two pieces of a puzzle that had finally found their place.

But it wasn't just lust, not anymore. There was something more in every touch, every kiss. A connection that went beyond the physical, something that spoke to the deeper bond they had forged through their shared struggles, their growing trust. It was in the way Mikhail looked at her, the way his fingers brushed over her skin as if memorizing every inch of her. He wasn't just claiming her—he was cherishing her.

Anya's mind raced, her heart pounding with the intensity of her feelings. Could she really do this? Could she really be with a man like Mikhail, someone who lived in a world of violence and danger? But as she looked into his eyes, she knew the answer. It wasn't a choice anymore. Her body, her heart—they had already made the decision for her.

"I'm yours," she whispered again, her voice barely more than a breath. And this time, she felt the truth of it settle deep within her.

Mikhail's grip on her tightened, his forehead resting against hers as he whispered back, "And I'll never let you go."

It was a promise, one that resonated in the quiet space between them. A vow that no matter what came next, no matter how dangerous the road ahead, they would face it together.

Mikhail's fingers intertwined with hers as he silently led Anya toward the bedroom. The quiet intimacy of the moment made her pulse quicken. The air between them was thick with unspoken desire, but there was no urgency in his steps. This time, it felt different—slower, more deliberate, as though they both understood the gravity of what was about to unfold.

The door to the bedroom clicked softly shut behind them, cocooning them in their own private world. Mikhail stopped just inside the room, turning to face her with an intensity that made her breath hitch. His eyes held hers, the dark desire there simmering beneath the surface, but he didn't rush. Instead, he lifted a hand to her cheek, brushing a thumb across her skin as if committing the feel of her to memory.

Their lips met in a kiss that was slow and deep, full of emotion that neither of them had to speak aloud.

Anya melted into it, her body pressing against his as she let herself get lost in the feel of him. His mouth was gentle but firm, each kiss a silent promise, a vow of his unwavering possession of her. The slow rhythm of their lips sent a shiver down her spine, her body coming alive with every touch.

Mikhail's hands began to roam, slipping to her waist as he pulled her closer, his warmth seeping into her. The brush of his fingers against the fabric of her clothes made her skin tingle beneath, the anticipation growing with each passing second. Slowly, he reached for the hem of her shirt, tugging it up, but not hurriedly. Every movement was purposeful, as if he wanted to savor every moment, every inch of skin he uncovered.

He pulled the fabric over her head, revealing the smooth expanse of her shoulders and the curve of her collarbone. His lips found the newly exposed skin, pressing soft kisses there that made her breath hitch in her throat. Anya's fingers gripped his arms, steadying herself as his mouth moved lower, tasting, exploring.

As Mikhail's hands slid down her sides, she felt the heat of his touch, the possessive yet gentle way he claimed her. His fingers brushed along the waistband of her pants, his eyes flicking up to meet hers. He didn't need to say anything; the look in his eyes told her everything. He wanted her—all of her—and not just in the primal, physical sense. This was deeper, more intimate than anything they had shared before.

Anya's pulse raced as Mikhail slowly unbuttoned her pants, his fingers grazing the sensitive skin of her lower belly as he pushed them down, leaving her standing before him in just her underwear. She felt vulnerable and exposed under his gaze, but at the same time, she felt powerful. The way he looked at her, as if she were the only thing that mattered in the world, made her feel like she was the one in control.

Mikhail's hands slid over her hips, his touch firm but reverent, as though he were worshipping her. He stood back for a moment, his eyes dark with hunger as they roamed over her body, taking in every curve, every inch of bare skin. The heat between them was palpable, but he didn't rush to close the distance again. Instead, he took his time, savoring the sight of her before him, the tension between them building with every second that passed.

He reached out, his fingers slipping beneath the straps of her bra, slowly pulling them down her shoulders. The soft fabric slid away, and Mikhail's eyes darkened even more as her breasts were revealed to him. His thumb grazed over one of her hardened nipples, sending a jolt of pleasure through her that made her gasp.

Anya's hands moved to his shirt, her fingers
trembling slightly as she tugged it over his head,
revealing the hard planes of his chest. She had
seen him bare before, but now, in this moment, it
felt different. It felt like every inch of him belonged
to her, just as she belonged to him.

Mikhail's hands found the waistband of her
underwear, and with a slow, deliberate movement,
he pulled them down her legs. Anya stepped out of
them, her skin tingling with anticipation. The air was
thick with desire, the weight of what was about to
happen settling over them like a blanket.

Without breaking their gaze, Mikhail unbuttoned his
pants, pushing them down along with his briefs.
The sight of him fully revealed sent a wave of heat
through Anya, her pulse quickening as he stepped
out of the remaining clothes. He was hard, ready
for her, and the tension between them intensified
with every breath.

Mikhail stood back for a moment, his gaze
sweeping over her body again, as if he couldn't
quite believe she was his. Then, with a low growl,
he reached for her, pulling her flush against him.
The heat of his body was intoxicating, the hard
length of his erection pressing against her thigh as
he kissed her again, this time with more intensity,
more need.

Slowly, Mikhail guided her toward the bed, their lips
never breaking contact. He laid her down gently, his

body hovering over hers as he kissed his way down her neck, his lips lingering at her collarbone before moving lower. Anya arched her back, her hands tangling in his hair as he made his way down her body, leaving a trail of fire in his wake.

When he reached her breasts, Mikhail took his time, his mouth closing over one hardened nipple as his hand moved to the other. The sensation was overwhelming, a mix of pleasure and tenderness that made her moan softly. His tongue flicked against her sensitive skin, his teeth grazing just enough to send a shock of pleasure through her.

He moved lower, his lips trailing down her abdomen, his breath hot against her skin. Anya's heart raced, her body trembling with anticipation as he kissed her lower stomach, his mouth hovering just above the place where she needed him most. Her hips lifted off the bed slightly, a silent plea for him to continue.

Mikhail's eyes met hers as he moved between her legs, his gaze intense, filled with a mix of desire and something deeper. He didn't break eye contact as his tongue found her slick folds, swirling over her clit in slow, deliberate circles. Anya gasped, her head falling back against the pillow as pleasure surged through her.

His hands gripped her hips, holding her in place as he continued his slow, torturous assault on her senses. His tongue moved expertly, alternating between gentle flicks and harder, more insistent strokes that made her hips buck against him.

The world around them disappeared, and in that moment, there was nothing but the two of them. Nothing but the heat, the desire, and the growing connection between them. Anya felt herself spiraling, her body teetering on the edge of release, but Mikhail wasn't done yet. He was savoring her, just as she was savoring every second of this slow, intimate dance.

With each touch, each kiss, Anya knew she was his—completely, utterly, his.

Anya's hands gripped the sheets beneath her, her knuckles turning white as she fought to contain the surge of emotion rising within her. The pleasure was immediate, but it was the way Mikhail touched her, with deliberate, slow movements, that unraveled her completely. His tongue moved in torturous circles, not rushing, savoring every second, every reaction. Her pulse raced, and each swirl of his tongue over her clit sent her spiraling deeper into the abyss of her desire for him.

Mikhail didn't let up. He teased her relentlessly, his tongue flicking over her sensitive bundle of nerves, while his fingers slid inside her, curling upward with a precision that left her gasping. It was like he knew exactly what she needed before she could even ask for it, every touch sending her higher, pushing her closer to the edge.

Anya's hips bucked instinctively, desperate for more, her body acting on pure need. Mikhail responded with a low growl of satisfaction, the sound vibrating against her core, amplifying the sensation. His fingers thrust deeper, matching the rhythm of his tongue as it swirled over her clit, his movements becoming more urgent, more demanding. She moaned his name, the sound broken and breathless, the pleasure building with a raw intensity that left her trembling beneath him.

The way he watched her—his deep brown eyes locked on hers, never wavering—made the experience even more overwhelming. His gaze held her in place, those eyes filled with heat and possession, and it only made the sensations coursing through her that much more powerful. There was something in that look, something that told her he wasn't just taking her body—he was claiming her completely, body, heart, and soul.

Each flick of his tongue, each stroke of his fingers sent her higher, the tight coil in her abdomen growing tighter with every second. She was helpless to stop it, her legs quivering as the tension mounted, threatening to snap at any moment. Anya's breath came in short, ragged gasps, her body trembling under his relentless touch.

"God, Mikhail," she gasped, her voice breaking, her body surrendering completely to the pleasure he gave her. She was his in every way, lost in the ecstasy he brought her, and she didn't care. The intensity of the moment was overwhelming, drowning her in sensations so powerful she could barely think.

He held her firmly, his grip on her hips possessive and strong, guiding her through every wave of pleasure. It wasn't just about control—it was about making sure she knew exactly who was in control. His control was absolute, but she trusted him with it, knowing he would take her to heights she'd never imagined.

Her climax hit her like a tidal wave, crashing over her with a force that left her breathless. Her body arched off the bed, her fingers twisting in the sheets as she cried out his name, her vision blurring as the orgasm consumed her. Every nerve in her body was on fire, the pleasure so intense it left her trembling, her chest heaving as she struggled to catch her breath.

But Mikhail wasn't done with her. Not yet.

Mikhail's body hovered over hers, his muscles taut with desire, his deep brown eyes burning with an intensity that took Anya's breath away. The air around them was thick, heavy with anticipation and need. Her body still trembled from the climax he had pulled from her, her pulse racing in time with the heat radiating from him. But it wasn't over. She could feel it—the way he looked at her, the way his hands moved over her skin—there was more to come.

Slowly, he positioned himself between her legs, his body pressing down on hers just enough for her to feel his weight, his strength. His hard, throbbing cock brushed against her slick entrance, and a gasp escaped her lips. Mikhail paused for a moment, as if savoring the moment, his gaze locking onto hers, filled with a hunger so raw it sent a shiver down her spine.

"You're mine," he growled, his voice low and possessive, a declaration that sent a surge of heat through her. His hands gripped her hips tightly, as if anchoring her in place, claiming her in every way that mattered. She was his, and the truth of that settled deep in her bones.

"Yes," she whispered, her breath coming in short gasps as her body arched toward him. Her hands found his shoulders, gripping his hard muscles as she pulled him closer. "I'm yours."

With that, Mikhail thrust into her, slow and deliberate, filling her completely. Anya's back arched off the bed as the sensation hit her, a low moan spilling from her lips. He was big, stretching her in a way that made her feel every inch of him, his cock throbbing inside her as he sank deeper. The feeling was overwhelming, but she welcomed it, her body opening to him, her legs wrapping around his waist to pull him closer.

He moved slowly at first, savoring the way her body clenched around him, his gaze never leaving hers. The intimacy of it all made her heart pound, the way he looked at her, the way he moved inside her—it was more than just physical. She could feel the depth of his need for her in every thrust, the way his hands tightened on her hips, his grip almost bruising as he pulled her against him. It wasn't just about lust—it was about something deeper, something that bound them together in a way that went beyond the bedroom.

"God, Anya," he groaned, his voice rough with need, as his pace began to quicken. His hips moved with a steady rhythm, each thrust harder than the last, driving deeper into her, pushing her closer to the edge with every stroke. Anya's breath hitched, her body tightening around him as the pleasure built, her fingers digging into his shoulders as she held on.

The room filled with the sound of their bodies coming together, the slap of skin against skin, the low moans that escaped her lips with every thrust. Mikhail's eyes never left hers, his focus entirely on her, on the way her body responded to him. He shifted his angle slightly, his cock hitting a spot deep inside her that made her cry out, her head falling back as a wave of pleasure washed over her.

Mikhail's hands gripped her hips even tighter, his fingers digging into her skin as he lifted her slightly off the bed, angling her hips upward so he could drive even deeper. The new position sent shockwaves through her, the pleasure intensifying as he thrust harder, faster, his movements more urgent now. Anya's moans grew louder, her body trembling beneath him as he pushed her closer to the edge.

She could feel it building again, the tension coiling deep in her abdomen, tightening with every thrust, every flick of his hips as he moved inside her. Her legs tightened around his waist, pulling him even closer as her body begged for release. She was so close, teetering on the edge, every nerve in her body on fire, her breath coming in short, ragged gasps.

"Mikhail," she moaned, her voice breaking as the pleasure became too much, her body unable to contain it any longer. "Please…"

He responded with a growl, his movements becoming even more intense, his hips slamming into hers with a force that made her see stars. His cock filled her completely, stretching her in a way that made her feel owned, claimed, and she loved it. Every thrust was a reminder that she belonged to him, that she was his in every way that mattered.

Anya's body tightened, her muscles clenching around him as her second orgasm hit her like a tidal wave. She cried out his name, her body arching off the bed as the pleasure tore through her, leaving her breathless and trembling. The sensation was overwhelming, her vision blurring as her body shook with the force of her release.

Mikhail followed soon after, his own release triggered by the way she clenched around him. He let out a low, guttural moan, his body tensing as he buried himself deep inside her, his cock throbbing as he came, spilling into her with a force that made his entire body shudder. His hands tightened on her hips, holding her close as he rode out the waves of his orgasm, their bodies locked together in the heat of the moment.

For a moment, neither of them moved, their bodies still intertwined, their breaths coming in short, ragged gasps. The intensity of what they had just shared lingered in the air, heavy and charged, the connection between them deepened in a way that left Anya feeling raw and vulnerable.

Mikhail lowered himself onto her, his body pressing against hers as he buried his face in the crook of her neck. His breath was warm against her skin, and she could feel his heartbeat pounding in his chest, still racing from the intensity of their lovemaking.

"I'm yours," she whispered, her voice soft but filled with emotion as she ran her fingers through his hair, her body still trembling from the aftershocks of her release. "I'm yours, Mikhail… always."

Mikhail lifted his head, his brown eyes locking onto hers with a fierce intensity that sent a shiver down her spine. "And I'm yours," he murmured, his voice low and raw. "Forever."

In that moment, Anya knew that no matter what happened next, no matter the danger that lay ahead, she was exactly where she was meant to be. In his arms, she felt safe. She felt loved. And she knew, without a doubt, that she belonged to him—body, heart, and soul.

Mikhail and Anya lay together in the quiet aftermath, their bodies still entwined, the heat of their passion lingering in the air. The room was filled with the soft, rhythmic sound of their breathing, slowly calming after the intensity of what they had shared. Anya's head rested on Mikhail's broad chest, the steady beat of his heart thudding beneath her ear like a calming lullaby. For the first time in what felt like forever, there was a sense of peace. The world outside, with all its danger and uncertainty, seemed far away.

Mikhail's hand moved gently along her back, tracing idle patterns on her skin, his touch soft and protective. There was no urgency now, no tension—just the quiet intimacy of two people who had found solace in each other. Anya's fingers played absently with the edge of the sheet draped over them, her thoughts wandering back over the whirlwind of events that had brought her here, to this moment, in his arms.

She never thought she could feel this way about someone like him—someone whose life was steeped in violence and danger. Mikhail was everything she should have run from, everything she had been taught to fear. And yet, with him, she felt safe. Loved. Protected in a way she had never known before.

Her gaze drifted up to his face, taking in the strong lines of his jaw, the way his brown eyes had softened as he looked down at her. There was a vulnerability in his expression now, something raw and unguarded that made her heart swell. He wasn't just the dangerous enforcer she had first met—he was so much more. He was her protector, her lover, and, in this quiet moment, the man she realized she was falling in love with.

The thought made her chest tighten with emotion, a feeling so intense it almost frightened her. She had been alone for so long, moving through life without truly knowing what it meant to belong to someone, to feel this deep connection. But here, with Mikhail, it all felt different. The walls she had built around herself had crumbled, and in their place was a newfound certainty. This was where she was meant to be—by his side, in his arms, no matter what the future held.

Mikhail's fingers brushed through her hair, his voice a low rumble that sent a warmth through her. "You're quiet," he murmured, his lips grazing her forehead in a tender kiss. "What are you thinking about?"

Anya smiled softly, her fingers splaying over his chest. "Just... everything," she replied, her voice quiet but filled with emotion. "I never thought... I'd feel this way. About you. About any of this."

His brow furrowed slightly, a hint of concern flickering in his eyes. "Does it scare you?"

She paused for a moment, considering her answer. In some ways, it did. The intensity of what she felt for him, the danger that surrounded their lives—it was overwhelming. But at the same time, it gave her a sense of purpose, a sense of belonging she had never known before.

"No," she whispered, shaking her head as she met his gaze. "It doesn't scare me. Not anymore. It feels... right."

Mikhail's expression softened, his hand sliding from her back to rest over hers on his chest. The look in his eyes was unlike anything she had ever seen before—tender, filled with a quiet devotion that made her heart ache with the sheer weight of it.

"Good," he murmured, his voice barely audible in the quiet room. "Because you're mine, Anya. And I'm not letting you go."

The words wrapped around her like a promise, sealing the connection between them in a way that felt unbreakable. She closed her eyes, sinking deeper into his embrace, letting the warmth of his body and the steady rhythm of his heartbeat lull her into a peaceful stillness.

She was his, and he was hers. They had faced so much together, and there was still more to come. But in this moment, lying in the quiet afterglow of their lovemaking, Anya knew that whatever challenges lay ahead, they would face them together. She had found her place, her person, and in his arms, she felt truly safe.

Chapter 18

Anya lay curled up beside Mikhail, her head resting on his chest, listening to the steady rhythm of his breathing. His arm draped protectively around her waist, his warmth seeping into her skin, calming the restless thoughts that had plagued her for weeks. In his embrace, she felt a sense of peace that had eluded her for what felt like a lifetime. It was strange, really—how someone as dangerous and intense as Mikhail could make her feel safer than she had ever felt before. But here she was, her body melting into his, her heart calming in the steady beat of his.

As the quiet enveloped them, her thoughts began to drift. She couldn't help but reflect on everything that had brought her to this moment. The chaos, the fear, the uncertainty that had defined her life since being dragged into the world of the Bratva felt so distant now. It wasn't just that Mikhail had protected her—he had become more than just a shield between her and the violence. He had become her anchor, her safety in a world that had been spiraling out of control.

Anya's fingers trailed absentmindedly across his chest, tracing the hard lines of his muscles, marveling at how far they had come. She hadn't expected to fall for him. It hadn't even seemed possible. Mikhail had been terrifying at first—cold, calculating, and so far removed from anything she'd ever known. But beneath that hardened exterior, she had found a man who was more than just the violence that surrounded him. He was fiercely loyal, protective, and even gentle in moments like these.

She loved him. The realization settled over her like a warm blanket, the weight of it surprising her even now. She hadn't said the words out loud, not yet, but they echoed in her heart. How could she not love him after everything they had been through? He had become her protector, yes, but more than that, he had become her everything.

Still, a tiny flicker of doubt lingered at the back of her mind, a creeping sense of dread she couldn't quite shake. Nothing was ever truly safe in this world. The peace she felt now—it felt fragile, like it could shatter at any moment. Her father, the Bratva, the constant danger—it was all still there, lurking just beneath the surface.

Anya squeezed her eyes shut, willing the unease to disappear. She didn't want to think about it, not tonight. Tonight, she just wanted to feel safe, wrapped in Mikhail's arms, knowing that, for now, she was where she was meant to be.

She took a deep breath, the rise and fall of Mikhail's chest beneath her soothing her frayed nerves. Slowly, the tension began to ebb away, her body relaxing against his. The weight of the day pulled her down into the softness of the bed, her eyelids growing heavier with each passing moment. Safe. She was safe.

And with that final thought, Anya drifted off to sleep, lulled by the steady heartbeat of the man who had become her world.

Anya was jolted awake by the sound of glass shattering, the sharp crack cutting through the quiet of the night like a gunshot. For a brief moment, she was disoriented, her mind struggling to catch up to the reality of the situation. But the pounding of her heart, the rush of adrenaline coursing through her veins, told her something was terribly wrong.

She sat up in bed, her breath catching in her throat as she strained to hear over the sudden silence that followed. Heavy footsteps echoed down the hallway, the unmistakable sound of intruders moving through the apartment. Panic surged through her.

Before she could fully react, the door to the bedroom exploded open, the wood splintering from the force of the impact. Four men stormed into the room, their faces covered by dark masks, their eyes cold and unreadable. The room was suddenly alive with motion, the air thick with danger.

Mikhail sprang out of bed with the speed of a predator, his body tense, ready for a fight. He launched himself at the nearest man, tackling him to the ground with a roar that sent shivers down Anya's spine. The two men collided with the floor, the force of the impact rattling the bedframe. But there were too many of them—too many to fight off at once.

Anya screamed, her voice raw with fear, but the sound barely registered over the chaos unfolding before her. Two of the intruders rushed toward her before she could move, grabbing her roughly by the arms and yanking her out of the bed. Her body jerked forward, her feet slipping on the cold floor as she fought to resist their grip. She kicked out wildly, clawing at their hands, but they held her fast, dragging her toward the door.

"Mikhail!" she screamed, her voice breaking with desperation.

She turned her head, her eyes locking on Mikhail as he fought like a man possessed. He had one of the men pinned beneath him, his fists driving into the intruder's face with a ferocity she'd never seen before. But even as he fought, another man came at him from behind, swinging a metal rod at his head. Mikhail ducked just in time, but the distraction was enough to give the second man the upper hand. The struggle between them was brutal, bodies colliding with bone-crunching force, the sounds of grunts and fists landing echoing in the confined space.

Anya kicked harder, her heel connecting with one of her captor's legs. He grunted in pain, but his grip didn't loosen. They dragged her closer to the door, further from Mikhail, and her heart pounded in her chest with terror. She couldn't be taken—not like this, not away from him.

"Mikhail!" she screamed again, her voice hoarse now, the panic clawing at her throat. She could see the desperation in his eyes as he caught sight of her being pulled away. But there was nothing he could do—he was trapped in his own battle, the other men relentless in their assault.

The room was chaos, the sound of fists connecting with flesh, the shuffling of feet against the floor as Mikhail fought to regain control. One of the intruders had a knife, the gleam of the blade catching the faint light from the window as he swung it toward Mikhail's side. Mikhail twisted at the last second, avoiding the worst of the strike, but the edge of the blade grazed his arm, slicing through the skin. Blood welled from the wound, but Mikhail didn't falter. With a snarl of rage, he drove his elbow into the man's throat, sending him staggering back, gasping for air.

But it wasn't enough.

Anya's captors were pulling her through the door now, their grips tightening as she thrashed against them. Her mind was a blur of fear and desperation. She couldn't let them take her. She couldn't be separated from Mikhail. Not now. Not when everything between them was just beginning to feel real, solid.

Her bare feet scraped against the cold floor, and she managed to plant her heel against the doorframe, using it as leverage to try and yank herself free. One of the men cursed, pulling harder, his hand clamping down painfully on her wrist.

"Let go of me!" she cried, her voice shaking with fury and fear. She swung her other hand wildly, her nails catching skin as she scratched at his face. He grunted, his grip loosening just enough for her to twist her arm free. But the other man was stronger, his hold unyielding as he dragged her backward.

Her heart pounded in her ears, the world spinning around her as she fought with everything she had. But it wasn't enough. She was losing the fight, the strength draining from her limbs as they pulled her further from Mikhail.

"Mikhail!" she screamed one last time, her voice cracking with despair.

She saw him turn toward her, his eyes wild with desperation, but he was still locked in the brutal struggle with the two men. One of them had managed to get him in a chokehold, and Mikhail's face was turning red as he fought to free himself. But even then, his eyes were on her, the anguish clear in his gaze.

And then, before she could blink, the men dragged her out the door, her body jerking as they shoved her down the hallway toward the front entrance of the apartment. She kicked and struggled, but they were stronger, their hands like iron as they pushed her toward the waiting vehicle outside.

Her mind raced, a thousand thoughts crashing into each other as she was forced toward the car. Was this it? Was this how it ended? Where were they taking her? And Mikhail—would he survive the fight? The thought that they might have killed him made her chest tighten with grief. She couldn't lose him. Not now.

And then she heard it—the unmistakable sound of gunshots echoing from the apartment.

Her blood ran cold.

Had they killed him? Had the last glimpse of his desperate face, his body locked in a fight for both of their lives, been the final image she'd ever see of him?

Her heart hammered painfully against her ribs, the taste of fear bitter on her tongue.

Anya's body hit the seat hard as the men shoved her into the back of the car. The door slammed shut with a violent thud, sealing her in. Her breath came in ragged gasps, her pulse thundering in her ears as she struggled to make sense of what had just happened. The tires screeched against the pavement as the car peeled away from the apartment, the speed throwing her against the door. She leaned her forehead against the cold window, the glass fogging from her breath as she watched Mikhail's apartment shrink into the distance, disappearing into the night.

Panic gripped her chest, her thoughts spiraling out of control. *The gunshot.* It echoed through her mind like a death knell, ringing in her ears, haunting her. Her stomach twisted painfully as the question she dreaded more than anything else took hold of her: *Did they kill him?* Mikhail's face flashed in her mind, desperate and determined as he fought to protect her. She had watched him fight for their lives, for their future, and now… Was he gone? Was he lying on the floor of that apartment, lifeless and cold? The very thought stole the air from her lungs.

She pressed harder against the window, as if sheer force of will could somehow let her see what was happening back in the apartment. But it was gone, swallowed by the darkness. Her reflection stared back at her in the glass, her face pale and streaked with tears. The helplessness was suffocating. She had never felt so lost, so powerless.

The men in the front seat said nothing. Their silence only amplified her fear, the quiet inside the car a sharp contrast to the chaos that had just unfolded. The weight of everything crashed down on her, crushing her under its relentless pressure. *Mikhail… I can't lose him. Not now. Not ever.*

But as fear clawed at her insides, another emotion rose to the surface, fierce and burning. Anger. Hatred. It was like a fire spreading through her veins, giving her a sense of focus amid the chaos. She knew who was responsible for this. *Konstantin Morozov.* Her father. The man who was supposed to love her, to protect her, but instead, he had betrayed her in the cruelest way imaginable. He had sent these men—*his* men—to rip her away from the only happiness she had ever known. He had orchestrated this nightmare, pulling the strings from behind the scenes like a master manipulator. And for what? To control her? To destroy everything she had begun to build with Mikhail?

Her father's betrayal felt like a blade twisting in her chest. She had known he was ruthless, that he had no qualms about using her as a pawn in his brutal world, but this? This was unforgivable. Her hatred for him deepened with every mile they drove, with every second that pulled her further from Mikhail.

A tear slipped down her cheek, but it wasn't just a tear of fear—it was a tear of fury. She gritted her teeth, her hands balling into fists in her lap as the rage coursed through her. Her father had taken everything from her, had tried to control every aspect of her life. But this time, he had gone too far. This time, it was personal.

And yet, beneath the anger, beneath the hatred, there was something even stronger—a realization that hit her like a punch to the gut. She loved Mikhail. She loved him with a depth she hadn't even known she was capable of. It wasn't just lust, or the heat of their physical connection. It was more than that. He had become her protector, her anchor in the storm, and somewhere along the way, he had also become her heart.

The thought of never seeing him again, never hearing his voice or feeling his touch, sent a fresh wave of grief crashing over her. The tears came faster now, streaming down her face as the car sped through the dark streets. *I love him.* She hadn't been able to tell him. She hadn't said the words that had been building inside her for days, the words she now knew with absolute certainty. And now… now she might never get the chance.

Her body trembled with a mix of emotions—fear, anger, and a deep, aching sense of loss. She had been ready to give herself to Mikhail completely, to build a future with him, and now, in the blink of an eye, it had all been ripped away from her. The devastation was almost too much to bear.

The city blurred past the window, the lights flashing by like ghosts, but Anya didn't care where they were taking her. All she could think about was Mikhail—his face, his strength, the way he had made her feel safe even in the most dangerous of circumstances. And now he was gone. She was being torn from him, from the life they had just begun to build.

A sob escaped her, but she quickly bit down on her lip, trying to silence the sound. She couldn't show weakness. Not now. Not when everything was falling apart. She had to hold on, had to stay strong. For Mikhail. For herself. For the life that was growing inside her.

Her hands rested protectively over her stomach as the car turned onto a new road, the tires squealing against the asphalt. Her heart ached, not just for herself but for the future she had envisioned with Mikhail. A future that now seemed to be slipping further and further out of reach with every second.

But deep inside, beneath the fear, beneath the devastation, there was still a flicker of defiance. She wouldn't give up. She couldn't. Mikhail had fought for her, had risked everything to protect her, and now she would do the same. She would fight, no matter what it took. Because she wasn't just a pawn in her father's game anymore. She was Mikhail's, and he was hers. And no one—not even her father—could take that away from her.

As the car sped into the night, Anya wiped her tears, her jaw set with determination. *I will survive this. I will fight for him, for us.*

Chapter 19

Mikhail barely had time to react before the door to the bedroom burst open, splintering under the force of the intruders. His instincts kicked in the moment he saw them—four men, masked, armed, and ready to tear everything he'd built apart. They were prepared, more organized, and had the advantage of surprise. But Mikhail was no stranger to violence, no stranger to defending what was his.

The chaos exploded in seconds. Anya screamed, her voice cutting through the confusion, and Mikhail launched himself at the first man with the ferocity of someone who had everything to lose. His fist connected with the man's jaw, sending him crashing into the dresser, but Mikhail didn't stop to check the damage. He turned just in time to see the second man charging toward him, swinging a metal rod aimed straight for his head.

Mikhail ducked, the whoosh of air brushing past his ear as the rod missed by inches. He retaliated with a quick, brutal elbow to the man's ribs, the satisfying crack of bone reverberating in the small space. But the fight was far from over.

From the corner of his eye, he caught sight of Anya—two of the men had grabbed her, dragging her from the bed. She kicked and screamed, her voice filled with terror, and Mikhail's heart seized. He had to get to her. He had to stop them.

But the two men he was fighting were relentless, trained, and they weren't going to make it easy. The first man was already back on his feet, lunging at Mikhail with a blade. Mikhail sidestepped just in time, grabbing the man's arm and twisting it until the knife clattered to the floor. He delivered a swift punch to the man's throat, cutting off his air, but the second man was already on him, wrapping an arm around Mikhail's neck in a chokehold.

Mikhail's vision blurred as the pressure cut off his oxygen, but he fought back with every ounce of strength he had left. His hands clawed at the arm around his neck, muscles straining as he tried to break free. Anya's screams echoed in his ears, filling him with a surge of desperation.

The thought of losing her, of them taking her away while he lay defeated on the floor, was more than he could bear. She wasn't just someone he needed to protect—she was everything now. He loved her. The realization hit him like a punch to the gut, igniting a primal rage deep inside him.

With a guttural growl, Mikhail slammed his head back into the man behind him, the sharp impact of his skull connecting with the intruder's face. The man grunted in pain, his grip loosening just enough for Mikhail to twist free. Without hesitation, Mikhail whirled around, landing a crushing blow to the man's temple. The intruder staggered, his eyes glazing over as he crumpled to the ground.

But Mikhail had no time to celebrate the small victory. The first man was already advancing again, blood streaming from his nose but still determined to take Mikhail down. They grappled, fists flying, the sound of bone hitting flesh filling the room. Every movement, every punch was fueled by Mikhail's desperation to get to Anya.

He caught another glimpse of her—she was being dragged toward the door, her feet slipping on the floor as she struggled against the men holding her. Her eyes locked with his for a split second, wide with fear, and it sent a bolt of terror straight through him.

"Mikhail!" she screamed, her voice raw with panic.

He couldn't lose her. Not like this. Not ever.

The second man was still down, unconscious, but the first was fighting like a cornered animal, desperate to finish the job. Mikhail delivered a sharp knee to the man's stomach, doubling him over, and followed it up with a vicious uppercut that sent the man sprawling to the ground.

His lungs burned, every muscle in his body aching, but there was no time to stop. He had to get to Anya.

Mikhail's eyes darted to his gun, lying just out of reach on the floor. He lunged for it, diving across the room as the remaining intruder staggered to his feet. His fingers wrapped around the grip of the weapon, and he swung it up just as the man charged.

The gunshot echoed through the room, deafening in the small space. The man's body jerked as the bullet tore through his chest, his momentum carrying him forward for a split second before he collapsed at Mikhail's feet.

For a moment, the world seemed to stop. The only sound was Mikhail's ragged breathing, the sharp, metallic scent of blood thick in the air. His vision blurred with the adrenaline coursing through his veins, but then it cleared just as quickly, sharpened by the one thought racing through his mind—Anya.

His heart lurched as he turned toward the door, but the apartment was eerily silent now. No more screams. No more scuffling. The hallway was empty.

Panic surged through him. Where was she?

Mikhail bolted toward the front door, his boots pounding against the floor as he desperately searched for any sign of her. But the apartment was already too quiet, too still, and when he stepped out into the night, the street was empty. The car—the men who had taken Anya—were long gone.

His fists clenched at his sides as the weight of realization crashed down on him. He was too late.

They had taken her.

For a moment, he stood frozen, staring at the desolate street where the taillights had disappeared into the distance, his breath coming in ragged gasps. He'd failed. The image of Anya being dragged away, her terrified eyes pleading for him to save her, flashed in his mind, over and over again.

A low, primal growl built in Mikhail's chest. The rage inside him burned like wildfire, threatening to consume him whole. He had never felt fear like this before—fear and fury so entwined that they felt like the same emotion. The woman he loved, the woman carrying his child, had been ripped from him.

He would get her back. He would tear through anyone in his way. And he would make them pay for touching her.

Mikhail stormed back into the apartment, his entire body trembling with fury. His breaths came in harsh, uneven bursts as his gaze locked on the unconscious man slumped against the wall. One of the attackers was still alive, blood dripping from his mouth, groaning in pain as he tried to regain consciousness.

Without thinking, Mikhail walked over, his boots heavy against the floor. His vision narrowed on the man, and before any rational thought could surface, he raised his gun.

The man's eyes fluttered open, groggy, confused—but Mikhail didn't hesitate. The rage boiled over, a dark cloud that clouded every ounce of his judgment. Without a word, he pulled the trigger, and the crack of the gunshot shattered the silence again.

The attacker's head snapped back, blood splattering against the wall as his body went limp.

Mikhail stood over him, his chest still heaving, the gun hanging loosely in his grip as his pulse thundered in his ears. He felt the rage simmer beneath his skin, but it had transformed—morphed into something darker, something more controlled. The real enemy, Konstantin Morozov, was still out there. He was the one responsible for all of this. For Anya's kidnapping. For the threat looming over them all.

The apartment was too quiet now, the silence punctuated by the sound of his own labored breathing. Blood soaked into the floorboards, the metallic scent heavy in the air. The destruction around him seemed inconsequential compared to the gnawing ache in his chest.

He had failed to protect her. But this wasn't over. Not by a long shot.

Mikhail turned, holstering his gun, and crossed the room. He needed to think, to act. There was no time for hesitation. His mind was already calculating, planning, and preparing for what came next. He had to get Anya back. But he couldn't do it alone.

Reaching for his phone, Mikhail's fingers trembled for a split second before he steadied himself. He dialed Nikolai's number, his jaw clenched tight as he waited. The phone rang once, twice, then clicked.

"Mikhail." Nikolai's voice came through, rough and alert, even in the late hours.

For a brief moment, Mikhail didn't know how to start. His chest tightened with the weight of what had happened, of what he was about to say. He wasn't used to this—he wasn't used to being so desperate.

"They took her." Mikhail's voice was low, gruff, each word laced with a rage he could barely contain. "Konstantin's men… they broke into the apartment. Four of them. I managed to kill two, but the others—" His breath caught for a moment, his fists clenching at his sides. "They took her."

There was a long silence on the other end of the line, the kind that made Mikhail's blood run cold. He could almost picture Nikolai sitting there, calculating, weighing the consequences of what this meant.

"You're sure it was Konstantin's men?" Nikolai finally asked, his voice measured, calm despite the weight of the situation.

"I'm sure," Mikhail replied, his voice raw with the emotion he was trying to keep in check. "This was an organized hit. It wasn't random. They were here for her."

Another pause followed, and Mikhail could hear the unspoken tension in the silence. He knew Nikolai was processing the gravity of the situation—what it meant for the Volkov Bratva, for their standing in the war against Konstantin.

But for Mikhail, none of that mattered. This wasn't about territory or politics. This was about Anya.

"I'm going after her," Mikhail said, the words spilling out like a vow. "I'm going after Konstantin himself if I have to."

"Mikhail..." Nikolai's tone was a warning, a note of caution that sent a surge of impatience through Mikhail's veins.

"I don't care about the consequences. I don't care what I have to do, or who I have to go through. I'm getting her back." Mikhail's voice rose, his desperation clear now. "And if Konstantin wants to turn this into a war, so be it. I'll burn his entire operation to the ground."

There was a beat of silence, then the faintest sigh from Nikolai. "You're thinking with your heart, not your head. You realize what this will escalate into?"

"I know." Mikhail's voice was like steel. "But this is personal."

Nikolai let out a slow breath, the weight of the decision he was about to make hanging heavily in the air. "And if you fail?" he asked quietly, his voice carrying the cold truth of their world.

"I won't," Mikhail shot back, the determination in his voice unshakable. He couldn't afford to fail. Failure wasn't an option, not when Anya's life hung in the balance.

Another pause stretched between them, heavy and foreboding, before Nikolai finally spoke again.

"You have my blessing," he said slowly, the words carrying a sense of finality. "I'll send men to your place within the hour to help you and I'll have someone come over to clean up the apartment. But Mikhail—" His voice grew harder, his tone turning lethal. "You need to end this."

Mikhail exhaled, the tension in his shoulders easing just slightly as relief coursed through him. He had Nikolai's backing. He had the strength of the Volkov Bratva behind him. But he also knew that this was now a full-scale war, one that couldn't end with just a few dead men. This was about Konstantin, about destroying the man who had started all of this.

"Understood," Mikhail replied, his voice low, but the determination burning bright.

The line clicked dead, and Mikhail slowly lowered the phone from his ear, his heart pounding in his chest. The apartment was eerily quiet now, the aftermath of the fight still fresh, the air heavy with the scent of blood and sweat.

But he couldn't stop. He didn't have time to process the devastation around him. All that mattered now was getting Anya back.

His mind raced with plans, strategies. He needed men. Weapons. Everything at his disposal. Konstantin Morozov had made a fatal mistake, and Mikhail would make sure he paid for it in blood.

He shoved the phone into his pocket, the fire inside him blazing hotter than ever. He had Nikolai's support, but this was still his fight—his war. Anya was his. His to protect. His to love.

And Mikhail would burn the world down if that's what it took to bring her home.

Mikhail stood in the middle of his apartment, the once-familiar space now a battlefield, littered with blood and broken furniture. The adrenaline still pulsed through his veins, but beneath the physical exhaustion, there was a sharper, more dangerous energy building inside him—a primal rage, unlike anything he had ever known. It wasn't just fury; it was something far deeper, more visceral. It was love, twisted and fused with vengeance.

His hands shook as he methodically grabbed his weapons, checking each one with precision, his thoughts consumed by a single, all-encompassing goal: get Anya back. As he moved through the apartment, collecting the tools of violence that had become second nature to him over the years, his mind kept flashing to her. Anya—her soft voice, her warmth, the way she fit perfectly against him as they lay together just hours earlier. She had been right there, in his arms, and now she was gone.

And it was his fault.

The thought hit him like a punch to the gut. He had failed her. He should have been faster, stronger—he should have seen the attack coming. He should have protected her, but instead, they had taken her from him. The image of her being dragged away, her eyes wide with terror, her screams still echoing in his ears, filled him with a sickening guilt. But even more than that, it stoked the fire of his rage.

Mikhail yanked open a drawer, grabbing a knife and sliding it into his belt, his jaw clenched so tightly it hurt. He would find her. There was no other option. And when he did, there would be hell to pay for the men who dared lay a hand on her, for Konstantin Morozov, the man who had orchestrated it all.

Love. It was a word he hadn't let himself think about, not seriously, not until now. But in this moment, with the weight of what had happened pressing down on him, he knew. He loved her. Anya had become his everything. She was no longer just the woman he was supposed to protect—she was the woman he couldn't live without.

That realization made the rage burn hotter, fueling him as he grabbed his gun, loading it with quick, practiced movements. There was no room for hesitation. The second he left this apartment, it would be war. Not just between Bratvas, but personal, primal—between him and anyone who stood between him and Anya.

Mikhail's mind raced with violent thoughts, each one more savage than the last. He could picture it—Konstantin's men falling before him, one by one. Their blood on his hands, their bodies dropping like flies as he tore through them with the single-minded focus of a predator hunting his prey. There would be no mercy, no hesitation. Anyone who got in his way would be dead before they even knew what hit them.

He grabbed another gun, tucking it into the back of his waistband. There was no telling how many men Konstantin had with him, but it didn't matter. Mikhail would go through every last one of them to get to Anya.

His chest tightened as he thought about her—what she must be feeling right now. The fear. The helplessness. It made him sick to his stomach. He had to believe she was still alive, that she was still fighting, holding on for him. He had to believe that he could get to her in time, that it wasn't too late.

And when he found Konstantin...

Mikhail's fingers clenched around the gun, his knuckles turning white. He would make Konstantin suffer. The man would regret ever crossing him, regret the day he decided to use Anya as a pawn in his sick game. Mikhail would look him in the eyes before he killed him, make sure he knew exactly who had come for him, and why.

The rage was almost blinding now, a steady pulse in his veins that drowned out everything else. He moved with purpose, his entire body coiled like a spring ready to snap. Every muscle was tense, his senses heightened, every breath filled with the promise of violence. He had lived this life for years—violence, bloodshed, war. But never had it been this personal, this deeply rooted in something other than duty or loyalty. This was for her. For Anya.

Mikhail grabbed a bulletproof vest from the closet, strapping it on with quick, efficient movements. He didn't care about the risks anymore. He would take them all if it meant getting her back. His life didn't matter—not if she was gone. He would trade it in a heartbeat if it meant keeping her safe.

He paused for a moment, standing in the center of the room, his chest rising and falling with deep, controlled breaths. His mind flashed to Anya's smile, the way her eyes lit up when she laughed. The way she had looked at him earlier, as if he was her whole world.

And he realized then, with startling clarity, that he would do anything for her.

Mikhail turned toward the door, taking in the destruction around him. The apartment, which had once been a brief haven for him and Anya, now felt like a hollow shell. The bed they had shared was in disarray, the remnants of their quiet life together shattered by the violence that had invaded their world. It hadn't been much, but it had been theirs. And now, it was gone.

His chest tightened as he thought about the moments they had shared here—the laughter, the intimacy, the quiet nights when it had felt like, just for a moment, the world outside didn't exist. But now it was time to face reality. Anya was gone, and if he didn't act quickly, she could be lost forever.

He heard the sound of cars pulling up out front and he knew his help had arrived. He moved toward the door, his body tense with purpose. Each step felt heavier than the last, but there was no room for doubt. This wasn't just about Anya's safety. It was about their future together.

Mikhail paused for a second, glancing over his shoulder at the apartment one last time. The space, now wrecked and bloodied, had been their sanctuary for a brief time. But that time was over.

His heart ached with the weight of everything that had happened, the guilt of not protecting her gnawing at him, but there was no time to dwell on it. He was a man on a mission now. There was no room for regret, only action.

Taking a deep breath, he steeled himself.

As he stepped over the threshold and into the night, the cold air hit his face, a stark reminder of the reality that awaited him. His jaw set, his muscles tense, and his mind focused on only one thing: getting Anya back.

This rescue wasn't just about her survival. It was about the life they could have together—a life that had barely begun. And Mikhail was ready to fight for it with everything he had.

With one final glance at the apartment, Mikhail set off into the darkness, the primal need to save her guiding every step.

Chapter 20

The car came to a screeching halt, jolting Anya forward, her heart pounding as the reality of her situation settled like a heavy stone in her chest. The sharp scent of leather and sweat filled the cramped vehicle, her captors' voices low and steady, as if kidnapping her was just another routine job. She tried to breathe through the growing panic, but it felt impossible—the walls of the car seemed to close in on her, trapping her in this nightmare.

Before she could fully prepare herself for what came next, the door flung open. Rough hands grabbed her by the arms, yanking her out of the car and onto the gravel drive. Her feet stumbled beneath her, the cold bite of the night air cutting through the thin fabric of her clothing as she fought to keep her balance. She looked up, her breath catching in her throat as she saw it—the tall iron gates of the Morozov estate, standing like sentinels before her.

Her stomach twisted with dread. She knew this place well. It was once her home, a place where she'd lived under the constant shadow of her father's control. Now, it felt more like a prison, the heavy gates and sprawling lawns a cruel reminder

of what she had escaped—only to be dragged
back.

The two men gripping her arms didn't slow their
pace as they marched her toward the stone steps
leading to the front door. She dug her heels into the
gravel, resisting their forceful pulls, but it was futile.
They were stronger, more prepared for her
struggle. She had no chance against them, not
physically at least.

Her thoughts raced, her mind a chaotic storm of
fear, anger, and hatred. The familiar crunch of
gravel under her shoes was a sound she used to
associate with her father's return home, a signal to
brace herself for his cold detachment, his icy
commands. Now, that sound was a cruel mockery
of the life she'd thought she could escape. The
estate stood silent and imposing, the dim light from
the windows casting eerie shadows across the
perfectly manicured lawn.

They dragged her up the steps, and the wooden
door creaked open, revealing the grand entryway
beyond. Anya's breath hitched as they pulled her
inside. The air here was heavy, oppressive with the
weight of her father's control. She remembered the
countless times she had stood in this very hallway,
under the watchful eyes of her father's guards, her
every move scrutinized, her every word calculated
to avoid his wrath.

But things were different now. She was different now.

The men's grips tightened as they steered her down the familiar corridor, her body tense with the weight of what was to come. The walls seemed to close in around her, the portraits of her family staring down at her like silent judges. Her heart pounded in her chest, her pulse racing as the inevitable approached. She knew where they were taking her—to her father's study, the very place where he had always issued his commands, as if his word was law.

As they neared the heavy wooden doors of the study, Anya felt the oppressive weight of her father's presence bearing down on her. The air felt colder here, the scent of polished wood and old leather hanging in the air like a ghost of the past. Her stomach churned with a mixture of terror and defiance. She knew what her father wanted—to regain control, to force her back into the life she had so desperately tried to escape. But she wasn't the same obedient daughter she had once been. She wouldn't let him win this time.

Her mind flickered to Mikhail. Where was he? Was he still alive? Was he coming for her? The thought of him fueled her, gave her the strength to keep resisting, even as the men pulled her closer to the doors. She could still feel the warmth of his embrace from earlier, the safety she had felt in his arms. He had promised to protect her, and she believed him. She had to believe he was on his way, that he survived, that he wouldn't let her face this alone.

The doors to the study loomed in front of her now, tall and imposing, much like her father himself. Her heart thudded painfully in her chest, the fear gnawing at her insides, but alongside that fear, there was something else—anger. How dare her father do this to her? How dare he treat her like a possession to be reclaimed, like a piece of property he could control?

Her body tensed, the fight building inside her. She wasn't going to walk into that room and surrender. No, not this time. She was no longer the submissive daughter who obeyed without question. She was stronger now, hardened by the life she had built with Mikhail, by the love she had found in his arms. Her father may think he could take that from her, but he was wrong. She wasn't a pawn in his game anymore.

One of the men knocked on the door, the sound echoing down the hallway like a death knell. Anya's chest tightened, her mind racing as she braced herself for what was to come. She didn't know what awaited her on the other side of that door, but she knew one thing for certain—she wasn't the same woman who had left this house. She had found something stronger, something worth fighting for, and she wasn't going to let her father strip that away from her.

The door creaked open, the dim light from inside spilling out into the hallway. The men pulled her forward, their hands firm on her arms as they pushed her into the study. Anya's breath caught in her throat as she stepped inside, the familiar scent of whiskey and cigar smoke hitting her like a wave. Her father was waiting.

Anya's mind snapped to one thought: Mikhail. She had to believe he was coming. She had to hold on, to resist.

The heavy door of her father's study slammed shut behind Anya, the sound reverberating through the room like the closing of a prison cell. She stumbled slightly as the men pushed her forward, her breath catching in her throat as she looked around the familiar, oppressive space. The dark wood-paneled walls, the towering bookshelves lined with expensive, unread volumes, the thick Persian rug beneath her feet—it was all the same as she remembered. A room designed to intimidate, to enforce control.

And there he was. Konstantin Morozov, her father, sitting behind his grand mahogany desk, a glass of whiskey in hand, his eyes cold and calculating as they settled on her. He looked every bit the powerful man who ruled an empire, his posture relaxed, as if he had been waiting for this moment with all the confidence of a man who knew he would win. He always won.

The moment Anya's eyes met his, her stomach twisted with a mixture of dread and anger. Fear clawed at her chest, but something else rose within her too—defiance. She had spent her entire life being molded into the obedient daughter, the perfect extension of his will, never questioning, never fighting back. But that girl no longer existed.

"Ah," Konstantin said, his voice calm and unnervingly composed. He set his glass down with a soft clink, his eyes never leaving hers. "Anya. Finally, back where you belong."

The air in the room felt colder, heavier. Anya's heart pounded in her chest, her pulse thrumming in her ears as she stared at the man who had shaped so much of her life. The man who now intended to control her future—who had already decided her fate without so much as asking what she wanted.

Her father stood up slowly, adjusting his suit jacket as he moved around the desk with an air of casual authority. He looked at her like she was an object, something to be managed and dealt with, not a person with her own desires, her own will.

"I've thought long and hard about this situation," he continued, his tone disturbingly measured. "The matter of the baby will be taken care of. You don't need to worry yourself about it. I'll handle everything, as I always do."

Anya's body went rigid at his words, her mind reeling. He spoke of her child—the life growing inside her—with the same cold detachment he used when talking about business deals or strategic alliances. Her hands balled into fists at her sides, trembling with the force of the emotions coursing through her. Fear. Rage. And something more—something primal and protective.

"If it's a family you want," Konstantin went on, as if he hadn't noticed the fire building in her eyes, "I'll find you a suitable husband. Someone who can give me the heir this empire deserves. This isn't your decision, Anya. It never was."

His voice was soft but lethal, like a blade sliding between her ribs. And for a moment, just a moment, the old fear bubbled up inside her—the fear that had always silenced her when she was younger, the fear that made her bend to his will without question. But as quickly as it rose, it vanished, replaced by a burning defiance that she could no longer suppress.

Anya's vision blurred with anger, her breath coming in short, sharp bursts. She wasn't a child anymore. She wasn't his pawn, his tool to be used and discarded as he saw fit. She had chosen her path, and it wasn't with him.

Her father looked at her, his cold eyes narrowing as if he sensed the shift in her. His lips pressed into a thin line, his control absolute, as if daring her to speak against him.

The words tore from her throat before she could stop them, her voice shaking but fierce. "No."

Konstantin's gaze sharpened, his body stilling, the air in the room growing thick with tension. "What did you say?"

Anya swallowed hard, but there was no going back now. The fear was still there, gnawing at the edges of her mind, but something stronger was driving her forward. She straightened her spine, forcing her chin up as she met his gaze head-on.

"I said no," she repeated, her voice steadier now, her heart pounding with defiance. "I'm not going to let you control me anymore. I'm not your daughter—not in the way you think I am. I've chosen my life, and it's with Mikhail. I belong to him now. Not you."

The words hung in the air, heavy with finality, and Anya braced herself for her father's reaction. For the first time in her life, she had openly defied him. She had torn down the walls he had built around her, thrown off the chains of his control, and claimed her own future.

For a moment, Konstantin just stared at her, his eyes darkening with something she couldn't quite read. His jaw tightened, the lines of his face growing sharp as he processed her words. And then, slowly, his expression hardened, his eyes narrowing to slits.

"You foolish girl," he hissed, his voice low and dangerous. "You think you can just walk away from me? You think you can choose some thug over your own blood? Over your family?"

Anya's heart pounded in her chest, but she didn't back down. "Mikhail is my family now," she said, her voice firm. "He's the father of my child, and I would rather die than let you take that away from me."

Her father's face twisted into a snarl, his fists clenching at his sides. "You don't know what you're saying," he growled. "You've always been obedient, Anya. You've always known your place. But this… this ends now. You will have no say in what happens next. The baby will be taken care of, and I will decide who you marry. You are my daughter, and you will do as I command."

Anya's body trembled, the weight of his words crashing over her like a tidal wave. But she wasn't the girl who had always bowed to his will. She had found strength, found love in Mikhail, and she couldn't go back to being the puppet her father had controlled for so long.

Before she could respond, the sharp crack of gunfire echoed through the house.

Anya froze, her heart leaping into her throat as the sound reverberated through the walls. Her father's expression flickered with something like confusion, but Anya knew immediately what it was. Mikhail. He had come for her.

"That's him," she whispered, her voice trembling with both fear and hope. "That's Mikhail. He's come for me."

Konstantin's eyes darkened, his face twisting with rage. But Anya barely saw him anymore. Her thoughts were on Mikhail—the man who had promised to protect her, to keep her safe. The man who had risked everything to come after her.

She just prayed he wasn't too late.

The study door exploded open with a deafening crash, the force of it reverberating through the walls. Anya's heart leapt into her throat, her pulse pounding in her ears as her eyes darted to the doorway. There he was. Mikhail. His broad frame filled the space, bloodstained and breathing hard, his dark eyes locking onto hers the moment he stepped inside. Relief surged through her, but it was tempered by the violence that clung to the air around him. Mikhail looked like a man possessed—like a storm given form.

Her father's grip on her tightened instantly, yanking her roughly back against his chest, his arm coiling around her throat like a vice. She gasped, her hands instinctively clawing at his arm, but his hold was unyielding. The cold, familiar scent of her father's cologne filled her senses, mixed now with the sharp tang of gunpowder and blood. The moment stretched into an eternity, the air between them charged with tension so thick it was suffocating.

Konstantin's voice, low and venomous, cut through the silence. "Stay back, Mikhail. Unless you want to see her dead."

Mikhail didn't move. His eyes flicked between Anya and Konstantin, calculating, his jaw clenched so tightly the muscles in his neck stood out in sharp relief. His chest heaved with every breath, but he was utterly still, his entire body coiled with barely contained rage.

The sounds of gunfire echoed from the hallways beyond, but in the study, everything seemed to narrow down to this moment—this confrontation between Mikhail and Konstantin. Anya could feel her father's breath hot against her ear, his grip tightening as if daring Mikhail to take another step.

"You think you can take her from me?" Konstantin spat, his voice dripping with contempt. "She's mine. She's always been mine, and she always will be."

Mikhail's gaze hardened, his voice low and lethal when he finally spoke. "She doesn't belong to you."

The words were simple, but the weight behind them was undeniable. Anya could feel the tension ratchet up, a deadly promise hanging in the air between the two men.

Konstantin sneered, his grip tightening around Anya's throat until she could barely breathe. "You're nothing but a brute—a thug. You'll never be anything more. Anya is Morozov. She belongs to this family, to me. You think you can walk into my home and take her from me? You think you've won?"

Mikhail's eyes burned with fury, but his voice remained calm, a dangerous undercurrent beneath the surface. "I'm not here to take her from you. I'm here to end you."

For a brief moment, fear flickered across Konstantin's face, but it was gone as quickly as it appeared. His arm shifted slightly, his grip loosening just enough for Anya to draw a shaky breath.

And that was when Anya felt it—the shift inside her. The fear that had controlled her for so long, the terror of her father's wrath, it all melted away. In its place, a new strength rose. Mikhail wasn't the only one who had changed her. She had changed herself. She wasn't the obedient, terrified daughter anymore. She was something more. And she was no longer willing to be a pawn in Konstantin's game.

Without thinking, without hesitation, Anya sank her teeth into her father's arm with all the force she could muster. The taste of blood filled her mouth, hot and metallic, as she bit down hard, her teeth cutting into his flesh.

Konstantin roared in pain, jerking back instinctively and loosening his hold on her. Anya twisted free of his grip, stumbling forward as the sudden release of pressure left her dizzy. Her heart thundered in her chest, the adrenaline coursing through her like fire, but she didn't stop. She couldn't stop.

Konstantin's furious scream filled the room, his hand clutching his bleeding arm as he glared at her with pure malice. "You little—!"

But he didn't get the chance to finish.

The sound of a gunshot rang out, loud and final, cutting through the tension like a knife. Anya's breath caught in her throat as she whipped around, her eyes wide with shock. She saw Mikhail standing there, his gun raised, his face set in grim determination.

Another shot fired.

Then another.

Each bullet struck true, slamming into Konstantin's chest with brutal force. His body jerked with the impact, his face twisting in disbelief as he staggered backward, blood blossoming across his pristine white shirt. For a moment, he swayed on his feet, his eyes wide with shock and rage.

Then, slowly, he crumpled to the floor, his body hitting the ground with a sickening thud. The room fell into a heavy, suffocating silence, broken only by the sound of Anya's ragged breathing.

Her father was dead.

Anya stared at the lifeless body, her mind struggling to catch up with what had just happened. She had dreamed of this moment—of being free from her father's control—but now that it was here, it felt surreal. Unbelievable.

Her hands shook at her sides, her heart racing as the reality of the situation began to sink in. Konstantin Morozov, the man who had ruled her life with an iron fist, was gone. Mikhail had killed him. And she... she had played her part.

Her gaze shifted to Mikhail, who was still standing over Konstantin's body, his gun lowered but his face hard with resolve. His chest heaved with the effort of the fight, blood staining his shirt, but his eyes were only on her.

"Anya," he whispered, his voice rough with emotion.

She took a shaky step forward, her body trembling from the adrenaline, from the overwhelming relief that flooded through her veins. The man who had been her tormentor, her father, was gone. And Mikhail—her protector, her lover—had come for her.

Anya's legs gave out, and she collapsed into Mikhail's arms, her body pressing into his as he wrapped her tightly against his chest. His warmth, his strength, enveloped her, grounding her in the reality of what had just happened.

"It's over," Mikhail whispered into her hair, his voice rough and strained. "You're safe now."

Anya clung to him, her face buried in his chest as the tears finally came. It was over. It was really, truly over. And for the first time in what felt like forever, she could breathe.

But even as she cried into Mikhail's arms, the weight of everything that had happened pressed down on her. Yes, her father was dead, and yes, she was free from his control. But the battle wasn't over. There were still enemies out there, still threats lurking in the shadows.

But for now, in this moment, she let herself be held. She let herself feel the relief, the safety of being in Mikhail's arms. Because in this moment, they had won.

And that was all that mattered.

Chapter 21

Mikhail's apartment was quiet, the stillness of the room a stark contrast to the chaos they had just left behind. The moment Anya stepped inside, the familiar surroundings washed over her like a balm. The tension from the night still lingered in the air, but there was a deeper sense of calm now, one that came with knowing they had survived. They were both here, alive, and together.

Anya's heart slowed its frantic pace as she took in the details of the apartment—the same walls, the same furniture, but everything felt different now. The space that had once been a place of refuge from danger now felt like something more. For the first time, it wasn't just a temporary shelter. It was home.

She could feel the shift in the air between her and Mikhail as they stood in the entrance. The connection they shared had deepened, something that was far beyond the heat of lust or the protective instincts Mikhail had always shown her. Now, it was rooted in something stronger—trust, loyalty, and the fragile beginnings of love.

Mikhail closed the door behind them, locking it with a sense of finality, as if closing the door on the nightmare that had almost torn them apart. His broad shoulders slumped slightly, the weight of the night's events finally settling in. For a moment, he stayed by the door, his hand resting on the knob as he exhaled a deep breath. The exhaustion was clear in the lines of his face, but it was more than just physical fatigue. The emotional toll had been heavy, too.

Anya watched him closely, feeling her heart ache for the man who had fought so hard for her, the man who had killed to keep her safe. Mikhail had always been a protector, but now, as he stood before her, there was a vulnerability in his silence that tugged at her. This was no longer about duty. It was about something much more personal.

"I'm sorry," Mikhail said quietly, his voice barely above a whisper. His eyes remained fixed on the floor for a moment before he looked up at her. "I should have—"

"Don't," Anya interrupted, shaking her head as she stepped toward him. Her hand reached for his, her fingers sliding into his as she gave him a gentle squeeze. "You don't have to apologize. You saved me."

Her words seemed to break through the wall of guilt that had settled over him. He met her gaze, those deep brown eyes softening as he searched her face. "I almost lost you," he admitted, his voice rough with emotion. "I... I don't think I've ever been so afraid."

Anya's heart clenched at his words. Mikhail had always been so strong, so composed, even in the most dangerous situations. To hear him admit his fear now, after everything, made her realize just how much she meant to him. He wasn't just a hardened enforcer of the Bratva anymore—he was a man who had risked everything for her.

"You didn't lose me," she whispered, stepping closer until her body pressed against his. She tilted her head up, looking into his eyes. "I'm here, Mikhail. We both are."

He nodded, his jaw clenched as he struggled to find the right words. The intensity in his gaze spoke volumes, but Anya could sense there was something else he wanted to say—something deeper.

"I've never felt this way before," he finally said, his voice low and rough, as if each word was pulled from somewhere deep within him. "About anyone. Not like this." His free hand came up, gently cupping her face, his thumb brushing lightly against her cheek. "The thought of losing you... I couldn't stand it. I don't think I've ever been so terrified."

Anya leaned into his touch, her chest tightening with emotion. She could feel the rawness in his confession, the honesty of it cutting through all the chaos and violence that had surrounded them. For so long, she had seen Mikhail as this untouchable force, a man made of steel and shadows. But now, she saw the man underneath all that—a man who cared for her deeply, who was as vulnerable as she was.

"I'm not going anywhere," she said softly, her voice steady despite the emotion swelling inside her. "Not without you."

Mikhail's hand tightened around hers, his grip firm but gentle, as if grounding himself in her presence. "Anya, I—" His voice cracked slightly, but he didn't look away. "I love you."

The words hung in the air between them, heavy and powerful. For a moment, Anya couldn't breathe. She had sensed the shift in their relationship, felt the bond between them grow stronger with each passing day, but hearing those words from Mikhail—words she never thought she'd hear from him—made her heart swell with a warmth she hadn't realized she was craving.

"I love you," he repeated, his voice firmer this time, as if he needed to say it again to make it real, to make sure she understood. "I've never said that to anyone before. But I need you to know it. I love you, Anya."

Tears welled up in her eyes, not from sadness or fear, but from the overwhelming joy of hearing those words from the man she had come to care for so deeply. Without thinking, she wrapped her arms around his neck, pulling him close as she pressed her lips to his. The kiss was soft at first, but it quickly deepened, their emotions pouring into each other as they clung to one another.

When they finally pulled apart, breathless but smiling, Anya rested her forehead against his. "I love you, too," she whispered, her voice thick with emotion. "I've loved you for a while now, but I didn't know how to say it."

Mikhail's arms wrapped around her, holding her tightly against his chest. For a long moment, they just stood there, wrapped in each other's arms, the weight of everything they'd been through slowly melting away.

For the first time since all of this had begun, Anya felt truly safe. Safe in Mikhail's arms, safe in the knowledge that they loved each other, and safe in the belief that, no matter what came next, they would face it together.

The air between them had shifted, thick with the weight of everything they had just confessed to one another. The raw emotion of Mikhail's words—his declaration of love—wrapped around Anya, grounding her in a way she hadn't felt in so long. Her heart was racing, but not from fear. It was from the warmth spreading through her, the undeniable pull toward him that had only grown stronger.

They stood there for a moment, still wrapped in each other's arms, the silence between them comfortable, heavy with the anticipation of what was to come. Anya tilted her head up, her gaze meeting Mikhail's, and in his deep brown eyes, she saw the same longing mirrored back at her. It was no longer just a physical need—it was deeper, more profound, a hunger for connection, for reassurance, for love.

She moved first, her hand sliding up to cup his cheek, her thumb brushing gently across his rough skin. His eyes darkened with desire, and before she could say another word, Mikhail's lips were on hers, slow and tender, as if savoring the moment, as if they had all the time in the world. His kiss was gentle, but she could feel the passion simmering just beneath the surface, ready to ignite at any second.

Her heart fluttered in her chest as she pressed herself closer to him, her body molding against his like it was where she had always belonged. His hands slid down her back, possessive and firm, as if he was holding on to the most precious thing in his world. And to Mikhail, she was.

The kiss deepened, becoming more urgent, more heated, as their emotions spilled over. His fingers threaded through her hair, tugging gently as his other hand gripped her waist, pulling her against him with a fervor that made her knees weak. Anya moaned softly into his mouth, her body arching toward him, her need for him growing with every second. It wasn't just about lust anymore—it was about the overwhelming love that had blossomed between them, the trust, the safety.

Mikhail broke the kiss just long enough to catch his breath, his forehead resting against hers as they stood there, their breaths mingling in the quiet space. His eyes were dark with desire, his voice low and rough when he spoke. "I need you, Anya," he whispered, his words sending a shiver down her spine. "I need you so much."

"I'm yours," she breathed, the words coming out before she could think. And she meant it. In every way that mattered, she belonged to him—body, heart, and soul.

The tension between them snapped, and Mikhail's lips found hers again, this time with more intensity. His hands roamed over her body, sliding up under her shirt, his rough palms grazing the bare skin of her back, her ribs, her waist. The feeling of his touch, so possessive and tender, made her gasp, her own hands moving to the hem of his shirt, tugging it up and over his head.

Her fingers trembled slightly as she tossed the shirt aside, revealing the hard planes of his chest, the tattoos that adorned his skin, the scars that told the story of the life he had lived. She had seen him like this before, but now, it felt different. Now, he was hers. Completely.

Mikhail's hands slid down to the waistband of her pants, his fingers deftly unbuttoning them before he pulled them down her legs in one smooth motion. She stepped out of them, her heart pounding as she stood before him, wearing nothing but her underwear. His gaze traveled over her body, a mixture of desire and reverence in his eyes.

"You're so beautiful," he murmured, his voice rough with emotion. He stepped closer, his hand reaching up to gently cup her face, his thumb brushing across her cheek. "You have no idea how much I've wanted this."

Her breath hitched at his words, the sincerity in his voice sending warmth flooding through her. She leaned into his touch, her own hands sliding down his chest, her fingers tracing the lines of his muscles before moving to the waistband of his jeans. She undid them slowly, teasingly, her fingers brushing against the bare skin of his abdomen as she pushed them down, revealing the hard, straining length of him.

Mikhail groaned softly at the contact, his eyes darkening as he kicked off his jeans, his hands immediately finding their way back to her body. He kissed her again, harder this time, his mouth hungry as his hands roamed over her curves, pulling her closer, pressing her against him as if he couldn't get enough.

Anya gasped as his fingers slipped beneath the waistband of her underwear, his touch sending sparks of pleasure shooting through her. He slid them down her legs slowly, deliberately, his lips never leaving hers as he undressed her completely. She stood before him, bare and vulnerable, but she had never felt safer, never felt more desired.

Mikhail's hands were everywhere, exploring her skin, his touch both gentle and possessive. He pulled her closer, his lips trailing down her neck, his teeth grazing the sensitive skin there, drawing soft moans from her lips. His mouth moved lower, over her collarbone, down to her breasts, his lips closing around one of her nipples, his tongue flicking over the sensitive peak.

Anya moaned, her hands tangling in his hair as her head fell back, her body arching into his touch. The pleasure was overwhelming, every flick of his tongue sending waves of heat coursing through her. His other hand slid down her body, his fingers finding her wet folds, rubbing her clit in slow, deliberate circles.

She gasped, her body reacting instantly as Mikhail thrust two fingers inside her, his thumb swirling over her slit, grazing her clit with each slow, deliberate movement. He curled his fingers perfectly, finding the spot that made her toes curl and her breath hitch in her throat. The pleasure shot through her,

her hips bucking instinctively as he maintained the steady rhythm, driving her higher with every stroke.

Her moans grew louder, the sound echoing in the quiet room, but Mikhail didn't rush. His mouth continued to tease her breasts, his lips closing around one hardened nipple as his tongue flicked over it, sending shivers down her spine. His fingers worked her in slow, tantalizing circles, the pad of his thumb brushing against her clit in a way that made her body tremble.

"Mikhail," she whimpered, her voice trembling with need. "Please…"

He growled softly in response, lifting his head to look at her, his eyes burning with desire. "Tell me what you want," he whispered, his fingers never stopping their torturous rhythm. "Tell me, Anya."

"I want you," she gasped, her hands gripping his shoulders as her hips bucked against his hand. "I want all of you."

A slow, satisfied smile spread across his lips, and he pressed a gentle kiss to her lips before whispering, "You'll have me, every part of me."

And as he laid her down on the bed, his body covering hers, she knew he meant it. Mikhail hovered above her, his gaze locked onto hers, the intensity in his brown eyes making her heart race. Every inch of him was focused on her, and as he positioned himself between her legs, the heat between them became palpable. He moved slowly, deliberately, lowering himself until his cock pressed against her entrance. Anya's breath caught in her throat as she felt the tip of him push inside, the sensation electric and overwhelming.

Mikhail paused for a moment, his eyes still holding hers, as if silently asking for permission, as if making sure she knew that this moment was about more than just physical need. It was about everything they had been through, the danger, the pain, the fear—but also the love and trust that had grown between them. He wanted her to know that she was safe with him, that she was cherished.

Anya's fingers gripped his shoulders, her nails digging into his skin as she nodded, her lips parting in anticipation. She wanted him. She needed him. Every part of her body ached for him to claim her completely. And then, with a slow, deliberate thrust, Mikhail pushed deeper inside her, filling her inch by inch.

The sensation of him stretching her, filling her completely, was overwhelming. Anya's eyes fluttered closed as she moaned softly, her hips instinctively lifting to meet him. Mikhail moved slowly at first, his body trembling slightly as he savored the tightness of her warmth around him. His hands gripped her hips, holding her steady as he began to move, each slow thrust deep and purposeful, making sure she felt every inch of him.

Her legs wrapped around his waist, pulling him closer, wanting more of him. Their bodies moved together in perfect rhythm, a slow, steady build of heat and intensity. Mikhail leaned down, pressing his lips against her neck, his breath hot against her skin as he kissed her, his teeth grazing lightly across her throat. Anya's moans grew louder, her body responding to him with every thrust, every touch.

"Mikhail," she whispered, her voice trembling with need. "Please... more."

Her plea was all he needed. Mikhail's pace quickened, his hips driving into her harder now, each thrust deeper than the last. The bed creaked beneath them as their bodies moved together, faster and more urgent, their need for each other overwhelming everything else. Anya clung to him, her fingers digging into his back as she gasped for air, the pleasure building inside her, higher and higher with each movement.

Mikhail's breath was ragged in her ear, his hands gripping her hips so tightly she knew there would be bruises, but she didn't care. She wanted it. She wanted all of him, every ounce of his strength, his power, his love. The primal need in his movements, the way he claimed her with every thrust, made her feel alive in a way she had never known before.

His cock was relentless, driving into her harder and faster, pushing her closer and closer to the edge. Anya's body responded instinctively, her hips lifting to meet his thrusts, her back arching off the bed as the pleasure built to an unbearable intensity. She could feel the tension coiling inside her, tighter and tighter, her body trembling with the anticipation of release.

"Mikhail," she moaned again, her voice desperate now. "I'm so close…"

His response was a low growl, his lips finding hers in a heated kiss as he continued to drive into her, his pace quickening as he brought them both closer to the edge. The intensity between them was all-consuming, the sensation of his body moving inside hers, the sound of their heavy breathing and moans filling the room.

Anya's heart pounded in her chest, her hands clutching at him, her nails raking down his back as the pleasure surged through her, wave after wave of heat crashing over her, pushing her closer and closer to the brink.

"I've got you," Mikhail whispered, his voice hoarse with need. "You're mine."

And with those words, she fell apart.

Her orgasm hit her with blinding intensity, her body shaking uncontrollably as the pleasure tore through her, her moans turning into cries as she clung to him, her hips bucking wildly beneath him. The release was overwhelming, her body tightening around him as wave after wave of ecstasy crashed over her, her mind going blank with the sheer force of it.

Mikhail wasn't far behind. He thrust into her one last time, deep and hard, his body shuddering as he reached his own climax, his release mingling with hers as they came together. The intensity of their shared orgasm left them both breathless, their bodies trembling as they held onto each other, lost in the moment.

He collapsed onto her, his weight pressing her into the mattress, his breath hot against her skin as they both struggled to catch their breath. Anya wrapped her arms around him, pulling him closer, wanting to feel every part of him, wanting to hold onto this moment for as long as possible. She could still feel the aftershocks of her orgasm pulsing through her, her body still trembling from the intensity of their lovemaking.

Mikhail's lips brushed against her neck, soft and tender now, a stark contrast to the raw intensity of the moment before. His body was still inside hers, their connection still strong, still unbroken. Anya could feel his heart pounding against her chest, could hear the soft rasp of his breath in her ear, and she knew that this wasn't just about sex. This was about something much deeper, something that went beyond physical need.

She was his, and he was hers. Completely.

As they lay together, the quiet of the room wrapped around them like a soft blanket, their bodies still intertwined, Mikhail's steady breathing the only sound in the stillness. Anya rested her head on his chest, the strong, rhythmic beat of his heart grounding her in the moment. She closed her eyes, letting herself sink into the peace that filled the space between them, her body still humming from the intensity of their lovemaking.

It was strange, this feeling of calm that settled over her, considering everything they had been through. Just hours ago, her world had been torn apart—she had been kidnapped, ripped away from the man she had come to love, unsure if she would ever see him again. The terror she had felt was still fresh in her mind, but now, in the safety of Mikhail's arms, it felt distant, like a nightmare that couldn't touch her anymore.

Mikhail's hand slid lazily through her hair, his fingers brushing against her scalp in a soothing rhythm. His touch was gentle, so different from the intensity he had shown earlier, and it reminded her of just how multifaceted he was. He could be fierce, dangerous, and possessive, but he could also be tender, loving, and protective. He was everything to her now, and the realization settled deep in her chest, warm and steady, like the beat of his heart beneath her ear.

"I never thought it would be like this," she whispered, her voice barely audible in the quiet room.

Mikhail's hand stilled for a moment, then resumed its soft caress. "Like what?"

Anya lifted her head slightly, her emerald green eyes meeting his dark brown ones. "I never thought I could feel this way about anyone. Especially not about someone like you."

He raised an eyebrow, the corner of his mouth quirking into a small, amused smile. "Someone like me?"

"You know what I mean," she said softly, her hand tracing lazy circles on his chest. "You're dangerous. Fierce. Everything about you should terrify me. But it doesn't. It never has."

Mikhail's gaze softened, his hand moving from her hair to cup her cheek, his thumb brushing against her skin. "You're not afraid of me?"

She shook her head. "No. Not anymore. Because I know you, Mikhail. I know your heart, even if you try to hide it from the rest of the world."

For a moment, they simply stared at each other, the weight of their journey—everything they had been through, everything they had survived—hanging between them. Anya thought back to the first time she had met him, how they had been nothing but enemies, both trapped in a world of violence and power. She had been so afraid then, so unsure of what her future held. But now, here in this moment, she felt none of that fear. All she felt was love.

"I'll never let anything happen to you," Mikhail said quietly, his voice filled with a fierce determination that sent a shiver down her spine. "You're mine, Anya. And I'll protect you. Always."

Anya's heart swelled at his words, a rush of warmth spreading through her. She believed him. She trusted him with her life, and that was something she had never imagined she would feel for anyone. Not after everything she had been through.

"I know," she whispered, her fingers tightening on his chest. "And I'm yours, Mikhail. Completely."

They lay there in the quiet for a while longer, the world outside forgotten, the dangers they had faced fading into the background. Anya let herself relax into the feeling of being held, of being safe. For so long, she had been running—running from her father, from her past, from the life she had never wanted. But now, she realized, there was no more running. This was her new life, her new beginning, and it was with Mikhail.

She pressed a soft kiss to his chest, the warmth of his skin against her lips anchoring her to the present. She had found her place, her home. It wasn't the apartment they were in or the life they had left behind—it was Mikhail. He was her home. He was the place where she felt safe, loved, and cherished.

Anya closed her eyes, her body sinking deeper into his as the exhaustion of the day began to catch up with her. But this time, as sleep began to pull her under, she felt none of the anxiety or fear that had haunted her for so long. Instead, she felt only peace, a deep, unwavering sense of belonging. She was exactly where she was meant to be.

In Mikhail's arms. Safe. Loved. And finally, complete.

Chapter 22

The fluorescent lights of the hospital room hummed softly, contrasting with the tense, quiet energy that filled the air. Anya lay in the hospital bed, her breathing labored but steady as she clutched Mikhail's hand. His strong fingers were intertwined with hers, and despite his usual stoic demeanor, there was an unmistakable flicker of anxiety in his deep brown eyes. This moment—this life they were about to bring into the world—was unlike anything he had ever faced before.

"You're doing great," he murmured, his voice low and soothing. He had faced violence, betrayal, and the constant danger of the Bratva world, but nothing compared to this. This was a different kind of battle, and the stakes felt higher than ever.

Anya squeezed his hand, her eyes locking onto his for a brief second. She drew strength from him, knowing that, despite the pain, she wasn't alone. Mikhail had been there for her in every way that mattered. As the contractions came harder and faster, she gritted her teeth, trying to focus on the rhythm of her breathing, but her mind kept slipping into thoughts of everything they'd been through to get here.

Seven months had passed since Konstantin's death, and though the memories of that violent night still haunted her dreams, she had found solace in Mikhail's presence. He had become her rock, her protector, and now they were about to bring their son into the world.

The nurse's voice broke through her haze of thoughts. "Okay, Anya, on the next contraction, we need you to push."

Anya's heart raced, fear and excitement swirling together in her chest. She nodded, gripping Mikhail's hand tighter as another wave of pain hit her. She bore down, pushing with all her strength, her entire body consumed with the effort. Mikhail's calm presence steadied her, his thumb gently rubbing the back of her hand.

"You've got this," he whispered, his eyes full of encouragement and something else—something deeper. For Mikhail, this wasn't just about bringing a baby into the world. This was the moment his life would change forever. He had never imagined this for himself—a family, a child, love. But now, as he watched Anya fighting to give life to their son, he felt something inside him soften.

With another push, Anya let out a sharp cry, her body trembling with the strain. The room buzzed with quiet urgency, and then, suddenly, there was a new sound—a baby's first cry.

The nurse smiled as she held up the tiny, wriggling form, still covered in a slick coat of birth. "It's a boy," she announced, the joy in her voice filling the room.

Anya collapsed back onto the bed, her body weak with exhaustion, but her heart soared as the baby's cries filled her ears. Tears welled in her eyes, and she glanced at Mikhail, who was staring at their son with a look she had never seen on his face before. Awe. Pure, unfiltered awe.

Mikhail's chest rose and fell with uneven breaths, and for a moment, he seemed frozen in place, his mind struggling to wrap around the reality of what had just happened. Then, as the nurse placed the baby into Anya's arms, he moved closer, his large frame casting a protective shadow over both of them.

Anya gazed down at their newborn son, her heart swelling with a love so fierce it brought more tears to her eyes. The baby's tiny fingers curled instinctively, and his face, red and wrinkled, was the most beautiful thing she had ever seen.

Mikhail's hand hovered above the baby for a moment before he reached out, his fingers gently brushing over the soft, delicate skin of his son's head. The baby quieted under his touch, and Mikhail's breath hitched. His usual hard exterior had melted away completely, leaving only the raw, vulnerable man beneath.

"He's perfect," Anya whispered, her voice thick with emotion. She looked up at Mikhail, her gaze soft and filled with gratitude.

Mikhail's eyes never left their son as he replied, his voice rough but tender, "You did it." His fingers lingered on the baby's tiny head for a moment longer before he leaned down, pressing a gentle kiss to Anya's forehead. "You're incredible."

Anya smiled, exhausted but happy, as she cradled their son against her chest. She could feel Mikhail's love radiating from him, stronger and more certain than she had ever imagined. In that moment, everything they had been through—the pain, the danger, the fear—it had all led to this. To them. To their family.

Mikhail stood by her side, his hand resting on her shoulder, and together they stared at the little life they had created. For the first time in what felt like forever, Anya felt truly at peace. This was her future—Mikhail and their son—and she knew in her heart that, no matter what came next, they would face it together.

"Have you thought of a name?" the nurse asked softly, her kind eyes glancing between the two of them.

Anya looked up at Mikhail, who finally tore his gaze away from their baby to meet hers. They hadn't talked about names much, but now, in the quiet of the hospital room, it felt like the most important decision in the world.

"I think…" Anya began, her voice trailing off as she considered the weight of the moment. Then she smiled, her eyes sparkling with love and certainty. "His name is Aleksandr."

Mikhail's lips curled into a soft smile, and he nodded, his voice low and full of emotion. "Aleksandr," he repeated, the name rolling off his tongue with reverence. It was perfect—a strong name for their son, a new beginning for them all.

As they sat there together, watching Aleksandr drift off to sleep, Mikhail leaned down and kissed Anya again, this time on the lips, a promise in every touch. He had found something he never thought possible—peace, love, and family—and he knew he would do whatever it took to protect them.

And in that quiet, tender moment, with their son cradled between them, Anya knew that this was exactly where she was meant to be.

Several weeks had passed since that life-changing night in the hospital, and Anya stood in the doorway of their new home, cradling Aleksandr in her arms. The house was beautiful—larger than the apartment, with sprawling windows that let in the soft glow of the morning light and a peaceful silence that wrapped around them like a protective shield.

It still amazed her sometimes, how much their lives had changed. From the violence and chaos of their beginning to the calm that had settled over them now. This house, with its open rooms and cozy corners, felt like a real home. It wasn't just a place to hide, to survive—it was a sanctuary for their little family.

And Mikhail had played a large part in creating that sanctuary. Since the day he had put Konstantin Morozov in the ground, everything had shifted. The killing of the rival Bratva leader hadn't just secured Anya's freedom—it had catapulted Mikhail to a new level of power and respect within the Volkov Bratva. Word had spread quickly about how he had taken down Konstantin, a man who had been a menace for years, without hesitation. The act had been brutal, decisive, and necessary, and it had sealed Mikhail's reputation as one of the most formidable men in the organization.

His standing in the Bratva had been strong before, but now it was stronger than ever. Even Nikolai, the head of the Volkov Bratva, had acknowledged Mikhail's prowess, giving him more responsibility, more trust. Mikhail wasn't just an enforcer anymore—he was a leader, a man whose name commanded respect, whose presence could make enemies tremble.

Anya looked down at Aleksandr, whose tiny fist had curled around a piece of her shirt. His eyes were closed, his breathing soft and even. She smiled, feeling the warmth of his body against hers. The love she felt for him was unlike anything she had ever known—fierce, protective, and overwhelming.

From across the room, Mikhail watched them both with a soft intensity that Anya had come to recognize. He had been quieter since Aleksandr's birth, more reflective, as if the weight of being a father had shifted something deep within him. Yet, there was still that underlying fierceness, the sense of danger that came with being who he was, but it was tempered now by something else—by love.

He stepped forward, his gaze never leaving her as he moved toward them. When he reached her, Mikhail brushed a hand gently against Aleksandr's head, the tenderness in his touch contrasting with the power that always seemed to radiate from him.

"How is he?" Mikhail asked softly, his voice a low rumble that sent a shiver down Anya's spine.

"Sleeping," Anya whispered, her lips curving into a smile. "Finally."

Mikhail chuckled quietly, leaning down to press a kiss to Aleksandr's forehead. His hand lingered on their son's head before he straightened up and met Anya's gaze. There was something different in his eyes today—something deeper than the usual protectiveness she had come to expect.

"He's perfect," Mikhail said, his voice filled with pride. "Just like his mother."

Anya blushed under his praise, but she couldn't stop the warmth that spread through her chest. Mikhail had always made her feel cherished, but now, with their son in the picture, it felt even more intense.

"You've given me everything," Mikhail murmured, his hand moving from Aleksandr to rest lightly on Anya's waist. "I never thought this would be my life."

Anya's heart fluttered at his words. She understood what he meant. For so long, Mikhail had lived in the shadow of the Bratva, bound by loyalty, violence, and a constant need for control. But now, with her and Aleksandr, his world had expanded. He had found something beyond the life he had always known—something worth fighting for, but also something that gave him peace.

"You deserve this," Anya whispered, her hand reaching up to cup his face. "We deserve this."

Mikhail leaned into her touch, his eyes closing briefly as he absorbed the weight of her words. "I never thought I'd have a family," he admitted quietly, his voice raw with emotion. "But now that I do, I'll protect you both with everything I am."

Anya's breath caught in her throat. There was such sincerity in his words, such conviction, that it made her heart swell. She knew that Mikhail would move mountains to keep them safe—he already had. They had faced more than most couples ever would, and yet, here they were, standing together, stronger than ever.

She rested her head against his chest, listening to the steady rhythm of his heartbeat. It was a sound she had come to rely on, a reminder that, no matter what, Mikhail was always there. He was her protector, her lover, her partner in every way. And now, he was a father, too.

As they stood there, wrapped in the quiet of their home, Anya felt a profound sense of contentment. For so long, she had lived under the oppressive control of her father, constantly afraid, always wondering if she would ever find a way out. But now, she was free—truly free. And she had Mikhail to thank for that.

But it wasn't just freedom that she had found—it was love. The kind of love that was unbreakable, that had been forged in the fires of hardship and danger. She had never expected to find this with someone like Mikhail, but now she couldn't imagine her life without him.

"This is our future," Anya said softly, lifting her head to look up at him. "Me, you, and Aleksandr. No more running. No more fear."

Mikhail's eyes softened as he looked down at her. "No more running," he agreed, his hand tightening on her waist. "We're a family now, Anya. And nothing will ever change that."

Tears prickled at the corners of her eyes, but they weren't tears of sadness or fear. They were tears of joy—tears of relief. After everything they had been through, they had finally found their peace. And Anya knew, without a shadow of a doubt, that this was where she was meant to be.

Mikhail bent down and kissed her gently, the warmth of his lips reminding her of the love they shared. It was a kiss that promised forever, that spoke of the life they had built together and the future they would protect at all costs.

As the sun filtered through the windows, casting a soft glow over their new home, Anya smiled. This was the life she had fought for, the life she had chosen. And she wouldn't trade it for anything.

I hope you enjoyed
Knocked Up by the Bratva
Enforcer. Scan the QR
code below and share
your love with a review!

Look For The New Book In The Volkov Bratva Series Coming Soon!

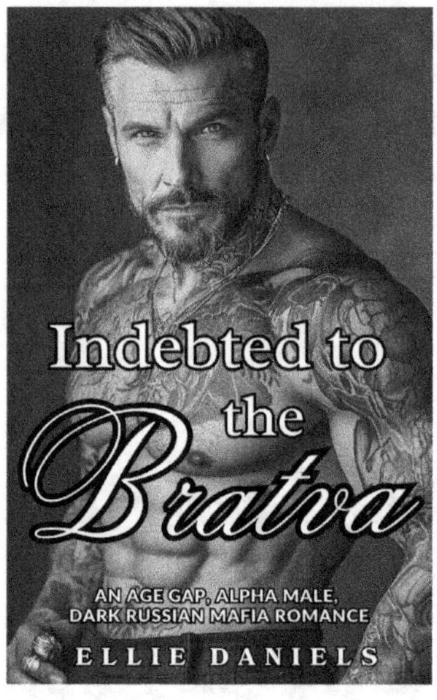

Bound by debt, consumed by desire. When a young woman is sent from Russia to pay off her father's crippling debt, she's thrust into the dark world of the Russian Mafia as a nanny for the ruthless head of the Los Angeles Bratva. But as passion ignites between them, her debt is no longer just financial… it's a matter of the heart. He's a man who's used to getting what he wants— and he won't stop until she's his—body and soul.

About the Author

Ellie Daniels is a Colorado author who ignites passion and desire through her captivating erotic romance novels and sizzling short stories. When she's not crafting worlds of desire and intimacy, Ellie enjoys quiet moments at home with her loving husband, their devoted chihuahua, and four playful cats. A sensualist at heart, she believes in the transformative power of passion and connection. Cherishing close relationships, Ellie finds inspiration in the complexities of love.